Copyright © 2024 by Amy W. Vogel

All rights reserved.

No part of this publication may be reproduced, distributed, or transmitted in any form or by any means, including photocopying, recording, or other electronic or mechanical methods, without the prior written permission of the publisher, except as permitted by U.S. copyright law. For permission requests, contact: info@amywvogel.com

The story, all names, characters, and incidents portrayed in this production are fictitious.

No identification with actual persons (living or deceased), places, buildings, and products is intended or should be inferred.

Book Cover by Kelly Carter

1st edition 2024

Contents

Dedication		1
1.	Chapter 1	2
2.	Chapter 2	11
3.	Chapter 3	19
4.	Chapter 4	28
5.	Chapter 5	37
6.	Chapter 6	46
7.	Chapter 7	58
8.	Chapter 8	71
9.	Chapter 9	76
10.	Chapter 10	84
11.	Chapter 11	95
12.	Chapter 12	105
13.	Chapter 13	115
14.	Chapter 14	122
15.	Chapter 15	142

16. Chapter 16   150
17. Chapter 17   160
18. Chapter 18   170
19. Chapter 19   179
20. Chapter 20   185
21. Chapter 21   197
22. Chapter 22   206
23. Chapter 23   214
24. Chapter 24   223
25. Chapter 25   231
26. Chapter 26   245
27. Chapter 27   260
28. Chapter 28   272
29. Chapter 29   280
30. Chapter 30   288
31. Chapter 31   296
32. Chapter 32   304
33. Chapter 33   311
34. Chapter 34   327
35. Chapter 35   337
36. Chapter 36   348
37. Chapter 37   359

38.	Chapter 38	366
39.	Chapter 39	379
40.	Chapter 40	390
41.	Chapter 41	403
42.	Chapter 42	415
43.	Chapter 43	426
44.	Chapter 44	434
45.	Chapter 45	442
46.	Chapter 46	451
47.	Chapter 47	460
48.	Chapter 48	468
49.	Chapter 49	475
50.	Chapter 50	481
51.	Chapter 51	489
52.	Chapter 52	502
53.	Chapter 53	513
54.	Chapter 54	523
55.	Epilogue	534
	Acknowledgements	539
	About the Author	542
	Surprise Bonus Section	544

For the Good Girls...Love Awaits!

Chapter 1

Conner

Talk about the worst timing. The worst possible timing.

This is the year my team and I win it all. I don't have time to fall in love.

Here I am, sitting in the ridiculously comfortable office chairs of the gorgeous and inspiring state-of-the-art Athletic Complex at the University of Coastal Cove in Northern California. I'm not thinking about the future I've spent five years planning and put my personal life on hold for.

I'm thinking about her, the woman I just saw. The woman I know I will spend the rest of my life with.

And my guts twist wretchedly, as I wait for my staff and team to arrive for our first meeting before training and classes start.

In the unexpected quiet, my mind's eye unwittingly caresses the form I saw. She is tall, strong with feminine curves that make my mouth water. She was radiant, with her brown locks shimmering. I only saw her face for a moment, but she was smiling and it cracked my heart wide open.

My body is at odds with my mind. I am normally in complete sync, a well-oiled soccer machine. I haven't thought about dating for two years, after a one-night stand that left me running out the door with my clothes in my hand, fear of the past repeating itself close on my heels. I have given no woman, much less my dream woman, a thought since. Turns out, I didn't have to go looking for her–she showed up outside the women's athletic dorm, moving her daughter in for her freshman year.

This is bad. It's so bad. Coach-parent relationships are frowned upon, especially when the coach is trying to take his team to the national championship.

Here I sit with the reality that twenty minutes ago, this chance encounter across the courtyard changed my life. I completely missed whatever my assistant coach said to me.

"Conner!" My right-hand woman, Inanna, and her sharp voice pull me from my trance as I stare.

"Are you listening to me? There's Elise Vokler, our new striker. I guess that's her mom with her. Let's go say hello." She walks to them, waving to our star freshman player, but I stand there, struck stupid.

I couldn't risk making any kind of connection, so I made an excuse and hightailed it, fear once again driving me forward, like a coward. I know I'll have to explain my behavior. I acted like an idiot, especially when Elise is an enormous piece of the puzzle to our team's success, current and future success.

She led her high school team to the State Championship and was recruited by all the major Division One teams. Six feet tall, with dark blonde hair, striking green eyes and an academic record to position her to be our first All-American; she is also smart, funny and driven to be an excellent leader on and off the field.

Inanna couldn't stop singing her praises after her scouting trip to watch her play. Inanna was incredibly impressed, since she played through the sudden loss of her father in her sophomore year.

Suddenly restless with all these thoughts in my head, I decide to walk to the coffee bar and make myself an afternoon cup. I don't really need caffeine. My mother always said I was naturally caffeinated. But the movement helps me and I know I'll have to explain my erratic behavior.

I cannot, at all costs, learn more about this woman.

Yet, that's exactly what I do as I'm waiting for my cappuccino to brew. I look up Elise's socials and easily find her mother tagged in several posts.

Now, I know her name - Carrie.

I'm done for.

***

Carrie

Well, that was rude.

Here we are, moving into Elise's dorm, sticky after lugging boxes of her stuff we shipped from Texas, when two of her new coaches' approach; well, one at least. Coach Inanna, the assistant coach, was all serious smiles. The Head Coach, Conner Doreland, was standoffish. I tried to appear confident and presentable, despite sweating like a whore in church. Elise was nervous because her voice went up two octaves as she waved and greeted them. I plastered a smile on my face, dealing with the inner freak out of not being fully put together.

He mumbled some excuse and ran off; not a great first impression at all.

Doing my best to be present during this happy first for my youngest daughter, I have work to do. Women who run their own businesses rarely get a day off. I have twenty emails to respond to before I can think about dinner... and then I probably need to send out five more before bed.

I love being here with Elise but I'm ready for a shower, some food and hopefully a nice long sleep after I respond to what I'm missing at the office.

It hits me then, the pang of loss. It always comes out of nowhere these days. I miss her dad being here with us to see his youngest grow into a young woman. Elise and I are both doing well after three years of therapy. Elise had to grow up way faster than her sisters. They, too, faced their own struggles with life and grief.

As we chat with Inanna, who is pleasant, though not warm, I mentally shake off the melancholy. I turn my attention back to the moment at hand and how strange it was that Coach Doreland just ran off. I'm going to have to trust he isn't a weirdo. Elise loved this program above any other, so he must be doing something right.

I'd been looking forward to meeting Coach Conner, as the girls know him. Of course, I'd done my research. His past was interesting, with a player who stalked him while he coached at Michigan State. It led to him losing his coaching spot before being hired here, at the University of Coastal Cove. My google search also turned up pictures of when he was a Premier League player. He is so hot.

I know women in their forties with grown children are supposed to be asexual, but we are the opposite, in fact. As he ran off, I got a magnificent view of his backside, and it was scrumptious.

Geez Carrie– thirsty much? I need to handle this lust tonight before I end up having a wet dream about him. It has been too long since I've gotten laid.

I think about this as I remind myself, I shouldn't be lusting after a man who will have an enormous impact on my youngest daughter's future, but I can't help it. I'm a widow with no prospects in my prime. The man is perfect imaginative fodder.

I ask Coach Inanna about him, and she shrugs. "We have our first team meeting shortly. He was probably overthinking it. He is the job."

I tell Inanna, "Well, Elise and I have had so many late-night talks about what lies ahead of her. I know she is in expert hands with you, Coach."

Elise and Inanna continue to chat for another minute until Inanna begs off to head to the meeting. Elise turns to me and says, "That's my cue too, Mama."

I nod and give her a long hug. Her sisters became very hug-resistant when they were this age, but Elise has never lost her desire for closeness. I lean into her ear to remind her about her virtual therapy session tomorrow with her therapist back in Texas.

She nods and says in a slightly exasperated tone, "I know, Mama. It's on my calendar and I have a session every two weeks this first semester."

"You've got it - I just know how home sick kids can get their first semester of college." I pull back and look at her with a critical eye. "I've been through this twice before, you know."

Elise rolls her eyes and says, "Oh, I know." Then we smile at each other, all levity restored.

I'm thankful for my work flexibility and the team Scott and I built around us. My company, which provides backend office support services to individual and small mental health providers, runs smoothly, truthfully whether or not I'm there. It is a huge part of Scott's legacy and why we still had a business after he passed so suddenly. A heart attack while the fucker was swimming.

He got out of the pool but died right there on the deck. They still took him to the hospital and tried to revive him. I watched it all and have worked through that trauma. I can call him a fucker for dying on me with minimal guilt now. I've learned to express all my feelings when they come up and how they show up. I've never apologized for how we've dealt with our grief, and we won't be running from it now.

"Mama, we did a lot of work today. Dad probably would have made this a game of Tetris." I'm glad she is thinking about him too and my eyes mist up a little.

"He crossed my mind too, while we were talking to your coach. Alright, get gone so you'll be there on time. I'll see you tomorrow, sweetheart. Be radiant!"

She hugs me again, makes the "I Love You" ASL sign with her hand–our habit since she could form it with her fingers - and springs off to the Athletic complex. I go inside her cozy dorm room in the middle of campus, decorated with various shades of teals, yellows and purples, and stack the boxes in her closet. I pat her bed on my way out and close the door behind me. It feels like the end and the beginning.

When I get back to Houston, I'll be completely alone, with all three of my girls out of our thirty-two-square-foot Houston home. They are all growing up and my heart pings as I walk to my rental car across the beautiful California campus, lush with green, just before summer shifts into fall.

The sunset is orange-pink and reminds me the endings are beautiful too. As I drive into it on the way to my hotel, my mind retraces the past few years and how much Elise has grown up following the horrific year after her dad died. Her sisters were dealing with their own grief in their own ways. Elise went off the deep end into partying and boys. Her sisters came to her rescue.

I wouldn't say I abdicated my role when Scott died, but I was completely overwhelmed. My girls and I now have the relationship I never dreamed in those months of devastation, depression. Scott and I weren't perfect, but we were in a good place. His death shook us all down to the bedrock. We have all done our work and continue to do it to stay balanced, not living in fear of the future.

Our family mantra is "Expect the best possible outcome."

As I drive to my hotel, I ponder how I haven't always liked how we've gotten here, but we are indeed living in the best for all of us. I even admitted in my last therapy session the desire to start dating.

I know finding someone who is open and accepting of my complicated life is a tall order. I know dating in your forties will lead to a whole other level of self-care and love. Three kids don't do a body any favors.

Here's hoping for a man who likes squishy.

I walk into my posh hotel room, grateful I chose it. I'm grateful I can afford it and be comfortable during these difficult times of transition. I order my room service, shower while I wait for the food and after it arrives, I tackle my emails as I eat.

With my work finished, I snuggle into the big, soft bed. I dive into the new book I brought. It's an unusual genre, a women's fiction modern fantasy thriller that has Booktok all abuzz. As I read a passage about how the main character deals with her trauma, the escape from reality I thought I was getting becomes a reminder as grief once again walks up and pats me on the back.

I take a deep breath as a couple of tears leak down my cheek. Propped up against my pillows, halfway sitting up, I put the book down and place my hands on my heart. I ask Spirit of Love to be close to us all, especially Elise on her first night away from home..

The only confirmation I get is the beat of my heart. I've done all I can and now it is time to let my last little birdie fly.

Chapter 2

Conner

Our very first team meeting goes very well with all the Senior and Junior players meeting their "adopted" underclassman. Each player is a "big" to a "little." Inanna put this in place five years ago when I hired her. She is the heart of the team, even if from the outside, she doesn't come off that way. She can coach her ass off, but taking care of the players is her specialty. If Inanna is the heart, I'm the brains.

The brawn is the monstrosity of a man the ladies finally get to meet -our conditioning coach, Erik Martin. He played professional rugby in Australia until he couldn't anymore. He is still just as fit as he was in his professional days. Plus, he has become my workout buddy. As a result, we are the fittest coaches on campus.

I heard about his methods when I was at Michigan State and recruited him when I started at UCC. His conditioning tactics are very similar to Gene Hackman's character from the movie Hoosiers: *No team of mine will ever run out of steam before their opponents.*

Welcome to hell week girls, I think as Erik lays out the training schedule. Most of the freshmen thought this would be a fun week before classes start, but tomorrow afternoon is our first workout. It is a doozy with a timed five-kilometer run, followed by ninety minutes in the weight room. That's the routine for the first two weeks, and only then do we train.

My requirement is simple: every player must memorize our playbook; They get tested on it. I'm that serious.

It was a stroke of brilliance for the "Big and Little Sister" program because the first two weeks are like drinking out of the firehose, for the freshmen. They are all looking at the coaching staff like deer in headlights.

As Erik lays out what will most certainly mean regular ibuprofen consumption, I contemplate saying something to Elise. A part of me suspects I want to get on her good side because I'm fucking gone for her mother with one look. I just barely convince myself it's just professional because I did act like an ass. She's my player and I don't want her (or her mother) thinking I'm a douche bag.

As everyone gathers their team manuals, I call out, "Hey Volker, can I talk to you for a minute?"

There is a pointed silence from the upperclassmen but the rest of the freshmen and most of the sophomores are oblivious because its sinking in they joined up with the toughest program in the country. Inanna gives me the side eye. For Elise's part, her light brown eyebrows knit over her green eyes, and she says unsteadily, "Uh, sure Coach."

She walks over from her "Big", my team captain, Alyssa Narcissus. It never hurts to make sure the underclassmen leaders are entrenched in the program from the start. My program is built on this: no bullshit, no drama, no secrets.

Boy, I'm doing fantastic with that philosophy.

I clear my throat. "Elise–I'm glad you are here. You are a great addition to our team and our program. We haven't settled on the starting roster yet, but you'll do your best to get ready for the season. You have a huge heart, and I expect to see that in play for us, yah?"

My mouth is in overdrive. I need to shut this down before I ask about her mom and give it all away.

Elise gives me a smile that is the same one I saw her mother wear and my heart catches a little. "Yes, Coach Doreland—I mean Coach Conner—I am ready. My family and I are very grateful for the opportunity to be here. My dad would have loved it, and my sisters can't wait to see me play."

I take a second and look at her; *really* look at Elise. She is young, of course, but there is something about her face that shows wisdom beyond her years. There is also a heaviness in her eyes I hadn't noticed before. She has been through some shit, as has her mom.

Her mom…. her mom. Those brilliant blue eyes…

I snap back when I hear, "Coach Conner?"

I cough a little into my hand. "Yes, sorry, I've got a lot on my mind. I'm sorry I had to rush away before meeting your mom. Is she coming up for a game?"

Oh. My. God. I'm fishing. This is so bad.

Elise responds proudly, "She is super busy, but she is going to make it to as many games as she can. She might not always be able to come to my games like in the past, but at least for my freshman year, that is her plan. When she puts her mind to something, she never fails to do it."

My heart drops into my stomach. I would love to feel what it is like to be the center of her mother's attention. Then I want to smack myself in the face. I redirect and hope it works so no one catches on.

"It sounds like she's rubbed off on you." I smile at her, and she smiles back. She is a class act as she replies, "Yes, Coach. I want to make a difference here. "

I nod. "We will do everything to help you develop into the person you are meant to be, Elise. You better get some rest tonight. Tomorrow ends the fun!" I smile at her again, and she nods back seriously.

"Oh, by the way," I add surreptitiously, "What's your mom's name so I can meet her at our first game and make up for being a total dummy today?"

"Her name is Carrie. And she is coming up for parents' weekend in a little over a month. I'm going to catch up with Alyssa. Bye Coach!"

I can hear the kids of my California school yard chanting in my mind, "Conner and Carrie sittin' in a tree – K-I-S-S-I-N-G!"

This time, I do slap my forehead to knock some sense in my addled brain. I need a hard ride on my bike, and I need it now. I need to burn through this hot-blooded lust thinking of Carrie Vokler. It'll be six weeks before I see her again. Plenty of time to get my head on straight or I am fucked.

***

Carrie

Waking up this morning, I thought I would be completely refreshed. I slept like shit and I'm so glad I get to see Elise one more time before I head out. At breakfast, I tell her how proud I am of her and all she's accomplished.

"I'm super satisfied with what I know about the soccer program and the university. No need to rush into choosing a major. This first semester is for figuring things out."

She nods and between chews says, It's a toss-up between history and poly-sci."

I think my little girl is going to be a lawyer.

"As happy as I am for you, sweetheart, I'm sad. We've walked through these last few years hand in hand."

She smiles and looks down, uncomfortable with the emotion. She pushes her omelet around on her plate before she says, "Take good care of Schroeder."

Our black cat, Schroeder, was flea-bitten and fooled my husband into thinking he was normal. He is not. Cats are definitely on some kind of spectrum. Between his midnight snacking on my hair, loud vocalizations in the morning when I make my coffee, and the habit of stealing my robe to go hump it in a dark corner, this cat makes life interesting. He adores Elise, and she loves him.

Even though he annoys me, for her, I keep him around.

Clearing my throat and changing the subject, I tell her, "I am so grateful I'll have groceries waiting for me. They'll be on my doorstep when I get home!"

Elise smiles and says, "D-say is great. I'm going to miss her. Hope she can come to a game this season—her and Brian." My best friend Dulce is a second Mom to my girls.

Dulce and my other close friends offered to come over tonight, but I told them I want time to be in the house myself. Well, with the ridiculous cat lurking and probably waking me up as he chews on my hair in the middle of the night.

We say our goodbyes as Elise prepares for her first workout with the team, and I cry a little on my drive to the airport. My flight home is uneventful, but my book, *Teleosis*, is indeed a hit. I didn't get very far before I fell asleep last night, but Booktok didn't lead me astray. The author deserves big sales because the entire four-hour flight kept me engrossed.

After I put my book away as we prepare to land in Houston, my mind drifts back to Conner Doreland. I indulge my continued morbid curiosity and search his socials. He doesn't post much, only about the team and their success. I scan a few articles about the timeline of events. It would have made a great Law and Order SVU episode, with the twist as the girl was the perp. She sent him a ton of sexts, which he blocked and reported. But then she started videoing him and manipulating those videos to make it look like he was watching her. She had a private YouTube channel where she posted everything and would send out invites to her team and other sports teams in Michigan State.

She kept posting on her socials about their supposed affair long after she was kicked off the team and expelled. It all came to a head one night when she showed up at his house and attacked him, but when the police showed up, they arrested him. Conner paid a hefty price for someone else's serious mental health issues.

In one picture from the trial, he looks 30 pounds lighter in it with a pallor to his cheeks. Like a much older version of the man I saw yesterday, even though it was over five years ago. From my not-so-quick look at his backside, I could tell he put back on all the muscles he lost and then some. Those joggers clung to his thick thighs, which is an enormous benefit to being a soccer player.

According to Wikipedia, he Is taller than me, which reports 6'2" or 6'3". Not much taller than my own 5'11", but enough.

I'll have to deal with that again if I date, not that Conner is an option. He lives across the country and coaches are definitely off-limits.

I finally find a close-up of Conner's face and see he has golden-brown eyes and dark brown curly hair, which hits just below the nape of his neck. *Yummy.* I close my eyes as we wait on the tarmac for our gate to be cleared and imagine what it would feel like to run my hands through those curls.

I envision pulling a curl down his forehead and then stroking his face with a feather-light touch around his ear to land on the back of his neck. I get lost in the imagined sensations of my hands on his neck; the hair tickling my fingers and wrapping the tendrils in my fingertips. My fingers skate down his cervical spine, and he shivers. He looks down at me, his eyes full of intent, like twin flames, and his mouth curved in a smile. He leans forward, and just before his lips reach mine…

DING!

We arrive at the gate, and the center aisle shuffle begins. My fantasy evaporates, but maybe I can recreate it tonight. I am clearly in lust when I should not be. But since it's all in my head, Conner Doreland Fantasyland, here I come.

Chapter 3

Conner

The first week is always a blur. There are administrative duties, making sure the team and their professors are current on game schedules. Weekly study sessions are required for the team because my soccer program isn't slacking on academics. Academic excellence raises the profile of the entire school, and I expect the most from my players.

This program is a godsend, but it is not my goal. What I'm working towards is to get called up to be a U.S. Women's National Team coach. I love coaching women. They are smart, complicated, and so much less dramatic than men. They put in four times the effort and play through injuries with more grit than the men. To coach them at the highest level? That's the real prize.

The only thing chewing my ass up is Elise Vokler. Or rather my major, hot-blooded crush on her mother, whom I've spent nearly every night internet stalking for the last week. We are not supposed to get involved with families and parents. You don't want to be a coach who is seen to play favorites.

That had never been an issue until I saw Carrie. Her Instagram account doesn't do her justice. In-person - she is fucking *alive,* and I want to bask in her glow. She looks like a woman in total control of herself, but I could have told you that from working these last two weeks with her daughter. Queens raise queens. Elise might be eighteen, but her maturity outstrips her years. She is self-possessed and knows her strengths and weaknesses.

The thought hits me - *when was the last time I was excited about something other than soccer?*

In my obsessive search for information about Carrie, I discover she recently changed her Peleton username from CaVo to CoCoSoccerMom. It's cute. I saw the IG Reel with her on a Peleton, sweating it out to one of my favorite instructors. Her curves are perfect, even with her expression that states she might be a little uncertain about her physique. The caption reads, "Trying this out and not sure it's my style."

Oh pretty girl, you are just my style.

God, I hope we end up in a class together and please help me get a grip because this desire for her needs to stop. Not just because my hand is numb and my cock is raw, since I started fantasizing about all the nasty things I could do to her. The vision of pulling down her shorts and seeing if she wears panties underneath is a major distraction.

"Coach! What the hell are you doing?"

I turn beet red as I realize Erik has caught me staring at that picture of Carrie Vokler in her Peloton gear. I realize I've got my hand on my rock-hard dick under my desk, so I scramble to distract Erik with an insult.

"Why are you here, Dickhead? You forget I have office hours now, or did someone crash and burn on box jumps?"

He grins at me in a way that tells me he knows exactly what I am doing. He walks over, but thankfully before he can see what I was looking at, the screen times out.

I smirk at him.

Still grinning at me like a fool, he replies, "I'm here to remind you that you are late for the team meeting." He leaves the next word unsaid, but the message is crystal clear.

Again. Shit.

Smoothly, he continues, "And... we're dying to know if you're ready to present the plan for the team dinner on the Saturday night of Family Weekend before the exhibition game with UCL on Sunday morning?"

The hand that was on my dick comes up to slap across my forehead. I completely lost track of time. Thankfully, in a lucid moment, before I went to Carrie Vokler Fantasyland, I prepared for this meeting.

I give him an annoyed look. "Erik, are we still doing that ridiculous Coaches-only flag football game that Friday afternoon? It's not like we don't have enough going on that weekend."

I try to relax, as I know this is part of the gig as a head coach. I must be *social*. It gives me a taste of the massive gender discrimination in sports my players have to deal with when I get comments like, "Oh, your little program is doing so great!"

I know Erik feels the same way when he mentions a pairing for the flag football game. "Yes. The Football program is teaming up with the men's soccer team."

I smile darkly. "Good, connect us with the swim team. Those coaches are fit, and it's a bonus that they aren't total misogynists. Football and those morons in the men's program won't know what hit them."

As I go around the desk to meet him, he puts a bear paw-sized hand on my shoulder. "Excellent plan, as usual, Coach. I can't wait to scare the shit out of the floppy cock men's soccer coaches. Serves them right for getting first dibs on the weight room schedule."

Erik will never forgive Arlo, our Athletic Director and my boss, for letting that long-standing chauvinistic tradition of the men's teams getting to pick weight training schedules first.

He gives me a sideways gaze as we walk out of my office. "Oh, and Conner, I expect an update soon on who you were about to jerk off to when I walked in. You better close the door next time, mate."

I turn beet red again and put a hand over my face as Erik's deep chuckle echoes in my chest. I will do that when thinking about fucking our star freshman's mother on a Peloton again.

***

Carrie

The week back at the office passes quickly and I get to look forward to my oldest daughter, Maley, coming this weekend. Business is great, my team reports. We can double the number of clients if we want, but we are in the sweet spot at managing thirty individual or small group mental health practitioners.

Our back-office processes are still stabilizing to scale above that number, so holding it for now is best. I have an ongoing debate with my second in command about what the next steps with the business are. She wants to go big or go home, but I'm not ready for that yet.

When I tell her this, Gena rolls her eyes and says, "Well, we will see."

Maley, as always, arrives early on Thursday night. I took Friday off again, loving a four-day work week.

"Mama! What have you been doing here all alone??" she asks as she blows in the front door.

I have her favorite meal, spaghetti Bolognese, prepared and reply, "Sweetheart, I've only been an empty nester for four days and I talk to your sisters twice a day. Y'all are all scared I don't know what to do with myself. Plus, I'm not exactly alone, there is always Schroeder."

Dumping her overnight bag on the first chair she comes to, she gets right to it. "Mama, you need something or someone to keep you busy. Have you signed up for any dating apps yet?"

I hold my hands up and say, "Whoa, whoa. Come in, have dinner, and tell me about your life. Then we can talk about my non-existent love life. Ok?"

She laughs and takes the next two hours to tell me about her work, the guy she is dating, and where she thinks she wants her career to go. She is a physical therapist specializing in helping children recover from severe brain injuries. "I enjoy working with the people, I really do. I also think I could be good at research and presentations. I just don't know if my clinic is the right place to pursue those goals."

"You've stayed in contact with all your professors from undergrad and PT school, so why don't you ask one of them to mentor you? You could meet with them and see what wisdom they offer."

"Yes, but I'm not sure which one would be the best one." She bites her thumbnail, which is one of her tells. She is overthinking and nervous. I don't pry, but I make a mental note to ask her towards the end of the weekend if she doesn't bring it up again.

We end up making popcorn to watch a movie, then eat our dessert - Magnum Double Carmel Popsicles. I end up falling asleep before the movie even gets to the halfway mark. She waits till the end, then taps me on the arm to signal its time for bed;

just as she did every night she came home late in high school and on college breaks

I wash my face and brush my teeth before I climb into my big California King sized bed. Then Maley comes down in her pajamas to say goodnight, hair up in a high messy bun from her nightly routine.

Maley pauses at the door and turns to me. "Do you want me to sleep with you, Mama? Are you ok? It feels kind of empty and sad. It is so quiet."

"Maley, sweetheart, there is plenty of room. I'm happy to share the space if you feel you need it. I'm ok, though. I know you are worried about me, but I keep myself busy, you know." I give her a long, knowing wink.

"EWWW, MOM! I know you DO that stuff, but you don't have to talk about it."

"I know you know I take care of myself–specifically of my beautiful female parts. Should I say the word to mortify you even further?"

"NO! It's fine when I say it, but to hear you say the P-word, it's just weird."

"Which one–you mean–Pussy?"

"UGH MAMA."

"You have one too you know, and I expect you are taking care of it. It's your great power source as a woman."

"Ok, Ok, Ok. I get it. Yes, I take care of my pu...yes, yes, I do. I know ALL THE THINGS you taught me. I just don't want to hear you say it!"

"I guess that means I'm sleeping alone?"

She gives me a look. "I'll still sleep here if you need me."

"Thank you, Darling, but no. I need to do my regular maintenance." I wink at her again.

"UUUUGGGGGHHHHH, ok, goodnight, I love you, Mama."

"Goodnight, Darling. You are seen, loved, and powerful. Sleep tight. Oh! Maley, wait. You will probably sleep in, but if you don't, I'm doing an early Peloton ride, so I'll make us some biscuit sausage sandwiches when I'm done."

"Sounds delicious, Mama, and have fun on your ride. I am sleeping in!"

She is smiling as she goes upstairs to her childhood bedroom. However, all the upstairs bedrooms are now more or less luxurious guest suites, maybe now nicer than mine.

I grab my phone to put it on the charging plate on my bedside table when I notice an unusual notification I'd missed. It came through a few hours ago. I tap on it and my Peloton app opens. I'm a little confused as I've never used the app other than in class. I take a beat to realize it's a private message. Everyone I know who has a Peloton has my number, so they wouldn't contact me here.

When I finally realize who the message is from, I am in utter shock and disbelief. The message is from a user named ConDore.

No. Fucking. Way.

I take a few minutes and an extra trip to the bathroom for a glass of water to gather my courage to open the message and read it. It is sweet and simple.

> *Hi – this is Connor Doreland. I saw your username and wondered if it was because your daughter is one of my new players. I'm happy to have her and glad we share another interest. I'm doing an early class tomorrow – I hope to see you there.*

Chapter 4

Conner

I'm going to hell in a handbasket, and it is the size of my nut sack.

I keep repeating this in my head as I type out the message on the Peloton app to Carrie. I can't believe I'm doing this. I can't believe I'm being this bold with a woman who is most definitely off-limits. Yet, I can't shake the thought of her. I need to see if she is someone real. If not, I can put this fantasy away.

If not...well, I do not know what to do about that.

When I saw her log onto the same ride as me this morning, I couldn't believe it. I couldn't see anything but her stats, but I liked what I saw.

This woman is a beast on this bike.

That just intrigues me more. I knew she had a Peloton. I've seen her in the gear. But now I know we have a similar schedule, and it makes me wonder what else we have in common. It makes me want to get to know her. It makes me wonder if I could take her out in the hills behind the university for a ride, or maybe a hike, with a picnic stop in the middle on the plateau overlooking the ocean.

The pressure of this season maybe making me mentally unstable because I feel obsessed with these thoughts of her. I should call my brother Joel. He is practically my best friend and also the closest in age to me, of my four brothers. Only two years separate us. He gets me in a way the other two don't. He could talk me off this ledge that I'm teetering on, with an abyss of a bad idea on either side.

Joel would help me sort myself out. Call Joel. Yes, I'll call Joel. Right after I send her a text message, I think as I exit my bike and go grab some water.

I take an hour of writing, erasing, and rewriting the simple, professional and hopefully earnest message to her. This is an hour I should spend reviewing tapes or something.

Once I push send, it's done. I'm done for and I know I've crossed a line. I can't go back. I end up going for a run and then I do review a tape. It's too late in the day to call Joel, so I send him a text telling him I need to talk to him tomorrow. I will tell someone what is going on in my crazy head because I kept it all a secret with Miranda.

With Miranda, I thought I could handle it and was taking the appropriate action. Yet, with me in isolation, she manipulated the system, me and everything else. I kept my mouth shut until it was too late. This time, I will be smart and get some clear advice, even if Joel will just tell me to get my head out of my ass.

While I'm winding down for bed close to eleven pm, I notice the notification and my heart leaps into my throat.

Holy shit! She responded.

My hands are shaking a little when I open the app and click on the message. It is nice, a little flirty, just as I realize I expected her to be.

> Hey Coach, yes, this is Elise's Mom. I'm just so damn proud of her and also...am a soccer mom. I'm glad to connect with you! Peloton is a mainstays of my workouts even though I much prefer riding outdoors. I can do it here in Houston till it just gets too damn hot. Do you ride outdoors in California? The hills behind the University looked beautiful while I was there.

I groan as I finish reading her message. It was like she read my mind. Who is this woman?

I send her another message back and then she surprises the hell out of me.

> Here's my number. If you'd like to talk, give me a call.

Bold, brazen and a bad bitch in the best way. She set the tone and left the ball in my court.

I do a lap around my house, then another, before I decide what to do. Maybe I should call Joel because this might become an emergency. I decide if she is going to let me make the next move, even if it is with super sweaty hands, and adrenaline pumping through my, I'm going to do it. I have been thinking about this woman for days and she invited me to contact her.

I will not waste my shot. Taking a deep breath to steady my racing heart and so my voice doesn't squeak, I hit the "call" button.

She answers on the second ring, and her voice is melodious.

"Hello?"

"Hey Ms. Vokler, it's Conner Doreland." I know my voice is shaky. I hope she isn't picking it up. "Is this too late for you?"

She laughs quietly but easily, and I'm instantly more settled. She explains, "Please, Coach—call me Carrie. It's not too late tonight, since it's Friday. My oldest daughter is visiting, so I'll keep my voice lower so as not to disturb her. How is your night going?"

She doesn't seem to ask about me to make polite conversation. She seems to want to know. Her tone is warm and seemingly vulnerable, especially given she is considering her daughter being in the house. She doesn't have to talk to me, so maybe there is some interest in her side too. I decide to continue to be bold but in a softer way, like she is.

"Please, call me Conner. I feel like a late-night call should put us on a first name basis, don't you?"

She laughs again and my heart swells. We have the best two hours of conversation I've ever had with anyone in my entire life. Our words, thoughts and feelings just flow. We keep it away from her former married life and my love life. We also don't talk a lot about her kids. I don't mind, I just want to get to know her and how her mind works.

It doesn't look like we will lack for conversational topics soon, if ever. It gives me hope there is something more here to explore. When I look at the clock and realize it's one a.m. her time, I get concerned.

"It's getting really late for you Carrie, are you usually a night owl?"

There's that melody of her laugh again.

"No, Conner, absolutely not. I'm usually in bed and asleep pretty early. I guess you intrigued me, and it's kept me up. It's been a long time since I had an invigorating conversation with a man, especially when work wasn't involved!"

"Well, I would love to learn more about your business, but we have time for that. Do you want to talk more tomorrow? You can just text me and let me know."

Her giggle is small, but it makes my cock get hard. What I wouldn't give to hear that sound in person. "Conner, it already is tomorrow for me."

I huff out a laugh and say, "You're right. Just text me later when you have time during your day with your daughter." I want her to feel comfortable talking to me about anything so I close with, "And you can tell me all about her–and your other two girls–whenever you want."

She is quiet for a beat and then says, "Thank you. They are my world. I'd like that, eventually."

I smile, "Of course, when you are ready. Sleep well, Sunshine." Then, with a confidence I'm not sure I feel, I tell her, "I look forward to seeing where this goes."

I can hear her smile and it my mind's eye, it's like the wattage in the room got turned up. "Yes, Conner, me too. This was – you are – a sweet treat."

I quirk an eyebrow she can't see at her words and respond only with, "See you in the morning for the ride." She says the same and we hang up.

Plans made an early ride for her, and for me. My legs might be torched, but I'll be there – with bells on if she asked.

It takes me another two hours to wind down enough to fall asleep. I lie there thinking about her, that Carrie might be somebody I could, one day, share my deeper stuff with. It would be a miracle. Other than the therapist I had after the trial, rebuilding myself and my mind, I never go too deep. I know I'm pent up with words, but I haven't been sure anyone would want to hear them, to receive them.

Carrie feels like someone who could keep them safe. A ray of delicious, warm sunshine in my hard, cold life.

Yep, that handbasket to hell is getting smaller and smaller.

***

Carrie

As I lie in bed, my mind races with so many *"shoulds"*.

I should not have stayed up till one a.m. talking with Conner Doreland.

I should have not even messaged him back in the first place.

He has to be fifteen years younger than me.

And he is so smoking hot. There is no way he would be interested in a woman at my age and stage.

Well, wait a minute, why the hell not? I have a lot to offer the right man.

Plus, didn't I think I was maybe possibly ready for this?

Maybe the universe is telling me something I need to get on board with–that a woman in her 40s could be just as hot – maybe hotter – than a younger woman.

I certainly know what I want and maybe, possibly given half the chance, I might want Conner Doreland.

That doesn't change the fact that he is Elise's coach.

But what's the harm in a little flirting and conversation with a hot young man? I'm not dead yet and this shit makes me feel more alive than I have in years!

The whole mental debate eventually makes me pass out from exhaustion. However, three hours of sleep is not my normal amount of beauty rest. But Conner asked me in our conversation to join him for a class and then said he couldn't wait to see me there.

I will not be a disappointment!

Now he has my number. I decided I'd rather talk than text, and he was happy to oblige. Our conversation flowed easily and heartily. It felt like we had both been waiting to talk to someone for a long time. Plus, Conner is even sexy over the phone. He has a deep rumble, but not a typical coach's baritone. It felt like warm butter sliding on my overheated skin.

He told me about how he grew up and how he made it over to England.

I told him about my life before Scott and the girls and what I hope to accomplish with the rest of my life. I didn't think he would want to hear about my married life, but he said something to me to make me think he wants to hear it all.

"Carrie–You can talk to me about anything. You don't have to hold back. I know y'all have been through a lot and I won't judge you or do anything but listen when you want to share."

I was quiet for a long time. I had a hard time breathing. No one had made me feel this seen as a woman in a long, long time.

"Carrie? Are you still there? I didn't say the wrong thing, did I?"

I was blinking so hard, in shock. *Is this guy for real or am I being catfished or something?*

I continue, taking the risk of opening my heart a tiny bit more, "You feel so genuine, and I hope that stays true. Yes, you are right, we – I – have been through a lot. I didn't share about my married life because I didn't think you would want to hear that. Plus, that is a whole can of worms I'm not entirely sure I'm ready to open."

We talked a little longer, then he let me go with, "When you are ready to talk, I'm ready to listen, even over text. Sleep well, Sunshine." Then, "I look forward to seeing where this goes."

Did he just give me a nickname?

If I know anything from reading the racy, romantic books I read, the nickname is a big deal.

I am stunned speechless, so it took me a second to reply, "Yes, Conner, me too. This was – you are – a sweet treat."

Sweet treat? What am I? A grandma?

But he was so sweet. Strong and sweet and that is delightful in a man.

Don't get ahead of yourself Carrie, it was just one conversation.

Yet, I get ahead of myself. Before I know my hand is in my pajama bottoms and once again, I climax with Conner's name on my lips. It's only after I come down from an orgasm powerful enough to light up my block that I settle and finally, fall asleep.

Chapter 5

Conner

After finally winding down, I sleep like the dead, which is unusual. I'm always tossing and turning. Something about her voice, talking to her, soothes me in a way that I haven't experienced, maybe ever. I feel like I can offer her what she needs and give her that safety in return. There is a deep peace – what my oldest brother who is in recovery–calls *serenity*.

Even after four hours, when my alarm goes off, I wake up completely refreshed. And excited because I know she won't let me down. I know she will make the ride. Maybe she'll want to talk for a few minutes afterwards and I can start my day with a ray of Sunshine to carry me through.

I called her Sunshine. That's what she is. Pure Sunshine. Warmth and light and beauty and strength and power all wrapped up in one. My Sunshine.

During the cool down portion of the class, I see that my brother Joel has responded to my text. He can talk this morning as he drives to work. He knows I'm up. I haven't slept past six am since I was sixteen years old. There was always practice or a match or something to do. Having a lot of natural energy benefits me, even though knowing when to rest has been a struggle to learn.

Carrie texts me she can talk for a couple of minutes before she starts her day. I pump my fist in the air and tell her to call me when she is ready. Then I send a text to Joel that I'll call him in fifteen minutes, getting a thumbs up in response.'

I'm brushing my teeth as the phone rings. I quickly spit out the toothpaste and answer on speaker.

"Good morning, Sunshine. How did you sleep?" The smile in my voice is matched by hers. She sounds energized and I like it.

"Well, not much. A certain handsome young man occupied my thoughts, so I'm going to running on a lot of coffee today. But I don't regret it."

That comment zings straight to my dick. I hope she means she thought of me the way I want her to be thinking of me.

She continues, "So, you've already nicknamed me, huh? That's a very book boyfriend thing to do, you know."

"Well, I'm glad I know what you mean by that and yes, I think Sunshine is perfect. I describe how I felt last night and this morning. I slept like the dead which is unusual for me."

"Wait a minute, how do you know about book boyfriends??" She sounds incredulous.

I laugh darkly. "I've been coaching young women for over fifteen years, so you pick up a few things. And some of the stuff y'all read is just plain porn on the page."

I sense the flush in her face and voice, even as she brazenly says, "Well, I hope you've picked up some pointers."

"Oh, trust me, I have copious notes. Maybe we should trade book lists sometime and see if we match up?"

I can almost picture her cheeks turning an even deeper shade of red. She clears her throat. "Well, that's unexpected and yes, sure, maybe we should do that. And you've been coaching for fifteen years? How old are you?"

I smile such a wicked smile. I knew this was coming. I know I don't look my age and most people assume I'm at least 5 years younger than I actually am. "I'm 41."

She splutters like she swallowed wrong and maybe she did. She breathes for a second to regain her composure. "Well, that is also unexpected. I thought I was much older than you. We are in the same decade of life, at least."

"Yes ma'am, we are. That and I've always, always had a thing for older women. England was perfect and fertile ground for that." I hope she can hear the smile in my voice. I'm also laying the flirt on a little thick for before eight a.m.

She swallows audibly. "Ok. Again, unexpected. Let's move on. Whew." In my imagination, I picture her fanning herself. She sounds like she is moving around the room – the kitchen?

"You making coffee, Sunshine? I only have another minute before I need to call my brother. How do you take your coffee?"

"Ummm," she takes a few seconds to think. I can almost hear her brain overheating. "Well, I use almond milk creamer, I like my coffee a little sweet, with a hint of bitter and very hot." She pauses, "Just like I like my men." And then she giggles at her own joke, and I can't help but chuckle with her.

She continues, "So, you have a brother?"

"Three actually, I'm the baby of four."

"Oh wow, that was a busy house! Having three girls was a lot. I can only imagine the repair costs with 4 boys!"

"Yah, there was some of that, but my older brothers are a lot older, so it was almost like there were two sets of boys. Joel and I are the closest in age. He is probably my best friend, too."

"That's really special. I'm glad y'all have each other. My brothers and I aren't close. Well, I am close to one, the oldest. My younger brother, Craig, and I don't get along." Her voice had gotten lower, sadder as she mentioned her siblings. Abruptly turning back into sunshine, even if it felt a little forced, she tells me, "That's a whole story you don't have time for, and I need to get on making biscuits as I don't think my oldest sleeps as late as she used to."

I can tell she is smiling for real now, as she always does when she mentions her girls. I really like that she has that much pride and closeness with her daughters. It speaks volumes about her – and them.

"Ok, yah, I better call Joel while he is on the road. It's been a brilliant morning, Carrie. Can I text you later to see how your day is going? I don't want to be a stalker."

She trills a little laugh, and her voice drops an octave. "Oh, sweet Conner, don't worry, baby. I'll tell you if you bug me." And the way she says baby makes my blood heat and I sway on my feet in the bathroom. She is something else.

"Later, then, Sunshine."

"Later, then, Sweetness."

"Did you just give me a nickname, Carrie?"

She laughs low again, "Men don't get to have all the fun!"

The promise in her voice is enough to have me taking myself in hand in the shower and thinking about all the fun she could have with me.

***

Carrie

As I prepare breakfast for Maley and I, I really hope Conner checks in later. I really hope to talk to him again tonight. I really hope to hear about how his conversation with his brother Joel went. I really hope he tells him about me.

I really hope...

When was the last time I got my hopes up about something? Scott and I were in a good place after several years of a tepid, almost roommate-like existence. Being married to your business partner is difficult because you are both "on" all the time. When we started the therapy clinic support business together, we were both excited, and it helped fuel our connection.

I suggested starting the business after noticing the struggle my therapist was having keeping up with the administrative side, especially with filing insurance claims. Scott jumped right in. It was like a new lease on our life until it got overwhelming for me. We were fifty-fifty at work, but I was doing ninety percent of the work raising the girls and the household chores. I got so lonely because either I was working late and he was asleep, or vice versa.

Five years into the business began a very dry spell in our marriage. We separated for a bit to get some distance and clarity. He moved out for just over three months. We still saw each other every day at work and kept it professional. Maley had just started college, Sabrina was in high school, with Elise was in middle school. It was hard on them because they loved their Daddy, and he wasn't home each night.

Three months to the day of our separation, I was in my office at work when a gigantic bouquet of sunflowers was delivered with a note that says, "Can I take you out on Saturday night?"

I wasn't sure I wanted to reconcile, but he always was a great salesman. He was the dynamic visionary behind the early growth of our company. So, by the night's end, he had wooed me just like all our clients. We started making out in his Volvo and took it to the backseat. Just before things went too far,

I stopped it and left him wanting. I'd done that early in our relationship, which drove him wild.

He looked at me as I exited the car and says, "My Darling Wife, two can play that game." He even watched me walk on jelly legs back to our house. He courted me from that moment forward. He asked me out every night thereafter. It took two weeks for us to decide for him to move back in. Mostly because we were fucking each other's brains out in his tiny, rented guesthouse a neighborhood over from ours. But I couldn't keep leaving the girls every night to have sex with my husband, as hot as it was.

So, one night, after another fancy dinner and mind-blowing love-making session, I rolled off him and asked,

"Is it time for us to be a family again?"

Scott got serious and looked me directly in the eyes. "Yes, but I need to do better at home. As fantastic as it has been to have a "mistress," he said with finger air quotes, "I need to go back home to my wife and girls. I miss sleeping and waking up with you, Carrie. I miss hearing your silly stories. I miss my girls and being in their lives. I miss us so much. Please take me back, and I promise I'll never make you regret it."

And he never did. He lived every day working to make all of us happy and took our company through another record round of growth, letting me have more and more control and input while, at the same time, building the team around us so we could work less. We hired the right people and learned to leave the office at the office.

That happened three years before he died, as now both Maley and Sabrina were thriving at college and Elise was in high school. Those three years were the best in our marriage. For a long time and maybe a little even now, it felt almost as if the fucker knew. Indeed, I've wondered many times in my lowest moments of grief if there was anything I, he, or we could have done to prevent his death.

In the end, what I've had to make my peace with is that there wasn't. We lived our life together, and now that season of my life is over. It is time to move forward.

It occurs to me that at around the same time; I was in hell. Conner was rebuilding his life. I make a mental note to ask him about that when he opens up about his stalker in Michigan State. I don't think it is an "if" he opens up, but a "when."

But if this is just a passing fancy to him…

That's scary as fuck, but I am reminded that I don't have to project my feelings or my fear about this new relationship into a "when." I've learned to rest in what is—worrying about what could be never get me anywhere but anxious and upset. I lived for too long like that before Scott and I healed. I won't go back there again if I can help it.

When Maley comes down a little after eight am, I've showered and made the homemade biscuits she loves. They would feed an army, and once upon a time, when the five of us were together, there was never a biscuit left behind. I'll pack most of them and send them home with her to freeze. I'm cooking the cheesy eggs and turkey sausage we both eat when she walks in, still in pajamas, and I hand her a coffee cup.

"So, Missy, when you get some caffeine, I want to hear everything about your new beau. I want every detail because I need to ensure he is mature enough to handle a woman like you who has all her shit together!"

She rolls her eyes and adds her favorite oat milk into her mug, with a maple syrup splash. "Yes, Mama, I'll tell you all about Jered. It's still early though. Sab isn't convinced."

She knows what to look for in a man after the last two, including the same one through all of undergrad. They were both duds. Young men who wanted her to do all the work to cater to their needs–another Mommy, basically. The second one didn't last nearly as long as the first, thank goodness.

"I guess we will see if Jered makes the cut!"

She takes a few sips of her coffee and eyes me over the rim. Then she makes a statement that has my jaw hitting the floor.

"First though, you must tell me who the guy you talked to till one am was. THAT is by far the more important question to me."

Chapter 6

Conner

"Brother! How are you, man? I feel like it's been forever since we caught up. How's the pre-season?"

My brother Joel, in a booming voice, answers the phone. He looks like a biker or a bear–maybe both. He is taller than I am and has a huge black bushy beard with long curly hair. He takes after our dad, like our two brothers. I'm leaner and have lighter hair, like our mom.

"Joel, the ladies are smashing. The team should rise to the occasion, gotta get them to a cohesive unit. We have our first exhibition game in about a month."

He listens with rapt attention. He played American Football in college, but he is now just as into soccer as I am. He leaned it when I started playing in England and got hooked.

"Which game should I come in for? I need to see my work schedule and if Misty wants to come." How this guy found a woman more fanatic about athletics; I don't know. Their three kids are all involved in multiple sports despite all being under eleven.

"If you really want to celebrate after, come to the match against Michigan State. I'll send you the schedule." Every time we play against my former employer, we destroy them, which couldn't make me happier. "How is the family doing?"

"Busy, so busy. Between work, school, and Misty's business, we run a full schedule from sunup to sundown. She is killing it, and I'm super proud of her. Where she finds the energy, I don't know. She keeps it spicy, too–when we won't get caught. That's a real danger nowadays."

He chuckles, and my chest gets warm for him. His adjustment to life after being a college football star to a blue-collar worker was emotionally rough. The family life suits him.

"I need to make my plans to come for Thanksgiving, for sure. I miss you guys. Have you talked to Derek or James?"

"Yeah, they are good. You should probably respond more on the group text, little bro."

"Yes, I should. I saw them both over the summer."

"Yeah, and they gave you the lecture, I'm sure."

I grimace, and Joel laughs because he can hear it in my voice. "Yes, of course. Their favorite topic. They are like old bitties. They tried introducing me to three women while I was at the summer cottage. It was gross. Zero of them were my type."

He laughs even harder at this. "They haven't learned after all these years that you prefer cougars. Were they all blonde and skinny?"

"No, even worse. They didn't even know anything about sports, much less soccer." I shudder. I would never want a woman who was clueless about sports.

"Yeah, I mean, they didn't marry your type, but still. Respectfully, women need a brain." This is a huge reason Joel and I are so close. Our tastes in women are very similar. His wife was a high school athlete before a car accident forced her to learn to walk again. She is a few years younger than Joel, but I respect Misty and all she's accomplished–after the accident and in her life overall.

Joel titters like only a massive grown man can and says, "So, is there any news on the dating front? You sound different, not your usual grumpy-do-shit-all-on-my-own self."

I pause because this is a big deal. I am more than interested in someone. How complicated it could be suddenly makes me sweat bullets. I already know Joel will be concerned because he was right beside me through every second of the fiasco in Michigan State. I take a deep breath and draw up some courage to face my fears, "Yeah, man. I have met someone. It's complicated, so I need your wisdom on handling it."

Joel lets out a long whistle. "How many years has Misty been on her knees praying for this? I know it can't be a passing fancy if you called me for help. You never do that."

I sigh, "Yah, I know. But I'm in deep, and it's happening fast. She's incredible, but it's complicated."

"Ok. Complicated. I can work with that. All relationships are at some point. How long have you been seeing her?"

"Um, well, we are just talking. But she checks every box for me. It would be long distance as she lives in Texas." I desperately hope he picks up on what I'm saying, so I don't have to admit out loud that I'm falling for the mother of one of my players. I cross my fingers. He is quiet before he says, "Checks every box, huh? Long distance isn't a big deal if she is ok with it. She's not married, is she?"

I laugh, "Fuck no, brother, I wouldn't touch that with a ten-foot pole. She's a widow."

"A widow, huh? She has to be hot, or you wouldn't be interested. A hot widow, now I'm really curious. What's the complication then?"

Dammit, he is going to make me say it. I take a couple of breaths to calm my anxiety. When I don't answer right away, Joel speaks in a worried tone. "Conner–man, what's up? I can't see anything else being a problem."

I take another deep breath and man up to tell him. "Well, Joel, she's the mom of one of my players."

Joel lets out a low whistle, which makes more beads of sweat pop out on my forehead. I nervously I ask him, "Are you mad? What is going through your mind?" I don't want to feel like I've disappointed him again.

"No, no, nothing like that. Taken aback, maybe." He chuckles. "It just never occurred to me that a player's parent would be your style."

"It never has been before. She came out of nowhere, and I was hooked when I saw her. We've had two amazing conversations, and I want this relationship to move forward however it can. She is just as into me as I am her."

"You 1000% sure about that, little brother? Because this is a tremendous risk. I don't want this to end up like Michigan State. No job, no prospects, and practically suicidal. Look, I'm all for this if she is it for you. You've been alone for too long, so if you've found someone worth taking a chance on, do it. Have you talked to her about it?"

"No, not yet. I swear, I'll talk to her before anything goes too far."

"Can I give you some advice, then?"

"Yes, please, Joel. I need it."

"Assume nothing. Keep giving her an out until she tells you she is in this for the long haul. You are a stand-up guy in every way, so I wouldn't expect any less from you. Can you be straight with her daughter, too?"

"Yeah, I don't know if that's a good idea until we decide to take the risk."

He sighs. "I understand, but remember, secrets will blow up in your face. Be upfront with everyone involved. It's not strictly forbidden, right?"

"No, it's not, but it is frowned upon."

"Ok, then be smart. Be the man you are, Conner. You've grown so much in the last few years and have an incredible future. Don't fuck it up now, little brother."

I sigh and wipe the tears out of my eyes. I want to make this guy proud.

We take a moment to let the feelings settle. It's a lot for two guys to share like this, even as close as we are. I move around my kitchen to make coffee and, as I do, my stomach growls loudly. It's time to feed my body, after that ride–both the Peloton and all the emotions.

Joel calls me back with, "Now, you little fucker. I still have another ten minutes till I get to work on this lonely interstate. Tell me about your girl....or should I say, your woman."

I put down the carafe I was using to pour water into the coffee maker and pause. I take a deep inhale. This–talking to, and now, about Carrie–is quickly becoming my favorite topic. I smile as I think about her. And how open she makes me feel even after such a short period.

"Brother, she is a fucking goddess."

***

Carrie

"How do you know I was talking to a man?" Maley's first question before enough coffee has me shaken.

I didn't think she would hear a word because she was upstairs and on the opposite side of the house. I whirl to face her. "Maley Susan Vokler, were you spying on me?"

She grins like a cat with a canary in its mouth when suddenly Schroder appears and weaves between her legs, shaking his tail and meowing loudly to be picked up and scratched.

She obliges him, and he purrs for a few seconds before he sinks his sharp kitty fangs into her hand. She shrieks and immediately drops him. He runs for his favorite hiding place under my bed. He stops, turns around to eye her and meows loudly, as if he is letting her know that the whole interaction was her fault.

She scowls at him and makes an obscene hand gesture. I chuckle before I return to the question at hand, wagging a finger. "I'm waiting, Missy. What do you have to say for yourself?"

She doesn't give an inch, but her scowl turns back into a mischievous smile. I hear her stomach growl loudly and she reaches past me to snatch a piece of turkey sausage. Chomping on it further delays her response, so I plant my hands on my hips, spatula still in hand, and stare her down.

The tension stretches out for a bit between us, and I must turn away from her to flip the sausage patties browning in the pan. My oldest knows I'm pretty much all bark and no bite when there are no–or low–stakes. I'm a terrible poker player and I note she has gotten good at uncomfortable silence.

She continues to chew up her stolen sausage patty like she has all the time in the world. She stands there, waiting me out.

I bring my coffee cup to my nose to smell the combination of the coffee and the chocolate protein powder and almond milk creamer I mix in to give myself a little boost to get the day going.

We continue like this, in our silent face off, as we prepare our breakfast. She butters her biscuits, adding jelly to one side of one half and planting a sausage patty in the middle before mushing it all together like a sandwich. It's exactly how I eat mine. Maley tops off her coffee, and then brings both our plates to our sunny breakfast nook.

It's September in Texas, so it's still hot as Hades and we are only comfortable sitting here in the sun drinking coffee because I haven't yet turned the air conditioner up.

Finally, after finishing one of her biscuit sandwich, Maley breaks the silence. "Ok. Ok, Mama, you got me."

"Ha! I knew you'd break first."

"Don't think this means I will let you off the hook. Don't think I won't ask again."

I look at her critically, knowing I could tell her. She is the family secret keeper, so if I asked her not to say anything about Conner to her sisters, she wouldn't. I need to prepare myself for her opinion. She can have very strong ones about how other people handle their lives. She is a true oldest daughter–and a Libra - in that.

I sigh, take a bite of my breakfast sandwich, and after I finish chewing, I jokingly say, "I don't think I've had enough coffee yet to discuss what my love life could look like."

"So, you have a love life?"

"Darling girl, I may have an ice cube's chance in hell of a love life, but at least it is a chance."

"For what it's worth, and whenever you feel like telling me–BEFORE I leave for the weekend–I am happy for you. You've been alone through some tough stuff. You deserve someone to love you, Mama. I know you don't need it; you are radiant on your own, but you deserve a man worthy of matching your energy."

The tears sting the corner of my eyes. I'm used to being the one who encourages my girls; it is a little overwhelming to be the object of their praise. I squeak out a "Thank you, baby" and focus on eating my breakfast. It doesn't take long; I'm starving from that ride and not eating much when I get home.

After a few more sips of coffee in the contented silence before I say, "I'm pretty excited about this guy. He is already someone in his world. He doesn't live here so it would be long distance. I know he is very interested in me, and it's early in our conversations."

I look her in the eye before I continue. "Sweetheart, it is more than a little complicated. But I am extremely attracted to him. And after talking to him last night, it isn't just physical. I'm attracted to ALL of him." I pause for effect as she sips her coffee, "Oh, and he is younger than me."

Maley spits some coffee back into her mug, and her eyes bug out. She takes a choking breath, swallowing the hot liquid and then leveling me with a glare.

I smile into my cup as I quietly retort, "Maley Susan, you deserved that."

She admits, "You're probably right. And you shouldn't talk so damn loud at one am!"

I chuckle, "Fair, fair. I'll keep it down tonight." *I hope,* I think as I swallow one of my own hot gulps.

As if she is reading my mind, "It's ok to hope again, Mama. Dad would want you to be happy. In fact, I had a dream about him the other night."

I raise an eyebrow. I dream a lot too, but Maley has the most vivid. I dreamed of Scott once or twice after he passed, two very short dreams, almost identical. In the dream, we were just hugging, and I felt at peace. I know dreams tell us a lot about ourselves. Between the two of us though, Maley has always been the one with the stronger gift.

She continues, "Yes, it was so striking. I texted it to myself so I would remember to tell you."

She fishes her phone out of her PJ pocket, opening it to her notes app.

She reads it to me, "I was in a field of tall grass, walking along and running my hands over the top, and I could feel the tickling feeling. I kept walking, and I was wearing a long gown. It wasn't white exactly, but it was the same cut of dress as the one I wore to Dad's service. It trailed out behind me, and I felt very centered. I felt like I had walked for a long time before I came to a doorway. I was still a way off from it, but I could see someone standing before it. It took me a moment to realize it was Dad." She paused.

"Did he say anything? What did he do?"

She swallows. "That was the weird thing. He didn't talk or say anything. He just stood there, smiling at me from the doorway. I called out to him and started to move forward, but he stopped me. I was standing in the grass field when he blew me a kiss and then raised his hand to make the 'I love you' hand sign. He turned and went through the doorway. Then I woke up."

As she finished, her voice got thicker with emotion. I reached over and took her hand. Her eyes were a little misty, and while I knew Scott was with us, to have so close an encounter with him as she did, even in sleep, the hair on the back stood up.

It's one thing to know the dead are just beyond our field of vision, only a breath away from the living. It's another thing to experience it.

We sat in silence as she recovered herself, tears leaking down her cheeks. I reached up to wipe them away, and she held my palm to her cheek.

"He is so proud of you, little bud," using his nickname for her. He started calling her 'little bud' while she was in my womb.

"He didn't love me anymore than my sisters, but he loved me the longest." That made a couple more tears leak out of both our eyes. He used to say that to her, too.

She let go of my hand and wiped her face. After taking another drink of her coffee to clear her throat, she says, "Now that

I hear it aloud, I think it was for all of us. I think it was a kind of see you later and a blessing to get on with our lives. Mama, you are the only one who hasn't done that. Maybe this younger man coming into your life is at the right time?"

I couldn't answer her. *Could it be that I was ready? Could Scott want me to loosen my grip and try to love again?*

This time, it was Maley's turn to reach over and take my hand. We'd learned that comfort is a give and take, always moving back and forth between us. My girls give and I've learned to take from them. They draw strength from me, and now, I can draw it from them when I need it.

It is an incredible blessing.

I take a couple of deep, steadying breaths and nod my assent. We sit for another ten minutes in contemplative silence. Then, as if we had one mind, we look up, smile, and rise to get ready for our day at the Zoo. It's Maley's favorite place in Houston and a Vokler family tradition.

Now, it feels like our family is about to begin a new adventure together.

CHAPTER 7

Conner
Make it to noon.
Don't be a stalker.
Make it to noon.
Don't be a stalker.

I keep repeating this mantra to myself as I go through my meetings. My leg is bouncing like a pogo stick under the table when Inanna looks at me and says in her typical prickly fashion,

"Conner, what's your problem? You've been acting like you have ants in your jockstrap all morning."

"Inanna, it's 'ants in your pants'." I correct.

She scoffs, "You are a dude." And rolls her eyes before continuing, "If you were one of my players and were acting like this, I would make sure you ended up with ants in your jock strap."

"You are unnecessarily cruel, Coach." Inanna may be a hard ass but she is really the good cop on the coaching staff. She is the player favorite. They know she has their back no matter what.

"So, what the actual fuck is up, Coach?" She also lets nothing go.

I sigh. "I have a lot on my mind." It's a cop out but if I tell her about Carrie, ants in my jockstrap will be the least of my worries. She would serve me my own balls sauteed in butter with mashed potatoes on the side.

She reads right through it. "BULLSHIT. What's up? You aren't expecting the sky to fall again, are you?"

It's my turn because she would bring that up because thinking something is going to go wrong, especially when things are going well, is a very classic trauma response. That used to be my standard operating procedure when we first started coaching together. She made me go back to therapy because it turns out, I not only had a fear of failure but also a fear of success. I dealt with it and now we are positioned to be the top program in the country.

It was the right call.

We work so well together because we play to our strengths, and I usually stay out of her way. The ladies trust her completely. She makes them feel safe even as she watches them like a hawk. It's the craziest kind of coach-player dynamic but it hasn't failed us yet. Over the years she has been coaching with me, she has grown into the type of leader who could easily lead the next phase of this program.

And she is exactly who I will recommend when I get called up to the National Team. I know that will happen in my bones. I plan to make sure she gets her shot and any others she wants. She doesn't need me but I sure as hell need her.

So, I better keep her happy-ish. "It's nothing. I-i-i just met someone."

She is working on play formation on our whiteboard, facing away from me. At this stuttering statement, she deliberately puts the cap on the expo marker slowly, sets it gently down in the tray and then, at a glacial pace, turns around to face me. The look she levels at me makes my armpits sweat.

"And why should that matter at all during our planning session? We have an exhibition coming up in a few weeks then the season starts a month later. We have a lot of fucking work to do, Conner."

Curtly, I respond, verbally meeting her alpha tone, "Inanna, I understand that. I also would appreciate you knowing this a huge fucking deal for me. I know we've both always been about the job, but this is someone who could end up changing my life. I will rein it in, but you don't have to make me feel like shit about maybe, potentially, hopefully, for the first time since you've known me, having a personal life."

She is staring at me like she can see through my skin, down to my chromosomes.

"Inanna, stop, I'm not a criminal."

"No, but you might have been body snatched. The Conner Doreland I know has NEVER been interested in a woman. Well, it is a woman?"

"Yes, Inanna. It is a woman. And there has been no one even remotely like her. She is one of a kind, which is why she has my attention. But I'll focus, I promise."

She continues to stare at me for another full minute and I almost flip her off, stand up and walk to the bathroom to splash some water on my face. But she breaks the stare and turns back to the board.

I breathe out a slow breath of relief.

"I heard that!"

"Well, why did you make my balls feel like they were being microwaved?"

"I needed to see how much you squirmed. Tell me about her when you are ready. She better be fucking outstanding."

I look down at my notes and mutter, "I'm pretty sure she is outstanding enough that you would fuck her."

She is quiet for long enough that I look up to see the side of her face and she's cocked an eyebrow. "Maybe I will."

I narrow my eyes at her and continue our playful, if not borderline inappropriate discussion, with a challenge. "You wouldn't dare to try."

Inanna fully faces me, adopts an angelic face, and bats her eyelashes while she says, "Scared I'll flip her, Conner? She'll have to blow the dust off your dick before y'all do anything, anyway."

She smiles like the freaking devil.

I smile back at her with all my teeth and say, "I hate you."

She laughs loud at this fake admission and tells me, "No you don't. You love me and owe all your success to me. Now, can we go back to planning if I promise not to fuck your girlfriend?"

I scrub my hand over my face and grit out, "Stop talking about her like that, and then yes."

She tuts her tongue at me, "Touchy, aren't we? She must be something special."

I look at my watch. Only thirty more minutes till I can text her without looking like a stalker. Thankfully, I already have the message ready to hit send. I typed it out the second I hung up with Joel.

> *How's your day going, Sunshine? Things going well with your girl? I look forward to hearing about it later, once you have the time. I hope it's not too forward to say, but I've been thinking about you.*

Refocusing my attention to the whiteboard, I notice Inanna arranged another set of possible plays, so I say, putting bass in my voice to assert my authority, "Inanna, you have thirty minutes to work your magic. Get on it."

Inanna rolls her eyes again, a trademark response, and we hammer out our plan for the exhibition game on Parent's Weekend.

***

Carrie

After a wonderful time at the Zoo and then a picnic lunch in Hermann Park, Maley and I find a shaded spot with plenty of cover against a September day that is hot as hell. She takes a sip of her Dr. Pepper while I try not to chug my sparkling water to quench my parched throat.

Maley echoes my thoughts. "I'm going to need to shower again when we get home. It's so hot!"

As if in confirmation, I feel the steady stream of sweat run down the channel of my spine into my underwear. I wore underwear today for this reason. Despite the political idiots running the state, Texas is a decent place to live and Houston is an open, inviting place to be thanks to enterprise and diversity. I love it even though I complain about the heat.

We Texans just have to hang on a few more weeks till the first cold front pushes through. Relief is on the way, the meteorologist said on the news this morning. That is much preferable to a hurricane.

Hopefully.

There is that word again in my thoughts — hope.

As I finish my tacos and wipe my hands, a text buzzes through. It's from Conner, and my heart soars.

> *How's your day going, Sunshine? Things going well with your girl? I look forward to hearing about it later once you have the time. I hope it's not too forward to say, but I've been thinking about you.*

I don't realize I am grinning ear to ear until my daughter calls me out, "Well, well, well. The mystery guy must not have gotten enough of you last night."

I look up at her and she is gazing at me with an amused expression, full of curiosity.

I decide to indulge her by giving her a few more details. "Actually, we took a Peloton class together this morning. I'd already planned to ride, when he messaged me on the app. Then we started talking, so he made plans to join me. It was at five in the morning for him, but he is an early riser, apparently."

"Wait, you met him on the Peloton app? How do you know this guy isn't a freak or a stalker or catfishing you??"

"Well, those are all likely scenarios IF I hadn't already met him. Or rather, know who he was."

"So, where did you meet him?"

I shift nervously on the table bench. While I didn't want to keep anything from my girls, I suddenly realize I don't want to be talked out getting to know Conner despite the obvious risk. I don't want to hear the truth that it is a bad idea to be in a situation-ship with my daughter's new coach.

"Mama, what is it? I know I said I'd wait till you were ready to tell me, but I need to know you're making smart, safe decisions."

I burst out laughing, "Maley, darling, that's my line. Yes, of course I'm making safe, smart decisions. This guy is vetted. Us being in any kind of relationship could be tricky."

I knew the question was coming as soon as the words left my mouth.

"Why?"

I sigh. "Can I respond to him and then I'll tell you about it?"

She sighs and says, "Fine. I need to make a call, anyway." For her, that was code that she wants to call her own guy. She walks a few steps away and I pick up my phone to text Conner. It didn't take me but a split second to put on my flirty hat. Thinking of him makes me want to flirt.

> Hey, Sweetness. Things are going well here. We've had some great talks and went to the zoo. Just finished a late lunch. Going to head home soon but I might need a nap. Some sexy guy kept me up late. Not that I minded. <wink emoji>

The three dots appeared almost immediately. His reply is indeed sweet.

> I'm glad you have this time with her. I really love how close your family is. It's impressive given how I've seen it go with mothers and daughters.

Then another message comes through, proving he is just as much of a flirt as I am.

> I'd love to take a nap with you someday. And keep you up late again too. Last night and this morning have made me want to get to know you – all of you – more than what the internet has told me.

I huff a laugh. So, he internet stalked me. Fair is fair, I guess – and smart.

> Oh yah? The internet? And what have you discovered, pray tell?

It doesn't take him long. When I read what he writes, I get a little lightheaded and my heart squeezes.

> Three words: Gifted. Gorgeous. Goddess.

I actually think I might swoon. It takes a beat to catch my breath and respond with,

> I think I like you even more now. You want to know what my internet stalking has told me about you?

Three dots and then.

> I'm a little afraid but yes.

I type out my three words for him:

> Bright. Brilliant. Badass.

I chase it with another text that says,

> But I reserve the right to add more than three words to this list.

It takes a full minute for his text to come back, although the dots are there the entire time. He is typing a lot...or tying and retyping.

> Sunshine, you have no idea what you do to me. I feel all, Idk, squishy inside?

I hit the laugh auto-response on his message and then type,

> Well, your insides match mine and the state of certain parts of my outside. Mom bods have some hard-earned squish to them.

What I get back makes the sweat channel down my back go from a stream to a river and I feel a different heat building at the apex of my thighs.

> Baby, there is nothing 'squishy' about any part of you. You are all woman and there is nothing I would like more than to take the time worshiping every inch of your body. And you get to pick the order.

I question back.

> The order?

His response is again quick,

> Yes, Sunshine. You get to pick what I use first: fingers, tongue, or cock. I would make sure to follow your order but then it's my choice what comes next to ensure I please you fully.

Holy hell. This man is going to be the death of me. I fan myself and it is not because of the Texas heat. I think I'm going to spontaneously combust. But if I'm going to go down in flames, I'm going to take him down with me.

> Conner, you can certainly have your way with me as long as I get my turn to wor-

> ship every inch of you and I will start with my tongue.

I have never texted with a man like this before and I hope we keep it up. Fuck, if we keep it up, we are going to have phone sex before the week is up.

> *Fucking hell, Sunshine.*

Then....

> *I can't wait to bask in your glow, Carrie. I also don't know how I'm going to function at work the rest of the day with this concrete erection.*

I laugh. I adore his honesty and tell him so.

> *I don't know what I did to deserve you being so open with me, but I adore it, Sweetness.*

Again, the quick response:

> *You didn't have to do anything, Sunshine. You being you allows me be more me than I think I have been for a long time. Do you have to get back to your girl?*

I also adore that he remembers I have a life.

> *I appreciate you remembering I've got company. I definitely want to talk to you later. Can I ask a potentially off-putting question?*

Ask me anything, anytime, anywhere. I'm yours.

Those last two words do something funny in my chest. I see Maley gesturing in a frustrated way and know my time with Conner is running out for now.

> Would you be ok if I told Maley about us getting to know one another? I know we haven't discussed the risks and if we need to keep it a secret. I want/need to be as honest as I can be with her. She has noticed something different about me – and she heard me talking to you last night. :D She wants details, of course, now that she knows I'm interested in someone. I don't have to mention anything, but you should know, she is our family secret-keeper. It wouldn't go beyond her unless she had my expressed permission. I mean, she wouldn't tell her sisters if I told her not to. And plus, you said you were going to tell your brother about me. About us. So, it would be nice for me to share with someone close to me too.

I hit send, see the length of the text and slap a hand to my forehead before I type out an explanation.

> I'm not usually a rambler, sorry. Just trying to live in truth. And I'm nervous. :D

I look up from my phone to see Maley punch her screen to end the call and take some long, slow breaths. It apparently was not an easy conversation with her new man.

I stare at her back a little longer because I know Conner has responded. My phone buzzed, but I don't want to look down at the message. I'm afraid he will want to hide whatever this is. I'm afraid that if he does, what that will mean for me? I'm afraid that even though we haven't hit the twenty-four-hour mark yet. I hope that this is something special; that what I've read about him and the feeling that he is a man of integrity, was wrong. I'm afraid I was wrong.

Holding my breath, I mentally hype myself and open my screen that timed out. As I read his message, I release the breath all at once because all my fears were unfounded.

> *Sunshine, yes, I want to talk more about this - where we are and what that means, what we should do, etc. We both know this is complicated. It's also moving fast for me, and I sense you feel the same. I trust you. I trust you know what makes sense for you.*

With an expression like a storm cloud, Maley plops down across from me as another message comes through. I take the opportunity to read it while my daughter's ire gathers steam.

As I read it, my head gets light, so I grip the table while my heart does a massive backflip.

> *Carrie, I can't wait to tell the world about us.*

Chapter 8

Conner

Our two-hour time difference means Carrie calls while I'm eating dinner, and she is in bed. I showered after running but am still quite warm. I've got on a pair of lightweight gray sleeping joggers and no shirt.

It's a moment before she looks up while she puts in her air pods. When I see her face, my breath catches. She is absolutely stunning. I say nothing as I'm transported back to the first time I saw her. Her face is clean, hair is a messy little bun and wearing a pair of soft looking dark purple pajamas. I bet she smells incredible.

I bet she feels like home. The thought floats across my brain space as she says, "Conner? Are you ok? Am I frozen?"

I shake myself loose and say, "Carrie, goddamn. I literally can't think of the words to tell you how stunning you are. Your pictures don't do you justice. Holy shit, Carrie."

Standing with the phone in front of her, it is her turn to freeze. Then I hear her mumble, "The things you say, Conner Doreland. I can't understand...." Pausing, she says a little more clearly, "I think I mean to say thank you, but now words escape me. Though I might need you to put a shirt on so I can concentrate."

I grin at her as I hold the camera up high enough to give her an aerial view of my face and torso before I flex. I'm not as cut as when I was playing, but I'm in fine shape. Erik, as a workout partner, helps with that. If she wants an eye full, I am happy to oblige.

"That's not fair." She pouts a little.

"Fair? I said nothing about being fair, Sunshine. If you like what you see, then triple it and maybe then you'll understand how I feel about who I'm looking at. I've never seen someone heading to bed who looks so.... fresh."

She laughs, "Well, it helps I fell asleep watching a movie with Maley again." She winks at the camera, and I stop with my glass of water halfway to my mouth. My cock liked that wink a lot. If I gave her another aerial shot, my joggers wouldn't hide a damn thing.

I blow out a long breath. "Well, you can fall asleep watching a movie with me anytime. Is that usual for you?"

"Falling asleep in movies? Yes, absolutely. I've dozed off in theaters. If it's dark and I'm warm and comfortable, I'm out like a light. I talk in my sleep, too."

"Oh yah, about what?"

My cock also responds when she giggles, "I've been told I tell stories, but they make no sense, like I'm speaking in tongues. My kids used to love to pretend to be asleep when I put them down for naps, because I would fall asleep before them and talk. Even when they were little, they thought it was hilarious."

"That is the cutest thing I've ever heard. Are you going to fall asleep on the phone with me so I get a story? I see you are getting comfortable."

Another giggle at a lower octave and my dick pulses. I wonder how many times I'm going to have to jerk off tonight to sleep. "I'm leaving my light on, so hopefully I will stay awake, but no guarantees."

Another low giggle and another pulse. Yes, it's going to be a long night.

***

Carrie

Conner shirtless is so damn distracting. Never in a million years would I think someone this good-looking would be face timing with me. He tells me about his day and what the next few weeks look like for him and the team. His openness makes it seem like there is a light shining on his face. He is so fucking handsome; it makes my chest ache. And my pussy is dripping. We haven't even done any real flirting or sexy talk yet.

I felt good when I called him but now, hearing his voice, it makes me want to hear him whisper my name, my nickname, or anything else, like "good girl," he wants to call me.

"What are the next few weeks like for you?" He asks and I startle out of my Conner Doreland erotic fantasy land.

He notices, "You ok there, Sunshine? I'm not boring you, am I? I don't want my story to start too early." He smiles a real, genuine grin. Oh God, he has a dimple in his left cheek. All I want to do is stick my tongue in it.

I can feel he likes me as much as I like him. I decide this is the time to be bold. I tell him, "Yes, Conner, I'm paying attention. I want to tell you something. Maybe it is going to seem a little out of character. So let me start by asking you a question."

"Okaayy" he says but a playful smile remains on his face. "I told you, Sunshine, ask me anything, anytime, anywhere."

I take a deep breath and pull my luminous self-up to the surface of my skin. I feel alive and I know what I want. Now, to see if he wants the same thing, too. "Conner, do you want to keep talking?"

He responds with, "I think you have something else in mind. Let's hear it."

Taking a deep breath, closing my eyes briefly to envision my radiance, I tell him, "Well, I'd like to suggest something I've been envisioning for a week now every night before I go to sleep."

He stares into the screen, meeting my eyes with a gaze that makes his golden-brown eyes looking like molten lava. That gaze has me pinned, breathless, waiting for his reply.

I want to jump straight into that molten flow and burn up.

"Carrie, I really hope you are thinking what I'm thinking, but you already have me, Sunshine. I'll do anything you want."

At that comment, I catch the scent of my desire, and it is intoxicating. I'm desperate to know what he smells like. I close my eyes and let out a little breathless moan at the thought of what he tastes like.

"Carrie," Conner says with a dangerous edge, "Pretty girl, look at me and tell me what you want."

Electricity zings through me with that slight bass added to enforce the dominance in his voice. Beyond wanting me, I know he cares about me. I feel safe and wanted.

I'm about to be my rockstar self and Conner's gaze makes it possible. Even though a part of me wants to explain–or maybe even apologize–for what I want; I just go for it. "Conner, I want to fuck myself while you watch. I've been imagining us together for a week now. Then I want to watch you fuck yourself while you think about me."

Chapter 9

Conner

 I feel my whole lower half clench, then pulse. Pre-cum soaks the front of my pants and I can smell myself, the tang and musk of my attraction to her.

 I bet her skin tastes like heaven and the flavor of her pussy high inducing.

 At her confidence, it would take an instant for me to have my dick in my hand and pop off. I am more turned on than I have ever been in my whole life.

 Yet, she invites me to this incredible dance by asking for permission, letting me lead but telling me exactly what she needs. I've never experienced this with a woman, which takes this to a whole other level of desire.

I grind out a gruff response, "Put your phone somewhere; to see everything. I want to see your body, Carrie. I want to see you to map what I can and then fill in the rest when we are together. This is your opportunity to teach me exactly what you like, so do a good job, Sunshine."

She moans, which zaps my dick like I'm wearing a buzzer. She gives me a beaming smile as she begins her preparations. I nearly explode at the sight of her face. That smile was glorious, and it was all for me. Fucking hell, I will not last long when we are together.

She is positively gleeful at the thought of pleasuring herself in front of me as she sets her phone up on the table by her bed. I will see everything from here, as if I was right next to her. She keeps her eyes on the screen as she reaches down, opens a drawer, and holds up a bottle of coconut oil and a glass dildo.

I close my eyes and inhale to hold my breath and calm the raging, pulsing desire.

She leans forward towards the camera, giving me an eyeful of her fantastic cleavage. She dangles the dildo in front of me as she whispers loudly, "Do you like my wand? I usually set an intention before I start, but this wand has a name now. I call it Sweetness."

She winks and I close my eyes, swaying slightly. I grip the edge of the table and, with my other hand, clench the phone so hard it shakes.

"Conner, why don't you put the phone down where I can see you?" Her voice is low and full, just a hint of a command and the vibration sings through me, like a song.

I obey, moving to my favorite chair in the living room. My house is cozy, so I take about 3 seconds. I prop the phone on the box on top of the mahogany coffee table in front of the chair. It is the perfect angle to give her full access to my entire body. My joggers are in a full tent. And my cock is ready to come out and play with this beauty.

As I sit down, I say, "I'm doing everything in my power to hold on to my control. I have never, ever, ever been this turned on. Do you have a vibrator, Sunshine?"

She shakes her head. "I've never tried one."

A moan from deep inside my chest erupts and then I say, "Good God, a first. Maybe we can try that together."

Her sweet giggle comes out and I'm going to die unless I hear that sound in person. It is going to be sheer torture to wait another 3 weeks to get her in my arms. I am already planning a weekend alone together.

We may never leave the bed. We could die of dehydration, and I wouldn't care one bit.

She lays down on her fluffy dove gray duvet, head on the pillow and I stop her. "No, no, no, Pretty Girl. Flip around. When I say I want to see everything, I mean it. I want the view I'll have when we are in person. I'll be looking up at you from between those soft, lovely thighs. And you won't be clothed when that happens, so take off that cute pajama top."

She looks up at me with surprise and an adorable wrinkle appears between her brows as she thinks through the logistics. She adjusts the phone and as she undresses; I see the concern pass over her face. She hadn't expected to be naked.

I don't want her to be uncomfortable, so I ask her, "Are you ok with that? Or would you prefer something else?"

That concentration wrinkle between her brows remains for a minute while she decides. "As comfortable as I am in my skin, could I keep my top on? I was prepared to take my bottoms off. How else could I show you what Sweetness does to me?" That crinkle on her face relaxes as she smiles at me and winks.

Her self-understanding and vulnerable expression take my breath away.

"Sunshine, make yourself comfortable, please. But know when I get you to myself, I want to see all of you without a stitch on. I'm going to worship all of you with no clothing in the way. Every piece of you available to me, deal?"

"Yes, sir!" And she does a brief salute, which unravels me further.

I growl out, "Be careful with that kind of response, Pretty Girl. That does unholy things inside of me."

She gives me a wicked grin. "Pay attention, Conner. Class is about to start. And we are going to move fast."

***

Carrie

This is the most exhibitionist I've ever been, a complete first, and it's so fucking hot. It is so exhilarating; I feel light-headed. I couldn't do this with just anyone. Conner's openness this possible. He wants to see me. So, I will show him.

I don't even need the lube. I'm that wet. I shimmy out of my pajama bottoms while I look at the camera. Positioning myself on the bed, I rest lightly to the side, with one leg bent, bracing on the headboard and one leg resting on the rail near the floor. I'm naked from the waist down and, at this angle, stretched open wide. He can see every inch, just like he wants.

He groans so loud. "Carrie, you are gorgeous. You are the hottest woman I've ever seen. I swear to God when I touch my dick, I'm going to come. You are perfection, Sunshine."

I lean forward a little, taking the wand in my hand, and say, "I am picturing this wand as your cock, Conner." I open my mouth, laying my tongue out flat and dragging the tip of the wand from the back near my throat down to the tip of my tongue. I then wrap my mouth around it, working my saliva all over it. I close my eyes and sigh loudly.

I hear Conner moan my name before he says, "Sunshine, hurry, I can't take much more. When I come, what do you want me to picture—in your mouth, chest or pussy? Because I'm going to do all of those."

I smile around the wand and look straight at the camera. As I pull it out, I tell him, "Mouth."

He groans again.

I slide the tip down over my throat, between my breasts, over my shirt and stomach, finally to rest on top of the little triangle of hair at the apex of my thighs. He is breathing hard. I feel the anticipation of a drug.

I don't wait any longer, as I part my labia with my right hand and use my left to position the wand at my entrance.

"Carrie, oh my god. Carrie." Conner's gaze is flying over me.

My pussy is soaking wet, open, and ready. I slide the tip of the wand in and as I do, my pussy immediately sucks it in tighter. I groan from my center, feeling my abs flex as I curl up slightly around the wand. I suck in a deep breath as I relax back and my legs widen, giving him a better view. My pussy clenches around the wand, and I exhale his name.

I swirl my fingers around and bring them to the epicenter of my pleasure. My clit is swollen, a button just ready for me to push. Using my index and middle finger in a circular motion, the pressure builds swiftly as I pump the wand in and out with growing force.

I look up into the screen and I can see the burning of his eyes as he watches me. I bite out, "Conner, let me see your cock in your hand."

He obeys instantly and takes out his glorious cock. It is swollen, springing up at full attention. It is a little longer than my wand and with a little more girth. I groan, knowing it is going to feel unimaginably good inside of me. At the thought of him filling me, I nearly hit my peak.

I concentrate on him as he uses the trickle of pre-cum leaking out of the tip to slick his hand and he pumps himself, squeezing hard, up, and down, once, twice, three times.

In a rush, I say, "Conner, oh my God, Conner. Oh my God. Oh, my God."

He commands, "Look at me, Sunshine. I want your eyes on me while you picture me fucking you senseless."

I do as he says, and I hear him grind out, "Such a good girl."

With one last circle around my clit, I rupture. My back bows and my hips come completely off the bed. Pumping the wand in and out as I stroke out my climax, I look back at the screen and witness Conner join me. He yells my name like a prayer, with his head thrown back against the back of the overstuffed chair. Cum sprays all over his muscled chest and abdomen. He continues to pump himself through the climax, as I draw mine out as well.

He is a stunning sight.

He picks his head up to meet my eyes and with quiet command says, "Yes, my darling Sunshine, come again and squirt for me."

Seeing him come, then with his words, my eyes slam shut and my back bows again. I try to keep my voice down, so I hold my breath before grinding out, "Oh fuck! Sweetness!" I see stars while I feel the gush of wetness around the wand.

I take a couple of minutes to calm down, still breathing hard as I look at the screen to see Conner watching me. He has his phone in his hand. He says nothing, and I don't have any words either. It's as if there is no screen between us. His face tells me everything I need to know about how he feels.

I can feel my connected heart, pussy and spirit shining right back at him.

Chapter 10

Conner

It seems easier to take another quick shower, as I am covered in cum. I tell Carrie I'll call her back in five minutes.

What I just experienced only confirmed deep down what I knew at a cellular level. I must be with this woman. I do not know how to work that out, but I feel at peace and know it will be alright. We might have to fight like hell for it, but we will. It's like the first time I saw a soccer ball and knew that's what I would do with my life.

My soul knows it: Carrie, and I are meant to be.

This certainty is a rarity for me and a fucking dream I don't want to wake up from. I brush my teeth and roughly comb down my hair, which is standing up on its own. I lie down in my bed and immediately feel a desire to go to sleep. That's another first for me.

A night of firsts.

I hit the Facetime call button, already smiling. I can only imagine what it is going to feel like when we are together. I want that so badly. My smile gets bigger when she answers, lying down, facing the phone. Like my head is on the pillow next to her. The first thing that comes out of my mouth is the truth from my soul, "I can't wait to fall asleep with you, Sunshine."

She smiles a warm, sleepy grin at me. It is incredible how much a person can glow.

"I want to hear about this nighttime routine of yours."

She giggles softly and impossibly; my dick gets a little hard. That giggle is an aphrodisiac. She sighs sweetly, content. "It depends on the day. Tonight, I had a little nap, which helps and since I knew I was going to talk to you; and I wanted to feel…" she pauses, "I don't know if sexy is the right word, but I wanted to feel alive. So, before we talked, I got into my pajamas, and I danced."

"You danced? What kind of dancing?"

"I put on some music that makes me feel good and I move-however my body wants to move. I'm not a dancer by training, I just let my body do what it wants. It usually feels cathartic. Whatever I'm feeling, there is music for it, which helps me positively channel my emotions. I used it a lot when I was grieving. Elise and I both did."

"Wow, I've never thought of doing that."

"I can feel out of control sometimes and I started dancing to channel it. I always wanted to dance with a partner but, well, you know." She doesn't want to mention her husband's name but continues, "He never wanted to dance with me. Only just a few seconds at a time. It felt like he was humoring me, even when we were having fun. He had other ways of preferred ways of channeling his energy–masculine ways–probably like you do."

"Yes, I am a very masculine guy." At that, she laughs loudly and tells me, "Yes, Conner, I can tell."

The thought that pops out of my head comes right out of my mouth. "Sunshine, I would consider it the highest honor if you would dance with me. I bet you look hot as hell doing it. And maybe it could help me."

"I would love that." She gets quiet. I wonder if she is lost in thought.

I want to continue the conversation, so I ask, "Ok, you dance. Anything else that settles you and makes you feel cozy? I want to wrap you up in my arms and let your warmth seep into me."

Being still and quiet feels like she is on the brink of sleep, and I can see her eyes are closed. She mumbles something I don't catch. "What was that, Sunshine? Am I getting a story already?"

"No." she says the word a little sadly, takes a deep breath, and opens her eyes. The blue is dark, like the depth of the ocean.

"What is it, Carrie?" I whisper as an ache to hold her spreads across my chest.

She sits up on her elbow and swipes her bangs off her face. This is her serious and brave face; I'm learning. She starts, her voice a little shaky, "I haven't mentioned my marriage before because I don't want it to be a downer. It doesn't bother me, being a widow. You get used to it, to the looks and the pity. When that happens and I can't handle it, I rage dance or curse about it to my best friend, Dulce." She smiles and laughs a little.

"But?" I say, knowing it is coming.

"No, Conner, there isn't a 'but'. I hope to have no equivocations with you that require a 'but.'"

I stare at her through the screen. "Ok, so what is it? You have a past. I do too and I want to share it with you. I know you were married for a long time and that he died suddenly. Inanna told me. Hell, Elise mentioned it to me, too. She wasn't sure she wanted to go to a school so far away. She was worried you would be lonely."

She laughs softly, her mind switching gears for a second. "Elise would worry about me. But, Conner, that's the thing. I'm not lonely. I live a very full life. Having the chance to share that with someone is a gift. The other thing I do before I fall asleep is say prayers of gratitude. Between the dancing and the gratitude, that is what I consider my mojo, my power."

"Sunshine, you have a lot. I think it is what caught my eye, and I have a lot to learn from you."

She smiles at me. "I think we have a lot to teach each other, my sweet, gorgeous young man." She winks and fuck if my heart doesn't leap into my throat. I still sense a lingering sadness, so I press her gently. "There is something you were going to say that made you sad. Will you tell me?"

She smiles tightly and tears up. She wipes her eyes before sharing. "Grief is funny. It hits out of nowhere. I was so happy when we started talking–and I am happy. When you said you couldn't wait to hold me, I realized how much I'd missed that. I can't wait to share that with you, and I am glad I'm finding it again."

I don't have any words, so I put my fingers to my lips and then to the screen. She catches me off guard with her next statement, "I bet you are a fucking amazing kisser–too. Those lips look divine."

I laugh. "Ok, I guess we are back to flirting, which is one of my favorite things to do with you. Yes, I have been told I am a superb kisser. I must admit it's been a while, but I think I can remember how for you." It's my turn to wink. She whistles.

"Well, that's going to be something we do a lot of when we get the chance. Now, my mind is going again. How about you tell me a story?"

I grin as I say, "It would be my pleasure. I'm going to tell you what I'm going to do on my day off tomorrow. It is an exceedingly boring routine I've kept up for years, always on the day before the training starts. It hasn't failed me yet and the perfect pillow talk to put you out like a light."

I tell her about my meal planning, grocery shopping, and meal prepping. I tell her about the list of the old games I watch and take notes on, then stretch out and then read for a couple of hours about strategy and leadership. Then I go to bed early because I'll be up to do a Peloton class at 4 am before I go to the office at 6 am Monday morning.

The next thing I know, her eyes are closed, and she is indeed mumbling something that isn't English. I watch her sleeping face for a minute, trying hard to make out the words she is saying, until my own eyelids get heavy.

As I fall asleep, I whisper a song that bubbles up in my mind, one my mom used to sing to me when I was tiny, "You are my sunshine, my only sunshine. You make me happy when skies are gray. You'll never know, dear, how much I love you. Please don't take my sunshine away."

***

Carrie

I wake up around five am with my hand on the phone next to me on the pillow. I haven't moved at all; I slept so deeply. My left hip and side ache. I picture Conner on the bed beside me, all strength, steel, and bright hope. Picturing him there gives me a vision–for a happy life with someone. I think I might have been living without a vision for a long time.

I can hear Conner breathing. He snuffles more than snores, like he sleeps with his face in the pillow. Like everything I'm discovering about him, it is so sweet. It will be wonderful to open my eyes and be with him. I'm going for Parent's Weekend in a few weeks, and I wonder if I can see him and Elise in one weekend.

With these thoughts blooming like fresh-cut roses in my head, I won't be able to go back to sleep. I listen to Conner breathe for a while; then my phone buzzes. It's nearly out of juice, so I pick it up, kiss the screen, and whisper, "Sleep well, Sweetness," before I hang up.

Vaguely, I remember him telling me his plans for today, a pre-season ritual.

Since this is my last day with Maley, I decide to get up even though it's early. I meditate and read, then decide to go out for a ride on one of my favorite trails. The sun is rising, and it is gorgeous in Houston.

As I ride, I feel something stirring in me. I love this company, and what we do, but I hunger for a new direction and challenge. I let that feeling remain where it is without trying to change it. I've learned the hard way not to force anything, to let it flow. It will be a busy week in the office and my second in command, Gena, who truly runs the place, wants to meet to talk. It's nearly September and time to plan for the next year and beyond. Scott and I were the founders, but Gena is the heart that keeps it running.

Maybe she loves what we do more than I do.

I think about what I love to do—which is empower women. It has been my strength and passion for why our business management services work. Most of our clients are women therapists. our sliding scale of offerings gives a level of partnership that allows us to get to know and care for them. Our service enables them to do what they do best, heal and serve their clients.

The ride is hot but rewarding. I get back to the house and peel off my cycling gear to shower and get ready for brunch. After I get out, I hear Maley packing up. Our brunch at a cute little bistro a minute from our house. It is fun and delicious, one of our favorite places. Most of our conversation focuses on her guy dilemma. She will see him tonight and that has her thinking about whether he stays or goes.

We are almost ready for the check when she says, "Mama, I didn't forget. I want to hear about your guy!"

I laugh and tell her, "Of course. How about we plan a dinner phone date and it'll be my turn, maybe later in the week after I see Sabrina? After her two thousand questions, I'll need time to recover."

I'm joking and quite serious. My middle daughter is a delight and a half but insanely curious. She asks questions at a level of depth few can perceive. It is what makes her an excellent pediatric oncology nurse.

Maley huffs, unhappy with this response. "Ok, at least tell me his name."

This is the complication I thought I was prepared to discuss, but suddenly I'm hesitant.

"Mama, tell me." Maley gives me a piercing look and I know I must be honest.

"Ok, but I need you to do two things for me. One–keep this quiet because it involves Elise and I want to tell her myself. I am going for Parent's Weekend, and I'll tell her."

Maley puts her hands up in a surrender position, "Ok, done. I don't tell other people's business, you know." She eyes me again because we all know Sabrina and I tie for the loosest lips in the family.

I hold up my index and middle finger, "Well, Two–I am aware of the complications of this relationship and don't need a lecture. I'm anxious about telling you because I don't want judgment. I am feeling hopeful for the first time in a long time. But I'm not naïve."

She is eyeing me like a hawk assessing prey. She can't help it, it's who she is. She is the oldest, after all. She sighs and speaks as if she lost a court case, "Ok, no telling my sisters anything and no commentary."

I smile as I reach over and pat her hand. Then I pause and take a deep breath. "His name is Conner Doreland. I knew who he was before that because he is her head soccer coach."

Maley's jaw hits the table, and her eyes bug out in her head. "Mama!"

I hold my hand up, and she stops immediately. "Sweetheart, I'm a grown woman. Not to mention, Conner is a grown man." *Conner is a very grown man;* I think back to him in his chair and the look of hunger on his face last night. I squirm in my seat out of desire at the image, which Maley takes for unease.

She starts, "But Mama…"

Still holding up my hand, I give her a pointed look and say, "Maley, you agreed, no lectures."

She blows frustrated breath upward through her lips. "Ok, well, if I find anything I don't like about him, can I ask?"

"Yes, my darling. I don't know if I'll have the answer, but we can discuss it. I'm sure I'll be answering many questions between you and your sisters. I don't know if I'll be able to avoid it. The only reason I don't want to tell Elise is because it is so new, and she is in a big transition moment right now. Let's just see what happens, ok?"

She agrees, and we finish brunch while I tell her all about Elise's life at school. Maley seems satisfied that I am not being reckless or stupid. We hug outside her car, and I get a little teary. I hope that one day, she will live closer. When I pull into my garage, I send my other daughters' texts to ask to check-in. Sabrina calls immediately to confirm our plans for the week and asks what we will have for dinner.

While I'm ordering my groceries, I get a text from Conner. My face nearly breaks in half from the smile.

Morning Sunshine and happy Sunday. I loved falling asleep with you. I told you about my day last night, but I may have bored you to sleep. The short version is I'll be busy and can call later. Is 9 pm your time too late?

I sigh. I had hoped to talk to him earlier because I can feel the late nights with him catching up.

Good morning, Sweetness <kissing emoji> Would 8 be ok? I want to get some rest tonight. For the office tomorrow.

He writes back immediately.

> *Anything for you, Sunshine. <winking emoji>*

> *You sure? I don't want to mess up your flow.*

> *You can mess me up anytime, Sunshine. Talking to you at night is my new favorite thing. What are you doing today?*

> *LOL. <kissing emoji> Just said goodbye to Maley after lunch. Now, going through emails, prepping my schedule, then reading. I'll start making a reading list?*

His response is instant.

> *Fuck yes. Let's compare notes because I think I'll surprise you. Till later, my Goddess.*

I sigh again. I have all afternoon to myself and will count the minutes till I hear his voice again.

Chapter 11

Conner

The day flies by and I know it's going to be a great season; I feel it in my bones. This is a good routine for Carrie and me to establish. If I can start and end each day with her, I can make it through the next eighteen days until I see her again.

Oh, yes, I've already done that math.

How we are going to make Parent's Weekend work to be together is going to be a topic of discussion. It's non-negotiable for me to see her. I already know when I'm going to see her again after that. There is a three-day weekend holiday a week after Parents' Weekend.

She can fly in on a Thursday night and I'll have her all to myself through Sunday. The team's big sisters take their new little sisters' home to meet their families, so Elise will be occupied. I can't wait to talk to her about it. It makes sense, and she strikes me as the type of woman who likes it when things are easy.

Preparation sets the tone for the season because a focused coach is an excellent coach. We have three and a half months before the NCAA tournament. Our goal is an undefeated season and winning that tournament. If we do that, we will be the top soccer program in the country. We've gotten close the last two years but have yet to clinch the title. When we do, an entire world of possibilities opens.

That's not my focus; little steps towards that goal every day ensure a secure foundation. The next three weeks are about integrating freshmen and gelling as a team. Unity means execution, on and off the field. Our first chance to test out our team will be the exhibition Parent's Weekend. My mind drifts back to how much time I can squeeze in with Carrie. We might not be in the same city yet, but I will work with everything I have to ensure that happens at the right time.

Before I know it, I look up and I've completed everything I've wanted to and more. It has taken me right on through to just before six pm–eight Carrie time. I message her I'm going to put my dinner on a plate, then FaceTime her. She sends back that kissing emoji that makes my heart bounce. As the dinner I prepared earlier warms up in the microwave, I close my eyes and picture kissing her.

The slow side of my tongue across the seam of her lips while the warmth of her pressed up against me. I picture pinning her back against a wall, grinding my hips into her as she opens her mouth and threads her fingers in my hair. The image of us pressed together sends a jolt of electricity through me. My dick is immediately at attention. He may earn a permanent spot tucked into the waistband of my pants when Carrie is around.

Before this fantasy goes too far, the microwave dings. I grab my food and hit the call button. Her gorgeous face with those hypnotizing blue eyes is before me. I hear, "Hey Sweetness" and even though it has been less than a day since I heard her voice, I feel the tension in me drain out like water in the bathtub.

She has some kind of magic.

We update each other on the day. I'm intrigued by her telling Maley about me–us. We agree to handle this situation with care. I agree with her not to tell Elise until Parent's Weekend. I haven't had time to get to know her, as a player or person. I'm not doing anything to jeopardize what this could be. I know I'm falling in love with Carrie. I never believed in love at first sight. Now I know it is real.

I want this woman in my life permanently.

My boss needs to know, as I want to do everything in my power to be the man Carrie deserves and that starts with this very important piece of our relationship–going public. She commits to talking about Parent's Weekend when we both have the capacity for it next weekend. One more conversation with Joel will not hurt, either.

It's a fucking trip and I'm strapped in for the ride.

After we've been talking for about forty-five minutes, she gives me a tour of her house and I give her one of mine. Our spaces couldn't be more different. Hers is a family home, big and spacious, with a full main suite downstairs and three rooms upstairs. It was the house her girls needed to grow. I know mine is a bachelor pad with only two bedrooms. It serves me well. Our spaces reflect who we have been and will help us get to know each other better when we are in them.

She gets ready for bed and I watch as she sticks her phone to the mirror so I can witness her charming bedtime routine. I won't get to sleep for another several hours. She did indeed make me a reading list, so I have some books to order when we hang up.

After she completes her routine, I ask, "You gonna dance tonight, Lovely?" I grin widely and she laughs.

"Sorry to disappoint, but I'm tired. Plus, talking to you helps settle my brain so I'll be telling stories fast tonight. Schroeder will enjoy it for sure."

The black cat is already on the bed, apparently on her side. I hear him protest as I see her shoo him over to my side.

Huh, well already thinking about sides of the bed, apparently.

She yawns and props the phone on the bedside table like last night when the thought of me made her come; then made me come. Then she came again. My cock hasn't forgotten at all. It is hard in an instant at the memory of her spread out, using that her glass wand to fuck her wet, exquisite pussy. I cough to clear my head and realize I'm going to need to jack off before I fall asleep tonight.

"Hey, Sunshine." She yawns behind her hand and sleepily says, "Yes, sweet Conner?" Dammit, my name on her lips does nothing to help my erection.

"I want to make sure we have another date, like last night this week. You up for it?" I know my desire for her is written on my face.

She gives me a slow, seductive smile and then licks her lips. "Yes, I have some ideas about what to do. But I want to surprise you." She winks and goddamn if I don't lose my breath. "And Conner?"

I clear my throat to not sound like a 13-year-old boy who just saw his first pair of tits. "Yes, Lovely?"

"I would love to sext with you. I will make sure you know EXACTLY what to expect the next time we have phone sex. In vivid, graphic detail."

My vision blurs. *HOLY FUCK*. I could not have dreamed of a more perfect woman. "Carrie, fuck me. I don't know what I did to deserve you but thank God I did. We are having a date on Friday night, no matter what. Dinner, dancing, and multiple happy endings for you, Sunshine."

I stifle a groan. My dick is so fucking hard.

She purrs, "You gonna think about me tonight, Sweetness?"

"You fucking know it, Sunshine."

"Good, treat that cock of yours right. I want him in perfect form for when we are together. Goodnight, Sweetness. Talk in the morning?"

"Fucking hell, of course. I'll dream about you all night long...beneath me, on top of me, in front of me, above me, sideways, standing, sitting...."

She laughs low and breathy. "Good." She blows me a kiss, winks, and ends the call.

This woman may kill me, but I will die the happiest man on the planet. Older women are flawless.

***

Carrie

I wake up to a text from Conner as I start my day.

> *Good morning, Sunshine. Woke up with you on my mind. It's going to be hard to focus on soccer because I can't wait for our date on Friday night. I'll do my best, though. <winking emoji> Talk to you tonight, Gorgeous.*

I sigh in a lovesick way. A woman could get used to this. I can't wait to surprise him.

I also can't wait to hear what Elise says about her first practice–then from Conner, how she did. This is a delicious little triangle that fills my heart completely full. I'm thinking about all of this as I get ready for my day. I get dressed, eat breakfast, and put together a workout bag as I have a Pilates class later. Then I make my lunch and take my coffee out the door. My commute is less than twenty minutes, but it is enough time to get mentally ready in the morning and then disconnect from it at night.

Once at the office, I hit the ground running. There are meetings, reports and a few conflicts to resolve. We have a couple of new clients, so that always takes a soft touch, as they get used to our process. We need to figure out how to work best with them. We've only had to part ways with less than five clients in the last fifteen years, so our process is excellent. I'm super proud of that.

Eating lunch in my office with Gena, who brought a nearly identical lunch, starts quietly. We've been in several meetings together already and the energy output for women driving a company forward means we are usually starving when lunch rolls around.

However, as typical, Gena starts first, "Elise ok?"

"Yep."

"Maley doing well?"

"Yep."

"You see Sabrina this week?"

She knows I am because she has access to my calendar. What good is a second in command if she does not know what I'm up to?

"You know it."

Then she hits me with what she really wants to know. "So, who did you fuck?"

I choke on my sparkling lemonade and look at her incredulously. She loves to catch me off guard and, clearly, I'm out of practice. "Excuse me?" I ask between coughs to clear my throat.

"You have a glow. That's a freshly fucked glow. You got some dick. Who is it?"

My eyebrows are at my hairline. "I have fucked no one; I was only gone a week. Gena, for Christ's sake!"

She eyes me with a Cheshire cat grin. "Oh, no, you got some serious deep dicking. I've known you for a long time and even after you and Scott got back together and he was fucking you senseless, you didn't glow like this. Who is it?"

I'm totally gob smacked. "You really know how to mess with someone's head, don't you? You are such a bitch. I think I pay you too much."

"Bullshit, Carrie. You do not pay me enough. In fact, I need a fucking raise. So, are you going to tell me? I'm assuming Maley knows. Dulce know yet? I could text her."

Dulce, my best friend, introduced Gena and I. Dulce was Gena's roommate for a while before they were both married. Gena got married first, but then divorced. Not long after that, Dulce met and married the love of her life, Brian. Gena has since fallen in love with Krav Maga. It's her passion and is the reason I don't mess with Gena too much.

She could murder me with one finger.

"Gena, I don't think you need to start anything on a group chat about my sex life. I met someone, and we had a fantastic time on the phone the other night. He has potential."

She snorts. "From how loose and happy you are, I'd say he has more than potential. When do I get to meet him?"

My eyes bug out. "Well, you sure are forward, assuming that, one, he is someone I'm going to bring around the office; and two, that I'd expose him to an interrogation of your epic proportions. I have Sab for that."

She sneers, 'Epic proportions, my ass. I'd just get the information out of him you need to now and then tell you if he is worth your time or not."

I scoff at her. "I can decide if he is worth my time."

She looks hard at me. "You could use a second opinion."

I continue to scoff, "And that's what I pay you for, in business, not my love life."

She continues to stare at me but resumes eating her lunch. She chews for a moment before saying, somewhat quietly, "You haven't had a love life; so, this is a new opportunity for us both."

I sigh. "Ok, ok. When you jump between good cop and bad cop, it always gives me emotional whiplash. Just give me another week. I promise I'll tell you about him at the two-week mark, ok?"

She sniffs. "Fine. Set a meeting."

I throw my hands up and say, a little louder than I should, "I'm not scheduling a meeting for that!"

She doesn't even bother to look at me when she says, "Ok, then you can buy me a glass of wine after work next week. You don't drink anymore, but I do."

I sigh, defeated. "Fine. Now, let's eat so we can get back to work. It's going to be a long week, and I have a Reformer class at 6 pm."

We get ready for the team updates and, just as I predicted to myself and Conner, it is a long week in the office.

Chapter 12

Conner

This week has been incredible.

I have a beautiful woman who I am getting to know every morning and evening. Plus, I'm going to do my best to fuck her by proxy again this weekend. We might have to work on more dates during the week because this once-a-week shit is not enough. I take care of myself well enough, but to be face to face–even on-screen–with Carrie when I'm coming is the next level. Only two more weeks before I can touch her soft skin.

From our evening conversations, I know Carrie's work week has been intense and mine is no different. We hired a new goalie coach, and she is a perfect fit. Our senior keeper leads the team from the backfield and this new coach will bring up the backup goalies, a sophomore and now a freshman.

Speaking of freshmen, our first practice goes smashing. The ladies are hungry and ready to play. Their conditioning with Erik is paying off and I see the choices Inanna and I made to fill out our roster were right. In fact, Elise Vokler is even better than we thought. She has massive talent. She is fast, and she is coachable. She came prepared for today and the only thing I had to correct her on was how nervous she seemed.

She was practically vibrating during warm-up.

I feel a tug on my heart to pull her aside. I know that's because my desire to protect and provide for her mother extends out to her kids. But I can't act differently with her than anyone else, so I wait till post-practice warm down, after most of the girls had headed back to their dorms to shower and eat dinner, before saying anything to her.

"Elise, come here for a second."

She jogs over. Her cheeks are red from exertion and her face nearly as striking as her mother's. She is a younger version of Carrie with green eyes, and I can't help but smile; she is so cute. "Yes, Coach?"

"You did well today. I can see you working the plays and formations out in your mind. Don't overthink it, you will get it. We knew you would not only fit in well now, but certainly in the future. You gotta remember to have fun, though. This is a game we take seriously but this program is still about living well."

"Yes, sorry, Coach. Thanks. It's just a lot to adjust to. I'll try."

"Don't apologize. Women never need to apologize for being who they are and trying. It's a team policy. No apologies unless you fuck up." I wink at her.

She giggles, which makes me smile wider. It's cute and reminds me of Carrie's. "Ok, Coach. Is there anything else?"

"Yeah, how did your first day of classes go?"

She smiles and then her face gets serious. "I'm excited. I had two core classes today and one for my major. The core classes are going to be a breeze, and the other one will be a lot of research and writing. I like that though. My sisters told me just to do the work when it is assigned, and I shouldn't have a problem. I need to read through my syllabus' tonight."

I nod. "Sounds like your sisters gave you good advice. What's your major again? History?"

"Double major in history and political science. Basically, everything and then some for-law school."

I smile at her again. "Going to be a lawyer, then?"

She looks at me in the eyes, "Yes to start, but ultimately Chief Justice of the Supreme Court."

I let out a low whistle. "Well, remind me not to piss you off, ok? But if I do, remember I'm your coach." I hold up my hands in front of me. "Don't sue me, ok?"

She smiles and says, "Don't worry, I'm entering corporate law. I don't think you qualify as a corporation that needs accountability."

I nearly say, "I see you are motivated like your mother," but I catch myself at the last second.

That would have been a massive mistake because, as far as she knows, I haven't met her mother. Fuck, this is going to be harder than I thought.

I switch gears quickly. "Who do you get your drive from, Elise? Your mom or your dad?"

She answers instantly, toeing the turf with her cleat, "Oh, my mom. She is a badass. Can't wait for you to meet her."

I know I'm grinning like an idiot, so I'm glad her face is turned away from me. "Yes, I can't wait to meet her either."

She looks over to where her roommate and big sister are waiting for her. "Coach, can I go? I am sweaty and starving!"

I laugh. I forgot that I'm talking to a teenager who had just finished a two-hour training session. "Of course. Have a good night."

As she runs off with a little wave, Erik and Inanna flank me.

"Good practice today, Coach."

"Yes, Coach it was."

"I'm happy with our progress, Coach."

Saying 'coach' for the first three sentences of our conversation after training is our dumb little post-practice ritual, but soccer players are idiosyncratic, like our little conversation has some kind of power to ward off evil spirits that would make us lose games.

I look at Inanna, "New keeper coach doing, ok?"

"Yes, she is ready for us to debrief before we leave for the day, and I need a fucking shower, so let's get it over with."

As we walk to the training classroom where we watch films, Erik eyes me. "The freshmen are hard workers. Elise Vokler especially. I have my eye on one or two other girls, who could be the type to stir up trouble."

I nod and say, "Good plan."

I noticed one or two freshmen with some attitude, including Macieee Griggs. We've dealt with moods before.

Erik claps a hand on my shoulder. "I'm going to run them fucking ragged. You can't have drama if all you have time to do is study and sleep."

I chuckle. Erik's plan is part and parcel of our team's strategy. Not everyone can hack it here in our program. "You do that, Coach. Let's go get our new coaching addition and her feedback and call it a night."

Erik eyes me with a knowing grin on the side. "Hot date, Conner?"

I don't even look at him when I say, "None of your business, Dickhead. You either Inanna."

She holds her hands up in outrage. "I didn't say a word!"

"I know you were thinking it. Let's do the job, ok? We are the job."

They answer in unison. "Yes Coach! We are the job."

As we walk, I send Carrie a quick text.

> Hey my only Sunshine. Talk to you in an hour?

She responds about ten minutes later.

> *Sorry, Sweetness, I was finishing a workout. An hour sounds great. I'll be fed and showered, ready for you, baby.*

My pants go tight over the center. This woman is perfection.

***

Carrie

The week is too busy. By the time I reach Thursday night, I've been through the ringer. Sabrina filled in for someone and worked a double, so we rescheduled our dinner till Saturday. I am relieved because work has me ragged by the end of the day.

However, talking to Conner every night and texting during the day has done wonders for my outlook on life. Gena was right. I have a glow. The sweet way he speaks to me heals me in ways I never expected.

It's Thursday night and we both feel the relief of almost being done with the week. We are talking through our day as we wind down for the evening. I am staring at him in awe as he tells me how training is going. He looks flushed with joy, so handsome. I am mesmerized in a way that makes different parts of me purr.

Hello, Lover was all I could think of when I reached up to the buttons on the side of my phone and took a screenshot. It was a wonderful picture too. Conner was smiling and looking right at the camera.

His tone shifts in an instant. "Carrie, did you just take a screenshot of me?"

Not expecting this, I stumble to reply, "Y-y-yes?"

With a face as hard as steel, he looks straight at the camera, down to my bones, and asks me point blank. "Why? Why didn't you ask before you did it?"

Laughing nervously, all I can respond with is, "I-I-I don't know. I mean, I know. Um, I don't know." I run out of words but keep babbling, as his response is so unsettled. "How did you know? I mean, what's wrong? Are you mad?"

"I heard the click. Delete it, please. I'll wait." His voice is so formal, it makes my chest ice over and then felt so much heartburn. I'd never seen him upset before. Granted, we had only known each other for nearly two weeks now. I feel tears forming in the corners of my eyes, but I wouldn't cry. I realize that this is a very tender spot for him–and I should have realized it might have triggered his past trauma from Michigan State State.

Still, a part of me is scrambling. I don't want him to think I am manipulating him. I try to breathe through it because I know that when I cause harm; I own it because I am a woman who owns her shit, good, bad and ugly.

That small part of me, that remembers growing up in a household where disappointment was constantly leveraged as a weapon, still wants to cry and beg forgiveness.

Doing what he asks makes me nearly drop my phone as I tell him, "Um, okay, hang on."

"I'll wait, Carrie," as he takes himself off video. I hate the tone of his voice. Tears leak out of my eyes as he takes himself off the video. I fumble around in my apps until I get to the photos, then promptly delete the photo I took.

"Ok, I deleted it. Conner, I am so sorry. I was wrong and if there is anything else I can do to make it right, please let me know."

"Carrie, I'm going to have to talk to you later." With that, he hangs up.

I sigh and let a few big tears roll down my face. I hate upsetting him. The only thing I could do, the best thing for both of us, was to give him space. I busy myself to keep my mind occupied and to let the emotional energy out, so it didn't get stuck. An hour later, I have my bearings again. While doing some laundry and texting 'good night' to all three of my girls, it occurs to me that this is most definitely an overreaction on Conner's part.

I dance to a sad song, praying for him through the movement. I am sorry I triggered him, even if it was unintentional. I must tend to myself in the space between us. I crawl into my bed, drained from the surge of emotions. I wonder if this will be the end for us and resign myself to letting him make his own choices.

I put my phone on the charging plate and lie there in the dark, working through, trying to accept whatever is to come. I am always quick to forgive people, and I do my best not to hold grudges. I hope I'll hear from Conner tomorrow, but that little girl inside me is afraid she will be rejected, just like I was in fourth grade when my crush told me I was ugly.

I picture myself holding and comforting my inner child for a while, like I used to hold the girls when they were little. But sleep doesn't come, so I grab my book from the other room, a historical fiction novel about a young woman trying to find her family after being separated during World War II after fleeing the Nazis. It is good and sad, which matches my mood.

I am ok and I am sad, both at once.

After reading for thirty minutes, my screen flashes. It's an incoming Facetime call from Conner. My hands shake a bit as I picked up.

His voice is low, sad and sheepish. "Hey, Sunshine."

"Hey Sweetness. Are you ok?"

"Yeah, I'm sorry I reacted that way. That was triggering for me."

"Do you want to tell me about it? You don't have to."

"No, I do. And I appreciate you showing me you deleted it. I was hurt you would do that, but it was not about you."

My eyes prickle a little, "I thought as much. I hear you and that's completely reasonable. I am so sorry."

He continues like he didn't hear me, "Miranda did that shit. She took pictures of me. She manipulated our coach-player communication systems to make it look like I was saying things I wasn't and as if we were talking secretly one-on-one offline. Then she put it all on the internet for everyone to see. I hadn't told you about what that time in my life was like, how broken I was, and what it took to recover from her lies. I lost so much over it, and I want to trust you, Carrie. I know you are not Miranda, but what you did brought back those terrible memories. I know you did it innocently, it just...you know?"

Yes, I hear the pain in his voice and wipe my face on my pajama sleeve before I whisper, "What can I do, Conner?"

He is silent for a long time. As torturous as it was, all I could do was wait.

He finally says, "I am going to let it go. It isn't about you, just stabbed at an old wound. I'm sorry I was so harsh with you. You didn't deserve that. Even if you did something major, I know I would forgive you, Sunshine. You are certainly not Miranda and not like any other woman I've ever met. Thank you for giving me space and talking it through with me."

The vulnerability in his tone choked me up, so all that came out was a tiny, "You're welcome."

We say nothing to each other, letting the emotion of it all settle. As a result, I get sleepy.

Before I knew it, I heard him say, "That's a good story, Sunshine."

I am out for the rest of the night.

Chapter 13

Conner

    I lie awake, listening to Carrie mumble over the phone and think about what happened. I overacted. She didn't deserve that harsh of a response. She did it on a whim, with no intention of harming me or my reputation. I know at a cellular level this woman is only for me, never against me.

What the fuck was that visceral response all about?

I concentrate on the swirling in the middle of my chest. It is difficult for me, tapping into my emotions. We were raised to be "manly men," no crying, no being a wimp. I've been on my own for so long that is hard to trust in the safety of another.

But, with Carrie, I want to. She makes me want to. She wants me as I am but makes me want to be better–to not just tell her how I feel but understand it myself.

To see how much she loves herself and takes care of herself—mind, body, and soul—makes me want to do the same. I've got tools for that, so I use one from my time after the trial when I was having panic attacks.

I put my hand on my chest and ground myself into my bed, feeling my back against the sheets, my bare legs, and wiggling my toes. I use my other hand to fist the sheet, and I smile. That reminds me of watching Carrie come for me. My dick hardens because that's what he does. I don't let myself get distracted.

I ask a question of myself and wait for all the thoughts and feelings swirling around to settle. It's like going through the eye of a hurricane, pressing through each band of wind and finally through the eye wall. There is only peace, and I breathe in and out deeply. I stay like that, clearing my mind and readying myself for the answer. When I did this with my therapist, there was always an answer.

I'm counting on that now.

After what feels like an eternity, the answer floats to the surface like a bar of Ivory soap in the bathtub. It bobs there, waiting for me to scoop it into my palm. I must be gentle with it or it will pop right out of my hand and out of my mind.

Slowly, I reach into the water to get it. When I bring it up towards my face, I see what's written on that little bar of soap. A clicking inside me happens because when the truth is made known, another piece of the puzzle of yourself locks in place.

You want it all with her or nothing.

Then the words melt and shift for a second until I can read the second part of the truth my soul reveals to my conscious mind.

You are afraid to fail–and succeed.

With a whimper in my throat. I fear that she'll hurt me, yes, but what does my life look like if this all works out? I fear I'll hurt her, but what if all our dreams come true?

I've never engaged too long with a woman because I didn't want to get hurt and I didn't want to change my goals to accommodate for anyone else. I never gave it a chance. It made sense to be the one that got out before things got serious; before anyone got hurt or I had to adapt my dreams to someone else's vision for our life together. I had a lot of fun but absolutely no commitment. I provide for and protect my team and staff, but it only goes so far. I only take it so far, get so close.

Now, I've found someone who is strong, yet gentle enough to be the anchor I need to build an actual life. Not the life I have now, all work and no play, but a life with the fullness I never knew I wanted. Yes, I want to win it all, but I want to win it with Carrie by my side.

With this new insight into myself, I continue to breathe. I relax in bed, into myself again. Then an idea hits me. This relationship is an act of trust. Not only with Carrie but also in myself, so I don't have to live in fear and that I will be ok. We will be ok. We can work through shit like this when it comes up.

I sit up and position the phone so I can take a picture of myself from the waist up. I'm not wearing a shirt; I never sleep in a shirt. If Carrie wants to see me, I'm going to give her something to drool over. I tuck my arm behind my head and arch my back just a little. I open my mouth, with my tongue just touching the tip of my upper lip, right under my cupid's bow. I smile cockily and snap the pic.

It's pretty good, if I say so myself. I sent it to her with a note,

> Here's your pic of me, Sunshine. It's just for you. I hope we will have plenty of pictures together we can share. And I expect an equally sexy one back tomorrow before our date. I'll be waiting.

***

Carrie

I wake up to a text from Conner and, surprisingly, a picture.

"FUCK THIS MAN IS GORGEOUS!" I scream as I bolt out of bed.

What an incredible way to wake up. He looks like a Magic Mike dancer. He wants a sexy picture back. Standing in my bathroom, I take off my pajama bottoms and unbutton my pajama top until only one button is left. Fluffing my hair, and then shimmy the shirt down so most of my breasts are exposed. Turning to the side to get my ass in the shot, I take three pics before I lean forward, and it's the perfect angle.

I send him a response without the picture, saying,

> I promise you are going to get a pic today. But I'm going to torture you a little and wait for the perfect moment to send it. I can't wait for our date!

I'm being a little evil—delightfully so. So, I add the devil's face. There is a big surprise waiting for him after dinner, so I want to build the anticipation and be a bit of a brat to see what he'll do. I schedule the picture to go through about lunchtime and get ready for work. I say a prayer of gratitude and a little blessing over my girls. I add Conner to the end.

***

Conner

I woke up to a text but no picture. I'm a little pissed she didn't do as instructed but excited because she is playing a game. I am going to have to punish this naughty woman for disobeying me. She is ruining me for anyone else, but I want her to know exactly who is in control of the bedroom.

It's not until I'm in the middle of my morning meeting that the picture comes through. I don't immediately pull out my phone because if I do, I might embarrass myself. No one is getting to see any part of my woman except me. I go back to my office and close the door. I sit down at my desk, take a deep breath to prepare and open the message.

HOLY FUCKING SHIT ON A CRACKER.

She is an absolute vision, and I can see everything I've been missing, including that sweet ass I'm going to bite. Then another text comes through.

> *If you like what you see, I'm prepared to show you everything tonight.*

I close my eyes and before I know it; I've thrust my hips, rolling the chair at my desk so my dick gets enough friction for release. No. I cannot explain the stain on my work pants. I hang on a few more hours till I see her. Maybe I should jerk off when I get home just to take the edge off. I look again at the picture she sent me. I can't wait for that body, that gorgeous pussy, to be all mine.

***

Carrie

Friday night has FINALLY arrived. The anticipation of seeing what Conner has set up on his end is intoxicating. I have everything set up for my dinner. I'm wearing a turquoise silk robe with my bathing suit underneath. Immediately after we finish, I'm going to take him outside so I can swim while he watches. Then, I'll strip down to nothing and then I'll step out, giving him the full view of my naked body before I put back on the robe. You know, in case neighbors. This part makes me nervous.

What woman isn't a little shy the first time? I've walked through my body image healing, yet there are parts of me that aren't perfect. I vow to embrace my inner Aphrodite and give him the show he deserves.

I'm having a light meal tonight: fish, rice and a few vegetables. I let my girls know that I'm busy tonight, so I'll have no interruptions. They were curious, but I played it off, just saying I was hanging out with a friend. They each responded with an emoji; Maley was a thumbs up, Sabrina the ok sign and Elise with two exclamation points. I have a couple of chocolate-covered strawberries to eat like a fucking porn star.

Chapter 14

Conner

    I get all the candles lit and my dinner set up with about five minutes to spare. I am dressed in my three-piece navy suit. I had it dry-cleaned this week to make sure it was fresh and prepped. It usually only gets worn at the end of the year banquets, but I thought that tonight, Carrie deserved the full Conner Doreland effect.

    Joel texted me earlier with the "thumbs up" sign. He doesn't know everything we planned, but he knows I'm going to have a date with her. It feels good to be supported by my big bro.

    I got my haircut and a straight-razor shave, which was one way I took the edge off my adrenaline. The other was working out for two hours with Erik. We lifted so much after I ran for an hour, normally I would collapse in bed. My Sunshine–and the excitement of being with her–gives me all the energy I need.

I've got a delicious meal ready, light. A steak with a sweet potato. It's one of my favorites. I want nothing distracting me, especially my stomach rumbling, so I also had a protein shake after the workout with Erik and then another an hour ago. After that workout, I need to fuel my body so I can be at my peak for her.

God, I wish I was fucking her all night long. I would eat these chocolate covered strawberries out of her belly button. Or her pussy. Or both. Or whatever she wants.

I can't help the thoughts, and my cock balloons through my pants. I shift around because this suit is a European cut, which means they are already tight in the crotch. Oh man, I'm glad I jerked off in the shower and clearly, I will not have any problems being ready for her. My dick is as ready as the rest of me.

I make one more check in the mirror and am pleased with what stares back at me. This woman deserves a fucking heart-throb, and she is going to get one.

***

Carrie

At exactly seven pm, a Facetime call comes through. Before I click it on the stand on the table, I take a deep breath, fluff my hair one more time and answer.

He is a god. And I'm underdressed.

My core immediately clenches upon seeing him and if the thought of what we are going to do tonight wasn't enough to get me dripping wet, the sight of Conner Doreland in a three-piece navy suit with a white shirt and aquamarine paisley tie is enough to make me faint.

I stutter out a breath, "Hi–you look exquisite Sweetness. Will you wear that suit for me again, so I can rip it off you?"

His pupils are already dilated when he answers low. "Baby, you can rip it to shreds and I'll buy a new one. Please tell me if you bring that robe with you to California. Are you naked under there, Sunshine?"

I snicker into my hand and say, "No, but once we finish dinner, I'll show you what's underneath. Do you like it?"

He looks directly into my eyes. "Carrie, I am utterly entranced by you. Are you a witch?"

I giggle again, and he coughs to clear his throat as he pours himself a glass of Pellegrino. He lifts the glass for a toast. I grab mine, filled with my favorite sparkling lemonade, and raise it as well.

"Here's to you, Sunshine. You must sparkle. You are like a candle, with a light that outstrips anyone I've ever met. I want to bask in your light as often as I can. I want you for mine, Carrie."

A tear leaks out at his incredible words. It is my turn to clear my throat and all I manage is, "Sweetness, I'm all yours."

"Then let's eat. I want you to know though, if you were here with me, I don't think I'd want to eat anything but you."

OH GOD. I can feel the middle of my chair getting wet. My eyes roll back in my head for a second, and I say his name in a breathy way. "Conner"

"Carrie, I'm going to need you to say my name like that every time now. Let's eat."

I am not sure if I can eat anything with what I'm feeling, but once I take the first bite, I realize I'm starving. He uses a knife to slice and enjoy his steak, and eventually, he takes off his jacket and rolls up his sleeves. Who isn't seduced by a man in a dress shirt with his sleeves rolled up? It should be illegal.

When I see his grin, I realize he knows exactly what he is doing. I toy with the collar of my robe, stroking and rubbing a finger around it and over my chest.

He grumbles, "I'll never eat if you keep distracting me, Sunshine."

I flash him a wicked grin. "You've clearly studied women enough to know what the sight of forearms does to us."

He nods and smiles at me. He sighs and we recover from our haze of lust enough to hold a conversation. It is slightly painful to act normally. We finish our main meals, and I show him the chocolate-covered–strawberries. To my surprise, he laughs, deep and from his belly.

"What's so funny, Sweetness?"

With that wide grin that makes his dimple pop out, he lifts a small package wrapped in a bow. When he opens it, I laugh too. We both bought strawberries. His eyes darken and he looks at me. "You eat yours first, Carrie." Then as I run my tongue over the chocolate, flicking the tip of my tongue on the end a few times before bringing it between my lips and sucking, he grits out,

"Such a good girl. I can't wait for that to be my cock."

I'm definitely soaking the chair now. "Me either, Sweetness. I bet you taste better than this berry."

He groans. "Show me my surprise, Carrie. And pray I don't come on sight."

"Let the games begin."

***

Conner

That dinner was the most delightful torture I've ever endured. Her in a pale turquoise silk robe, teasing me, watching her mouth, her eyes, scrambles my brain. Then witnessing her give that strawberry head basically completely undoes me. She stands in her robe and grabs the camera stick. She holds it to her face, and I see her walk outside.

"We going on a field trip, Sunshine?" I ask curiously.

She flips the view on the camera so I can see what she is looking at. We are outside looking at a lush backyard with twinkling lights, a grassy area with a couple of loungers, and a pool. I hear her say, "It is just nice enough to be out here, finally, but still hot. I think I'm going to go for a swim. You mind?"

This woman is indeed a witch.

She places the camera down at an angle where I can see the complete pool, then stands in front of it in her robe and then she drops it. She is in a stylish one-piece swimsuit of emerald green, her full cleavage is on display.

"Carrie, Carrie, Carrie. Wow. You look fantastic."

She fluffs her hair a bit, pulling it up into a messy bun and securing it with a clip. With her arms up, it makes her breasts pop. She asks me, "You like it?"

"I love it, Sunshine." I almost say "I love you" but I catch myself. She descends the steps into the pool and swims around. She does breaststroke and I can tell she is a strong swimmer. "You swim a lot, Sunshine?"

Her voice is a little far away since she is on the other side of the pool, but I hear her say, "Yes, in high school and in college. Taught all my girls to swim. I love it but chlorine doesn't love my hair. I'm vain like that."

I chuckle. "You could go gray for me. I like it."

She snorts, "Well, that makes one of us. I'm not ready to embrace all my old lady colors yet."

I smile at her sweetly, even if she can't see it. "You showing me your stroke, Baby?"

At this, she gives me this look of full intent. "Absolutely not. I just wanted to get a feel for the water. It's time for your surprise."

She swims over to the shallower side of the pool and stands up. She pulls her hair out of the clip and lets it fall around her shoulders. The ends get wet, but it only adds to the effect. I think I'm going to pass out when she gingerly slips the ends of the suit down her arms, over her chest, and gingerly reaches down to pull it off her legs.

She stands back upright and tosses the suit on the side of the pool. She is naked in front of me and the image of her beauty will be burned into my brain till the end of time.

***

Carrie

Standing in front of Conner, naked as the day I was born, is liberating. As soon as I got in the pool, started swimming around, my nerves settle, and I pulled that strong self-up to the surface. I heard a voice in my head whisper, *Shine for him. Shine for you.*

So, I do.

I feel like Aphrodite when she emerged from the ocean on a seashell. I feel powerful and I'm not thinking about my body. I can't, with the way Conner is looking at me. He is just staring, like I'm a heavenly vision of awe and wonder. I move around a little, swim around again, feeling the water touch all of me and it is so sensual, erotic.

"Come, let me see you again, my darling." Conner whispers so tenderly, but his voice carries and is full of command. I obey and this time come a little closer to the camera so he can get a closer look.

His throat is working, like his mouth is dry. His forearms are so vascular and powerful. I can't wait to have them wrapped around me, his strong fingers pushing inside of me. I groan at that thought and reach up to cup my breasts with both hands, gently twisting my nipples just a little. I can't help it. Just him watching me has me so ready for him.

"Carrie, you are the most superb woman. My mouth is watering, just thinking about what I would do to taste those luscious tits of yours."

I sigh at his word choice. "You are kind of dirty, aren't you, Coach Doreland?"

"You do not know, my Sunshine. I'm going to whisper the most lovingly disgusting words into your ear as you fuck yourself and come for me. You understand?"

"Yes, sir."

"Good girl. Now, get inside before anyone sees you. You're mine."

As I get out, he groans loudly. "Fucking hell, Carrie. Your body is perfect. You must spend the night with me, Parent's Weekend."

I look at him as I put on my robe to go back inside. "You want to spend the night with me on Parent's Weekend?"

"Hell yes. I want to spend every day with you too. I will make it work; I promise. Do you trust me?"

I laugh, low and slow. "Conner Doreland, I just bared my entire self to you. I think that's a pretty good sign of how much I trust you."

"Good girl. You ok with that being the plan?"

I think for a minute, cautious. "Yes, I am. I know you will take care of the details, so we will both have privacy. It's going to be hard for me to be around you without climbing you like a tree, though."

He looks at me, "I'll make sure you have plenty of time to do that, my Sunshine. Now, go inside and lay down on your bed. I want to fuck you properly, but until then, your wand will have to do."

***

Conner

She is the most gorgeous person I've ever seen. I honestly can't believe there is a human woman who looks more perfect–and she is just for me.

She is soft in all the right places I like and clearly works out. The basic evidence of that is her toned and tight legs, arms and back. Her ass is divine. Her big, full breasts are more than a handful and I can't wait to get my hands on them.

Speaking of my hands, they are shaking as I get undressed and lay my suit out on the chair. Carrie is positioning herself on the bed and I groan out loud again. She is a work of art.

"You ok, Sweetness?"

She asks me with a note of concern in her voice. I can't stop groaning at the sight of her. And how I would sell my soul to be in person with her right now.

I speak so low it's a wonder if she can hear me, "Yes, my perfect Sunshine. I would sell my soul to be with you right now. The next two weeks will not go by fast enough."

She blows me a kiss as she lays down, her pretty wand by her side. "No lube tonight, goddess?"

She blushes at me, which is just as cute as it is sexy. "No, Sweetness, I've been wet for you for hours."

I groan again. I can't help it. The thought of her dripping for me is remaking me in real time. She is watching me get undressed and my dick is so red, the tip is angry. He is angry to not be able to be inside of her and I can't say I blame him. I'm finally standing in front of her in my boxer briefs.

She looks so hungry; she could be drooling. *FFFFUUUUC-CCKKKK.*

She gets up and leans into the camera so I can hear her clearly, "You are a god – my soccer god, Conner. And if you don't get out of those briefs, I'm going to start without you."

I growl at her, "No, you won't. You are a good girl."

She giggles and lets out a loose breath. "You know I have such a praise kink when it comes to you."

"Oh rrreeeeallllllyyyyy," I drawl out. "I'm not into much dominance play, but I can make use of a healthy praise kink." I say all of this while I'm stepping out of my underwear, and she lets loose a wolf whistle.

"Yes sir, please do. I don't have any words for your cock, Conner. He looks like he needs attention. I want to worship and adore you. I think I could kneel at the altar of your cock for hours. I'm all yours and so ready for you, Conner. Tell me what you want me to do."

"Then kneel, Sunshine. I want to see what you look like when you are genuflecting."

She gets on her knees, and I get a straight shot down her cleavage. Then she proceeds to deep throat that fucking wand, moaning on it, humming, moving along the flat of her tongue. She gags a little and I grunt in approval. I finally hold my cock in my hand and imagining being down her throat has me hissing through my teeth. I can see how wet her inner thighs are. "You want me inside of you, Carrie? Is that what you want?"

She takes the dildo out of her mouth and looks up at me through her eyelashes. "Yes, please Sweetness. Please."

My tone is soft, just a touch of firmness, as I'm discovering she likes. "Lay back on the bed, my lovely prize. I want you to touch yourself, plunging that wand as deep as it can go, imagining it's me bottoming out inside of you. Your magnificent pussy loves that thought, doesn't it? Tell me what you smell like, Carrie."

She is on the bed, legs spread to the camera. There is so much moisture, her wand slides right in. She turns her head from side to side, moaning. I know as soon as she touches her clit, she may come.

"Slow down, my love. This will not last long anyway, but let's try to keep going for another minute or two." The second I lay down and think about Carrie sliding down on top of me, my hips start to thrust and rock.

She is still moaning but is now looking at me. "Conner, I smell earthy, like spice, and I'm so warm. I want to bounce on top of you so bad. Just over and over again, with you driving up into me from below. Would you let me be on top, Sweetness?"

"Carrie, fuck, you can have me upside down, sideways, on top, bottom–any position you can think of. I want every one of them, especially the ones you've never done."

She laughs a little and I make a note to ask her about what was so funny at that moment.

"And gggooooddddd, I bet you taste better than anything that has ever been on my tongue. Fucccck, Carrie. You want to touch your clit? How swollen is it? Tell me what it feels like?"

She rubs as she continues to thrust the wand in deep. She again uses those same fingers I saw her use before, the middle and index. I'm trying to concentrate to see if I can tell how hard she is pressing, but I can't. I will get her to show me.

I pump my hand on my dick a little faster. "Tell me, Carrie, how close are you now that you touch that juicy little nub?"

***

Carrie

I'm going to rip in half when I come. The orgasm building inside of me is like nothing I've ever experienced. And Conner's voice pushes me higher and higher. I'm wetter than I've ever been. He asked me a question, and I tried to make my brain work to answer him. I want to submit to him, to obey. I feel so cared for, desired and wanted.

This is a fucking spiritual encounter. And we are about to awaken to bliss together.

"Oh Conner, oh god. It is so plump, like a button. Oooo-hhhh, Conner, I don't think.... Oh Conner...."

I'm moaning his name repeatedly now. I can hear him stroking himself, and I look up to see his eyes locked on me. When he says the magic words, I detonate. "Come for me, my love. Now."

He joins me and groans out his release, loud and feral. He comes all over his chest and stomach again. He sounds like an animal when he yells my name and yells it so loud, I can't take it. I fall over the edge into another orgasm, if the first one ever stopped. I am barely breathing, and my hips are completely in the air. I'm shaking with the force of this, and I hear his soft words.

"That's it, Baby. That's it, Baby. That's it, Baby. Oh, goddddd-dd Carrie, you are so beautiful when you come for me."

I stay in that orgasmic paradise for a little longer, and then my butt hits the mattress with a thud. I'm panting like I've run a marathon. I look over at the phone camera and he is looking at me.

"What's wrong, lovely?" He asks with a tinge of concern in his voice.

It's then I realize I have tears running out of the corners of my eyes, falling into my hair.

"That was astonishing and otherworldly, Conner. I've never felt like that." And it is in this moment I recognize just how far gone for this man I am. I am fully and completely in love with him, and I've never met him in person, for real. He makes me feel understood and seen, it is mind-blowing. I was married for over twenty years and never felt this complete.

It is scary and yet I want it. I want it. I want him. I want it all with him.

"Conner, it scares me how strongly I feel about you. Does it scare you?"

"Absolutely, it does, but I can't think of my life without you in it anymore. How about we clean up and talk a little? I like the idea of some heart after-care for you. It would make this tonight complete for me to reassure you."

We do that, and I'm still sniffling when I lay back down under the covers. I am sleeping naked, as is he, which was his idea. A prelude to how it will be when we are together, all snuggled up after the ascension to another world in body, mind, and soul. I can't wait.

We talk for a little while. He soothes my fears and worries with his wonderful, tender words. He knows just what to say.

"I know this is all so fast and so new, but I trust it. I trust you and I've trusted no one. I will let nothing bad happen to us. I will do everything I can to make sure this is all open and we can be together with no blow back. Let's just keep talking about it."

I don't yet want to tell him my darkest fear–that this will be taken from me, just like before. I know I will tell him eventually, but for now, I just listen to him reassure me and murmur loving words into my ear until I fall asleep.

Right before I do, I hear him sing. I crack my eyelids open as I don't want to disrupt him or make him feel embarrassed. It's the "You are my Sunshine" song.

As I listen, another tear, this one of joy and peace, slips out of my eye onto the pillow beneath. And I drift off to dream of lying in Conner's arms, and I know it will all be alright because this man loves me like I love him.

***

"I can't believe I just had five orgasms in less than twelve hours. This can't be normal."

On the way to the grocery store, I recount our date night with my best friend. I need to process what is happening and Dulce is always and ever my sounding board. Otherwise, I end up going around in circles in my head.

Her response is immediate and searing. "Who the fuck wants to live a normal life, Carrie?"

Her words ring through me, like an echo of some long-forgotten desire. That desire has been asleep, dormant but now reverberates around in my heart and in my body, like a super bouncy ball. It hits all the walls of my mind and soul, which I built up to survive.

With Conner, I don't just have to survive. Our relationship is healing me to thrive.

Dulce continues, "I love this for you. You deserve it, even if you abandoned all hope that the ship of love was ever going to make its way back to port. Now you sail off into the sunset with the man of your dreams. You gonna get on or are you too afraid? Friend, I don't want to be standing on dock with you as you watch that love sail away."

This is why she is my best friend. She paints a beautiful picture of what's really happening in my life. Her words are the brutal truth, but she delivers this with love. It's how she always calls me on my shit.

I sigh and say, "I know I've been holding myself back. But what if I end up being 'too much' is for him?"

She matches my sigh, but has a different take. "What if your 'too much,' is just right for Conner – and exactly what he wants?"

She pauses to let the words sink in and then says, "Look, I've known you for a long, long time. I know when you have been a wife and mother, you learn to compartmentalize and play the roles. That started breaking down when you and Scott took that break. Things were so different when you got back together. But now, he is gone, and the girls are off living their own lives too. It's time, Carrie, for you to be the complete you. You've never had the chance to truly live into her. Conner is helping you be all you can be."

I chuckle and after a moment, I whisper, "It scares the shit out of me, though."

"I know. You'll remember I felt the same way when Brian walked into my office and swept me off my feet. Took me a minute to get over myself. You helped me do that, and now it's my turn to help you."

I'm pulled into the grocery store parking space, but I make a point to bear witness to my feelings. There is a solidness in my chest, underneath the top of my rib cage, under my heart. I don't feel fear here–the fear of being my full self in front of Conner.

I feel at home.

I tell Dulce this and she says, "I know. You don't have to hide anything from anyone anymore. You don't have to fear getting hurt. You've been through hell. You may still smell a little like smoke, but you are on the other side."

We hang up and I get out of my car to head into the store. My body may be grocery shopping on autopilot, but my mind is spinning as I ponder it all.

Sabrina finally settled on chicken enchiladas with salad, Mexican rice and brownies for her favorite meal–for today, at least.

Conner checks in with me as always and tells me I'm going to have to recreate this dinner menu for him sometime.

When Sabrina makes it over to our family home after her extended shift, she is tired but happy. She worked out before coming over, which is a necessary part of her day, given her usual stress level. It helps her come down even as the hospital is a natural fit. There is always something happening, and she loves it.

Hospitals are a major trigger for me. I don't go to the doctor often because I have "White Coat Syndrome," and my blood pressure goes through the roof. It brings back all those memories of the chaos after Scott's death and how they tried to save him. They were doing their job, but it left me with invisible scars on my soul.

Sabrina takes a shower while I get our dinner plated. She will probably drive home to her apartment near the hospital in her pajamas after we eat, talk, and relax with each other. I love having her here as long as I can. She loves being around her family and she needs her space, too.

Not two seconds after we sit down at the table and I take a bite, she hits me with questions. My middle daughter doesn't beat around the bush. She never has, always seeing what other people don't. It's what makes her such an excellent pediatric oncology nurse. She is a younger nurse in terms of age and experience, but is at the top of her team because she notices the slightest changes in her patients and acts on it. She has never been wrong, and she has to fight plenty of doctors who don't listen. Apparently, one resident has taken more than a professional interest in her.

She has made a name for herself because of her track record. She has come a long way from the kid who struggled to find herself.

Her interrogation begins. "Ok Mama, what's different? What's going on? You seem different, lighter, happier? And why is your bathing suit on the ground outside? What HAVE you been doing by yourself for the last two weeks?"

I mentally facepalm myself for leaving my bathing suit outside on the ground after my striptease for Conner.

"Well, I've met someone."

"Yah, I know. Maley told me. Elise's soccer coach, right? She said he's super into you."

I blow out a breath of frustration and level at look at her, "I told her not to tell anyone! Did y'all say anything to Elise?"

Sabrina shakes her head. "No, she told me not to. Despite what everyone thinks, I can keep my mouth shut." She makes a face at me because she's worse than I am about keeping secrets. "I looked him up. You think you are in love with him? His past looks sketchy."

We spend another few minutes discussing my blossoming relationship with Conner before she says, "It's weird to picture you with someone other than Dad, but you deserve to be happy."

And just like that, the discussion about Conner is over and we are talking about this hot, young doctor who wants to be more than just colleagues with her.

After dessert, strawberry sparkle cake, which I've been making for her since she was eight, we start a movie. I feel my eyes drooping, but can do nothing to stop them. Halfway through the movie, I feel her lips on my temple. "Goodnight Mama, I'll text you when I get home."

"Ok, sweetheart, drive safe. I love you." I groggily say, rubbing my eyes and stretching, getting up with her to lock the door and set the alarm behind her.

She pauses midway out the door and turns back to me. "Oh, and Mama?"

"Yes, what is it, darling?"

"Go get this man. You deserve it. You deserve to be happy."

And with that, she breezes out to her car, leaving me smiling, and a little stunned.

I text Conner and get ready for bed. This is my absolute favorite way to end my day.

Chapter 15

Conner

The last two weeks have flown by. Carrie and I are continuing to grow together with morning and evening calls. We've also hit a few Peloton classes together. Add on planning for Parent's Weekend, plus Erik killing me with workouts, I've had more than enough to keep me busy.

I'm very encouraged that the freshmen are connecting with the program, and I am thrilled with everyone's control of the ball and passion for the game.

Carrie and I had another weekend that started with a phone date. We both set records. She came three times to my two. We started it off like our first one, eating dinner and talking about what the impending weekend would look like. We discussed how to handle interactions with Elise and my staff. It was good to talk it through, even if I know, just like in a game, you can do all the preparation you want, but the only thing you can trust is that what you've built will stand when reality hits.

She has an excellent mind for strategy. She would make a brilliant coach, which I fucking love. She seeks my advice and pushes back in all the right places. She doesn't resist, but she doesn't chase either. She is damn attractive on the outside, but what captivates me is her emotional health. Even during our first conflict over the screenshot, she handled it like a grown-up.

After the dinner portion of our date, she upped the ante. I wasn't sure how she was going to top the pool striptease, but I should have never doubted. She set the camera up on a tripod, took off her robe to reveal she was wearing a lingerie bodysuit, and then danced for me to Hozier's song "Movement." It took all I had not to touch myself while she moved. She was in her bedroom, using the end post of her bed like a stripper's pole.

Listening to me talk about all the ways I would lick and fuck her with my fingers gave her the first orgasm. The second was her kneeling on her bed and using her wand like she was straddling me. Watching her bounce on that glass dildo and touch herself, imagining it was me touching her tits and ass as she bounced on my cock, it took us both less than ten minutes to climax.

Neither one of us said much as we cleaned ourselves up and then we both crawled under our sheets and blankets, staring at each other on the screen. Dopey smile on my face, fuck me if I didn't almost say, "I love you." It was right there on the tip of my tongue when she whispers,

"Conner, the way I feel about you scares me."

Her admission made my heart pound for multiple reasons. First, she feels as strongly as I do. Second, she is in love with me too. Third, that is scary because it is so fast, and we haven't met in person yet. I take a deep breath and speak the truth I know.

"It doesn't scare me, Carrie. Nothing besides soccer has ever felt so right to me. It's ok to be scared though. You've been through a lot. And if you were worried about it, you won't disappoint me when we are together. I just want to be near you, to touch you, to hold you. Even if we never have sex."

She interrupts me with a giggle. "Like that would happen."

I stare at her. "Sunshine, I'm serious. Even if the only sex we ever have is what we've shared these last three weeks, I will be happy. I want you to be comfortable, to feel safe. You have become the most important thing to me. I don't know why or how; I just know that you are."

She sniffs loudly; moisture in her eyes. "I feel the same way. Other than my girls, you are all I think about. I have to tear my mind away from wondering what you are doing to focus on work. I'm not even putting a good effort into our reading list because all I can think about is when I can talk or text you. It's quite obsessive."

I laugh, "As long as it's mutual. I know we talked a lot about next weekend. I want you to know it's going to be hell on earth to not be able to touch you until we are alone. I'm not sure I'll be able to look anywhere else in the room but at you."

She sighs, "Oh, the things you say, Conner Doreland. I'm done for. Being with you in person is only going to solidify that."

At that admission, I puff my chest up with pride and say in a caveman-like voice, "Me Tarzan, make you Jane happy!"

She laughs musically, and I almost let out a sigh. "You go from Mr. Darcy to Tarzan pretty well, Sweetness."

I get a little serious about what I say next. "I'm going to take care of you, Carrie. I want to. I want to make this work, and I think you've figured that out. I want to make your girls happy. We will figure out whatever comes up between us but promise me we will do it together. Ok?"

She wipes a little tear away and says, "Together, always, Conner. I'm yours."

"And I am yours, Sunshine."

***

Carrie

After the longest work week where I drummed my fingers in every meeting, Gena finally yelled at me to stop before she cut off my hand.

It was Friday of Parent's Weekend and I'm leaving for the airport at 3:45 am. I am showered, dressed, and waiting outside for my Uber. After I land, I'll pick up my rental and drive the hour up the Coast in time to drool over Conner with no one being wiser while he plays flag football in the All-Athletics Coaches Game.

This game is a very popular event. Tickets were only available for purchase in a two-hour window this last Monday night. Elise said she tried to get tickets, but when she got to the Student Union after her last class and practice, the line was around the corner. They sold out before she even got inside the building. I was upset until she told me someone slipped two tickets under her door. They were in the front row, center Stadium.

My hands are twitching, thinking about him. I'm ovulating, which means my libido is on ten, maybe fifteen. I don't know why he promised that if I didn't want to have sex with him, we wouldn't. I appreciate the sentiment, but sex is all we are going to have tomorrow night. Maybe some conversation in between.

After going through multiple wardrobe options, I feel confident and ready. Today, I'm wearing a dark aqua jewel-toned silk shirt with dark wash jeans, an understated gray animal print belt, and gray suede ballet flats. I'm glad I'm leaving Houston early because it's warm even in October. It is cooler in California, so I have a sweater if I need it. I look nice, even for the early morning, and have a neck pillow, with a strong hope of a nap on the plane. I want to look my best when I see Conner for the first time and for Elise to be proud to introduce me, officially.

As I ride to the airport, I imagine what I want to do when I see him all sweaty. I send him a text, even though I know he won't see it for a few hours, describing licking the sweat from his neck, chest, abs and then letting him fuck my face right there on the Stadium field. I am so horny I can barely stand it.

My plane boards and I'm grateful to find I'm not sitting next to anyone. I nod off as we take to the air and sleep right until we land. When I check myself in the mirror in the terminal bathroom, I am frustrated. My hair is a little mushed and my makeup smeared. I call Dulce as I'm walking through the airport. She talks me off the ledge before telling me to get my head out of my ass. "Stop being a Reina del Drama!"

Only my best friend would call me a Drama Queen in Spanish.

I arrive at Elise's dorm with enough time to find a parking space. She is waiting outside her dorm for me with her roommate and Alyssa, her big sister. She gives me an enormous hug, which I return. She tried to pick me up like when she was little and we nearly fall, laughing so hard in our joy to be reunited again.

"Mama, I've missed you!" She says this while holding her stomach as her friend's grin at us.

"You've had so much fun and been so busy, sweetheart. I'm so proud of you for making this transition." I mean it too.

My youngest grows serious in a flash, "You've said you've been ok, have you? Not too lonely?"

I wave her off and laugh. "No, darling, I've been keeping myself busy, don't worry. I've got a lot to tell you about how busy I have been!'

She looks at me quizzically, ever the future lawyer, looking for chinks in my armor. She's never lost an argument, even when I was in the right. I know she will ask me about that statement later on when we are alone tonight, so I preempt questions and say, "C'mon, c'mon, introduce me to your friends, and then let's go drool over all the coaches!"

Elise turns her nose up and says, "EWWWW, Mama!" But she has a twinkle in her eye. The four of us fast-walk to the Stadium and find our seats, right in the front row, as Conner had provided. Alyssa, being the team captain, secured seats for the rest of the team and their parents, also with Conner's help. He said he called in a favor from his boss, the Athletic Director. Something about easing the sting of having to pick workout room times after the men's team coaches.

I am so full of nervous energy knowing I'm going to see him for the first time in person, I can barely sit still.

Elise, of course, notices. She leans over. "Mama, what is wrong with you? Did you have too much coffee on the flight?" She speaks loudly over the roar of the crowd as they introduce the coaches. Each team stands up, waves, and cheers. As the coaches line up in the center of the field, I see him.

He is the most gorgeous man I have ever laid eyes on. Tall, well over six feet, with wavy brown hair that is longer on the top and shorter on the sides. In the shorts he is wearing, I can see all his creamy, well-muscled thighs. His t-shirt hugs his shoulders. I can see he is big and super fit. I know his workouts with Erik have been intense. I've delighted watching him get more and more defined in the last three weeks, but through a screen doesn't hold a candle to what I see before me.

Conner, god of soccer.

I can barely see his molten milk chocolate eyes, but with a start, I realize he is looking right at me. I'm not sure if he can see me, but I take a chance. I wink and blow him a kiss. He blinks and rocks back on his heels just slightly before placing his left hand over his heart. I see Coach Inanna catch the movement out of the corner of her eye and follow his gaze. She finds me and I give her a little wave. She doesn't smile. I only get a curt, brief nod.

Conner's gaze never leaves my face. I stand there and smile like an idiot as they announce the Women's Soccer Team Coaches, and the players erupt around me.

Chapter 16

Conner

Carrie is here.

I drink her in before she realizes where I am on the field. What I see, I adore. Tall, well-dressed, fit with her long brown hair down, caught in the gentle breeze. Her heavenly blue eyes pierce my heart, even from this distance. When our gaze finally connects, my heart jumps. Then she winks and blows me a kiss.

My heart stops. I reach up to check if it is still beating. Then I realize she is giving Inanna a little wave but doesn't break our stare. The world falls away. It is like no other people exist. Everything and everyone else go blurry and quiet. The only thing I care about is her. I vaguely hear my team cheer, but I can't stop looking at her.

Looking right back at me and smiling. That smile I've seen grace her face a thousand times on screen over the last three weeks is real and all for me. Over the screen didn't do it justice–like taking a picture of the moon. Elise pulls her arm to get her to sit down. It's only when I hear Erik chuckle in my ear, I realize I'm rooted to the spot.

He elbows me in the side and says, "See someone you like, Coach? I guess now we know who the mystery woman is. Inanna, you owe me $50." I hear Inanna blow a tight breath through her teeth, but I don't take my eyes off Carrie.

"Really, Conner? Really!?!?! A PARENT??" She whisper-screams in my face. I meet her furious black eyes I have only seen like this one other time. During our first year of coaching together, we lost to LSU in the first round of the NCAA Tournament. It was a humiliating defeat, and she almost killed me.

It is nothing compared to the fury in her eyes now.

When I finally form words and open my mouth, she puts her hand across it. She hisses, "Not here, not now. We will play this ridiculous game. We will win. And then you are going to fucking explain to me why you are making goo-goo eyes at our new star freshman's mother!"

She looks homicidal and as the post LSU game memories flood my mind, I instinctually cover my balls with my hands. She is fucking scary when she is this mad, and I wouldn't put it past her to grab my privates and give them a good twist.

Erik chuckles again. "She is hot, though."

The speed at which I turn to look at Erik cracks my neck. The look on my face must be deadly, a match for Inna, as he puts his hands in defense. "Whoa, whoa brother, I am just saying. I admire her from afar. Fucking hell, man, you that far gone?"

I don't get the chance to answer before Inanna says, still radiating wrath, reminds me, "Arlo is going to have your balls in a jar on her desk when she finds out."

It is finally my turn to surprise them. "I have a meeting with her first thing Tuesday morning. I'm doing this right. No secrets, no hiding. It will not interfere with my ability to coach this team and at the end of the season, I'm going to propose to her."

Inanna chokes on her water and Erik stares at me as if he has never seen me before. Then his expression turns soft, "Conner, if she is it, why are you waiting for the season to end to ask her to marry you?"

My heart clenches a little, and I reach up to rub the center of my chest. I have thought about this. I've gone over and over it in my head a million times. I am sure of what I want to do, but I want to make sure I'm doing it at the right time and for the right reasons.

"We need to tell her kids. We need to tell Elise. I need to meet with Arlo. I need to do this right. I will not have the same shit happen as it did before at Michigan State State. This will all go well, just like our season. I am sorry you found out this way. I had intended to tell you after the game."

Inanna looks like she wants to rip me to shreds, but Erik just stares at me with a goofy grin. She elbows him in the gut to get moving and he "oofs" his assent. He matches her furious pace, and I know I have to follow, too. I cast one more look in the stands and see Carrie turn her beautiful face to me. It's like we are two poles of a magnet. She smiles again and this time, I smile back.

As I walk over to put on my flags, all I can think about is getting through the next forty minutes of this ridiculous game so that I can officially meet her. I say out loud to my assistant coaches, "We are winning this game. It will be the first win in an undefeated season. Get me?"

They both nod, Inanna still furious with Erik smiling. Inanna plays better when she is raging. It makes me feel bad for whoever is covering her. They are going to end up bloody.

We get in position to start the game, facing the massive–and extremely slow–football coaches. Erik, given his size, could play along with them, but he is nearly as fast as I am. It is mind-boggling how a man that big can run that fast. Between us and the Swim Team Coaches, we will run them through. The head swim coach, who also played football in high school, is our quarterback.

Erik is our center and as he snaps the ball to Coach Williams, I run a quick in-and-out pattern. Williams hits me in the chest, and I make a twenty-yard gain before they catch me. I look over at Carrie and flex with the ball in my hand just before I toss it to

Erik. There is a bevy of screams from the stands, from my team and other women with hopes. They can hope all they want.

I'm taken.

He laughs, "Showing off a touch, are we?"

I look over my shoulder to see Carrie grinning from ear to ear. Then I see her pointedly run the tip of her tongue over her top lip. Fuck me. My cock hardens and I inconspicuously adjust my shorts. One more glance and then I hear the snap. I run an x-pattern with Inanna and the other swim team coaches, crossing five yards downfield. Williams hits me and then I pitch it to Inanna, who sprints it in for the first touchdown.

It continues to go downhill for the football team from there. We end up beating the football team 12-3 and, sure enough, the guy they put on Inanna has bloody knees and elbows from missing her flags so many times and hitting the ground.

The temperature is cool. It's a nice day, so we aren't sweating that much. I decide I want to make an impression, so I look at Erik and nod. He and I both take our shirts off at the same time. Inanna hisses at me. She hates it when men are blatantly, being men, and she knows I have ulterior motives.

I hear her whisper-scream "Behave!" as we jog across the field towards the stands. As excited as I am to win, because I love winning, I have something more pressing to do. I have a visceral, world-ending need to meet the woman I'm in love with for the first time. I quickly high-five each of my players as I move past them on my way to Elise. Carrie is standing right by her side, an inch or so shorter than her daughter and a few shorter than me.

I can't help but look her over as I jog towards her. God, she is fine.

Carrie is looking up at me with stars in her eyes, and I realize I almost can't speak. My mouth feels dry and uncoordinated. I want to grab her and pull her to me. I have the football in my left hand and give it to Elise. "Here you go, Superstar, make sure the entire team signs this. We put it in the team training room as a reminder of our first win during our undefeated march to the NCAA title. Now, Elise, care to introduce me?"

***

Carrie

Conner takes my hand and a jolt of energy flows from his warm, large hand into mine. Looking at him is intoxicating, especially given that he took his shirt off. I can't form words and are hands are barely moving it up and down. Then it hits me.

I'm completely head over heels, wrecked for this man. I am in love with Conner Doreland.

Elise shakes me out of my reverie and practically shouts in my ear, "Mama! Mama! Are you ok? What kind of la-la land are you in? Can you please say hello to my head coach and let go of his hand?"

In a dreamy voice, I say, "No, darling, I don't think I can." Conner's smile gets broader and brighter. I hear the strain in Elise's voice, the embarrassment because this is not my usual. I try to clear my head, but it is so hard with Conner looking at me. "I'm sorry Coach, my mom seems to be having a stroke or something."

He laughs but says nothing, just keeps holding my hand. I try to pull myself together. "I'm sorry, Conner." I see Elise wince and adjust. "Ah–I mean Coach Doreland. I don't know what's come over me."

Impossibly, he smiles bigger. "You can call me Conner if you want to, Mrs. Vokler." I groan and say, "Oh god, please do not call me that. Please call me Carrie. Or whatever you want." Elise is looking back and forth between us, clueing into the weirdness.

She doesn't quite catch on, but wanting to end the awkwardness, says, "Ok, well, I'm glad you two finally met. Coach, good game. I'll take care of the ball. We will see you tomorrow at the Parent Dinner. Mama, c'mon on!"

I do not pull my hand away, and neither does Conner. I'm sure we are attracting stares, but I don't care. At least until my youngest daughter grabs my left arm and yanks me with her. When the connection to Conner's hand falls away, I sigh sadly. I look over my shoulder at him and he raises a hand, winks, and mouths, "I'll call you later."

The entire way back to her dorm and my rental car, she fusses at me. Then her fussing turns to worry. She asks me if I'm feeling alright.

She turns her head to look at me and asks, "Mama, did you eat this morning? I've never seen you act like that. Maybe you are coming down with something? Did you pick up a virus on the plane?"

I chuckle under my breath because Elise can switch her thought process in a flash. She goes from prosecutorial to motherly in a heartbeat. "Yes, Sweetheart, I'm ok. I ate, not much, but I'm hungry, so let's get lunch!"

She looks at me from over the roof of the car. "Ok, well, if you start feeling bad, we can call Coach Inanna and get in with the athletics doctor, I'm sure."

Internally, I cringe. I am not sure, given Conner and I's display, that Inanna would be keen on helping me. She looked like a pot of water about to boil over, as she has clearly figured out there is something between Conner and me. I don't envy him having to have that conversation.

We arrive at the cute bistro we found the last time I was here and get seated at the table. Elise has gotten over her concern for my odd behavior and started her regular chatting. She is quiet as she figures out what to order, but I am not surprised when she does. A chicken wrap with salad and French fries - and lots of ketchup. It seems my youngest's love for all things sweet began the moment she first tried the red condiment. She used to scream, "MORE," for it when she was in her highchair. It didn't matter what she was eating, she wanted ketchup with it.

I order the same thing, minus the ketchup, and switch out for sweet potato fries - with ranch dressing. If ketchup is Elise's thing, the ranch is mine. Especially with pizza. Elise talks the entire lunch, filling me in on all her classes, assignments, and the team drama. There is another freshman, Maciee Griggs, making waves, and not in a good way.

Elise has dealt with spoiled rich girls her entire life. She has a knack for being the one person on the field who can connect with them. I don't know if it is her graciousness off the pitch or her ferocity on it, but she garners respect. She can calm girls down from almost anything. She has gotten one red card her whole career. It was during her sophomore year of high school, right after Scott passed. None of us were in a good place, but Elise insisted on playing through it.

A Dad on the opposing team was yelling ugly comments and obscenities. I let it go, but he started directing his vitriol towards Elise. I got up to speak with him. It turned ugly quickly and when he got in my face and called me a "man-hating dyke who deserved to have her tits chopped off," I suddenly felt Elise by my side right before her fist collided with his face. She kicked him in the balls and then in the stomach. While the ref understood, she was out of line and got thrown out of the game. When we got to the car, she looked at me and says, "It was worth it." Then we got frozen yogurt with glee, while she iced her fist.

"Mama, I don't think Maciee learned how to be a good friend. I don't think I'll be the one to teach her, but I'll try. Maybe that will give her a glimpse of how to act."

I applaud her desire to help and give her with a word of caution, "Elise, I love your heart. I always have. Just remember, she doesn't know how to treat it well. She could turn on you.

She only knows one way to get what she wants, to hurt other people. She probably learned that at home. I'd be willing to bet her parents are a piece of work, too."

She smiles tightly, "Oh Mama, yes. You'll get to meet her dad tomorrow night. Her parents got divorced and her dad cut her mom off and out of Maciee's life. It's a very sad story."

We wrap up lunch, and I take her back to her dorm. She hugs me across the center console of my rental and tells me she will call when she is done studying. I make it back to the hotel and check in. There was not an opening to bring up my blossoming relationship with Conner and to stave off the anxiety and building exhaustion, I change to workout. There is no one in the hotel gym at this hour. I am grateful to zone out and do my favorite treadmill workout in peace.

Conner calls fifteen minutes into my workout. I sigh like a teenager with a crush as I reach for my phone to answer.

Chapter 17

Conner
   My life will never be the same.

It's all I can think of as I sit in a meeting with my staff. Between entertaining the parents and then making sure the team is ready for this exhibition game tomorrow; I should have enough to occupy my brain space.

Yet here I sit with only one thing in my mind's eye: Carrie.

Tomorrow night is going to do nothing but intensify my desire for her. She must come back next weekend. I will fly her here or go to see her. All that matters is I pack as much time with her into my schedule as humanly possible, which keeps my team focused on winning the NCAA Title. It is an excellent thing that I thrive under pressure.

Suddenly, Inanna slaps the back of my head.

"OW! What the FUCK was that for?" I rage at her.

"First, it's for falling in love with a parent." She makes a move to slap me again, and I stand up with a warning look on my face. She backs down only because I tower over her but keeps lecturing. "Second, for not preparing me. Elise doesn't know, does she?"

I blow out a frustrated breath, "No, not yet, but we are trying to figure out how to tell her. I'm sorry I didn't warn you, but this is MY LIFE, Inanna. The REST OF MY LIFE we are talking about. Can you cut me some slack? I was going to be completely honest with you after I talked to Arlo, but I guess the cat is out of the bag."

Inanna doesn't look happy with my answer. I know she is worried this will derail our hard work. She is the team mother, truly the mama bear. I love it, unless that intensity is directed at me. Erik makes a move to put up his hands in a conciliatory gesture. His deep baritone reverberates through the room. "I suggest we take a breather. Then we can come back and map out the strategy from this exhibition game tomorrow. That is where our focus truly needs to be."

Inanna has frustration radiating off of her, so I agree with Erik's plan. I give them both a nod, tell them to find our Keeper Coach and then exit the training room to call Carrie. She picks up on the second ring, and I hear a mechanical whirring in the background. Her voice is a little breathy, and my frustration rolls off of me when I hear it. "Hi Sweetness. I'm glad you called. How are you?"

"Well, I'm doing better now. The revelation of our relationship didn't go great, but I wasn't expecting it to whenever Inanna found out. She is intense."

She makes a non-committal sound in her throat and her breathing is elevated. "You on the treadmill, Sunshine? You didn't want to get on the bike?"

This time she giggles, and of course, my dick responds. "What was that cute little laugh for, Sunshine?"

She giggles again and then the reason hits me. I step farther down the hallway, away from the conference room doors, and in a whisper loud enough for her to hear, say. "My Sunshine, are you saving that perfect pussy for me?"

She lets out an indistinct sound, "Mmmmmmmm, Conner, I love you can read my mind. I wanted to make sure all was in tip-top condition for you."

I pull a hand through my hair and down my face. "This new information is going to make it hard for me to focus on problem-solving with you about Elise because all I'll be thinking about is how I'm going to make you so sore all night tomorrow."

Amused, she says, "That's the plan, lover. But who says I need you to help me problem-solve my situation with Elise?"

That comment is challenging. The energy of her voice shifted, and it makes me feel wary. Did I miss something in her last text?

"Sunshine, did I miss something?" I ask her and I can't shake the slight edge to my voice.

"No, Conner, you didn't. I want to TALK to you about it. I can figure out how to handle this with my daughter." She sounds a little stiff. I don't want to argue with her, but I need clarity. Even if her pushing back on me makes me feel like I want to push her against a wall and show her who is boss.

I clear my throat and say, "Okay, my Sunshine, I hear you. You want to tell me what's going on and I'll share my thoughts when you ask. Deal?"

She assents and tells me about how she feels. She wants to do it right and doesn't want to put any pressure on her. I feel uncomfortable, as maybe she doesn't want to tell Elise at all. I don't like secrets. They have burned me before.

I have a question ready when she finishes and says, "Ok, Conner. I'm sorry. I want your advice. I've gotten all the thoughts out of my head. Now I want to hear yours."

"Carrie, do you want to keep our relationship a secret?"

I hear the treadmill switch off. She is quiet, and I can feel the tension building between my shoulder blades. When she answers, they relax as my heart soars.

She confesses. "I do not want to keep us a secret. I'm falling for you, Conner. There is no way I could have expected this in any lifetime, but I want to be with you. I know how much it means to you to be completely honest at every level, and it's the same for me. I will tell Elise tonight."

I'm quiet for a long time and realize I need to walk back into my meeting. I know my silence probably makes her nervous, but

I appreciate her giving me the space. It allows me to be open with her in a way I've never been with anyone before.

"Carrie, I know you will do what is best. I have a meeting with Arlo on Tuesday, and I will work it out with my coaches and with Elise."

Her voice sounds a little small when she says, "Okay, I trust you."

"And Carrie?"

"Yes?"

"I've been in love with you from the first moment I laid eyes on you. I will turn the world upside to be with you. This is forever for me, and it pushes me–you push me–to be a better man. You deserve to live the rest of your life being loved in the fullest way possible. This is all or nothing for me, Sunshine."

I can hear her sniffling on the other end of the phone. I've said nothing close to this to another woman and while I know she has loved before; this is a first for me. She is brave to take on navigating this tricky situation with her daughter, so I will be brave and live how I feel.

"Conner, I can't wait to kiss you. You say the most holy and profane things. I can't wait for our life together."

I puff up my chest because those words make me want to take on the world. Which I need to do right this second as my coaching staff is waiting for me. "My Sunshine, I have to go back to my meeting. I will text you when I'm done and let me know how things go with Elise, yah?"

"Yes, of course, my Sweetness."

With those parting words in my ear, I walk back into my meeting. We are going to win the whole fucking thing–NCAA Tournament, Top Collegiate Program, and our lives together.

***

Carrie

To pass the time waiting for Elise, I walk around the quaint college main street near my hotel. Cooling down after my workout is easier in the California early fall temps, but I am in a daze. All I can think of is Conner. I never expected to feel this way. I never expected to find love again, or if I did, it would be more companionship. What I've found instead is the world-ending, epic, storybook love that can remake the world.

I loved Scott. We had passion and friendship. It was more than enough. We built so much together, and it was so good at the end.

Now, I've found my soulmate. I don't have to settle for less than what I need–what I deserve. It makes me feel funny, like I can't be this lucky. After what I went through with Scott, I can feel those fears and doubts creep their way forward in my mind. Just as quickly, I thank and remind those parts of myself that we don't need that kind of protection. We deserve a man like Conner, period and full stop. Conner is the complete package, and he is all mine.

I wander into this adorable bookstore called "The Book Nook." It is cozy, the place you expect to find in a picturesque college town. The whole place is decorated in soothing tones of yellow, teal, and dark blue. It has plenty of comfy chairs, as if they want you to sit and read a book. The shelves are packed, and they have tables with the latest releases. There is a table for independent authors front and center, rather than tucked away in the back.

I love it all ready, especially when I see my most recent favorite read, *Teleosis,* on the indie table. The author self-published and she's been vocal about bookstores giving the same upfront shelf space to authors like her. She wants to do away with the self-publishing bias.

I love an underdog and I'm glad the owner has great taste.

I notice a table with a sign that says, "Spicy Sports Romances." They have lots of hockey and football options, but I don't see any soccer. I dig around a bit until I hear a gentle voice say, "Looking for something?"

I look up to see a pair of wire-rimmed glasses framing blue eyes that sparkle with intensity. His salt and pepper hair falls into his eyes. The rest of his hair is pulled into a man bun, and he is tall and well-built. He is handsome in an unexpected way; like his features might have been mismatched on a smaller scale, but on his broad cheekbones, with plenty of room between his eyes, his look is remarkable. He smiles at me, and I smile back, immediately at ease with this gentleman who could be five years older than me - or twenty.

I cough and say, "Well, I was looking to see if you had any soccer stories?"

He smiles and says, "Not many. Unfortunately, that market hasn't been tapped yet, but it could end up being as big as hockey is right now. Boiling, these hockey romances are." He laughs an easy, deep, musical laugh that immediately makes me want to know more about him.

"I like you read your inventory," I say with a lascivious grin, and he doesn't exactly take the bait. I'm not flirting, more just feeling out of the situation, plus there is something about this man that puts me at ease.

"A shopkeeper would be remiss if he didn't keep up with trends. As good as Pride and Prejudice sold for Jane, it isn't exactly on the bestseller list now. I need to turn a profit, otherwise, who is going to supply the local college students with their regular dose of smut?"

He winks at me, and I laugh.

I reach out my hand and say, "Hi, I'm Carrie and I love your bookshop."

He takes my hand in his huge one and the rough callouses scrape against my palm. "I'm Samson. Welcome to the Book Nook. I'm glad you found us, and I can show you the couple of soccer romances I have. Are they for you or someone else?"

I blush a little as Samson quirked an eyebrow. "I pass no judgement on what my patrons read. I read it all. It's not only a job requirement but a calling."

I smile warmly and say, "OK, you are my new best friend, so I will tell you. It's for my man. We will finally get to spend tomorrow night together and I want to give it to him as a present–and for ideas for later." I wink.

He laughs loud this time and claps his hands together. "Oh, you special, wonderful girl! To have a man to trade smutty books with is a dream. You are one blessed woman." He looks at my side-eyed and whispers, "Does he have any brothers into age gaps?"

It is my turn to laugh. "Yes, he has brothers, but all of them are spoken for. I promise you this, though. I will return the favor you've done me here by scoping out the eligible population here in this town for candidates for you. Any specific requirements?"

He looks down and I see he is blushing now. When he meets my eye, he has a serious look. "I've kept my eye out for years and let me say this town is dryyyyyyy. I'm tired of making the trip to San Francisco. I'm ready to settle down. So, if you can find me a man who is tall, strong and ready to settle down, I'll be in your debt for life."

I smile broadly and commit to the search. He shows me around the store, which takes longer than I expect, as he tells me his history, including losing his first love to AIDS in the late 1980s; how he ended up as the owner of the Book Nook. He is such a beautiful, genuine soul. I give him the short version of my life and tell him about Conner. Between Conner's declarations, our bright future together, and meeting Samson, this day could not get any better.

When my phone vibrates with a message from Elise, I tell Samson about her, and he gives me some sage advice. "Tell her straight, Carrie. Trust her to handle the information in her own way and in her own time. And if Conner is as stand-up as you say, he will make this all right–for her and the entire team."

As I make my purchases, I commit to coming back the next time I'm in town.

I turn back as I open the shop door and call out, "We will find your man soon, Samson! I'm sure he is just around the corner!"

He waves me out with a bright, beaming smile that lights up his face. Everything in the world is perfect as I float to pick up my youngest daughter for our hotel movie night.

CHAPTER 18

Conner

Soccer strategy reminds me of choreography.

The difference is that dancers execute exactly as they have practiced. In a game, we have to rely on what we coached, with the execution being up to our players. Being a coach is like riding a roller coaster; a build-up, a sudden drop, and then a white-knuckle grip that leaves you exhilarated at the end.

There will be national and professional scouts at every single game we play this year. This is the most high-risk season we've ever played, and it should have me on edge like never before. Unusually, though, I can't seem to muster the energy to be worried, concerned, or insecure. This deep-seated feeling of contentment started when we completed our roster with all the freshmen committing. There was only one hold out and we are currently struggling to decide what to do about her.

Maciee Griggs is talented and has great potential. We recruited her straight out of one of the top private high schools in California. She seemed a natural fit.

Until we started practicing. I am not sure how she got this far on her talent alone because her attitude is abysmal. I'm wondering if her father, a very rich shipping magnate out of San Francisco, paid them to speak only about her good qualities. I don't know what game she and her father are playing–but her inability to show up on time to training or class and un-coachability has us seriously considering cutting her.

It's plenty early enough in the season to do so, but I'm not sure she knows that.

"It's terrible." Inanna says grimly as she blows the hair off her forehead. "Her on-time record is pitiful. She's missed almost all her classes. To top it off, there are whispers she is stirring up trouble with her teammates too. Comments in the locker room and on social media. I think we need to have a sit down with her and her father on Parent's Weekend. He isn't the easiest man to deal with, but if he has any influence over her, to get her to shape up."

My assistant coaches continue to discuss handling Maciee. She will ride the bench until we see massive improvement. The success or failure of this team starts and ends with me. If we are going to be the team we've worked tirelessly to be, that must be my sole focus–rich Daddy or not. I sit pensively, thinking about how Maciee responds to not playing, and then I'll make the call.

As my coaches draw their discussions to a close, I tell them straight away, "We scope out her father at dinner tomorrow night. She is not playing until there is a drastic improvement in her commitment to the team. Inanna, clarify that if she is having issues adjusting to college life, we will involve her academic advisor to give her a lighter load, but she has to go to class. We need to be on the lookout for any mental health concerns. We know what to look for when it comes to that."

Both Inanna and Erik nod seriously while I continue, "I do not think she has anything other than Rich Girl Bully Syndrome and we all know that will not fly in this program. Inanna, talk to her Big Sister. This is our time to shine, and I need every one of our ladies fully invested in doing just that. No. Matter. What."

I emphasize those last three words with a finger poke at the two of them. Inanna cocks her head thoughtfully at me, "Conner, not to change the subject, but I am. How do you think Arlo is going to take the news of your pending engagement to Elise Vokler's mother?"

I narrow my eyes at her and respond testily, "Her name is Carrie, Inanna."

She waves me off dismissively. "I know. I know. I knew her first. However, I want to hear how you will handle it with Arlo, because that will be a big deal."

I have given my meeting with Arlo an inordinate amount of headspace. I know the order of things: Parent's Weekend Dinner, fucking Carrie into a coma, the game, and then I'll talk to Arlo. I'm all set.

"Inanna, I am going to be completely honest with her. Then I will ask her how we should handle fallout or damage control. It's what she gets paid the big bucks to do. I'm going to trust her with what is happening in my life and seek her guidance."

Inanna lets out a low whistle, "That's mighty brave of you, Coach. What if it doesn't go as you plan?"

I stare at her for a beat. "Then I'm going to make a different one. I'm a soccer coach, Inanna. It's an inborn talent of mine to make quick decisions when the game is on the line."

She laughs heartily and loudly, startling Erik, whose head was bobbing back and forth between us like a ping-pong ball.

Inanna finishes her chortling and says, "I also know you can be a controlling son-of-a-bitch, and you hired me to navigate the hard times. So, if you need me to go with you to talk to Arlo, or you need me if anything comes up with Carrie at all, I have your back. I want all the wins just as much as you do, but you being happy and fulfilled means more. I don't say it much and I'm still pissed you didn't tell me before now, but I'll get over it. We are here for you."

Erik nods his agreement and I feel a weight come off my shoulders. With Inanna and Erik on board, the relief washes through me. They must have had their own conversation during our break while I talked with Carrie.

"Thank you, Coaches. Now, let's get through the next thirty-six hours and kick some ass. Shall we?"

***

Carrie

Elise is in a fantastic mood when I pick her up.

"Done with classes and homework, so it's only fun and soccer this weekend!" She pumps her fists in the air as I drive to our hotel. I cannot help but smile. My youngest is built to have fun, even low-key fun, like a movie night with her mom.

Elise has packed very little, knowing she can use whatever of my toiletries she needs. The girls and I share a very similar face and body care routine, and it makes it easy when we travel. We coordinate who is bringing what and share.

We order from room service, with Elise ordering her longtime favorite–chicken tenders and French fries with a root beer. I request a bottle of ketchup. I order the same thing, and we chose our movie while we wait for our food. We select a thriller movie about a killer shark, another one of her favorites, and fall into a companionable silence as the movie begins.

I recognize I'm nervous. I don't want to do is ruin our time together with the news about Conner and me. My youngest is the most empathetic out of all of my girls. It is when she gets in her feelings that things go sideways. She doesn't lash out in anger like her sister, Sabrina. She doesn't keep things to herself like Maley.

Elise melts down when she is upset—or if anyone is upset with her. I've dried thousands of tears and breathed with her to help her calm down. I don't want her to be upset, but I can smell it, like ozone in the air after a rain.

Suddenly, she whips her long, straight blonde hair around and looks me full in the face. She is back to wearing bangs, which softly frames her eyes. "Mama, what is it? You know I can tell when something is on your mind."

She is tuned into my wavelength like no one else. She and I have been buddies since the moment she was born; always on my hip, until she started walking, then running not long after. We've been partners for years, and while that has shifted as she'd gotten older, the connection is as deep and solid as it ever was.

She continues with her brows knitted together. "Mama, you were acting weird at the game earlier and now you are quiet. What is going on with you?"

I don't want her to see me take a deep breath and hold it because she knows all my anti-anxiety tricks and it'll tip her off. I put on a big, bright smile and say, "I'm enjoying being with you. I might be a little tired."

She nods, but she isn't buying it. "Ok. I get that. What else, though? What are you not telling me?"

This is the moment. Being so close to your children has its pros and cons. The pros are that when they become adults, there is a connection you both keep growing into. The con is the same—it requires you to live in a level of courage that sometimes feels superhuman, like it does now.

"Mama?" Her voice now carries the edge of concern and has gone up an octave.

It is now or never. "Elise, I need to tell you something. I'm scared because it's big. I'm so excited about it but it affects you. We will have to figure out how to navigate together."

"Okayyyyyy. I can handle it." She sounds confident, yet that twinge of concern remains. I move to face her, mirroring her crisscross applesauce posture. I take both of her hands in mine and gently rub my thumbs across her knuckles. Her long fingers curl into mine.

"Sweetheart, I've met someone. It's someone you know, and it happened fast. I haven't told you before this because you've had so much going on, plus, I wanted it to be an in-person conversation. We are in love and figure out a life together."

She is stunned and silent. It was only a few weeks ago, on our way here for her to start school, that I had even brought up the idea of dating again. Now, I'm telling her I'm in love with someone and I can see the dazed look in her eyes.

It lasts for a split second before she narrows her eyes at me in fury.

"NO! You cannot be in love with Coach Conner! Plus, you just met him!!" She pulls her hands back from me and gets off the bed. She paces around the room.

I am stunned by how quickly she made that leap. I expected tears and I'm getting rage. It feels like she slapped me across the face. I open my mouth but cannot say anything. She continues to pace and rant. "I literally just got here. I am starting over and now you drop this on me. Mama, this could ruin everything! Do you know how my teammates are going to look at me? What if they think I am only starting because of you and Coach Conner's relationship? This is the worst news ever!"

I want to tell her to calm down but know from the countless times that's been says to me as a woman; it is a bad idea. She continues to go on and on about it and then stops in her tracks and looks at me dead on again. "Do my sisters know?"

I blink. It is incredible how fast her mind works and the mental gymnastics she can do.

I stutter, "Y-y-y-yes. But we agreed I should wait to tell you in person. And I've not told anyone else his name or who he is besides Dulce."

She rolls her eyes and then narrows them. Her whole body is shaking with fury and asks tightly,

"Because y'all thought I couldn't handle it?"

I'm shocked, like she threw water in my face. "No–no–not at all. We wanted you to get settled, and this all happened after I dropped you off. He contacted me and it just took off from there."

She goes completely still, puts her hands on her hips, smiles at me in a way that doesn't even remotely reach her eyes, and says, "Well, stop it then."

"Excuse me?" I am floored by what I'm hearing.

"Mama, I'm saying that if you want me to do well here, you will stop seeing Coach Conner. I don't care who you tell or who you don't tell, someone is going to find out. Plus, how am I supposed to function around him knowing this?"

    I pick my jaw up off the ground. I thought she would be happy for me. I never would have expected a knock-down drag-out like I'm getting here. Unexpectedly, tears start coursing down my cheeks. "E-e-e-lise, I t-t-thought you would be h-h-happy for me." I am so hurt by how angry she is and I feel it rise in my chest. Tears start streaming down my face and I just ball up like a deflated balloon.

Chapter 19

Conner

I'm a nervous wreck when I think about Carrie telling Elise. I honestly don't think it will go very well. I've spent the last decade with women Elise's age as they grow and mature. It's incredible how much they grow mentally and emotionally in these college years. When the ladies from my program graduate to go take on the world, their brains are fully formed, and they have purpose.

An eighteen-year-old, no matter how self-aware, is still young. They don't think that, of course, and they are much more capable than their high school counterparts. They just haven't had the time yet to grapple with everything "adult." It's why Inanna stays so close to them. They need her in these first couple of semesters. I set up safety and direction. Inanna makes sure their hearts and heads are on straight.

Hell, here I am in my early forties, still figuring it out. Plus, I have more than a vested interest in one of my players dealing with a major home-life situation because I am in the home-life situation.

To manage my anxiety, I go for a run in the hills. I know it will be a few hours before I hear anything from Carrie. She had a fun night planned. It wasn't all about this romantic bomb drop. Plus, if I'm away from my car, it will keep me from jumping in it to go bang on Carrie's hotel room door to demand an update in person.

The only situation remotely close to telling Elise for me is telling my boss, Arlo, but that is not nearly as fraught with emotional entanglements. Telling Arlo is about business and protecting the program. It's easier to keep those conversations in check and a compromise to be found.

From what I've experienced in coaching Elise for the last month, she is all focus, drive, and strength. She has excelled on and off the field in her transition to collegiate life. I've never met someone who wants to win as badly as I and Inanna do until Elise. There is a tiger inside Elise Vokler and anyone who impedes her hunting down what she wants is going to get mauled.

I hope I'm wrong, but I think Elise is going to be furious.

If it were me in her position, I would be. She reminds me of myself at her age, in her competitive style and form. To top that off, with everything she has overcome, she is a force to be reckoned with, which is why I think we can build the program around her, why she is the little sister of our Team Captain and she has the talent and work ethic to go all the way to the Women's National Team and even play professionally.

Her goals are not small, and she still needs time to become the woman she is. Carrie may not completely see that yet. That was a tremendous driving force for my stalker–Miranda. She couldn't get her dad to see her as someone who could make her own choices. Pair that with serious mental illness and projecting her Daddy-issues onto me and, well, that shit hit the fan fast.

However, Elise responds, she and Carrie will work through it. They are healthy and have a very close relationship. Then I hope we will all be able to sit down and plan out what happens next.

When I get back from running, I shower, then check my messages one more time. Nothing yet from Carrie. I have my own difficult parental conversation not to have with Maciee Grigg's father. I would like to get ahead of any fallout in case Maciee throws a tantrum.

I dial the number and the man I'm calling picks up on the 2nd ring. He sounds just like I expect him to–a rich asshole. "Nelson Griggs here."

I grimace at the greeting and put on my manly, Coach voice. "Mr. Griggs, this is Coach Doreland from UCC. Do you have a moment to speak with me?"

"Oh, yes, yes, Coach, how can I help you? I'm surprised by your call. Is everything ok with Maciee and the team? Or are you calling for a donation, even though that seems like it would be your boss's job?"

I inwardly groan. What a douchebag. I don't let it show in my voice, though, and give him a gruff laugh. "Mr. Griggs, everything is fine. Yes, I leave the donation calls to my boss for sure. We are prepared for the exhibition game and think this season will be one for the record books. I called bec---"

He cuts me off and I wonder how many drinks at happy hour this man has already had. He lets out a high-pitched squeal of a laugh. "That's great to hear, my boy. And I know my Maciee will be a tremendous asset to your program."

I start in again, "Actually, sir, Maciee is why I was calling."

His laugh is like fingernails on a chalkboard. "Oh yes? Are you calling to tell me she is starting?"

I've met a lot of guys like Nelson Griggs. They can't imagine something wouldn't go their way. It always has, so why stop now? I'm not sure if he is listening, so I just say what I need to. My words pull his attention from his ego-and probably liquor-soaked perspective. "Actually, no, sir. I was hoping while you are here for Team Dinner and Exhibition, we could sit down to talk about some areas where Maciee needs to improve to continue to be a part of our program."

This sobers him and he grows serious. "I can't imagine any area that my Maciee would need to improve. But please enlightened me, young man."

I roll my eyes at the slight. I look younger than I am and by his general air and tone, I can pinpoint immediately why Maciee has attitude problems. Having a father who thinks flowers grow out of your ass, so your shit doesn't stink, does nothing for coachability.

"I would love to sit down and have that conversation with you, Maciee, and my Assistant Coach on Sunday. We think Maciee has potential, but we've had to talk with her several times over the last month about taking our program and her academics seriously. Making sure my players are set up for success is a huge part of our program—we produced not just elite athletes but great people. We have a window of an hour between the end of the game and the Team debrief and we can meet in my office. Will you be available?"

"Oh sure, Coach. But wouldn't this just be easier if I let your boss know I can see us donating for a new training center just for women's athletics?"

I slowly blow out a breath. "I appreciate that generous offer, as I'm sure the Athletic Director would. Our new training facilities serve our needs just fine. What do you say, Nelson? Can you stay for an hour after the game to make sure we all have the same understanding about Macieee's future with our program?

I hear him mumble something under his breath about uppity youngsters who think they know everything. "I'm sorry, what was that, sir?"

He putters his response, "Oh, oh, nothing. I'll see you tomorrow at the Parent Dinner, Coach. I'll let Maciee know about our meeting."

I smile a truly genuine smile, which I know he can't see, but hope he can feel through the phone. "Oh, Mr. Griggs, she already knows. Her attendance is a condition of her continuing to be a part of this team. I look forward to seeing you both tomorrow night."

I hang up and yell, "MOTHERFUCKER!!!!!" as loud as I can to no one in particular. I hate dealing with arrogant pricks who think they can just buy you off so they can continue to do what they want. Every sport has them and soccer is no exception. He is not doing his daughter any favors by spoiling her. She needs to face the consequences of her behavior and if I'm the one that has to start that domino effect, I will do so without hesitation. It will only be for the good of the program and hopefully Maciee's own good.

I check my messages one more time to see that Carrie still hasn't reached out. That concerns me, but I trust her. I make myself some dinner and watch the Real Madrid and Chelsea game I recorded earlier. As it gets later and I still don't hear from Carrie, my nerves get to me. It's hard to settle down, but I finally do just before midnight. I am itching to get my arms around Carrie.

I send her a goodnight text and tell her to call me at whatever time she needs me.

Lying down in bed, house dark and head on my pillow, I blow out a frustrated breath. Tomorrow will be a very long day.

Chapter 20

Elise

How could she do this to me?

I am furious with my mother. Normally, the sight of her curled up in a ball crying would be enough to make me rethink my outburst. I *never* see her cry. She is always the strongest one, the rock of our family.

Now, even the sound of her sniffling doesn't move me. I can't help it. She should *not* be in love with my coach. He should not be in love with her.

I wonder if Coach Conner will still let me play for him if I kick a ball straight into his crotch?

I've had my fair share of shitty coaches. My Mom and Dad supported me through those experiences. Still, I am in love with what I have here at UCC. It's not just about the soccer. I love learning, even the core classes I have to take. I've made great friends–on the team and around campus. My life finally feels like mine for all the right reasons.

This news makes me feel like it will all slip through my fingers like sand on the beach.

This opportunity, even though it is far from my family, is my chance to stand on my own. It is a wide, open space and with lots of room to make mistakes. It's about me, not my mom.

It was about her for so long after Dad died. Why can't she just let it be about me for once?

Those dark thoughts continue to build like a storm cloud in my mind. It is a dangerous path for me to walk mentally. I turn away from where my mom is lying on the bed and all I want to do is get out of here.

I walk over to the nightstand opposite to where my mom's bed is and grab my phone.

"Mama, I'm going to go for a walk. I am way too angry to work this out with you right now. I'll be back in a little while. Don't wait up."

She picks her head up from the bed and I meet her eyes before I break contact. I grab my shoes, then some socks and a sports bra out of my bag. I slip on a pair of running shorts as my Mama moves to sit up and say something to me, but I make my way out the hotel room door in a hurry. I don't hear what she says as the door closes, and I don't want to hear it. I need to get myself settled and back in a better frame of mind.

I get down to the hotel fitness center and realize I left my earbuds upstairs. I blow out a frustrated breath because I wanted to run my ass off to my death metal playlist. That would be a terrible idea, given that it's after ten pm and I have a game tomorrow. I need my legs fresh, but it also wouldn't be the first time I've done something stupid before a game.

I go to the corner of the fitness center and quickly put on my sports bra. I'm glad I sleep in one of my sister's old t-shirts. I don't look too ridiculous as I step onto the treadmill. I set it to a decent walking pace and after thirty minutes, the clouds in my head and heart clear just enough for me to make a call.

"Hey Kiddo, what's going on?"

My sponsor answers the phone on the second ring. Selene and I have been working together for almost two years since I joined with A.A. Therapy was helping process my grief over my dad's death but I was still feeling the compulsion to drink a lot–before school, sometimes at lunch and certainly to get to sleep at night. It wasn't sleep, more like passing out. I needed something different, because I knew this was going to be so bad for me, my family, and my future.

It was when I confessed to my mom's best friend, Dulce, and she packed me off to a young person's A.A. meeting, that I saw the lifeline I needed. I don't know why or how I ended up addicted so young. In the end, all that mattered was I knew I was powerless and there was a way out of it.

My entire perspective on life changed when I started working the Twelve Steps with Selene. There were a lot of late-night phone calls those first few months, but I've been in a good place. Calling her this late is definitely unusual. It's after midnight, her time back in Houston. Her voice is calm and reassuring as always, even though I can hear the concern in her voice. Out of respect for that, I don't waste time, just get right to the point of my call.

Despite the brisk pace I'm walking, my voice is even and hard as I tell her, "My Mom is in love with my new coach."

Selene lets out a whistle between her teeth before she says, "Wow, Elise, that's heavy. How are you feeling?"

Selene has a decade of sobriety and even though she is only twenty-eight, she has what I want in life. She is secure in herself, serves others and is successful in her career in the construction industry as a project manager. She and her boyfriend just got engaged and they are planning a sober wedding that will be a blast for everyone, no alcohol needed.

I tell her the truth. "Not good. I haven't felt this anger or dealt with these dark of thoughts in a while. I'm on the treadmill and that usually helps, but my head isn't clearing."

She asks the question I know I need to answer but dread facing, "Maybe it's your heart you should focus on."

Selene has taught my family a lot about learning to be gentle with ourselves. Between her and our family therapist, this has been the most important–and the hardest lesson–we've had to learn. Selene saw my mom tap her chest during a match and asked me about it later.

"My mom reminds me to play from the heart. She's done that since I was little." I told her. Selene never lets me forget. Now, it means I need to be gentle with myself–and others.

It is always the focus of her counsel to help me work through my emotions, which caused taking my first drink. I couldn't deal with all of them, and the conditions of my life certainly didn't help, so I drank to numb them out. Learning to feel them, to live from my heart, is a daily work in progress.

I keep walking in silence for a few minutes and Selene patiently waits on the phone for me to find the words. When I do, they come out in a rush. "I just can't believe she would rush into something. Everything has changed for me and now she wants to add something else to my plate. This could have a huge impact on how the team views me when it comes out. Because we both know it will come out. Everyone will find out. Everyone will know, and what if they stop being my friends because of it? What if they all end up hating me? What if what I'm building here all gets torn down because my mom is being selfish?"

Selene simply asks, "Are you not upset with your coach, too?"

At the thought of Coach Conner, the top of my head actually feels like it is going to come off. "Oh, I am. I completely read him wrong. Maybe I read this entire program wrong. He seemed so put together; the exact program I needed. But now? He seems like a fucking predator. I really want to kick a ball right to his face, balls or both!"

My heart rate has picked up–not from the pace but from my anger. I feel like I'm going to burn up from the inside out. I'm so angry with Conner. With my mom, too, and maybe the entire world.

Selene replies with, "I can totally understand that. This is a monumental shift in a season that was already full of big changes. You are on your own for the first time, so your mom dating someone, much less falling for someone, without you knowing from the jump, is really a massive bombshell."

She pauses before continuing, giving me some space to process. I breathe through the anger, even punching the air in front of me to move it through. I'm sweating for real now and I lean until the sensation, letting the waves of heat radiate off my skin to balance the fire I feel in my gut.

I'd love to kick a hundred balls into the net, maybe even picture Conner's face on all of them.

When I say this to Selene, she chuckles softly and asks me, "How did your mom take your reaction?"

At that question, the fantasy of kicking Conner's head through the upper ninety's crumbles. The recent memory of my mom's face, red and blotchy, which I've seen less than a handful of times in my whole life, returns and I immediately feel ashamed.

It's all I can do to whisper, "Not well. She thought I would be happy for her."

Selene again gives me some time to find my center before she says, "So, tell me the real reason you aren't happy about it?"

I blow out a breath and retort, "I think you know me well enough to know why."

She chuckles louder this time and says, "Yes, I do, but you know, I know you need to say it out loud."

For a third time, my sponsor doesn't press me, just waits patiently. After a minute of total silence, I switch off the treadmill and take a seat on a workout bench. I've been gone for close to an hour and the fuel of my emotion draining off like the last of the water in the bathtub. I hang my head as the busy day also catches up with me.

I make sure Selene is still on the line. We've been silent that long. Seeing that she is dashes my secret hope that we got disconnected so I don't have to fess up to what I feel underneath all that anger now that it's bled off.

This is the crucible of recovery. We feel the feelings, remember it is a gift to feel them. Then we ask for help when we don't know what to do.

I pluck up my courage from somewhere deep inside and speak the truth. "I'm scared everything will get messed up. I'm scared it will all get ruined again. I'm terrified of ending up in the dark place again and not know how to find my way into the light."

I add at the last second, "I like Coach Conner, too. I don't want him to hurt my mom. She's been through enough already. I've hurt her enough already." Tears slip down my face as I grapple with how I treated her.

My sponsor is smiling, I can tell through the phone. "Elise, I'm so proud of you. You are doing so well. This is big, and it is ok for it to be scary. It's the unknown and you are right. Your mom has been through a lot. She never stopped loving you and being there for you in your dark place. She won't leave you now. And what if everything goes better than you expect it to? If we are playing the 'what if' game–what if this ends up being the best thing that could have happened to you? You didn't think that was the case when you came into the rooms and had to admit, at sixteen, you were an alcoholic, but it was, wasn't it?"

I eke out a small, "Yes," around the knot in my throat.

Selene takes that as a prompt to continue, "Ok, then. You know I'm going to have you journal and then put it in your God Box. You can do that tomorrow. How are you going to handle things when you go back up to the room?"

I sniff loudly. "I'm going to make amends for the way I reacted and what I said. How selfish and fearful I got."

She murmurs, "Mmm-hmmm. Then what?"

After a few more tears fall, I take a beat to roll my shoulders and stretch the tension out of my neck, which cracks loudly. "I'm going to talk it out with her. I need to give her a chance to tell me how this happened–*in a month!*" I say the last bit with emphasis and Selene chortles.

"Stranger things have happened, kiddo. Your mom is a very smart lady, and your coach has never seemed like a slouch. They are going to do what is best, I believe that, and you should too. Besides, Michael fell for me the moment he grabbed my cup of coffee instead of his at my home group meeting. You know, he didn't have the balls to talk to me after, so he went back every day at the same time in case I'd be there, just to run into me again."

I laugh even though I've heard the story of how they met a hundred times, usually as a warning but sometimes as a promise of what could be.

Selene sends me off to apologize to my mom with five words, "Rest up for tomorrow's game."

I walk out of the fitness and punch the button on the elevator as I tell her, "I'll let you know the winning score."

***

Carrie

When I hear the key card in the lock, I'm instantly awake and sitting up. I drifted off after the Elise left. The tumult of emotion was overwhelming, and I was completely blindsided. I did not handle it well, which wasn't helped by the exhaustion of the long day. I feel like a wet towel, rung out and hanging funky over the shower curtain.

I'd gotten a text from Conner right after Elise left and while I thought about calling him, I was just too tired to speak. I gave him a summary of the situation and expressed my gratitude for his support.

> *It did not go well, Sweetness. She was furious and left. She will be back, but I've got to rest my eyes. They hurt. My heart hurts.*

He sends back the kissing face emoji, but I know there is more that he wants to say–and probably do–but after we talked earlier, he knows I need to handle this with Elise on my own.

Elise comes into the room, and her bangs are plastered to her head. She's been exercising and confirms it with a shrug. "I went to the Fitness Center for a while." She explains nothing else before she closes the bathroom door and takes a shower.

I lie back on the bed, an arm over my scratchy eyes. I hate crying. I especially hate crying in front of my girls. I've always been the one that holds it all together and I expected Elise to be emotional, but I didn't expect fury.

I'm glad she is back in the room though, and I'm hopeful we can talk it out. Quickly because as I glimpse the clock, time has marched well past midnight. I've been up for twenty hours straight, minus my recent brief nap.

Sighing, it occurs to me my daughter needs something to sleep in, so I get out from under the covers and walk over to my suitcase. I get out a second workout t-shirt, which I only brought as a just in case, and lay it on her bed. I immediately crawl back into my bed, returning my arm over my eyes to shut out the light. Elise comes out of the bathroom a few minutes later, steam billowing out.

She starts to ask me for a shirt, then realizes I've already put one out and mumbles, "Thanks, Mama."

I don't push her to talk to me at this moment. Given the level of her reaction, I don't expect us to talk again tonight, so I roll over, facing away from her bed, and close my eyes. I feel the touch of her hand on my leg and realize I'd fallen asleep again. I roll over to see her standing by my bed, holding out a washcloth.

"I thought you might want this for your eyes."

I nod and take it from her hand, laying it across my face. It is cool and I'm grateful. She sits down on the edge of her bed, near the side table. The relief of the cloth wears off quickly, my face heating the material. At about the same time, Elise speaks.

"Can we talk?"

I take the washcloth off my face and sit up, scooting back, so I'm propped up against the headboard. "Sure, sweetheart."

She pauses as I adjust and says, "I was wrong about the way I reacted. I shouldn't have lashed out at you like that, or made you feel you have to choose because I got scared of what could happen. I'm sorry, Mama."

I reach over and extend a hand to her in front of the table. She reluctantly takes it, not out of hesitation but guilt. Her shoulders are slumped forward, and she is looking down at her lap. Her face reflects how tired I feel. I keep it simple with my response, "I forgive you. I am sorry I didn't tell you before now. I just wanted you to establish your life here with no extra stress."

Still looking down at her lap, she says, "I know. I forgive you too."

We sit there, holding hands for a while longer, before I feel myself sink back into unconsciousness, the weight of the day taking over again.

Elise notices, of course, but has one last thing to say before she lets me drop off. "I want to hear the complete story, and we still have a lot to talk through about it all. I'm scared this will affect how the team treats me. I know it's not illegal or anything, but it feels wrong. Can we talk over breakfast when we are both rested?"

I shake my head yes and move towards the middle and open the covers, inviting Elise in for a snuggle. It's been a long while since she's wanted to do this, so I don't know if she will. It just feels right to make the offer.

She takes me up on it, climbing into bed with me. Her long body takes up all the space on her side of the bed, as she lays her head down on my right shoulder. I smooth out her hair and whisper, "Thank you."

As I drift off, I hear her quiet voice say, "I love you, Mama. I'll be happy for you soon."

I smile into her hair and while I know she gets up to go back to her own bed in the night; I wake up refreshed.

All night I dreamed of my little buddy with a blond bob and huge green eyes kicking a soccer ball with her chubby legs and yelling, "Mama! LERK!"

Chapter 21

Conner

It was a long night. I know I slept because even if I take a while to fall asleep; I don't have to sleep for over five hours to feel rested. I got slightly more than that, as it was after midnight when I got a text from Carrie.

Using my foam roller to iron out my muscles is essential. I learned this after blowing out my knee, which ended my Premier League career. Regardless of how much Erik and I have been working out together, running tonight, light yoga would not provide enough for my body—or my mind—to completely power down. My phone was on the floor in front of me and if I hadn't been in a chaturanga, I might have missed the message flash across the screen.

I focus on one phrase and my chest aches.

> *My heart hurts.*

My earlier desire to drive over to her hotel room and hold her ramps up again. I talked myself off the ledge, though. Carrie and Elise need to navigate this together, and I keep reminding myself to trust that they will. I want to fix the problem, but in this instance, it's not mine to fix.

I fall asleep hugging a pillow. Tomorrow, it will be Carrie in my arms.

When my alarm goes off at six, I try a little meditation like I know Carrie does every morning, but it doesn't connect. I'm too antsy–about the day, about tonight, and about the game tomorrow. The day before a game is one that is always busy. My schedule is packed from 9 am on. The Seniors plan the night before every first match.

Just a few more hours and she'll be mine. I can hold her, I can kiss her, make her heart feel better. Then, if she feels like, I can make her brain and body explode with pleasure.

My team meeting goes well, as planned. It's a long one. We don't get done till lunch time. All of us are hungry and the players peel off to hit the dining hall. As we are packing up, Elise hangs back. She asks to speak to Inanna and me. She seems nervous until I realize she isn't. She is focused, and it has her vibrating with energy. I know that feeling and say that to her.

"Thanks Coach. We have a lot in common now," she responds somewhat sarcastically, but with a full-faced smile.

Inanna looks at her sharply and says, "Ok, so we all know that we know we know. Are you ok, Elise?"

This makes Inanna a top-tier coach. Her concern for her players' emotional well-being is paramount to everything else. She has no hesitation kicking their asses in training, but their mental health is her number one priority.

Elise nods and says, "Yah, I am. I'm still kind of in shock, and it is making me jittery. Would I be able to be excused from the team bonding tonight to spend some more time with my mom?"

My first instinct is to grab her shoulders and shake her, then to tell her "NO" in a very loud voice. But I rein myself in and lower my level of panic at the thought of having to change plans with Carrie. We've waited so long for this. Just as I'm about to launch into a lecture about the importance of team bonding, Inanna beats me to it.

She shakes her head, "No, Elise. I understand how you are feeling. It is a big deal what you've just found out. However, this is part of the deal of being in our program. Team bonding is not optional, save a death in the family or other crisis. This is a shock, I get that. But it's a good thing. A very good thing. Your mom will be ok."

I feel an enormous sense of relief, not having to say anything, and Inanna's touch is always exactly what is needed with the ladies. Inanna isn't pushing the team bonding for my benefit because she doesn't know I'm spending my night with Carrie. She is only speaking the truth of our strategy. The team has to be one to win. We are family and families stick together.

I nod and agree, a very Coach-like look on my face. "I know it's been a lot, Elise. I think of myself as your Coach above all–the Head Coach of this team. Your team needs you to be there tonight and it will help settle your mind."

I hear Inanna sigh, knowing she is annoyed I say anything. It isn't annoyance at what I've said, just that I'm a man and validated what she said. She made it adamant she didn't need that from me. I look at her sideways and quirk a grin, which further annoys her.

She huffs out a breath and says, "Ok, Elise, now that 'THE HEAD COACH' has spoken, why don't you go get you some lunch and ask about any last-minute prep you can help with for tonight?"

Elise looks like she wants to argue but thinks better of it. I recognize she isn't so worried about her mom but needs reassurance herself. I quietly add, "Elise, why don't you call your mom on the way and check on her?"

She looks up at me with her big, round green eyes. She doesn't have to look up far. She is only an inch, maybe two, shorter than me. Still, the shape of her face reminds me so much of Carrie.

My heart catches and I want to add, "Go on, Sweetheart." Her connection to Carrie already has me in a paternal mindset.

But I don't as Elise speaks first. "Thanks Coach. That's a good idea. I will. My Mom means everything to me, you know that right?" Her eyes go a little glassy and far away, remembering all they've been through.

I say to her, "Trust me, it is one more thing we have in common, Elise."

Inanna breaks the tender tension with a sharp command. "Elise, if you miss out on lunch, I'll make sure the team has to run ten extra laps around the pitch before the game, while you watch. Get your ass to the Dining Hall!"

She startles and immediately looks chagrined. A true team player through and through. Never, ever cause your team to run extra laps. I chuckle as she bolts and say to Inna, "Well done, Coach."

Her face turns sour. "Oh, fuck you Conner. Don't validate me again." Then she gives me a serpentine grin as she says, "Speaking of fucking, I'm guessing that's what you will do tonight. You are welcome to make sure your love fest isn't disturbed."

It's all I can do to hug her. "Yes, I owe you big time. Name your price and, of course, lunch is on me."

Inanna gathers her bag and as we shut the door, she says, "Lunch is on you for the rest of your life, Conner."

I chuckle and agree. It is the least I can do to make sure our plans continue.

***

Carrie

As we wait for our breakfast to come to the table at the hotel restaurant around eight the next morning, I tell Elise the story of how Conner and I got here with our relationship. Now that we have slept and are both more centered, and both with coffee in us, this time she listens. She tells me how she feels about it, including her fears about what could happen. She wants us all to be smart and after Conner tells his boss, come clean with the team. She is terrified they might judge or exclude her.

I listen but reassure her, "This team loves you and while it might be a bit of a shock, I think you'll be surprised. These are not high school or overly privileged club players. Even before I knew Conner–and more about Inanna–I knew this was the right place for you. Give them a chance to surprise you."

She is quiet while we eat. I am still raw from last night, so I am relieved not to have to make conversation. As the wait staff is clearing our plates, Elise has one final question for me. I can feel it coming, just like I knew I was in labor with her.

When she finally speaks, I think we may be going to make it out of this, salvaging the night and the weekend. "Mama, are you both really in love?"

After Elise leaves for her team meeting a little before nine, I dance for a long time, first frenetically to get my energy out but soon I slow down. The song "Movement" by Hozier comes on, which was the song I stripped to on one of our phone sex dates.

My moves become very intentional, and I picture myself dancing in front of Conner, in person, while a stream of golden light fills me. I see the light reach out for him as he reclines on the bed. It is a delicious feeling, and my body feels yummy and alive.

It's as if the sorrow of last night alchemized into pure eros and all I want is him.

I continue to dance for a while longer before I know I'm done. I've missed a few texts from Conner and update him on how things ended up with Elise. I carry this aliveness with me as I answer emails, take a couple of work phone calls and finish a project I've been sitting on for one of our department heads.

It's past noon when Dulce calls to check in. She's had a slow morning too, after her five-mile run. We talk for a while as I share the story of how telling Elise went.

"I'm not surprised, actually. I kind of figured she would blow a gasket."

Annoyed, I respond, "Conner said the same thing. Why didn't either of you tell me? I might have been more prepared."

Dulce hits the nail on the head with her response, saying, "You were expecting her to react as you see her–the little girl who needs her Mama. But Carrie, Elise is growing up. You've got to adjust your picture of her in your head. We both know that's normal. You had to do to the same thing with Maley and Sabrina. Elise is figuring out who she is and you get to let her.

My chest feels like it is sinking. "I just don't want her not to need me anymore."

Dulce calls me up short, "We both know that would never happen. It's never happened with the older girls, and it definitely won't happen now with your little buddy. Create a different version of that little buddy in your mind."

I sigh, loudly and painfully. "I know. I know. I'll work on it."

Dulce swiftly changes the subject to something much more fun, "Ok, tell me again what you are wearing tonight. The whole thing, lingerie and all."

Just as I put my phone down from wrapping up with Dulce, Elise calls. She said Conner encouraged her to call me, just to check in. My heart melts.

"I'll be busy till I see you at the dinner, Mama. You getting on ok?"

"Yes, sweetheart, I'm doing fine. I may lie down for a bit. I'm feeling tired and there is still a lot of the day to go."

"All you have is the dinner, though." She points out.

I hurry to distract her. I don't think her finding out about Conner and I's plans for tonight would be a great idea. She will be busy with her teammates, anyway. "Oh, yes, but the last thirty-six hours have been a doozy. And we still have the game to go tomorrow, even if it's an exhibition!"

"Ok, I'll see you at the restaurant for dinner. You're the best, Mama. I love you most!"

I chuckle at this statement. She used to say it every day before she went to sleep for her nap, as a toddler. "Yes, my darling girl, I know. I love you too."

Three hours later, after almost a two-hour nap, I'm dressed and ready to go. I'm wearing a long emerald green dress with a gold chain belt and camel wedges. It is my favorite dress up outfit, which I've only worn once to my high school reunion last year.

My long dark brown hair is straight down my back and my makeup is all smoky eyes, soft blush and a nude lip gloss. Gold hoop earrings with a never-worn long platinum and gold accent necklace complete the look.

When I finally arrive at the restaurant downtown, near to my new favorite bookstore, I am impressed. They reserved a private dining room. It is all wood paneling; the smell of the oak wine racks permeates the air as I walk through.

The parents were supposed to arrive at 5:30 pm, and I'm late. I'm one of the last to arrive and immediately Elise comes over. "Mama, you look so beautiful! That's my favorite dress of yours. Come in, we are waiting for Maciee's Dad to come in. He is at the bar." She makes a face like she just smelled something awful, which is her cue to me to stay away from him. Apparently, he is a huge creep.

As Elise takes my arm to lead me to our seats, I can't help it. I look up to see Conner, and my heart stops.

He is wearing his navy-blue suit, minus a tie. He is so gorgeous; the color of his suit sets off his golden-brown eyes and stylishly wavy hair. I can't look anywhere but his face because he is staring at me like I'm the only thing he wants to eat from the menu.

CHAPTER 22

Conner

She is a fucking, ultimate vision. The second she walks in the door, the sunset lighting her entrance, I feel like I'm in a romance novel or a classic film. I have never, ever seen a woman this complete. She isn't just beautiful. She is so stunning, and I notice the entire room turn their attention to her as Elise rushes over. I see her daughter lean down to say something to her and take her arm.

Then she meets my eyes.

I'm frozen to the spot. All I can think of is walking over to her and taking her in my arms. Then, stripping that lovely dress from her body so I can see all of her. The naked hunger in my eyes has Erik elbowing me in the side.

"Easy boy. Let's not make it SO obvious that you want her as your dinner."

I let out a low growl, and he laughs. "Maciee's Dad finally left the bar and is seated. Open the dinner, Coach." I notice Inanna has a strangely composed face, which means I'm going to hear about this later, but I can't help it. Carrie is the only person in this room that matters to me.

My welcome speech is brief, to the point, and I do my best not to look at Carrie the entire time. The first time I do, I nearly forget what I was going to say. Her face is lit up like the moon. She is staring up at me from her seat and all I know is I better get through this dinner to get to her. I breathe through my nose and say the same speech I've said at every team dinner for the last five years.

"Thank you, Parents for joining us tonight and for supporting the first game of the season. We expect great things from the ladies. They have been working so hard. The seniors have done a spectacular job leading the rest of the team, especially our offensive and defensive captains." Both ladies stand, and everyone claps.

Then I continue, "Tonight is a night to celebrate all their hard work, but it is also a reminder of what is coming. We are beginning a journey tonight, a journey to the top of the mountain. To get there, we operate as a unit."

I had been meeting each pair of eyes around the room and finally come to rest on Carrie as I say the next words. "We are going into battle, and it only works if we are all in, together."

Then I break tradition with, which I know will be something else Inanna adds to her, "Discuss with Conner later," list.

My eyes still focused on Carrie, I ask the group, "I'm all in. Are you?"

I hear the chorus of "yes Coach!" from around the room, but only notice one person's response. Carrie's face lights up. She smiles at me and nods her head. She then mouths to me, "I'm in," and it is all I can do not to stand on the table and howl. I keep my composure but say a little louder than necessary, "Ok, let's eat!"

I try my best not to look at Carrie the whole time. Erik and Inanna draw my attention away. The dinner, as it has been every year we've hosted the team dinner here, is delicious. I will bring Carrie here when she comes back to town. The agenda for that trip is already well formed in my mind, but I would love to treat her here.

After dinner, as the parents and players are gathering up their belongings to head out for their bonding and get some rest before tomorrow, a very drunk Griggs approaches Carrie. He is swaying on his feet, and I can see he is talking right in her face.

She looks disgusted and extremely uncomfortable. She leans back when he leans toward her to ask her a question. She looks like she will be ok, but I still have a strong desire to check this dude, bodily. Carrie in her stylish wedges has two inches on him. He is an even bigger asshole than I thought.

When he grabs her elbow to drag her to the bar with him, I hear him say, "C'mon baby, we are both single. Let's have a little fun tonight. You know I'm rich, right?" My vision blurs as I see a red mist. I'm going to murder him for touching her and I'll gladly go to jail for it.

I hear her say, "Get your fucking hands off me. I am not your baby and I'm rich too, pencil dick."

It vaguely registers, but I still have to appreciate her insult. It was well-timed, but he still doesn't need to touch what is mine.

She pushes him back, and he stumbles thanks to five whiskey sours before dinner and several glasses of wine. He catches himself and the room goes silent, so everyone hears him drunkenly say, "Well, I guess what, my daughter is true. You are an uptight cunt, just like your precious little daughter." Carrie's face becomes a mask of shock, and it roots her to the spot.

I am going to carve this guy's heart out with a spoon for daring to speak to her like that. Then I am going to cut his balls off and feed them to him. His daughter is now officially off my team.

Without realizing it, I am moving towards them before I feel a hard yank on my arm, roughly pulling me back. I nearly swing until I realize it's Erik. He is ten feet tall at this moment, and it halts me. He stares down at me and says the only words I need to hear. "Conner, let me handle this. You go to Carrie."

Erik stalks over to Nelson Griggs and manhandles him outside the restaurant. He doesn't say a word to him, not even acknowledging his protests. He shoves him into a cab and tells him to get back to his hotel before he calls the cops.

I make it to Carrie and take her hands in mine; they are so soft and fit in mine like they were made to be there. I want to put my forehead to hers, to calm us both as we are both breathing hard. I have my wits about me, though, knowing everyone is watching us. I rub the backs of her hands with my thumbs in a soothing, circular motion. Her breathing returns to normal, and I let go of her left hand to turn to the room.

I meet everyone's eyes as I announce, "I think that's enough for one night. Players to your team bonding and parents, well, you don't have to go home, but you can't stay here."

Everyone is moving woodenly, deeply uncomfortable after the altercation, so I whisper to Carrie. "Sunshine, are you ok?"

She nods and finally meets my eyes. She is furious and I like it. That light inside of her will not tolerate any small dick energy. I have a feeling if Erik hadn't stepped in, she would have handed Nelson Grigg's his ass on a silver platter.

I smile at her and say, "Coach says it's time to leave. Are you ready to get out of here?"

She takes her hands out of mine, draws in a deep breath with her eyes closed, shakes her arms out, releasing the adrenaline. When she looks up into my face, her eyes are clear again and whispers the words I've been waiting a month to hear.

"Yes, I'll meet you at the hotel, Sweetness."

***

Carrie

The drive to my hotel takes me ten minutes, five minutes longer than it should. In the confrontation's aftermath with Maciee's Dad and my incredibly filthy thoughts about what is about to happen, I get confused on where to turn.

Conner is waiting for me in the parking lot at the back of the hotel. As if he could be any sexier, he is leaning, in his flaming hot suit, against his blacked out matte BMW 350i. He looks like Hades personified. I groan as I park my white Camry rental before remembering all the smutty books, I've read about how much Hades worships his woman.

I plan to be every bit of Persephone tonight.

As I get out of the car and walk towards him, I hear him laugh and ask me, "Get lost, my Sunshine?"

I don't answer. Instead, I walk straight to him, press my body completely up against his and pull his face down to mine. He is already rock hard, and I feel his tongue against the seam of my lips. I open my mouth to allow his tongue in and tilt my head to invite him to take it even deeper.

He does. This is the best kiss of my entire life. My hands are in his curly hair, and it feels just as I imagined it would. My brain goes quiet, and I am fully in my body as the world disappears. All that I know is that his hand is on me, holding me flush with him. All I can feel is his hard chest, abs, and solid steel cock. The universe shrinks down to just us, in this moment.

Nothing else exists or matters.

He smells like sandalwood and spice, and I feel my core pulsing as I breathe him in. I can feel my juices soaking the crotch of my lace shapewear under my dress. My hands are everywhere, inside his jacket, around his waist, on his chest, in his hair. I am sure I'm making a complete mess of him. We stay making out by his car for an indeterminable length of time. Kissing him is like breathing–both natural and necessary.

I moan into his mouth. His lips don't leave mine, but he pulls back enough to say, "Carrie, we need to get inside. NOW." He squeezes my ass and pushes me backwards, just a fraction.

He is as breathless as I am, like we've been drowning slowly in each other. "Get us inside, Sunshine. I need to strip you bare."

I obey his command and let him pull me to the back entrance of the hotel. I take out my room key to let us in, but my hands are shaking and I drop the keycard twice. He growls as I bend over to pick it up, my ass lining up perfectly with his hips.

"Carrie, if you don't get that door open, I'm going to fuck you from behind right here. I can't wait any longer, Sunshine. Now."

I finally get the door open and lead him up the stairs to my second-floor room at the end of the hall. I move to press my key card to the lock when Conner suddenly spins me around. The hallway is dark, and he kisses me again, pressing me against the door. His fingers draw up the long skirt of my dress. Our tongues devour each other, we can't get enough.

Suddenly, I feel the rush of cool air across my overly sensitive private parts. We don't stop kissing as Conner slides the bodysuit to the side and easily slides his fingers inside my pussy.

I moan his name so loud. I don't give a fuck who hears or sees. Conner is touching me, and I feel like I've waited my whole life for this; for him, for us to be together.

He leans over to nuzzle my neck and sucks on the skin right where my shoulder and neck meet. My hands grip his shoulders as his fingers move rhythmically in and out of my slick channel. I grind my hips against his palm. He puts his thumb against my clit and my legs shake. Just a few more seconds and I'll explode.

He leans into whisper into the shell of my ear, "Come for me, Gorgeous." He goes back to sucking my neck and I do exactly as he says. My orgasm rips through me as I scream his name until his mouth covers mine, swallowing the sound.

He keeps working in and out of me, making the most of this first orgasm, until I come down just enough. Then he whispers in my ear again, "Get me inside you, Carrie."

I can't form words or move well. I'm unmoored and he knows it. He chuckles, takes the keycard from my hand. He gets the door open and yanks me through. He sweeps me up into his arms, bridal style, kicks the door closed and carries me over to the bed.

CHAPTER 23

Conner

My dick is going to burst if I don't get inside this woman in the next two minutes. I really want to lick her from head to toe, from back to front, because she deserves that level of veneration. My mind can't even form how deep my feelings go for her after tonight. How she kissed me in the parking lot without a word unhinged me.

Verbal conversation no longer feels necessary. We've already shared so much. Plus, my cock has waited long enough. My tongue inside her beautiful pussy is going to have to wait till round two. The only reason I finger fucked her against the door is to make sure she had at least one orgasm before I do.

I carry her to the bed and gently set her down on the edge, her feet on the floor. She is trembling. That first orgasm barely took the edge off and while I am extremely proud I made her come within seconds. The reality is we've only just begun.

An atomic bomb of repressed sexual energy is about to go off.

I kneel in front of her and take off my suit jacket. Then I remove both her shoes and kick mine off across the room. As I run my hands up the outside of her legs, I drag her dress up with my fingers. She lets her head fall back and moans my name like it is holy writ. I will my hands to remain steady.

When my fingers, entwined with the soft material, reach her hips, I stop. I reach around and undo her belt. She is breathing so hard and when she lifts her lovely face to look into mine; I see pure trust in them. She has no reservations about what we are about to do. It floors me and my hands really shake.

I want her to know she is a treasure. I will just have to use my body to show her.

I drape her belt on her shoes and then lift the dress up over her hips and whisper, "Arms up, my love." She complies and I pull her dress off. I don't immediately look at her, but stand and lay her dress neatly on the back of the chair near the door. When I turn back around, I can't believe what I'm seeing.

She is wearing a black lace bodysuit that molds her sweet curves and sets off her pale skin. Her hair is slightly mussed from my undressing, and it is like I've been struck by lightning. She is captivating. She waits just a beat before she opens her legs and whispers, "Come to me, Sweetness."

That invitation propels me into motion. I make it back to her in one step and I'm all over her. I gently push her all the way to lie on her back. I can't touch enough of her, my mouth raining open-mouth kisses all over her neck, her chest, her abdomen. I drag my tongue over her perfect, slightly salty skin. She smells like the ocean at sunrise. Every sound she makes is like lighter fluid on a bonfire. It just winds me higher and tighter.

I slip one strap of her bodysuit off her shoulder and pull it down until her breast pops free. I take her nipple in my mouth as she winds her hands back in my hair. I suck and lick as I enjoy the feeling of her hands in my hair. It is the biggest turn on so far. I do the same with the other strap and blow on her other, dark rose-colored bud. At that, she chants my name, and I know neither of us can take much longer.

I had so wanted to take my time with her, explore every inch and learn to map what she likes from the sounds she makes. I'm grateful I have all night, and I plan to put every second to good use. And as hot as she looks in this bodysuit, I need to see her flesh.

I continue to pull the bodysuit off and down her legs. I kneel in front of her again as I fold her lingerie on top of her belt and shoes. She is completely naked in front of me, one arm behind her head so she can see me. As she looks at me over the top of her exquisite breasts, her eyes are aflame with devotion and desire. What I'm thinking just comes out of my mouth.

I say, in a voice full of reverence, "Carrie, you are a work of art."

She sits up and reaches for me. I come to her without hesitation, kissing her as she wraps her legs around my waist. It is only now that I realize I'm still fully dressed. She realizes it too and unbuttons my shirt. When she can touch my skin, she abandons my shirt and strokes her fingers over my chest and abs. I groan loudly and finish the job, throwing the shirt behind me, letting it crumple on the floor. I fumble off my belt and she helps me push my pants down. I do not know where they land.

"Oh Conner, you are perfection." She gasps as she takes me in. She reaches for my cock through my black boxer briefs with one hand and it spasms as she makes contact. With her other hand, she hooks her fingers into the waistband, and I use the hand I'm not bracing with to pull them all the way off.

Finally, we are face to face, flesh on flesh. I'm on top of her, most of my weight on my forearms, with my hips between her legs. I know what we are about to experience will change us irrevocably. We stare at each other for a long moment, just letting our breath synchronize and our heartbeats align. Her hands roam down my back, lower and lower until I feel her squeeze my ass and pull me even closer.

The movement lines the head of my cock with her entrance. As I continue to look at her, to stare into her eyes, I reach between us and rub the head of my cock in her wetness. She is soaking and we are both dizzy with in anticipation as I do it. I take the opportunity of her open mouth to kiss her again and she squeezes my hips with her legs, pulling the tip of my cock just inside her channel.

Stars appear at the edge of my vision.

It's like we are making our way to the precipice of a cliff. I kiss her so deeply, trying to use that kiss to communicate everything I feel about the past without her; this present moment in her arms and the future I dream of having with her. She holds me just as fiercely, and I know that in the space between us, we both have found our sanctuary.

She finally breaks the kiss, opens her mesmerizing blue eyes to meet mine, and says, "Please."

On that one word, I thrust forward and carve that promised channel inside her. Her whimpers and sighs of pleasure stoke my fire higher and higher. I can't get enough. It is so much more powerful than I could have ever imagined. I move back and forth, spurred on by her glorious noises and the body created to fit mine. I know I won't be able to last long, but I'm not even worried about it.

She is mine and I am hers forever. I have the rest of my life to adore this woman in the proper way.

With her ankles locked on the small of my back, I feel my balls tightening. My pace gets faster as Carrie calls out to me. She is calling me to join her as her pussy walls fluttering and squeezing me as her body climbs in synchronicity with mine.

I have never felt freedom like this. Being inside her has unlocked a level of depth I didn't know existed.

It is an eternal moment when we both reach the second just before climax. I feel a sensation in my chest as I look into her face, like a bell ringing. Time stops and the only thing I know is that I am right where I am supposed to be. Then I see her throw her head back, call out my name one more time, and I feel her orgasm hit. Waves and waves of liquid love spill in between and out of us.

The cosmos dances behind my eyes as I come so hard my heart feels like it will implode.

I continue to move inside of her, drawing out our pleasure as long as I can. She spasms against and again, until she is a whimpering mess. As we finally come into stillness, me still on top and inside her, I kiss her gently as I stroke her cheek with one hand. Her hands find their way back into my hair.

I raise my head to meet her eyes and we both say it, "I love you."

We continue this fully open, intimate stare until something catches her eye. She giggles and looks up at me again, with a bright smile on her face. I cock an eyebrow at her in question.

"Something funny, Sunshine?"

She kisses me through her smile and says, "Do you want to take your socks off or are your feet cold, Sweetness?"

***

Carrie

Conner laughs so loud, and I can feel it in every part. He is still inside of me, not wholly soft despite the nuclear level of orgasm we both just had. Climaxing together, staring into each other eyes was a complete spiritual experience. It was like a portal between our bodies opened up and now our souls are entwined.

"Sunshine, your timing is impeccable. We've just had the best sex of our lives, confessed our love, and then you make me laugh. Please never change. And please don't move. I know, for your sake, we probably need to untangle, but I have dreamed of this nonstop for a month. The last thing I want to do is pull out of you now."

As he talks, I can feel his hips move, slowly rocking against me. I moan. I can't help it because my body responds to his. His eyes darken and narrow, and I watch his head tilt and his tongue dart out to lick his lips. His face is still only a few inches from mine, so I push my face up. I kiss him and then move my mouth down his jawline and neck. My tongue decides it wants to taste him, so I do, licking a long column from where his shoulder and neck meet up to his ear.

I whisper, "Conner, are you ready to take me again? How do you want me? Just tell me, and I'm all yours."

I can feel him harden fully within me as he groans, "Oh God, Sunshine. I have too many ideas. Just keep licking and sucking my neck while I decide on how best to fuck you for round two."

I do exactly as he instructs, and my hips respond to his, rolling up and back to meet his thrusts. He is still gently moving inside of me. I know he is hard and ready, so I take a moment and just enjoy being together. One of his hands has moved down to rub and massage my ass like he is beginning his thorough exploration of each part of me.

As we continue to move together, he moves the hand from my ass to the outside of my thigh and pulls my leg up to bend, resting it against his side. It changes the angle and place he is hitting inside of me, and I let him know how good it feels.

"Oh, Conner. God. This feels like heaven."

We continue to move together in that slow, sweet way, building back up the tension. He leans down and kisses me as my hands explore his well-muscled back. Feeling his muscles flex and ripple beneath my touch has me panting for more. Conner is taking his time. The hand on my leg moves to my breast, and he sweeps along the outside, dragging calloused palms in a circle until he gets to my nipple. He pinches and rolls it between his thumb and middle finger, hard enough to feel it, but not hard enough for pain. His hand beside my head strokes my hair as his mouth murmurs.

"I knew you would feel like home. I knew there was a place inside of you only I can go. I knew your body was made for mine. I knew you were so good, so right, so perfect. I knew you were it for me the first time I saw you."

He keeps murmuring into my hair, almost as if he doesn't realize he is speaking. It is a stream of consciousness, all the pent-up words he has said. Maybe he has never felt them with anyone else. Every word he speaks, I feel at a cellular level, vibrating with truth.

I have never felt more loved, cherished, and safe.

All this slow and steady movement has kindled an unquenchable fire in me. All the words Conner is saying are like lighter fluid on a bonfire, and suddenly, I am so overstimulated I can't take another slow, steady movement, or I will go insane.

I kiss him deeply, trying to communicate the depth of my need. When his hand keeps rubbing up and down my leg and his thrusting remains patient and kind, I decide to take evasive action. I lick my way back to his ear and say, "Conner Doreland, you are a dream come true, and this time is so sacred to me." He just keeps rubbing my leg, hitting that spot with his perfect cock.

I feel the edge of demand come into my voice as I whisper, "And I have never wanted to be flipped over and fucked raw more than I do right now. I want to suffocate face down, screaming your name into the pillow."

Chapter 24

Conner

Carrie has cracked my soul wide open.

This first time was more than incredible. It was so much more than just sharing our bodies. A thread now connects us, a soul tie that I only want to build up. As I move inside her, stroke her smooth skin and feel her under me, I could die and go to heaven and not even know it.

This is heaven. She is soft, with her legs splayed out to make room for me. Her breasts are perfect, more than a handful. The feel of her soft hair in one hand and the smooth skin of her leg in the other is hypnotic. I want to stay here, between her legs, for eternity.

I feel like I finally belong.

I want to take it slow, to just feel her tenderness and expression of her pleasure. But that isn't what my goddess wants. I grin into her hair as I hear her words and feel myself sliding in and out of her. That she is more than ready. My Sunshine wants to get fucked.

And if I have anything to say about it, my Sunshine is going to get what she wants.

I pull back just enough to whisper, as my lips trail up her cheek and say, "Oh, really?"

In one motion, I push back onto my knees without removing my cock from her slick channel and pick her up by the waist. I flip her onto her stomach and say roughly, "On your hands and knees." She complies, pushing up, and dammit, if feeling her this new way doesn't drive me right up to the edge.

I run my hands over her shoulders, down her spine, and up again, only to drag my fingertips lightly down her sides. She shivers and says quietly, "Conner, that tickles."

I smile darkly. "You want me to show you what tickles?"

She shivers again and says, "Yes."

I bring my left hand to the curve of her waist, which fits like a glove. Her shape fits all parts of me. I take my right hand and slide it down from her waist over the delicious globe on her ass. I am going to have to bite it later. She deserves that for teasing me with that sexy picture a few weeks ago because I have not forgotten that.

I am still inside her but not moving, and she rocks her hips back toward me, trying to get some friction.

"Carrie, stop," I command, and she freezes, looking back at me over her shoulder. I reach up with my left hand to move her long golden hair off her neck. I smile at her, and then she squeaks as I use my right hand to circle her asshole.

"Conner!"

I chuckle, deep and low. "I asked you if you wanted me to show you what tickles."

She moans, and it is all the encouragement I need. I don't have any lube here but will get some for when she returns next weekend. I hope she will be into it, but I only want what she wants. Still, the thought of being buried in her ass has my cock straining to move. I maintain my control a few seconds longer as I continue stroking her entrance with my fingertips. The sounds Carrie makes are obscene.

"You want this? You want me here, Carrie?"

"Oh, God, yes, Conner, yes! I'm yours; take all of me."

At those words, it's all I need to snap. I grab her hips with both hands and thrust forward, seating myself fully into the most beautiful pussy ever created. I bottom out and pull back again, going a little faster each time I move. The force of my movements knocks her to her forearms, which she is resting on her forehead. Her moans get louder and louder as my balls slap against her pussy lips.

"Fuck Carrie, fuck Carrie."

I continue gripping her hips hard enough to bruise, railing her, and I feel like I could do this forever until I hear her whimper, "Conner, please."

I know exactly what she needs, and it makes my balls tighten. A bead of sweat rolls down my back, and the lighting gathers at the base of my spine. But I don't want to come yet. I want to give her maximum pleasure.

I reach around with one hand, down to her slick channel, gathering more than enough to slip and slide my fingers up to her clit.

With each pump, I circle her clit and say, "Show-me-just-how-much-you-want-me-Carrie. Be-the-best-girl-for-me-and-come-around-my-cock-while-I-paint-your-pussy-with-my-cum."

At that last phrase, I feel her pussy walls clamp down around me, and she lets out a near howl. A matching roar comes from my throat as release, losing all sense of time and space.

It takes a few moments to come back into my body, into this world, and I realize her legs are shaking.

I whisper to her, "Hang on, my love." As I pull out, I hear her mumble into the bed. She collapses boneless on the bed, and I stand up. My legs are a little wobbly, but I know I can take it. I approach her side of the bed and lean down to kiss her temple.

"What was that?"

Gathering just enough energy to turn her head, I hear her say, "Sadness."

I stroke down her spine as I chuckle, "Don't worry, my love. I'll be back inside your beautiful pussy soon enough. I guarantee it." For a second, I gaze at her creamy skin; the expanse of it, I'm going to use the rest of the night to memorize and mark with love bites. I want her to go home with many remembrances of me until I can do it all over again.

I press a hand into her hip and tell her, "Roll over, sweetheart." She does just enough, and I slide a hand under her upper back and then under her legs. I kneel on the bed to get leverage and then haul her up against my chest. I hear her say, in a little dreamy protest, "Conner"

"Shhhh, Sunshine, let me take care of you."

I carry her into the bathroom and lower her to the toilet. At this, she becomes a little more alert, looking slightly surprised, and I cock an eyebrow at her. I say, "You didn't think I'd risk you getting a UTI our first night together?"

She colors prettily, and I realize what this is about. So, I turn on the shower and prepare to step in. "It's fine to pee in front of me, Sunshine. But if it makes you more comfortable, I'll wait for you in the shower."

As I step in, I let out a high-pitched, "FUCKING HELL!"

"What? Conner, are you ok?" Carrie's voice is all concern and soft.

"Yes, Sunshine. I'm fine. Just will have to do my walk of shame barefoot since now my fucking socks are wet."

***

Carrie

Being with Conner is the fullest experience I couldn't have even imagined. Our connection is undeniable. I sit on the toilet, trying to hurry and pee so I can get in the shower with him.

My body just fits with him, melting and oh, so safe. There is no resistance in me to being with him. Even my worries about how I look naked have disappeared. My stretch marks, c-section scar and roundness that I've long thought unattractive haven't even been on my mind. I don't think Conner sees me the way I do.

He makes me feel like Aphrodite incarnate and I'm going to embrace it.

He beckons to me, "You coming in, Sunshine? It's nice and warm and so am I."

I call back to him, "Sweetness, warm is not what I would call you. More like scorching hot. I'm coming."

I giggle when I hear him mumble, "That's what she said."

I love his sense of humor. As the trust grows between us, I can't wait to see more of his silly side.

I finish what I'm doing and grab my special hair wash. It smells divine, and I want to use it on Conner. As I step into the shower with him, my breath hitches. God, he is a masterpiece. I take my time looking him over every inch of chiseled man flesh and I lick my lips when I see the cut of his shoulders and then again when my eyes land on the V-shape indentions just above his hips.

"I have seen no one sexier than you, Conner Doreland."

He looks me dead in the eyes, raises his arms to the back of his neck and poses for me. I feel the cascade of a mix of love and desire for him, like warm honey, start at the top of my head and move down my arms, to my torso, and rest directly in my center. I set the bottle down and step towards him. He doesn't move, just waits for me to do whatever I want in that cocky, very male model stance.

There isn't a centimeter of skin I don't run my fingertips over. His shoulders, chest, abs and his perfect bubble butt. He shivers as I trace with both my pointer fingers that V line on either side, from the outside of hip bone inward.

He whispers, "That tickles, Sunshine."

I look at him, full in the face, and my only response is, "I'll show you what really tickles in a bit. But I want to do something first. You trust me?"

He shivers again as my fingers twirl in his curly pubic hair, which makes his cock twitch and harden. He locks his eyes on mine and says, "With my entire self, Carrie."

That response feels like the most intimate exchange yet.

"Ok then, Big Boy, turn around." He drops his arms and turns around, facing the stream of water. I run my hands all over him again and then I can't help myself. I kiss where my hands touch, and he groans.

I press myself up against his back, wrapping my arms underneath his and pressing my hands flat against his chest, and he groans again. I lean up as close to his ear as I can get with our height difference and tell him, "You carry so much weight on these shoulders, Conner. So much responsibility. Let me ease a little of the burden by doing something for you."

He turns around and leans down to kiss me. Before I lose myself, I break the kiss and pull back. Time runs in slow motion, and I reach up to caress his cheek. I kiss his shoulder again and then grab the hair wash.

Getting a generous amount in my hand, I finger-comb it through his wavy, milk chocolate hair. I realize there is a bench in the shower and instruct him to sit. He turns around to face me and sits. It puts him eye level with my nipples, and he smiles a wicked grin before looking up at me. He brings his hands to my hips, and I smile back at him.

He allows me to care for him as he has cared for me, and it is intoxicating. He closes his eyes and sighs in contentment. The sensations I am experiencing between the fullness of my heart, the warm water at my back and the building pulse in my pussy make me a little woozy.

Being with Conner is a high I never want to come down from.

Chapter 25

Conner

I've never had a woman wash my hair. It is sensual and relaxing. Her hands are gentle but firm, lightly scraping with her nails. She is an expert from years of practice with her girls. I lean into her as I pull her closer. I can't stop myself from touching her. I massage her perfect little ass. She is more boob than butt and I adore it. Her breasts are directly in front of me, those dark rose-colored nipples erect and begging for my mouth. I plan to explore every inch of her and draw out every sound I've heard over the phone and more.

I close my eyes and rest my forehead against her soft stomach. She has a small patch of hair above her pussy, and I wonder if she would let me shave her. My mind is solely focused on what I will do next to bring her pleasure. I love how she treats me. Her hands move down to my neck, massaging and working her way through my traps and delts.

She speaks softly, "Conner, your shoulders are magnificent. This is my third favorite muscle group."

I slide my forehead up till my chin rests above her belly button and I'm looking up through her big, beautiful breasts. She tilts her face down to meet my eyes.

Curious, I ask. "Oh? Third favorite? What's number two?"

Without missing a beat, she says, "The Adonis Belt. Which makes perfect sense because you might be Adonis personified."

I pull back a few inches, still rubbing her ass, and ask, "What's the Adonis Belt?"

She giggles, and my cock responds instantly. She returns her hands to my hair, doing one last pass, as she tells me, "It's fun to have a daughter who is a physical therapist. You learn all kinds of cool names for muscle groups. The Adonis Belt is right next to my favorite muscle on you. Stand up so I can rinse your hair, and I'll show you."

I do as she bids, the hair wash rinsing out quickly. My cock is standing at attention. She puts her hands on my shoulders and her hands move down my sides, coming to rest on my hips. Then, she traces up and down those V-shaped indentions on either side. She leans up to press her lips to mine and says against them, "These are your Adonis belt, my glorious soccer god."

I smile, my lips still against hers. "What a wealth of knowledge you have, my love. But tell me, what's your favorite muscle on me?"

She drags one hand to cup my balls and uses the other to wrap around my cock. My head swims as her long, slender fingers squeeze me lightly before she reports, "Him. Yes, he is my favorite muscle on you. I think he likes me, too."

My dick throbs in her hand, eliciting a giggle. I let her stroke me back and forth for a minute, my head falling back and my eyes closing. I enjoy the feeling of her hand on me instead of my own. Jacking off will never be the same now that Carrie has touched me. I moan low as her hand moves and she massages my balls.

Finally, I raise my head and bring my hands up to cup her face. Her jaw fits inside my palms exactly. I lean forward and can't help myself. I kiss her hungrily. She gives me exactly what I want, in the tilt of her head, the movement and pressure of her tongue, and the width of her mouth.

I've never been so thankful for hotels that never run out of warm water. As good as cold showers are for our bodily systems, as well as ice baths; I don't want her shivering. I need to get her back to bed. Without breaking the kiss, I turn off the water, grab a towel, and rub her down. She pulls back and laughs. "Multi-task much?"

Smiling, I let her have the towel while I grab my own. Stepping out of the shower, I give her my hand to her. Once she is out, I grab her around her upper legs and lift her. She wraps her legs around me and we kiss again as I take her back to bed.

This night is cementing our bond and maybe Erik is right. Maybe I don't want to wait till the season is over to propose.

Maybe I want to make her mine as soon as possible. I pull my lips back from hers and lay her gently on the bed. She sighs contentedly and sums up how I feel. All is right in the world when we are together. Desire and lust darken her eyes. They are a deep blue, sparkling. She is completely open to whatever comes next.

"Conner," she breathes out my name as she moves back towards the middle of the bed, like a prayer or a moment of hope. It gives me a vision for a life with her. I swear her kiss wipes my memory of everything before her.

Finally, I taste her neck, her collarbone, and down her chest to between her luscious breasts. They are big and full. One of her hands remains in my hair. I want to meet my Maker, many years from now, with my face on her chest and her hands in my hair. With one hand, I massage her breast and bring the other hand up to her throat, just resting. Her moans turn guttural.

Having her submit to me, letting me use her body however I want, is so arousing. My cock throbs painfully. But he is going to have to wait. It's my tongue's turn.

Bringing my other hand to start work on its twin. I close my mouth over her nipple, and she gasps. I suck and lick, going back and forth between her two scrumptious tits while she writhes beneath me. I swear I can feel the nectar of life on my tongue as I suck harder and longer, consuming all her noises. I complete my time at her breasts with a sharp nip of my front teeth to both. Her hips buck up underneath me. I know she is soaked for me. God, I love this woman.

I continue my way down, past the abdominal scar from an early childhood surgery. I run my tongue along the horizontal length of it and she sucks in a breath. I know she is self-conscious about her abdominal area not being flat. I don't see what she sees. I see the complete opposite. The softness of her middle is divine. I know this body has molded and stretched itself to bring three lives into this world. Everything about her journey brought her to me and I take my time making the map of her in my memory.

Leaving one hand to rub her breast and the other to stroke her side as I bring my hand down to slide under and grip her ass. Her ass cheek fit in my hand, and I moan. "God, Carrie, your ass is flawless. I love your tits are twice as big." She giggles as I continue to move towards her center, wet and aching for me. I can smell her arousal, and it heightens the experience.

I push up slightly so I can use that hand on her ass to roll her towards my face. My other hand slides down her hip. Kissing my way over to where her cheek is exposed. I look up at her and she is watching me, both hands splayed, palms up above her head.

"God, Carrie, you are gorgeous."

She reaches down with one hand to stroke my face, and I continue to move over to the globe of her precious little ass. Her chest moves up and down more rapidly in anticipation of what I will do next. Her squeal turns into a low, deep moan as I sink my teeth into the meat of her ass. I give her a full hickey on her ass and she is writhing under me so much I have to hold her hips still to complete the job.

When I finish, I raise my head and come back to hovering over her center. "Carrie, look at me."

She does instantly. "That was for not sending me that naughty picture. When I tell you to do something, you do it, understand, my sweet?"

Her eyes narrow slightly but are so filled with want, so she nods. "Words, my love. Give me your words."

"If I promise to obey, will you please fuck me with your tongue? If so, then absolutely, I'll do whatever you want."

I laugh, "There she is–my greedy goddess. Are you ready for me to make you come again?" I have wanted to know what she tastes like for weeks; it's haunted my dreams. I take a moment to breathe her in, my nose in that small patch of hair just above her clit. She smells like incense, tangy, sweet, and so complex. And she is so wet. I can't wait any longer.

I run the tip of my tongue down her center, dip into her opening, and back up again. I tease her clit, and her moans threaten to undo me. Thinking about her physical prowess has my dick pulsing painfully.

I continue to lick, suck, and slurp at her core, bringing her right up to the edge of orgasm. She is holding her breath in anticipation, her body begging for release. At this moment, I stop and pull away, kissing on the inside of her thighs as she squeezes my ears between her soft, powerful thighs.

All I hear is "Oh, Conner nooooooo."

I rise on all fours, crawling up to look her in the face. She comes up to kiss me, ravenous, and we both moan as she tastes herself. She wraps her hands on my shoulders and brings me down on top of her, sucking herself off my tongue.

I pull back and say, "We aren't done, my Sunshine. I need you to come on my face and feel my cock pulse in your throat." I didn't think it was possible to be more turned on than I am right now.

"Oh, shit, Conner, yes." I give her room to sit up and I lay down in her spot. She straddles my face, her beautiful pussy right over my mouth. I hum as I contact her, and she pants. She stretches herself out over my body, licking her way down my Adonis Belt and cupping my balls. As her tongue dances across the tip of my cock, I feel her moan. She doesn't waste a moment, sliding her wet mouth down my length. She gags a little and inhales through her nose.

She is going to get all of me in her mouth. I nearly come undone. "Carrie, yes, oh my God, that feels so fucking good, Sunshine."

She moves her mouth up and down, getting me wet and then using her hand in that glorious twisting upstroke. My hips thrust in time with her hand. Her other hand continues to massage in and around my balls and I see stars out of the corner of my eyes. I feast as she coats my face and neck.

Suddenly, the base of my spine feels like it is on fire, and I realize she is humming. I croak out, "Carrie, I'm going to come but don't swallow, Ok?"

She hums her assent and moans around my dick. Her fingers press into the space between my balls, and it will only be another couple of seconds. I know she is close. I continue to fuck her with my tongue, as she used my chin to get friction. I can feel her whole body tense up at the same time as mine. She screams with my cock in her throat as she comes, and I explode into her mouth.

I slowly bring her down as she pulls off my dick, holding my cum in her mouth as instructed. Her hands rub up and down my legs as head into post-orgasmic bliss. She sniffs a little loudly and I move her hips, so she is laying on her side against me. She sits up and turns towards me, mouth still locked tight.

"Show me, pretty girl." She obeys, opens her mouth, and damn if I don't harden again at the sight of my cum on the inside of her mouth.

I rumble my approval at her, stroking her face. "Good fucking girl, now swallow." She does loudly and then with an angelic smile. I pull her forward and kiss her deeply, tasting myself in her mouth. We come up for air and I pull her into my side, her head lying in the dip of my shoulder.

One of her long arms drapes across my middle and her long fingers skim across and around my hip bone. It's been a long night, as it's probably closer to one a.m. I am relaxed but not sleepy. I hear her breath deepen and then I hear her mumble something.

"What's that, my darling?" Her answer makes no sense, and I realize she is asleep. I feel a warmth in my chest spread and realize it is pride. It reminds me of my first goal at every stage, knowing I've hit a major accomplishment in my life plan. As I lay there and try not to laugh at her low, silly gibberish, I feel an unusual peace anchor me into the bed, into her.

I cover us with the blankets, I quietly sing her song, "You are my Sunshine" She cracks her eyes just enough to meet mine as I settle back into cradling her.

In a voice thick with sleep, she says, "Conner?"

I whisper back, "Yes, my Sunshine?

Her voice is drifting off again and I know she is falling back asleep as she says, "Don't leave me."

My heart lurches within my chest, and I reassure her with the truth. "Never, ever, ever, Sunshine. I'm yours until my dying breath."

She sighs and I hug her tighter. I lay awake listening to her mumble till I drift off into a dreamless sleep.

***

Carrie

When I wake up, I don't have any idea what time it is. I can only see the barest of light peeking out around the curtains. All I know is Conner, his body against mine, and where we fit seamlessly. I'm not exactly awake, but I'm no longer asleep. It's like I'm in suspended animation–a world where it is only us and that's all that matters.

I say a prayer of gratitude in my mind and heart, sure that my guiding spirit hears me. I'm living a dream, and it is real.

It is a long time as I listen to Conner breathing next to me, peacefully snuffling. I adore how he sleeps and am so glad it is deep. He will need it for game day. Just before I feel his energy shift into waking, I turn my face to his and whisper, "I can't live without you."

He opens his gorgeous, sleepy brown eyes and gives me a warm smile. Then, I feel it. He comes fully awake because his mind has clicked on. It's game day and my glorious coach is coming into focus.

I roll the rest of my body over to face him, feeling the twinges and aches from our lovemaking. I stroke his face as he looks at mine, as if he is trying to memorize it.

I speak quietly and ask, "You ready for today?"

He nods and I can see the emotion play out on his face. His voice is low, "I don't want to get up, or leave you. I would give my both my nuts to stay here with you. I've never experienced what we've shared with anyone else."

My eyes get watery and as I look up at him, one escapes. I whisper, "Me either." Then I smile and say, "But don't get rid of anything, especially your balls. They are number three on my list of favorites."

He chuckles and says, "Well, far be it from me to deny you anything." His face turns somber again as he says, "But I have to go home to get ready."

It is my turn to nod, and I run my hands on every inch of skin I can reach before I say a little sadly. "Conner, I'm going to touch as much of you as I can to get me fill since I don't know when I'll see you again."

He beams, "That's easy. I'll see you next weekend."

I blink not once, not twice, but three times at him before I ask, "Next weekend? I can't come back that soon?"

He quirks an eyebrow. "Why not? Hear me out."

He explains his plan for me to come back next week. As he talks, my brain spins, words forming like an overfilled cup, ready to spill out. I am so surprised he decided something like this without clearing it with me. Even though it is a good plan, my mind gets sidetracked by the roadblocks. There won't be any flights that are affordable. What will I tell Elise? What about my job?

He finishes and while we are still lying face to face, that bubble of peace we were in has burst.

And with it, the dam of my words opens as I begin my arguments. Elise got her debate skills from me, and as I speak, part of me is wondering why I'm arguing and not just going with it. Conner is taking care of me, and I'm fighting it. But I'm too caught up in the spiral.

Conner pushes me flat on my back against the pillows and comes to lie on top of me, with his hips nestled securely between my thighs.

"Sunshine, you just told me you can't live without me, but you've just spent the last couple of minutes telling me how you plan on doing just that till you can figure out when to come back." His gaze is soft but darker that when he woke as he says, "What bothers you about this?"

I try to get out from under him, but he is too heavy. I feel like I need space, like I need to get away to think clearly. "You heard me say that? About not being able to live without you? Are you using that against me? Conner, that is not fair, and you know it. And get off me if we are going to argue." I push at his chest, and he just leans his weight on me a little more, just enough to pin me.

He looks deeply into my eyes, trying to read my soul. Calmly he tells me, "We aren't arguing, Sunshine. I think it's more of a discussion."

With those words, I push his weight off enough to take a deep breath. Tears prick my eyes for a different reason. This is the first time I have ever felt like Conner was not listening to me, and it is devastating. As I sit up, I turn away, but he grabs my hand, softly calling to me, "Don't run, Carrie. Talk to me."

I try to keep the emotion out of my voice, but it is unsuccessful. "You aren't listening to me. It's the first time I've ever felt like you aren't hearing me." I pause and take a deep breath; I don't need to cry over this, even though I really feel like it. I am tired, which heightens my emotions. "I know it's a good plan and you've thought it through. I just wish you'd not brought before you are about to walk out the door."

He pauses, now rubbing his thumb over the back of my hand. That calms me and as my breathing evens out, he puts his hand on my elbow and pulls me towards him. I don't resist. My body and soul need this closeness. I'm not trying to be stubborn. I just feel raw.

I lay down with him again, his arms wrapped around my shoulders, with my face on his chest. I sink into him as he rubs small circles into my lower back.

"Carrie, I wasn't trying to spring this on you. I have been so caught up in seeing you, it just slipped my mind to bring it up. I can book a flight for you tonight while you are on the plane home. I know you can take care of yourself–and your girls–and now I can help. Let me be your partner. Will you come back next weekend, and we can spend the whole time at my house? You can see my space, no need for an impersonal hotel."

He smiles a childlike smile–at the thought of me being in his space and a few tears slip out at his admission. That plus, I've been on the forefront of taking care of my family and the business for years. It requires a thousand different decisions, usually at the drop of a hat. Having to always have the answer for everyone is exhausting, but here is a man who wants to support me in all the ways I never knew I needed.

I whisper around my emotion-clogged throat, "I don't know how to let someone else take care of me. But I trust you." Then, a weepy mumble of, "I'm sorry."

He puts a finger under my chin to lift my face to his. He kisses me softly and says into my lips, "Don't apologize, my love. This is new for us both and we will figure it out together. But if you had kept arguing with me, I was seriously considering fucking the 'yes' out of you. Damn the consequences of being late to the first game of the season."

That makes me laugh, and he smiles. "Why do I suspect you are serious, Sweetness?"

He leans down to kiss me again, longer this time, then as he pulls back, his hands cup my face and his voice is deep as he says, "I will never miss an opportunity to fuck you. Being inside of you is heaven on earth. I want to do it forever."

We stay cuddled up together for probably longer than we should, and it makes me sleepy again. The next thing I know, he is kissing my forehead, dressed in his jacket over his rumpled shirt and pants. "I gotta go Sunshine. I will not stop thinking about you till I see you at the game. My poor ankles will be the price for being cold."

I giggle sleepily as I tell him, "I'll bring you a new pair of dress socks Friday to make up for the ones that got wet."

"It's a deal, my love. I'll see you soon, yah?" I nod and he is gone. Before I fall back asleep, I feel my heart fill with gratitude as I say a prayer for our team to win, my daughter to play her best without injury and my man to experience the joy of all his hard work.

Chapter 26

Conner

Getting up and leaving Carrie was more difficult than I ever imagined, especially given that I'm going to my second love–coaching soccer. My chest tightens in the best way when I realize soccer is now in second place in my life. That's never, ever been possible with any other woman, but I know it is true on a cellular level.

I am hers and she is mine and my soccer career will be all the better for it.

I am grateful we worked through the conflict without a big dramatic fight. It's proof we are both healthy. It doesn't taint the memory of the weekend one bit. It enhances it because this is the way couples who go the distance resolve issues.

I realize I should have told her my plan sooner. I will do that in the future. Genuine love is safe and makes room for both people to continue growing into all they are meant to become. I am grateful to be experiencing it after so long on my own.

As soon as the chilly morning air hits my bare ankles, I curse. I'm glad it will warm up and I will definitely wear socks with my coaching uniform. I get home, shower and get ready quickly. My hair is a little long, so I make a note to get a haircut this week, before Carrie comes back. I will order her products too, so she doesn't have to bring them with her. I snapped pictures of everything she uses. I want her to feel at home, like it is our home, until we can make one together.

I miraculously arrive at the stadium ten minutes early. I make myself some coffee and grab two protein shakes from the coaches' fridge. Inanna arrives with breakfast tacos for the team, a pre-game tradition, and I am starving. I grab three bacon, egg and cheese and she raises a brow at me.

"Hungry, are we? Busy night? You look like you have a freshly fucked glow." she says dryly.

I shook her a wicked grin but don't acknowledge her last comment. "I feel my metabolism ramping up after each workout with Erik. I'm sure that's it."

She gives me a rare, soft smile and says, "I do hope things work out for you. That's your only option, actually, to make sure it all works out. Nothing is going to fuck up this season, you understand?"

I give her a full-on salute, and she nods in approval.

The rest of the coaching staff arrive, and I settle into my comfort zone as Head Coach. Elise arrives early with almost all the team, which pleases me. I encourage them to be early for everything and they respect that.

There are only two missing players at the start of the meeting, both freshmen. One, a fullback named Chandler, walks in with a sheepish, "Sorry Coach, I was in the bathroom."

Pre-game nerves are real, so I don't call her out for it. In high school, I used to vomit before every game, but thankfully that subsided before my senior year. The only player missing is Maciee. That's her last strike, so this afternoon's meeting will be an easy one.

The meeting goes well until Maciee shows up twenty minutes in. She is wearing sunglasses, which is abhorrent as it is a sure signal of a hangover. You can hear a pin drop in the room as Inanna, in a threatening tone, tells her to take them off. She does, but then disturbs the rest of the meeting by getting up several times for food and coffee.

When the team heads out to warm up, I ask her to hang back. Pouting, she does and is face to face with all three coaches, unrepentant.

Inanna reads my thoughts. "Well, Maciee, this should make our meeting after the game with your father an easy one. You have been sufficiently warned and after this morning, you are out of the program. Go clean out your locker. You don't have to leave the school, but you won't be on a scholarship or play soccer at UCC."

She stiffens at this and then smiles, "My Dad already left because he has seen me play a thousand times. He made an appointment with the Athletic Director tomorrow to make a sizable donation, so I bet I stay on the team."

She has the audacity to wink at us.

I internally scream "FUCK!" Because this is a complication I do not need on the same day I tell Arlo about Carrie and I. I reply calmly, but I don't hide my edge, "Well, that's great to hear. Donation or not, that changes nothing. You are still out of the program. We don't play these games at UCC, Maciee. You should have listened a little better during our recruiting meetings."

Her youthful face turns beet red, and she actually stamps her foot. *How in the world did we miss this?* I see the same question reflected on Inanna's face. She points a finger at us before backing away. "I will make sure you regret this decision for the rest of your lives! I am not someone to be trifled with! My Dad will make sure you lose your fucking jobs over this insult. You think you run such a tight program? Don't worry, I know things and will make sure the world knows all about it!"

She spins around and storms out, slamming the door behind her. Inanna picks up the phone to let security know to see her out of the building. The hairs on the back of my neck are prickling. "That sounded a little too much like Miranda to me. I think I better push up my meeting with Arlo, in case Maciee knows anything about Carrie and I."

Inanna nods solemnly. "Do that. You are excused from the post-game wrap up sessions with the team."

"Gee, thanks. Good thing I can trust you to handle it all." I roll my eyes at her before she adds, "You just make sure this is airtight, *capich?*"

"*Capich,* Boss. Let's go kick some ass."

I look for Carrie as soon as I walk into the stadium. She catches my gaze and winks. The pitch always feels alive to me. The grass smells sweet, with the earthy smell of soil underneath. It's mid-morning, so the light is perfect, just beginning to add some heat to the air. That will grow within the next two hours of game time.

With the chill of the morning holding strong, the temperature is perfect and the coastal breeze we get will make this a very tolerable atmosphere to play in. There are spectators completely bundled up to ward off the early fall feel. It's nothing like some games in the Premier League, in the rainy spring of England, where the cold seeps into your bones.

Today, in California, we have a perfect day for a match. My heart swells with so much hope it might burst.

The moment the teams hit the pitch; we are locked in to win. The whistle blows. The other team maintains possession even as we press in, so I yell to close them down. As they do, we intercept a pass, which gives Elise and Alyssa, our team captain and her Big Sister, a clear lane.

These two move like they have one mind. Elise makes a run down the right flank, passing the ball with precision as she hits her stride. She lands a perfect cross kick into the no-man's-land in front of the opposing keeper. Alyssa receives the kick and kicks it high into the upper nineties, as it sails past the goalie, who tries to block with no success. The kick is just too good.

It's a goal in the first ten minutes. I look up to see Carrie screaming her head off with her arms in the air. I smile, knowing her passion for this game runs deep.

We stay up through the half, nearly through the half. Just before the referee calls halftime, Erik leans over and says, "They look like they are running out of steam."

I grin back at him, still pleased with our showing thus far, and say, "I guess you still have a job then."

In the locker room, Inanna walks the team through what needs to shift into the next half and I make a couple of changes to our projected starting eleven.

It turns into a magical combination. This will be the starting lineup for the rest of the season and take us all the way to the winner's circle. They move in sync, blowing past three defenders like they were standing still. One junior, playing right mid, slots to the left of the goalkeeper. We go up 2-0 in the first five minutes of the second half.

As we get close to the end of time, with no overage coming, they get chippy. They sense victory. One of the opposing players goes down with a cramp, so I call the team over to reset their focus.

"Ladies, we are minutes away from our first win in an undefeated season. Let's settle down, keep the ball, and play our game." They nod and return to position with their heads up.

The slight break gave the other team just enough recovery. With three minutes left, Elise has the ball and is fouled from behind. She goes down and my eyes immediately find Carrie. She is looking at Elise, a reservedly. Years of watching Elise baked in the need to pause and see if she gets up. She cuts her eyes to me. She doesn't look worried.

As a soccer mom, she's seen her daughter go down hundreds of times.

The moment Elise stands, Carrie visibly relaxes. The opposing team forms a wall to defend the penalty kick. A junior moves to take it, but I yell for her to step back. She reads my mind as she walks over and taps Elise on the elbow.

Without hesitation, Elise puts the ball where she wants it, steps back and takes a big breath. I sneak a peek at Carrie. She is holding hers. When her foot connects with the ball, it goes up and over, bending it with perfection into the upper nineties with no chance of their keeper saving it.

With that, the final whistle blows, and the team rushes Elise, but I look up at Carrie. She is beaming and when she turns that smile to me, a small puff of wind could blow me over. Erik walks up, puts a huge hand on my shoulder and says, "Nice work, Lover Boy. Now, let's celebrate. I'll cover for you. Go kiss your lady goodbye."

Carrie waits outside of the stadium. Stepping up behind her, she doesn't startle when I lean close to whisper, "Congratulations, Ms. Voekler."

She turns towards me, and we are practically in each other's arms. It's probably too close, but I couldn't care less. She looks into my eyes and says, "Thank you, Coach Conner. Congratulations to you too. You have done an excellent job preparing them. What will you do now?"

I can't describe what happens to my chest when she praises me. To have her respect and admiration makes me feel like I am capable of anything. I stare at her for a beat before my mind returns to me and I answer, "I'll go congratulate my team, and then see the love of my life off to the airport."

Carrie's hands twitch at her sides, like she wants to reach up and press them to the sides of my face. The lining of her eyes is silver. "You will you pick me up Thursday night? I can't wait to ride in that car of yours. I'll spend all week dreaming of the ways I want to have you in it."

My cock likes the sound of that, and I pull her away to an alcove under the stadium, dragging her against me. She hums at the feel of my hard dick in her lower abdomen. Taking the risk, I kiss her. I can't help myself. She opens for me and the world disappears. I don't know how long we stay locked together, but when I hear a soft cough behind us, I jerk my head up, furious to be interrupted even as it's idiotic to be kissing her in public.

"Can I interrupt this tender moment to say goodbye to my mom?" Elise looks mostly disgusted and slightly amused.

Carrie hugs me quickly but tightly and whispers, "I'll call you when I get to the airport."

She is true to her word, and we spend the hour before her flight planning her trip back for the long holiday weekend.

***

Carrie

Watching Elise hit the penalty kick was the icing on the cake of the entire weekend. I love watching her play. Watching her get coached by my dream man has me in the stratosphere. After I untangle from Conner and our risky embrace, Elise and I talk as she walks me to the car. I'm glad he is meeting with his boss to tell her about us, so we won't have to wait long to be public.

My departing words to my girl are filled with how proud I am of her. I've said some version of this after every game, win or lose, her whole life. I remind her to keep having fun and I'll call her when I land. She plans to go home with her Big Sister next weekend and I mentally commit to telling her my plans once I get home and get some sleep.

By the time I board my airplane, I'm so grateful Conner is making all the arrangements for my return flight. I am so tired I can't see straight. I knock out as we taxi off the runway and don't wake until the wheels hit the pavement of in Houston. I realize I'm starving and pray there is enough for a cheese sandwich at home, as I haven't eaten since breakfast.

Conner has everything arranged for me to come back, including already ordering all my products, so all I must bring back is a suitcase with clothes. He tells me, "A very, very, very small suitcase, only a carry-on. You need is one outfit for dinner and a hike, and something to fly home in. The rest of the time, you will be naked or something of mine. I want to see you in my clothes."

As I walk into my empty house, having updated my other girls and Dulce during my Uber right home, I sigh. Schroeder meows at me loudly, unhappy he had no company. He will have to have a visitor when I'm gone next week, or I'll find a "gift" on my pillow when I get home.

I make my cheese sandwich and eat in silence. This house is always peaceful. It is full of so many joyful memories from our family's time here. As my mind wanders, a text from an unknown number comes through.

> I saw you two today. Everyone is going to know.

I feel the shot of adrenaline go straight to my arms and legs, like a flash of fire spreading. My head feels light and I'm instantly ready to fight or run. I screenshot the text and, with shaky hands, send it to Conner.

I get his response in seconds.

> Whatever you do, don't reply. It's Maciee, and it's handled. I'll call you once I update the coaches.

I must deactivate my nervous system, so I take a shower with an icy blast at the end. When I get out, exhaustion sets in, but my mind is still whirling. What was that text about?

We weren't subtle this afternoon during that kiss, so maybe we were seen. I send up a prayer that this doesn't cause issues for Conner.

As I lie down in bed, my mind abruptly shifts and an unusual thought pops into my head.

What if I sold the house and moved to California? What if I sold the business and just started fresh?

I have been seeking guidance on my next season in life. I know I don't want to lead this company much longer. Gena is really more suited to it, especially without Scott to anchor me there. Now, with Conner and the life we want to start together, I reach for the sense of peace over turmoil about the text.

I close my eyes to visualize what's possible. I picture myself selling business, even my house, or giving it to the girls. My skin tingles as I see behind my eyes something like glitter settling over my skin. In my mind's eye, I see my skin catch the light reflecting overhead, like there are tiny specs of diamonds embedded in my pores. The vision to help other women build their businesses and have the success I have becomes clear, as I hear the words, "Women's Empowerment Coach."

I raise my hand to my mouth and realize I've been given the answer to the question I've been holding in my heart for several weeks now. I realize I can be a Business Coach from anywhere. Grateful tears roll down my cheeks as my chest gets tight.

I take a few steadying breaths before I realize my phone is vibrating, as I missed a call from Conner. I scrub a hand over my face and brush my hair out of my eyes before I Facetime him back.

"Hey, Sunshine, were you asleep?" He has an almost apologetic look on his handsome face. I face I already miss being inches from mine.

"No, not yet." I give him a smile and put the back of my hand over my mouth to stifle my yawn.

He chuckles, "I bet you were close, though. We are back to sleeping together over the phone, but not for long. I booked your flight and emailed you the details." His smile is light, but he looks serious.

"I know you are trying to be cute–and succeeding famously, but what's wrong? What did Maciee do besides send me a text?"

He looks away and then looks back at me. "Things did not go well with Maciee Griggs today. She was twenty minutes late to the pre-game meeting. We informed her we were cutting her from the program. She threatened us and has now sent a picture of the two of us to the entire team."

I stare at him in shock. I also immediately feel a deep sense of shame for kissing him in public today and probably jeopardizing his job. My hand is over my mouth when I whisper, "Oh, Conner, I am so sorry. I've ruined everything."

He furrows his brow in confusion. "Carrie, what in the world would you have anything to feel sorry for? Our privacy was invaded. We are two consenting adults. No one can threaten us, no matter what. This is all on Maciee, Sunshine."

I steady myself as he continues, "Plus, we've talked with every one of the players, and none of them have a problem with us being together." Elise's Big Sister made that very clear when she called a team meeting in the dorms after she received the picture. The team met and discussed it before we even knew there was an issue. And they all think it's fantastic. They completely support Elise as well and have plans to fuck anyone up that messes with her. Soccer girls do not take their teammates' mental health lightly.

He goes on, "Also, Maciee posted the picture to social media. It's been taken down, but she will be expelled. It violates our student code of conduct, which she and her douchebag Dad signed as part of her paperwork. She will be ushered off campus before dawn. I don't know how Maciee got your number, but you can bring her up on charges of stalking. It's thin with only one text, but I know how to leverage that, unfortunately."

His face sours, and I know he is thinking of his own stalker.

"How are you going to handle this with Arlo?" I ask quietly, looking down and playing with the hem of my PJs.

"Carrie, look at me." I do and it feels so big when I look into his warm, dark honey eyes. His tone is serious, but the emotion in it cascades over me. "Carrie, you've done nothing wrong. I'm ok. Elise is ok. Arlo knows, and she is furious. Not with me; well, ok a little with me. She is livid with Nelson Griggs. He was going to meet with her to pay her off. She is writing a letter to every Athletic Director on the West Coast to make sure Maciee is blackballed. UCC Soccer is a family. You fuck with one of us, you fuck with all of us."

I have knots in my stomach and Conner can tell. His entire face softens when he says, "Hey, you will not lose me over this. And I will lose nothing, either. Most of all, you."

I blow out a long breath and look at him. "It is an idiotic motherfucking motherfucker who would have the audacity to mess with you and your team!" He laughs then, and it diffuses all the tension between us. He wipes his eyes and replies, "Well said, Sunshine."

He continues, "The team handled it all. They got the pictures right after you got your text. I only had to call Arlo, with Inanna and Erik present. We talked it through in about ten minutes. That woman works absolute miracles."

His gaze turns a little dark. "All you ate for dinner was a cheese sandwich? No, no, my lovely. That will not do. I will make sure you go home stuffed next Sunday night."

I laugh, switching gears. "Stuff me in every way possible, promise?"

His pupils blow out at my double meaning, and he asks, "You sore, my darling?"

I bring up my hand, rotating it in a side-to-side motion. "Yes, a little. But I have a plan for a few Peloton rides this week to toughen those parts up for you."

He laughs again. "Well, as long as you are ready to ride me, I will be more than pleased."

I lean my face into the phone and whisper, "Conner, I may need to ride you in the backseat of that fantastically fuckable car before we ever leave the airport."

He leans in and his own whisper is husky when he says, "My cock, my fingers or my face, Sunshine?"

I give him a devilish grin and say, "Maybe all three."

Chapter 27

C onner

    I am so proud of my team. They all make a circle around Elise and pump her up about her mom finding love again. Most of the comments end with, "too bad it's Coach Conner," which always brings a smile. I'll let it go on for a day or so, being the butt of the joke, but then it's back to business.

    I can tell that Elise is avoiding me, so Inanna pulls her aside after the practice on Monday. They have a long conversation, and there are lots of hand gestures. I keep my distance and let Inanna do what she is going to do.

    "There are hearts in your eyes," Erik says, coming to stand beside me.

    I've never been in love, but there is no doubt in my mind I am head over heels. Knowing Carrie feels the same way allows all my parts to be in alignment. As I work to keep the ladies focused each day during training. Arlo and I now have a standing meeting for the rest of the season every Wednesday at three pm, to cover strategy and press.

This is the heat and pressure she lives for, which is what has allowed our athletic programs to flourish under her leadership. She saw my potential when I was broken by the Michigan State scandal. She blocked the opponents to my appointment and carved a path forward for this program to start fresh.

To say I owe her my career is an understatement. She wasn't thrilled about Carrie being a parent, but she even offered her mansion by the sea for our wedding. My people know true love when they see it and they will move heaven and earth to see it come to fruition.

I'm on a pink cloud, so I'm going to ride it all the way to the National Championship game.

"Coach?"

I turn and see my captain standing in front of me, two other seniors in tow.

I answer them straight away, "Yes, ladies, what can I do for you?"

"We need to ask you two questions."

"I'm all ears," as I smile at their bold approach.

Alyssa takes a deep breath. None of my players are afraid of me, but there is a coach-player dynamic that is to be respected. She starts and then stops.

Then she starts again, "Ok, so we've been discussing it. We all know what's coming with other teams. Maciee's post was up long enough, so we know other teams saw it. A few of the players are getting texts from friends around the country."

"Ok, so what's your question?" I ask her seriously because the acid churns in my gut. I hate this. My past is already scarlet, and I don't need to bring Carrie, or her family, into an orbit that would cause flack hitting them.

Alyssa looks at me, completely dead serious, "Ok, so, we were wondering how lenient you will be this season on red cards on teams that talk trash."

I blink. "I'm sorry? Red Cards?"

The defensive captain, Natalie, steps up now to say, "Yes, sir. We've been talking about what Elise might get on the field. They will take shots at her and make horrible comments. So, how hard are you going to make us run if we end up getting cards in her defense?"

We have a minimal yellow and red card policy. We play clean and fair. Sure, we know how to do things when the ref isn't looking, but as a program, we do not encourage violence.

Except in this case, I think darkly.

I pause for a few minutes, letting their inquiry settle in. "Well, ladies, it will be something the other coaches and I have to discuss. We couldn't condone retribution." They all nod, their ponytails swinging with the movement.

I continue, "However, I know that my relationship with Elise's mom puts a target on her." The ponytails continue to sway with the movement of their heads.

"Yet we are talking about my family. And it would apply to any of you." Ponytails are in full swing now as they agree and the protective urge swells in my chest. No one is going to touch what is mine, especially if that is Carrie or her girls.

"So, I'll say this in an unofficial capacity. You better use all the tricks in your bag to set the tone for the match and if there are repeated violations or attempts to intimidate Elise, I trust you three will make sure those players get taken out. No overt action if you can help it. Understood?"

They all have devilish gleams in their eyes. Soccer girls are the toughest athletes in the world, and they know how to get away with a lot of shit. It was eye-opening for me when I first started coaching. They get dirty when needed.

"What's your other question?"

This time, it is our keeper, Peyton, currently struggling with a hamstring pull and mentoring a sophomore who is starting till she recovers, who speaks up. "Well, Coach, you know there is a holiday weekend, so we were hoping you would call practice early so we could all head out?"

All nine eyeballs are glued to my face with such hopeful, wistful expressions. I don't tell them this suits me just fine and planned ending practice early on Thursday because I need time to get to the airport to pick up Carrie.

I drag out the moment, making them squirm, until I inhale and sigh in a very overdramatic fashion, then say, "Ok, fine. Practice will end at three instead of five. But everyone who can better get here early on Thursday and start running!"

They look at each other and squeal. I chuckle and tell them, "Alright ladies, get out of here and let me talk with the other coaches about your violent delights." I wink and they run off, chattering the entire way.

I meet up with Inanna and Erik and Inanna quirks a brow at me.

Erik calls it, "Going to need to hire an extra trainer for the bloodbaths that will ensure if someone tries to fuck with Elise, eh?" I laugh and Inanna rolls her shoulders. "I love it that our girls are planning to be so smart with their violence."

I slap Erik on the shoulder and tell him, "How much have you been hearing in the training room?"

He grins but only says, "A lot." I look at Inanna and tell her, "I'd be willing to bet a lot of money that he knows more about our players than you do."

She rolls her eyes and scoffs, "Only because he is the biggest gossip out of all of them. You are calling practice early on Thursday?"

"Yep, 3 pm. You ok with that?"

She nods her approval. "I'm catching a flight to see my college roommate. We are going to paint Seattle red."

I knit my brows together in confusion. "Seattle?"

She nods with an unusually cheeky grin on her face. "Yep, it has the second-best lesbian bar in the country. Wildrose, I believe, is the name."

I laugh and tell her, "Happy Hunting." Then I turn to Erik, who is looking at her a little abashedly. "You got any plans for your holiday weekend, Big Man?"

He shrugs, never one to comment on his personal life. "I plan to read some books; you know a quiet staycation."

I snap my fingers. "Damn, that reminds me. Carrie bought me a book. Said I need to read it for pleasure and ideas. I have to go buy her something at the bookstore in town. She mentioned the owner–a guy named Samuel; I think–was really nice."

Erik shrugs again. "I've been there–the Book Nook. And it's Samson. Yes, he is a nice guy. You'd like him. I'm sure Carrie did."

At that comment, we call it a day and go our separate ways. I need to grab some dinner, get to reading, and wait for my only Sunshine to call me.

***

Carrie

The week gets rolling quickly. It is a short week. I'm only working three and a half days, so I make them longer, staying till after seven pm each day. It's draining, but I know it's not forever. I can push through and do it for a few days. I'm still the CEO and need to model the work hard-play hard ethic we instilled when we founded this company.

I do early morning Peloton rides with Conner to get my workouts in. He is always so encouraging, and we've resumed our nightly phone pleasure sessions, even if they start early enough for me to get a full night's rest. I need more sleep than he does. We've created a joint playlist on Spotify and while our music tastes differ; it adds to the scorching atmosphere of our verbal sex.

I continue to feel the residual effects of the revelation I had about building a women's empowerment business. Letting it marinate–not thinking too hard on it or trying to figure it out – is something I try to practice. I'm not always successful at it, I have my meltdowns.

When I'm sitting with it one day during lunch, Gena calls me out.

"Carrie–what the fuck?"

I startle back into this reality and try to grasp my current circumstances. "What's up, Gena? What do you mean?"

She narrows her eyes at me. "Look, you've been in a dream state since you met this man. And you've been back two days since getting your brains fucked out, but I know it's not just that. I've known you for over a decade, and I know when something is up. So, WHAT THE FUCK IS UP?"

Sighing, I silently wish I wasn't so transparent to the people in my life. I shake my head, afraid to say what I've been thinking about for these last few days. This would be another massive shift in a very short amount of time.

Gena, as always, has other ideas on the timing of a discussion and starts tapping her foot. "Well, are you going to tell me? You know you have to. Girl code and all. I know it has to be more than Conner."

Gena is basically my work wife, but I still try to put her off. "I don't know if I'm ready to talk about it."

She reads me anyway. "Does this have something to do with work? You've been doing fine, but I can tell your heart isn't in this anymore. It hasn't been since Scott died. Let's get straight to the point. Do you want out?"

Fuck! How does she read me so easily? I internally cringe, but it all comes spilling out, like the dam was ready to burst. "This company was a joint dream with Scott. We built it together and then with you. You are as close to a partner as I've had these last few years. Between you and Dulce, I've made it through, and my girls are well taken care of. But you are right, this has not always been my vision for my life. I feel like there is something more I can do, for women especially."

I don't want to tell her I had a Divine revelation the other night, especially as I was in a transcendental state–somewhere between awake and asleep.

Like a dog with a bone, she keeps at me, "And? There is more to this. I can feel it."

I look at her as she takes a bite of her salad off her fork. I feel my fear of telling her I want to leave fluttering in my chest like a gigantic bird. I take stock and realize it's because I want her approval. I don't want her to think I'm a kook–some kind of religious nut. My church days are long over. After Scott died, many of our so-called friends disappeared, uncomfortable with my grief. My spirituality went in a different direction. I needed more openness than the church was willing to give. A few stuck around for a few months, but eventually I stopped hearing from them, too.

Gena is eating and staring at me, boring a hole into the middle of my forehead. I finally give up, sighing loudly, and she grins. She knows she won the standoff.

"Fine, I'll tell you." And so I do. I tell her about the revelation, about the vision and the network I want to build. She is unusually quiet for a moment and then blows air out of her lungs in a rush, which flutters her long, side swept bangs.

"I always knew this day would come, and I wanted to be ready for it. It's later than I thought."

She is almost talking to herself, so I wave my hand in front of her face and say, "Excuse me? What are you talking about?"

She snaps to attention, as if just realizing I'm still in the room, and promptly says, "I want to buy you out of the company."

Choking on the water I was sipping; I take a minute before I catch my breath again. "I'm sorry, what? I didn't hear you right. You said you wanted to buy me out of the company?"

Gena is as serious as a heart attack. "Yep. I have been saving for this for years. You just told me about your dream. Now,

I'm telling you mine. I want to own this company and scale it nationwide."

I never expected this in a million years, but it makes total sense. I say the only thing I can think of in the moment, "Well, let's get the paperwork together. Looks like my new life and yours are about to start now."

We take the rest of our lunch time to strategize how to do this as selling a company isn't a straightforward task.

Once we wrap up lunch, I send Conner a text, giving him a quick update that I will soon have more time to spend with him in person.

> *Hey Sweetness. I know this is sudden, but how would you feel about me living with you in California sooner rather than later?*

> *Sunshine, this better not be a joke. I will punish you for it, and it'll be more than a love bite on your ass.*

I giggle and Gena rolls her eyes as she packs up her stuff, hightailing it out of my office. She has learned that when I giggle like that, it's Conner and she doesn't want to be party to her boss' sexting session.

> *Call me when you can, my love.*

I didn't expect him to FaceTime me right then. I can see he is in his office, and he is by himself.

He greets me immediately, "Hey, gorgeous. This was perfect timing. I was here working through some plays. I have to say, seeing your beautiful face in the middle of my day is my new favorite thing."

Sighing as my heart melts, I tell him. "Conner, you know exactly what to say. I've never seen your office. Want to show me around?"

He smiles, and my heart skips a beat. I know it will always do that for that grin, one just for me. Before he turns the camera around he says, with a little of gravel in his voice, "You look delicious in your work clothes, my Sunshine."

He makes a quick walk around his medium-sized office. When he sits back down at his desk, I ask, "So, how sturdy is that desk?"

He growls out, "Plenty sturdy for me to fuck you on, that's for sure. If not, I'll have it reinforced. Now, all I'm going to think about all day, every day, are the ways I can take you on this desk. Boy, your pussy would sure look pretty spread out in front of me. I could just roll up in my chair and taste your sweet juices any time I wanted."

Fanning myself, which he sees and chuckles about, I try to get a hold of myself. "Ok, right? Yes. Whew, though. The images flooding my brain of the two of us together in your office are *very* tempting and distracting. Trust me, if I was in a skirt today, we'd be fucking ourselves for each other right now."

He laughs darkly. "I know my insatiable Goddess. Now, tell me your news."

He waits patiently for me to form the words, and they all come spilling out. I love this man, and I can't wait to show him in less than two days, a hundred different ways how much.

Chapter 28

Conner

When Carrie walks out of the SFO airport where I'm waiting for her in the garage, she is a vision. I am standing on the passenger side of my car, the one I bought to celebrate getting this job. It's my dream car, a matte blacked out BMW 350i with burgundy leather interior and nearly illegal dark tint on the windows.

I drink my fill of her as she moves towards me, the slightest sway in her hips. She is wearing a forest green wrap dress with a thin brown suede snakeskin belt and knee-high brown suede boots. Green, teal, and turquoise are her favorite colors, and she wears them as often as she can find something she likes. I love it, but I can't wait to rip it off her so I can fuck her properly in those sexy as hell boots.

As instructed, she brought only a small weekend bag. She plans to buy a UCC soccer t-shirt and already tells me she is stealing one of my "Head Soccer Coach" pullovers. She won't be able to wear it for a while in Houston, but if she is planning on spending a lot of time here in California, I want my mark literally written on her chest.

One of these days, we will get tattoos. I need her name inked over my heart and I want my name on her in a place only I can see.

She finally makes it to me and stops, a huge smile on her face.

"Whatcha' waitin' for, Sunshine?" I ask curiously.

"For you to sweep me off my feet, of course." She winks and throws her head back to laugh as I pull her in and up into my arms. I take a couple of steps in a circle, far enough away from my car door, and twirl her while we kiss. When I slide her down my body till her feet hit the ground, I know she can feel how much I want her. I unlock the car, toss her bag into the front seat and then slide into the back.

"You gonna fuck me in the airport parking garage, Sweetness? Let the cameras catch all our fun?"

I nod my head. "Yep. Sunshine, you are going to ride me in the backseat of my car like you promised."

Her eyes go molten blue, and as we position ourselves in the backseat–not an easy feat given, we are both so tall. She immediately crawls on top of me. I already had the front seats moved all the way forward, which gives us a little more leg room. I sprawl out as much as I can, as Carrie positions herself.

She scrambles to undo my belt and zipper on my jeans. She is practically squatting with her ass in the air till she can get my boxer briefs down.

"Shit, Conner, why did you even bother to wear underwear?" She mumbles in a slightly irritated tone.

I chuckle at her as I lift my hips and reply, "And here I was thinking I would be a gentleman and make sure if you were hungry, we could get something to eat before we humped in my car."

Completely focused on getting my pants off, she doesn't hear me. When she finally gets them to my ankles, she says, "Good enough," and drops to her knees on the floorboard.

She doesn't have a lot of room, but makes it work. She lands with her mouth right above my weeping, throbbing cock. Looking up at me with those sparking eyes, she says lowly, "Four days was too long. I need to taste you."

Not giving me a chance to respond, she drops her sweet, warm mouth straight down, taking me immediately to the back of her throat. I groan loudly, not caring if anyone hears me because this feels amazing. She comes back up, licking the length of me with the tip of her tongue and swirls it around the head.

She slides her perfect mouth down on me again as I thread my hands in her hair. I feel her pull up, making a gagging sound, and I smile darkly. I don't want her to choke, but there is something so hot about her gagging around my cock. I stroke her hair and let her know I approve. "Good girl, taking me so fucking deep. Oh, shit Sunshine."

She moves her mouth and hand together, alternating between sucking me down and then humming and licking me. As she moves her hand to my balls, my spine tingles. Fuck, this woman is worshipping me and making dirty as fuck sounds, like it is pleasing her to please me.

I gently pull on her hair and tell her, "Come here, my love. I want my ride." She gives the tip of my dick a playful kiss and comes up to straddle me.

I palm her pussy, which is soaking. Bracing her forearms above my head on the seat, as I'm lying in an "L" position, I undo her belt and lift her dress over her head. Seeing what she is wearing underneath leaves me breathless. "Oh, fuck Carrie, you are so hot."

In a burgundy lace bodysuit that molds her curves to perfection, she meets my eyes as I undo the clasps on the bottom. Her eyes roll back in her head as I slide two fingers inside her.

"Conner, oh my god, Conner." She moans as I pump in and out of her dripping pussy.

***

Carrie

Conner's fingers in my slick channel are heaven. Every part of him is heaven. Sucking his cock got me to the brink of orgasm. I love worshipping this man's body. He is my home and being with him brings me to the edge in no time flat.

I ride his fingers for a bit before I can't take anymore. Still looking in his eyes, I tell him what I want–what I need–breathlessly, "Need you inside me now."

My emotions are riding high. I can feel them as I slide down onto his beautiful cock. He raises his hips up to slam into me from underneath. The sound I make when he hits the deepest spot in me is obscene, but I couldn't care less. I can't see straight with the pleasure of him inside me achingly good. The waves of my orgasms build as I slam myself down on him over and over

As I feel like I'm about to break as the waves overtake me.

He reads me like a book and meets my eyes. "Touch yourself Carrie. I want you to come. Now."

I barely get close to my clit before the waves crest, and I am done for. I shake, nearly vibrating with pleasure so intensely I can't do anything but go with it.

Conner rams up into me from beneath and groans out, "Oh Carrie, fuckkkkkk!!" He pumps completely, warming me from the inside out, and for a moment, the world stands still.

Shaking as I come down, I start to cry.

My climax released something raw in my soul. I clutch his neck, sobbing into it and all I hear are small sounds like "shhh, shhhh" as one big hand rubs my back while the other braces me against him, cradling my rib cage.

I'm holding on for dear life. My makeup is ruined and I'm still sitting on his cock as it softens. Our combined release leaks out on us both, but Conner doesn't rush me.

When I finally meet his eyes, he takes my wet, snotty face in his hands and asks, "Good tears?"

He kisses my lips lightly, and I nod. Then, I feel a little awkward because of what just happened, so I gasp out a little laugh and say, "I made a mess in your car."

He does a cute little one-shoulder shrug. "You've never been more beautiful than you are right now. Plus, it takes two to make this kind of mess."

I give another little laugh, as he brings my lips to his, this time more forcefully, like he wants me to feel his love through the contact. He doesn't let me pull away, and it makes his face a mess, too.

When he lets me pull back, he keeps my face in between his huge hands before quietly asking, "Want to tell me what that was about?"

I look at him. "You don't want to clean up?"

He shakes his head, and my heart breaks a little wider open. He brings his lips to my space right between my collarbones and murmurs into my skin, "Sunshine, I would rather take care of your heart first."

With that permission, I launch into a full-on babble. "I didn't know a love like this was possible. I didn't think I would ever be loved like this. I didn't know if I deserved another chance." I sniffle again, my eyes welling back up and he brings his lips now to my collarbones, up my neck and finishes by kissing both cheeks.

He says six words full of hope as he stares deeply into my eyes. "You deserve this and much more." I can feel the tears running in between his fingers. He lets them fall. It isn't the torrent of before. It is the love I feel spilling over.

Finally, moving to clean up, Conner instructs me where the hand towel he brought is. I reach around the center console and our bodies come apart, leaving my core bare and cold. I tease him, "You had some forethought, eh - Sweetness?"

He looks at me and seriously says, "That was more than I could hope for, just like you. Plus, you promised."

He uses the towel to wipe my face before we fully untangle ourselves, then pats me down, gently stroking my labia and inner thighs before he takes the towel to himself. He deftly reaches between us to clip my bodysuit back together, then pulls me back down onto him, into an enormous bear hug. He whispers into my neck, "I am so happy you are here, Carrie." I choke up again as he releases me and climbs out of the car on the driver's side.

He pulls his pants up as I put my dress back in place. As I do, I send up a silent prayer the garage cameras didn't catch too much of our tryst. Connor unwinds his long legs and stands up, reaching in to help me out. Putting his hand on the small of my back, he walks me around to open the passenger door, grab my bag, and adjust the seat. Seeing me settled, he puts my bag in the trunk and walks around to get in the driver's seat.

I lean over the center as he starts the car and give him a deep kiss. He hums his approval and reaches over to buckle me up.

As he shifts into reverse, I smile into his eyes before telling him, "Take me back to our place, Sweetness."

He gives me a huge grin and says, "Indeed, my love." We start the drive home.

Chapter 29

Conner

The drive back to my place takes about an hour and a half. Carrie is quiet and we hold hands as I maneuver us up the scenic coastline. She is looking out the windows and looks at peace. I didn't really know what to do with her post-climax outburst. I knew there wasn't something wrong because we just had explosively gratifying sex.

When she was crying, my mind spun through scenarios and causes. The more she held on for dear life, I realized this was about pent-up emotion.

She's shared with me some about how hard it was being a single-mother and a widow, while still trying to run a successful business. She knows she's done the best she could—and also that her best was incredible. Her girls are fantastic, successful, kind humans. Everyone wants their children to grow up to be Carrie's daughters.

I can't imagine what she has been through–and to come out so full of integrity on this side. It's why I want to be with her. Holding her felt right. It always does, but especially when she was so upset. As we drive in silence, I can't help but think about what we will do next.

Tonight, I'm cooking dinner and while there will be more sex, I want to experience "couple things" with her. I want to nap with her. I want to watch a movie with her. I want to stroll downtown holding her hand. I want to cook her eggs and pancakes and watch her make the crazy coffee concoction she drinks every morning.

I want to take her for a night on the town and show her off as mine.

I want to plan and dream with her. Her mind is so sharp, I know she will color in the lines of the picture I draw. Her long, warm fingers are intertwined with mine, as my palm cups hers from the top. My thumb rubs gently against the back of her hand.

"You hungry, Sunshine?"

She gives me a drowsy little, "Hmmmm?" I realize she is asleep. I smile because this is another first, I'm discovering about her - she gets sleepy in the car. She looks like an angel with her head back against my tan leather seats and the orange light of the setting sun on her face. It makes me feel peaceful knowing she feels safe enough to fall asleep while I'm driving.

Driving home–which is wherever we are, together.

I repeat my question, "I asked if you were hungry, my darling."

She opens her eyes, and they are the same color as the ocean reflected out the front window. Her beauty catches me off guard again. Guys like me don't get many chances to be with a woman like this and I vow to not waste a moment of it, ever.

She smiles at me, and I squeeze her hand in return. "Yes, getting there. What are we having?"

***

Carrie

Conner describes a most delicious meal of surf and turf with baked sweet potatoes and chocolate soufflé for dessert, with coconut ice cream. He planned all my favorites.

The surf is for me, and he has spared no expense–redfish. He is having a center-cut steak filet.

He said the sweet potatoes are already done, staying warm in the oven. He won't tell me if he made the souffle himself, but it makes me smile to picture him baking. I bake my girls' favorites, but I've never tried something as ambitious as soufflé.

Conner Doreland is nothing if not ambitious.

The coconut ice cream is from an Instagram reel I sent him a few weeks back. He remembered, which seems like such a small thing but makes all the difference. He thinks about me.

He listens to me. He doesn't just say it, he shows me. I can't help but dream of what our future will be like.

That was a huge part of my emotion at the airport. It's been such a long time since I've truly felt cared for and desired. Our sexual chemistry is undeniable, yet it is more than that. His tender approach was perfect. He didn't try to fix it or talk me out of it or get defensive.

Conner, like the man he is, made space for me to feel. Conner is a miracle. A gorgeous, intelligent, focused, sexy as hell miracle and I plan to make sure he knows it all weekend and for the rest of our lives.

We pull into the driveway of his house and my eyes rake in every detail. I've seen what his house looks like in all our Facetime conversations, but now the puzzle pieces fall into place. It's bigger than a bungalow and tucked into the hills he is so often running or biking in.

A perfect, single Conner house.

We park in the garage, and he jumps out, grabs my bag, and opens the car door to help me out. He cradles my waist as he moves me inside, where we enter a mudroom off the kitchen. I take off my knee-high boots while he unlaces his dress shoes. He leaves them in a little cubbyhole and I put my boots on the floor next to them.

He smiles at me, "I can't help liking things neat, Sunshine, but mess up anything you want. I want to feel your touch in the house, so make it your home."

I stretch up to wrap my arms around his neck and kiss him. He deepens it for a moment, before he pulls back, enormous hands still around my waist and says, "C'mon. It's time for dinner after a quick tour."

He shows me, first, in the modern kitchen, which is open to the family room. It's clean and minimalistic, with all updated appliances and a wide island with two barstools. He has a dark oak kitchen table with four chairs, two settings already placed for our dinner. In the living room area, there are some masculine touches, including a faux bearskin rug on the floor before the fireplace. His little patio out back has two Adirondack chairs sitting in a small grassy area.

His bedroom has navy blackout curtains and a matching comforter, with four pillows, two in square navy patterned shams. There is a dark teal blanket across the foot of it. When I look at him questioningly, he shrugs. "It's your signature color, and I wanted you to feel at home."

I squeeze his hand, and he leads me into the bathroom to see how he set up all my products, at the two-person sink and in the drawers. I sigh. I really could not imagine a more perfect man, like he is out of one of my favorite romance books.

I peek into his shower, and he chuckles, "We will do our best in there, Sunshine, but the real action will have to be on the bed, couch, floor or a countertop. And I plan to have you on each of those surfaces." My core heats again as I can tell he has put a lot of thought into where and how he will make love to me this weekend.

He shows me to the second bedroom, which has no bed. It's more of a home office and workout room. The story of his player career is documented on the walls, with pictures, article clippings between his college and Premier League jerseys. His Peloton is there, with a yoga mat, bands and a few weights. He sees me noticing and says, "If I really want to work out, I have the gym on campus. And Erik, of course."

"Of course," I say, smiling. I love seeing his space with my own eyes.

We go back towards the kitchen, and I open the sliding glass door to the cool night air. It is wonderful to be in a place where you can smell the ocean without being smacked in the face by humidity. As I turn back, I comment about the rug in front of the fireplace. "That's a nice touch."

He grins devilishly as he lights a fire in the fireplace. "That's for later. My dessert after dessert."

He makes our dinner after serving me a glass of prickly pear sparkling lemonade. Watching him cook is a dream and sexy as hell. He is so at ease. He is a man who takes care of himself and now, me. I take my time watching him move. Seeing him like this, graceful and full of purpose, is an unexpected treat.

His intention and careful planning may arouse me as much as anything else. Seeing him in his element feels like another thread pulled taut as our lives are being knit together.

The fish and the steak are ready at the same time. Conner likes his steaks rare. He plates my fish and sweet potato, sprinkling some salt with a pinch of brown sugar over the butter. He plates his steak and potato, then pours himself a glass of lemonade, too.

He carries the plates to the table, commenting, "You've been smiling this whole time, Sunshine." I reach up to touch my face and realize that he is right.

Telling him what I was thinking about while watching him in the kitchen, he grins. "I want to make sure that smile never leaves your face." He leans over, kisses me before speaking a simple blessing over the food. "That this food will nourish our bodies, conversation and give us plenty of energy for what is about to come."

I mumble, "That's what she said." He catches it and chortles before he says, "Eat up, Buttercup."

Once we are finished, Conner puts the souffle in the oven. He fessed up to having some help from Inanna on how to prepare them. He takes my hand and leads me to the tile space between the kitchen and lounge area.

"While we wait, I want to do something I've been dreaming about since the first time we FaceTimed."

Confused, I say, "You want to see my glass dildo?"

He roars in laughter and says, "No, silly goose. I want to dance with you."

He presses a button on the remote he pulls from his pocket and the music starts. It's a good one too, "In Your Arms" by Illenium with X Ambassadors. We start slow dancing, my arms around his neck and face on his shoulder as he tugs me in close, hands kneading my hips and ass. As the music speeds up, he spins me out and as I laugh, he brings me back in.

I move my hips up against his in a figure-eight motion, and he tries to match me. We dance for the rest of the song, and it rolls into another, "Heaven" by Niall Horan. It's a little faster and we match the beat. Both delighted, we laugh as his smile looks like it will split his face in half.

He kisses me as the song ends and I lose myself in it. It doesn't even register right away what song it is. It is slower, "Movement" by Hozier. When it makes its way into my brain, I say, "This is the song I did my striptease to during one of our phone sex dates. "

He pulls back to grin wickedly, pausing the song before tucking a strand of hair behind my ear. "I know. After dessert, I want a lap dance."

Chapter 30

Conner

I overcooked the souffle. Man, that shit is hard to get right. Inanna walked me through it step by step. Baking French desserts is one of her superpowers. It got a little crunchy on top because I was dancing with–and then kissing Carrie - and not paying attention to the timer.

To her credit, she eats every bite. She goes on and on about how delicious everything was and how I can cook for her anytime. She punctuates every compliment with a kiss somewhere on my upper body. All I can think about is what's next.

Gone are the romantic thoughts. Gone are the dreams of our future. Gone is the normal OCD need to clean the kitchen after I eat.

All I want to do right now is fuck my woman. I didn't get enough earlier. I told her I wanted a lap dance and I really fucking do. This woman can move, and I want it all in the privacy of my own home.

Still trying to compliment me, I pull Carrie to her feet when I stand up. Giving me a seductive smile, knowing what I want, she says. "Why don't you press play, and we will get started, Sweetness."

Before the music starts up again, she is straddling me, her dress hiked up around her hips. "Just let me kiss you a minute longer," she begs, and I can't say no. She kisses me within an inch of my life, our tongues swirling together, and unbuttons my shirt. I put my hand on hers and say, "No, that's not what's next." She licks up the column of my neck. As if my dick could get any harder. That does it.

"I'm just getting us both prepared for our happy ending." She winks at me and stands a few feet away from me on the couch. I splay myself out, as she throws her hair over one shoulder and sways her hips in slow, sensual circles. She undulates her arms for a second before she reaches down and pulls her dress over her head, tossing it on the floor. Seeing that lace thong bodysuit from earlier makes my mouth water.

I can't wait to feel her skin under my fingers and taste every inch of her.

She continues her slow dance as the music shifts to "Continuum" by Tanerelle. Carrie is fully into what she is doing, almost belly dancing with her movements. I don't know where she learned to dance like this, but I am so fucking turned on and feeling lucky as hell she is mine. As she bends over to touch her toes, ass in my face, I can't help it.

I lean over, grab her hips and breathe her in. I smell our sex from earlier all over her pussy. It almost snaps my control, but I want this to be slow. She turns around to grind on my lap, her core moving forward and back over my concrete cock. Her big, beautiful tits are right at my mouth, so I lick her nipples through the lace. She moans and I feel the pre-cum soak the front of my boxers.

She grabs my hands, putting my right one on her right breast and my left one on her ass. I promptly start kneading it in time with the song and her gyrations. I pinch and roll her nipple between my thumb and index finger.

She drops her head back and lets out a guttural moan that tests my resolve to go slow once again. Her hair is long enough with her head back for me to fist it and hold her there as I take my right hand to her waist, sitting up to suck on her neck.

She is still moving on me with smaller thrusts, somewhat immobilized, with her head pulled back. She puts her hands on my shoulders, sliding them up my neck to tangle in my hair. I release her as I continue to suck on her neck while she grinds us into a state of delirium.

We continue with this as the music changes and Rihanna's "Skin" comes on.

It makes me want to do exactly what Ri-Ri sings about. I finish unbuttoning my shirt and pull it off. Carrie watches me and hisses through her front teeth, "Fucking Adonis. Conner, please." I know just what my baby needs and I'm going to give it to her.

***

Carrie

Dancing for Conner made me feel so sexy. This is the most alive I've ever felt and now that he is shirtless and I can touch him, I won't ever stop. Still straddling him as he grips my ass and whispers, "Hang on, my love." He stands us up and I wrap my legs around him. I can feel his glorious cock through his pants.

He walks us over to the rug, slowly letting me down to slide against him, unlocked in a standing embrace. His lips catch mine and then our mouths become urgent, devouring. I grip him to me, my palms splayed over his defined shoulders and his hands are running over my torso like mad. One second, he has my breasts in his hands; the next they are slipping down my sides.

We stay like that, making out for what could be an eternity or a split-second. Caught up in the whirlwind of desire for him, the universe is narrowed only to this moment, to the feeling of him.

When he slips his hand down my stomach to unclasp the crotch of my bodysuit, I sigh in relief. I unbuckle his belt, and he lets his pants fall to the ground. I back up a step to look at him, stripping for him as I admire his masculine form. I pull the body suit off till I am standing naked. Preening for him, his gaze completely wipes away any shame I have about my body. His eyes are reverent and ravenous.

As I also take my fill of him, I see his hard work in the gym. His pecs are a wonder, his abs cut like marble, and those delicious v slices lead me to look at how marvelous he is in his black boxer briefs. They are tight on his waist and the head of his cock slips through the slit in the front. His thick thighs glisten in the firelight, and I look to his defined calves and long feet. I drag my eyes back up to his face and say, "God made you so perfect, Conner. I'm all yours."

He answers with action. He strips off his boxers in record time and then scoops me up, bridal style, in his arms. He sets me down on the faux fur rug, right in front of the low warm fire. The screen door is open, letting in the cool night air and letting out the heat from this fire and oven in the kitchen.

I softly giggle. "It's just like in the romance books." He grins and hums in approval before coming in for one last kiss. He uses both hands to push my breasts together and sucks my nipples, and he uses his tongue to swirl around in such a way that my eyes roll back in my head.

He continues until I am begging him to touch me. My back arches into his mouth, and I feel my wetness slipping between my thighs. He finally relents his onslaught on my breasts, to kiss down my stomach.

I met his eyes as he hovers over my center and tell him, "Open me up, Conner. I want all of you."

He makes the same sound of approval, low in his throat as I open my legs around his body. He gets down to the strip of hair just above my pussy and runs his tongue all over the shaved skin. His voice is deep and commanding as he asks, "Would you let me shave you down here?"

He brings a hand up my leg, along my inner thigh. He twirls his index finger around my vulva, stroking me gently, dipping inside my channel when he needs some moisture.

I can't form words, but he stills, waiting for my response. I croak out, "Yes, you can do anything to me." His mouth lands on my clit as a reward and he hums. My hips come off the floor and his other arm wraps around my hips, holding me so tight against him as he slides two fingers into my wet heat, curling them to play with my g-spot. His mouth is alternating between licking and sucking.

I'm in a state of suspended animation, and he does one final pulse of his tongue in time with his fingers stroking my spot before I lose my breath. My scream is stuck in my throat as my orgasm detonates from my spine to my shaking legs, to where the tip of his tongue is now running in circles around my clit to draw out the climax. I grip the fur of the rug so hard I pull some out and I hear him say, "Such a good girl, squirting for me."

Barely letting me come down this time, he moves up over me. Kissing me with my cum on his face is the hottest thing ever. He picks up my leg and throws it over his shoulder, and slides his rock-hard cock straight into me, immediately bottoming out.

His mouth forms an "O," as his eyes close. He meets my eyes and says, "Heaven." He pauses for a second before he drives into me, and I brace my other heel on the floor to keep up with him.

Instantly, my vaginal walls tighten. All I know is his body moving into mine, eyes closed. He is whispering, but I can barely make out the words. He strokes my cheek and draws my attention. I open my eyes to his face right above mine and realize what he is saying.

"I love you, Carrie. Forever and ever and ever...I love you."

We are transcendent, lost in the feeling of love we are making. I feel him get faster, go harder. I run my hands down his back, cupping his bubble butt. He continues to pound me, and I can't help but moan, "Oh, Conner. Yes, baby."

After a few more thrusts, his orgasm hits him like a freight train. It makes mine crest, and he yells his pleasure into my neck. I'm boneless under him for a minute as we both breathe hard.

We come to stillness, and I rub light circles up and down his shoulders. Changing to drag my nails up and down his muscular back makes him groan, "Oh God, that's too much." I do it again until he melts his full weight onto me, shivering in sensation.

Eventually, I need to breathe, as his muscular form on top of me is getting heavy. "Conner"

I realize he is dozing. I laugh softly and I whisper into his ear, "Now who fucked who into a coma?" He inhales, kisses my shoulder and pushes up, his cock sliding out in our combined release. Losing him inside me makes me physically sad.

He looks down on me with pride and says, "C'mon Sunshine, let's get cleaned up and get into bed. I'll do the dishes before I make you breakfast in the morning."

Chapter 31

Conner

This bed has never felt so inviting.

But first, Carrie does her bedtime routine that takes four times as long as mine, which amounts to little more than brushing my teeth. I'm ready to settle my Sunshine in for the first time in my bed. I feel a rush of pride, as if this place is finally my home. It's her presence that makes it feel that way. As Carrie is settling in, I close the house, tidying up a bit but quickly, so I make it back to her. She is still awake, but barely, when I crawl under the covers with her.

She hisses a little as I pull her to me. "Conner, your hands are like ice!" I chuckle and try to pull them back, but she grabs my arms. She sticks one of my hands on her lower back and one between her legs, in the softest, warmest part. Then she sticks her feet in between mine.

I kiss the top of her head as I tell her, "Sunshine, your feet aren't much better."

She drapes one arm over my ribs and tucks the other along my torso so she can lay her head where my shoulder and chest meet. She hums a little cheerful sound, and I press my feet down firmer onto hers, willing them to warm them up faster. The warmth of her body from the ankles up and the fragrant pillow of her hair make me drowsy almost instantly.

Suddenly, her whole body convulses. It wakes me up completely and I hear her laugh quietly before she apologizes, "I'm so sorry, Sweetness. That hasn't happened in a long time! I felt like I was falling and was just about the hit the ground."

"I don't think that's normal, Sunshine. You have some interesting sleep habits. What else am I going to learn about you during our first weekend together?"

I can feel her lips turn upward. "Well, I have a couple of surprises. I can show you tomorrow. What else are we going to do?"

She yawns, which lets me know my time is limited. It's as if once she sets her mind to do something–even falling asleep–she makes it happen fast. She'll be mumbling in the next two to three minutes.

"Besides breakfast? I thought we could go on a hike and have a picnic. Then, if we feel like it, we could go to that bookstore you found, and I can pick out a book for you to take home. Something dark and smutty."

She hums with satisfaction and yawns again. "I love the sound of all of that. When are you taking me to dinner?" She yawns a third time; I can feel her body melting into mine and her icy feet are finally thawing. My hands are warm now, thanks to her soft skin.

"I'm going to take you out on Sunday. I thought we could drive around and look at houses. This place is great for me, but I'd want you to have space for you to make it your own. And for the girls to visit, of course."

"Conner?" She has a dreamy quality to her voice, all warm honey and milk.

"Yes, my love?" I lean down and give her forehead a peck. It feels as if I'm in my dream already.

Her voice is a little muffled and I know she is almost gone, but she says, "You make me feel so safe, so special. Thank you."

I can feel the tug of my body to rest and hold her a little tighter, trying to speak around the knot of emotion in my throat. I know she is asleep by the time I say it, but I speak out loud.

"Sunshine, you are healing places I didn't know were broken, just being with me. It should be me thanking you."

Then, as my eyes get heavy, I whisper-sing our bedtime song. I don't know if I finish it because the next thing I remember; I wake up and realize Carrie isn't in my arms. I'm confused, but only for a second before I feel her slide back in next to me.

***

Carrie

I slept like the dead, the entire night in Conner's arms. Neither of us moved. I think even our unconscious minds didn't want any space. We stayed pressed up against each other all night.

When I woke and looked at the clock, which read five am. To my body, that's seven am, so I'm awake. I slip out of bed to shower.

I'm not gone long, but when I come back into the room after finishing my post-shower routine, Conner is stirring. I hurry over, drop my towel and slide in next to him. He sighs contently and pulls me right up next to him again. I could stay like this all day, with no rush, no hurry. I thread the fingers of one of my hands up into his hair, his arm coming to rest on my biceps. He angles himself where I'm cradling him against my chest, as I wrap my other arm under his to stroke his back. He sighs heavily and happily.

I smile because with that exhalation, I can smell the sourness of sleep on his breath, but I don't mind. It's nice to know that this perfect man is still human. If he were an actual god, I could not deal with that.

I breathe the rest of him in as he snuggles his head onto my chest, right above the rise of my breasts. His hand comes up to cup my rear end, which really does fit in his hand. His cock is hard, but he isn't pressing to do anything. We are content to be skin-on-skin in these early morning hours.

I am not sure if I doze back off or enter a meditative state as we lie there together. Conner is asleep again. It is an untold blessing to be here with him this morning, enjoying the space and peace only lovers unified in heart can.

After an indeterminate length of time, we both rouse. I am sure my hair, after washing it, is probably a kinky mess of waves across his pillows. Conner pushes up on his elbow and looks down at me.

"Good morning, Sunshine. I've never slept so well." He continues to look down on me for a few long beats. I don't rush him. I can tell my face is open and I'm smiling. He reaches up to brush his fingertips across my lips and whispers, "This smile is why I call you Sunshine. It lights my heart up."

It's my turn to cup his face, and I lean forward to kiss him, maintaining eye contact. As I feel his tongue slip in between my lips, I tilt my head and close my eyes. I was never a fan of kissing Scott in the morning, but this urge to be open with Conner is unquenchable. I clear my mind and just feel.

As our tongues tangle, he uses his mouth to suck gently on mine. God, he is an amazing kisser, morning breath or no. I would gladly die of dehydration from kissing him for days. Our hands roam, sweeping across every plane, dip and arch of each other's bodies, until they finally find each other underneath the covers and interlace. Conner brings both my hands up into one of his, up over my head. His other hand strokes my inner thigh.

I moan at all the sensation, and I feel his cock hardening even more.

Then something very unsexy happens.

My stomach rumbles. Loudly. Normally, I've had coffee and breakfast by now. I try to ignore it and wiggle my hips underneath Conner to signal him to keep going. He pauses and looks down at me. I answer the unspoken question, whispering into his lips,

"No, it's fine. Keep going."

He tilts his face up to kiss me when my stomach growls again, horrifyingly louder than the first time.

Instead of a deep kiss like I want, he smiles into my lips. His hand is still pins mine above my head and I know the look in my eye is wanton. I can feel myself getting wet in anticipation of what he will do to me with his fingers stroking the juncture of my inner thigh.

To my frustration, he tells me, "Don't worry, my love. We can eat and come straight back to bed. I love dessert after breakfast, anyway. He releases my hands and pushes back onto his knees before leaning down, burying his face in my small strip of pubic hair.

Then he speaks to my pussy like they are old friends, "Don't fret, beautiful one. I'll be back here before you know it." He then looks up at me and his face that close to my core leaves aching until my fucking stomach growls. *AGAIN*.

He huffs and reaches for me. "Come on, my Sunshine. I'll make us a breakfast fit for my queen."

He gets up and pulls out a t-shirt and boxer briefs from his dresser. He hands me the t-shirt, which is large enough to hit my thighs, and then he steps into his boxers. He winks at me, "Don't want you to get cold and I fucking love seeing you in my clothes."

I step over to him and kiss him, palming his semi-hard cock through the material. "I fucking love seeing you without clothes, Sweetness. Let's eat so you can eat me." I wink at him and turn around to walk into the kitchen. He growls before catching me from behind, rolling his hips into my ass.

"Talk like that will get you everything you want and more, Sunshine." I snicker and look back at him, cradling his face in my palm.

"Promise?"

"Cross my heart."

He makes me coffee, cleans the dishes from last night, then whips up eggs and pancakes, the best I've ever had.

After we finish eating, with a smattering of conversation because we are both starving, Conner cleans up the kitchen again.

I tell him, "A lady could get used to this!"

He gives me a wicked little grin at me over his shoulder. Then, after a final swipe of the counter, he stalks to me, takes my coffee cup and sets it down. I let him take me by the hand and move me in front of the island he just cleaned off. Then he picks me up by the waist, sets me down and says, "Lie back, I want my morning dessert."

After the first orgasm, he pulls me to my feet, spins me around and bends me over the counter he just had me on.

I think a full stomach and two orgasms are the best way to start our day.

Chapter 32

Conner

I find myself slumped over Carrie in the kitchen after we both come together. Having her here and able to live out all the daydreams I've had about where I want to fuck her turns me into an animal.

I kiss the back of her neck and down her spine as I pull out. I pull up my boxer briefs from around my ankles and stand up straight. Carrie follows before I turn her around and crush her into my chest.

"Carrie, I will never get enough of you." That pussy is magnificent, so open and ready for me."

She hugs me back just as tight, arms around my back. Into my chest, I hear her mumble, "I'm all yours, Sweetness. I love you."

I tilt her face up with my fingers under her chin and kiss between her eyes, the bridge of her nose, and then tilt my head to meet her lips. "I love you, forever and ever. Amen."

My chest hurts from all the emotion flooding through me. I take a deep breath before I ask, "Sunshine, are you ready for a fun day outside? The weather should be beautiful, and I want to show you where I have my deepest and dirtiest thoughts about you."

"Ready for anything, Coach."

I can't help the growl that escapes my throat. I adore hearing that word from her mouth.

"Ok then, Sunshine. Go get yourself dressed. I'm going to pack our picnic and take a quick shower. Make sure you wear one of my hoodies. It's cool this morning, but we will warm up."

"Yes, Coach!"

"New kink unlocked, Sunshine?"

She giggles and my cock twitches. "Maybe so. Do you like it?"

"I'll show you how much later."

She smiles big and kisses me one more time before she is off. After cleaning the counter again, I pack up my backpack with trail snacks and our picnic lunch. I have a backpack for Carrie, but all it has in it is a blanket for the ground and the book she gave me. I haven't finished reading it yet, so I thought it would be fun to read to each other when we stop. It is supposed to be a gorgeous fall day in north coastal California, and I want her to experience it.

In the shower, I hum her song while I wash and rinse my hair.

***

Carrie

Conner is in the shower longer than expected, so I peek behind the shower curtain. He is standing in all his naked Adonis glory, his head under the stream of water. His lips are moving silently. I suck in my breath as I take a moment to admire the view. How a woman like me got a man like this, I'll never know, but I will never stop being grateful.

When I finally speak, I startle him. "You ok in here, Sweetness?" He brings his head out from under the water and smiles sheepishly before he says, "Was I taking too long? Sorry, I got lost in my prayers of gratitude for you."

Fuck, can I fall any farther for this guy? I lean in and we make a wet, smooching sound. I hope he feels every ounce of how much I cherish him, and I can't help but smile as I pull away to say, "Ready when you are."

"Give me 3 minutes. Start the clock."

Two minutes and fifty-four seconds later, he is dressed, with only his hiking boots to lace up. I did not think he could get any hotter but seeing him in joggers and hiking boots is better than him in gray sweatpants. After pulling his own hoodie over his head, he adds a baseball cap backwards.

I have a powerful urge to strip my leggings off, lie down on the bed and open my legs for him. He must be able to tell from the look on my face because he steps over, leans down, and licks the shell of my ear. I fall against him and feel a full body shiver race through me.

His breath in my ear makes me shiver more as he says, "Yes, you'll be ready for me later, won't you Sunshine?"

All I can do is nod, and he plants his hand on my lower back, holding our hips together. God, I can feel how hard he is through his joggers. He chuckles into my ear again, "Good." My inner slut is in control and her libido is through the roof. With our chemistry rooted in safety, I will try anything with him.

I know he is here for me and he knows I am here for him. It is the most erotic combination. I nearly faint.

He holds me up against him and hisses into my ear before he says, "But first, I'm going to take you on an adventure. Let's go, my love, and I promise, we will have plenty of fun along the way."

I sigh and take his hand. I'm suddenly too hot for my clothes. "You are making lots of promises, Sweetness. I am counting on you to follow through." He chuckles as we walk out of his house hand in hand. "I am a man of my word, Carrie. Let's go."

He locks the door, tucks the key into a pocket of his backpack, which looks heavy. Mine is not, and it's just one more way I see him caring for me. He takes the lead and sets an easy pace I can match as we set off in the hills.

As he said, it's not a strenuous hike, but being from Houston with zero elevation, I'm huffing and puffing up the hills. I stop and take off the hoodie, as I've warmed up considerably, as has the late morning temperature. Conner strips his off as well, giving me a glimpse of his Adonis belt. I must be licking my lips, because he does his model pose and smirks. I laugh as he walks over to tie the hoodie's arms around my waist.

"Like what you see, my Sunshine?"

"Good enough to eat!"

He leans down to steal a quick kiss and says, "I expect nothing left from my own personal Aphrodite."

When we set off again, we fall into a serene silence. The movement of my legs is meditative, and it quiets my mind. I take in the scenery, which is so gorgeous.

I breathe out, "Conner, I can't wait to do this all the time with you."

He turns around, eyes sparkling, and takes my hand. A few more minutes and we crest the hill and I see our destination. A crested plateau above the ocean with a view takes my breath away. I soak it all in.

Conner unloads our picnic and walks over to remove my backpack. He takes out the blanket and spreads it out. Then he reaches in and pulls out the steamy soccer romance I bought for him on Parent's Weekend.

It's a book called We'll Meet Again by Kelsey Painter. He tells me, "I don't read as fast as you do, Sunshine. Maybe we can read together so I can catch up. Hopefully, we will even get some ideas for later." He winks.

I grin at him and join him on the blanket. We talk as we eat our lunch. I gaze in wonder at the horizon, feeling all the possibilities of our future. My heart is so happy as he talks animatedly about his dream of becoming a U.S. Women's National Team Coach. He thinks it a few years off yet, with a few more winning seasons at UCC, but something in me tells me it will come to him sooner than later.

Our heart's desires are so close to becoming reality, if I close my eyes, I can almost touch them.

After we finish, he takes off his cap and lies down with his head in my lap. I feed him some grapes, which make us both laugh. With one of my hands threading through his hair, I scratch his scalp and pick up the book in my other hand.

Eventually, we switch places, and the sun is warm, but the air, with the ocean breeze, is so pleasant. I lie down on his chest. Conner is using the packs as a backrest, and he has one hand holding the book, the other rubbing circles on my side. Between the warm sunshine, the cool breeze and the melodic sound of his reading voice, I get drowsy and feel myself pulled into a dreamlike state.

I don't know when Conner puts the book down, but I wake sometime later to his arms wrapped around me, with us both on our sides. He is humming low, not asleep. He seems to do that when he is restful, but his body isn't ready to power down. I crack open my eyes and sneak a look at him. He feels my head move the slightest bit and looks down into my face. His eyes search mine with no urgency.

There is no need for words as I feel us both continue to open ourselves to each other. Our soul bond is strengthening. It is a transcendent moment, in which I feel completely seen and whole.

He rubs those same small circles on my back, and I lightly scratch him up and down. We spend the afternoon in this dreamlike state, taking turns reading, snuggling and touching, our hands memorizing what our hearts are learning.

This is our own once in a lifetime love story.

Chapter 33

Conner

Carrie and I are walking in a field holding hands till we see an arch in the distance. She is dressed in a flowing, soft teal gown with sandals and her hair is braided with flowers around the sides. I am in a soft ivory shirt with dark gray pants and dress shoes. There is a sunflower pinned over the left side of my chest and she is holding a bouquet of sunflowers and blue hydrangeas.

The light is hazy, either daybreak or twilight. I can't tell, but I am both excited and nervous. Getting closer to the arch, I notice all our friends and family are there, seated in concentric rings, with my brothers, Carrie's daughters and my coaches sitting nearest the structure.

There is a woman standing directly in front of us, and she smiles. She makes a hand motion, as if to invite us to join her.

Carrie looks at me, smiling and still holding my hand. I take a step forward, leading us into our future.

I wake up from the dream reluctantly and slowly. I rarely dream much at all, so to have such a vivid one of our wedding, I take several moments to savor it. The spot where Carrie was is slightly warm, which means she hasn't been gone long. Her body clock is still two hours ahead of mine.

We fell asleep on the couch watching one of her favorite movies, "Sabrina," after I made fish tacos and coconut rice. It was a wonderful end to a peaceful day, full of growing connection.

As I allow myself to become more awake, I smell the coffee she made, and she started a fire. I get up, slip on some boxer briefs and go out to find her curled up on the couch under a blanket.

She doesn't startle when I put my hands on her shoulders, just puts her coffee cup down, leans her head back to look up at me and smiles.

"Good morning, Sweetness, want to come cuddle me before the fire?"

She opens the blanket up and I see she is wearing the robe I bought her. Thicker than the one she has at home, but a perfect weight for chiller mornings. She is gorgeous and I tell her so. "Sunshine, I think you are the most beautiful in the mornings."

She raises an eyebrow at me and says, "Conner, I'm a mess."

I settle in between her legs, turning to kiss her collarbones, then tell her, "You are a vision, especially now. What are you doing out here by yourself this morning?"

She smiles and pulls me down into her, kissing me lightly on the top of my head while wrapping her legs around my hips. She speaks into my hair when she says, "Meditating on our future. It's very good, you know."

She threads her fingers in my hair and scratches my scalp gently. "Oh, god, Carrie, how can it be anything but good when you know exactly that I like?"

She does her sexy giggle and rubs the inside of her thigh along my hard cock. "I see my favorite part of you is awake. Do I need to pay him some attention?"

I scoot down her body so I can rest my head on her soft middle. My shoulders fit just right across her hips.

I sigh as I say, "Not yet. Sometimes snuggling is more important."

She responds in feigned shock, "You can't be sated yet, my glorious soccer god!"

I look up at her and say seriously, "I'll let you suck my divine cock after I bask in your light a little longer."

I feel her core tighten at my smutty words and know the thought of a morning blow job excites her as much as it does me.

Recalling my dream, I ask her, "Did you have any dreams last night?"

Her energy shifts and she sighs. "Yes, I had two. I'll tell you, but I hope it doesn't kill the mood."

I shake my head. "The mood is like a fire. We can always relight it. I heard you in your sleep. You clearly spoke and were upset. Then you talked to me. Tell me about both. I want to listen."

She sighs again. "One was my reoccurring nightmare–which is actually a memory of when I saw Scott after his heart attack. I never dream much more than this, probably because I lived it, but it's always when I beg him not to leave me. My dad wasn't around much when we were younger, so I think that traumatic memory and the childhood fear of abandonment surface once in a while. It reminds me there is still work to do."

As she speaks, I feel the need to reassure her, so I massage the outside of one of her legs, with light but firm pressure. All I can say is, "I'm so sorry you had to go through all of that."

My heart is so heavy for her and yet so proud of her strength. I press up onto my knees, taking the blanket with me and then pulling her into my lap so she is straddling me. I hug her tightly, locking one arm around her waist and sliding the other hand up under her hair and massaging her neck.

We stay like that for a long moment because I just want to hold her. She presses her face into my neck and breathes. I've learned that sometimes–maybe most of the time–this is exactly what she needs me to do. So, I give her the space for her emotion, full of warmth and understanding. I give her what I have, and I know it soothes her because her body melts into mine.

She sighs and kisses my neck, sitting up to face me. "Want to hear about the other dream?" I nod my assent.

She smiles and tells me, "Well, it was about you. We were walking in a field together, holding hands. We were going towards a semicircle of some kind and lots of people were there. I felt like we'd been apart, so I asked you where you'd been. Want to know what you said?"

This piques my interest as she is describing the same visual in my dream. I don't remember talking to her in mine, but I'm eager to hear what may be a joint dream. It's a crazy thought, but since all of this differs completely from any other relationship I've ever heard of, I will believe it. I nod my head at the same time as I bring my hands up her legs under her robe, to rest on her delicious full hips.

She sucks in a breath at the contact, and her voice comes out in a rush. "You smiled at me and said, 'Well, I have been looking for you, of course.'" She smiles and I have to laugh. It sounds like something I would say.

I lean forward, holding onto her so she doesn't topple off backwards and declare before I kiss her soundly, "Carrie, I've been looking for you my entire life and I'm so glad I found you."

She smiles into my mouth and then opens for my tongue to take control. We lose ourselves and as if they are on autopilot, my hands open her robe to cup her breasts.

She moans as I knead both and my thumbs rub her nipples to peaks. I keep massaging her breasts until as she rocks her hips back and forth over my hard cock. She pulls away from the kiss and pulls me close to her. She loops with one arm around my shoulders and the other around my neck with her hands in my hair and I use the opportunity to latch my mouth onto her nipples, going back and forth. I bring one hand between us and just barely brush her vagina, feeling the wetness.

For a split second, I can't decide what I want to do with her, and it is just enough time for her to moan, "Conner, I want to suck your cock. I need to."

I rumble out, "I will never deny you that, my love. Hold on." I move to stand, and she locks her legs around my hips. I kiss her as I walk us back to the bed. As I set her down, I tell her, "Drop your head off the side of the bed."

She looks slightly confused but obeys. Her robe is completely open, and I can see every inch of her creamy skin as I stand behind her head.

Thankfully, my bed is tall enough where her mouth is at cock height and I fist myself, pumping once or twice while she looks up at me from this new angle. "Want me to fuck your face while I finger-fuck you into oblivion, my Goddess?"

She nods and opens her mouth for me. I hiss out, "Such a good fucking girl," as I slid right in, and she takes me in all the way to the back.

She gags less this way, and I have just enough leverage and length to dip my fingers in-between her open legs to her wet and waiting pussy. She hollows her cheeks and sucks me as I pump my index and middle finger into her with my thumb, moving side to side on her clit.

I get close and my hips pump harder. I know this is rougher than she may have expected, so I back off. Her eyes are streaming, with saliva drips down her face.

Her eyes are unfocused, but then says, "Don't stop, I love it," answering my unspoken question.

I lean down to kiss her upside down and she pulls the back of my head hard into hers. After kissing her for a moment, I tell her, "I want to watch you get yourself off while I come down your throat. Let me get your wand."

I grab her glass wand from her suitcase and quickly smear it with the coconut oil from my nightstand, which she had informed me she prefers to lube. I hand it to her and notice she is panting, eyes wild. She takes the wand from me and lies her head back again, opening wide.

I watch her slide the wand into her waiting pussy and rub her clit. I take my fingers out of her mouth and lean down to kiss her sweetly and say, "I'm so glad I finally found you, my Sunshine."

Her eyes soften, then blaze again with lust as I tap my cock on her lips. She takes me full to the hilt and I can feel the extra slide of the coconut oil.

It only takes a minute or two of watching her suck my cock and fuck herself before I'm done. "Carrie, oh god, Carrie, I'm fucking going to come." At my words, she cries out, whole body shaking as I shoot myself down her throat.

She drinks me down and I pull out, walk around, grab her feet so I can tug her neck flush with the bed. Then I kneel, gingerly taking the wand in my hand. She whimpers as I lick her center where the wand is, to her clit and I bring her through to another orgasm, fucking her with the wand as I suck and lick her clit.

After she is spent, I take the wand out, lay it on the bed. I crawl up to hold her in my arms. I kiss the top of her head and say, "You deserved all of that and more. You are so fucking sexy, Carrie."

She sighs and hugs me closer. We lie there in the afterglow until both of our stomachs grumble.

I chuckle and tell her, "Let's jump in the shower and then I'll make my sex goddess a hearty breakfast."

***

Carrie

My spiritual body may be insatiable when it comes to Conner's body on mine, but my physical body feels every bit of our activity together. It's a delicious and erotic soreness. Similar to the fingertip bruises and love bites he has left all over my body.

With Conner, I feel fully alive, and I whispered that to him before I fell asleep. My fear of losing him has crept up into my dreams. What I went through with seeing Scott die in front of me and then the horror of them trying to revive him makes me fear losing Conner in the same way.

Logically, I know that's impossible, but traumatic responses don't follow logic. They hooked Scott up to so many wires, trying to bring him back. I don't think I can ever be in a hospital again without a severe emotional reactionary freakout.

I don't voice it very much, as this is still all so new to us both. I don't doubt or worry him, even as I'm rooted in the knowledge he understands. His fear is something or someone from the outside will tear us apart. They are related to his experience at Michigan State State, just as my fears are rooted in my journey.

I've committed to myself to continue working through it and not letting it hinder our future together. Because it is so good with Conner, the way he treats me like I'm priceless and precious–a woman of worth and value–my fears are alive and well.

I don't think there will ever be a time when I'm not afraid of loss–losing one of the girls or Conner or anyone else I'm close to.

This relationship is giving me another level of power to not let fear run my life.

As I watch this perfect man for me make breakfast, I feel worlds away from that fear I woke up with. I reheat my protein coffee as he cooks us turkey sausage and pancakes. He makes silver dollar pancakes this time and eats his turkey patty in between two pancakes like a sandwich. I can't help but laugh. This guy is so cute.

"Conner, I love we are learning more about each other this weekend. Seeing you–and the way you take care of me in the big and small ways - makes me fall that much harder for you."

When I tell him this, I'm laughing, but by the end, I have tears in my eyes. He leans across the table, hard muscled chest on full display and a mouth full of food, and kisses me. Our lips press hard and when he pulls away, he just looks at me in wonder.

He doesn't have to say anything. My heart knows exactly what he feels.

We finish breakfast and cuddle a little more. It's late morning, we've taken our time starting the day. Neither one of us is rushing to go anywhere or do anything. I send Elise a text message and she sends me a silly gif of a cat with crazy hair. It must be how she feels. I know she is having a good time with Alyssa. I can't wait to hear about it later.

As I finish texting, I hear Conner call my name from the second bedroom. I walk in and see him stretching on the yoga mat, shirtless in a pair of joggers. I am distracted by all the gorgeous man's flesh on display. He flexes for me and smiles before bringing my attention to the other empty yoga mat beside him. He looks at me from Warrior Two pose and asks, "Want to move a little with me, Sunshine?"

I hurry to his room and change into leggings, a sports bra and a t-shirt.

When I walk back in, he makes a displeased growl and says, "No shirt!" I giggle loudly and strip off the t-shirt and he nods approvingly. I come to the mat beside him, and he leads me through his favorite vinyasa flow. I am not as mobile as he is and can't hold some of the plank-like poses for as long as he can, but he encourages me all the way. I start sweating, but Conner isn't even remotely struggling.

When we turn around so that my back is to him, in the Warrior series, he comes to stand behind me. He adjusts my form and kneads my ass and legs, nearly knocking me off balance. He steadies me and leans down to suck my earlobe between his teeth before whispering, "Sorry, I couldn't help myself."

My smile is huge. I can't help it as I say, "I'll never be sorry to have you touch me." He grunts his praise, and we continue to flow for another thirty minutes. It feels good to stretch out of move my body, especially after all the sex. We finish up the practice lying on our backs and Conner takes my right hand to his left. We stay linked in corpse pose for a long time, just enjoying the silence and breathing with each other.

We both feel it when the energy shifts and it's time to get up and head out on our day date before a romantic dinner tonight. Conner adds a t-shirt and UCC soccer hoodie and invites me to do the same.

"I'm allowed to wear t-shirts out in public, but not at home with you?" Conner comes over to me, puts himself flush against my front and says, "When we are at home together, I want to all the skin. I love your body. Now, let's go have some fun, my Sunshine."

We start at one end of the downtown strip, and I realize halfway through our stroll through downtown, my cheeks hurt because I'm smiling so much. We had a little snack at a delicious coffeehouse, sharing scones and a croque monsieur. Conner had a protein shake before we left the house, otherwise I know he would be ravenous.

We continue to walk through the charming shops, when we come to a jewelry store. Conner tugs me inside and says, "Pick something."

I look at him, surprised, and say, "What? You are buying me jewelry? Why?" I am so surprised. I don't wear a lot of jewelry and now, feeling under pressure, I have a very hard time deciding on what to get. Conner peruses the selections and ends up at the opposite end of the store from me.

I keep looking, not having a clue what I want, and he comes up to whisper in my ear from behind, "Don't worry, Sunshine, I found it." I turn around to see him holding a ring and a necklace, both with the same design–two hearts connected in a filigree pattern. It isn't huge or gaudy, just a sweet, simple design that is, in fact, perfect.

My hand flies to my mouth with a surprised, "Oh!" and take it in for a moment. It is exactly the symbol I would want to represent our relationship visually with two intertwined hearts. They are both white and gold, which is my favorite. He says, "They have different sizes for the ring. I don't know which finger you want to wear it on, if you want to wear it at all. Or the necklace. I love the idea of you wearing something I've given you, but it's up to you."

His voice is laced with vulnerability. This is a big deal for him. Scott bought me lots of jewelry over the years, but I rarely ever wear any of it. I've given quite a bit to the girls and even sold some pieces I really didn't like.

But this, from Conner, I adore. It's classic and understated. It is my taste all rolled into one. As I stand there looking between the ring and the necklace, a decision crystallizes in my heart.

"I would be honored to wear them both, Sweetness. We can get the ring for my left middle finger." The smile I give him feels like it is going to split my face in half.

He wraps me up in the middle of the store in an enormous bear hug. We stay like that for a while before we finally separate to go size the ring and check out. He puts the ring on my finger and the necklace gently around my neck. His fingers linger as he closes the clasp.

On the way out of the store, I spot a bracelet that just seemed to fit him, with a black leather strap connected with white gold clasps inscribed with "Hold Fast." He wanted to wear something I bought him, to keep me close.

We are like giddy teenagers walking out of the store, our arms around each other's waists. We stroll down main street towards the Book Nook and I'm so excited to introduce him to Samson. As we enter, with the bell over the front door ringing, Samson is nowhere to be found. I walk in a little farther and come around the corner, just in time to see Erik backing away from Samson, his cheeks flushed.

He quickly grabs a book, looks in my direction, and pales as Conner walks up behind me. I can feel Conner tense as Erik looks around like he wants to escape. The moment hangs like that - awkward and unresolved.

I'm free in this moment to choose the best way to help my man—and his assistant coach—navigate what could be a life-altering situation for Erik. I don't hesitate to speak up.

"Hi Samson! I made it back sooner than expected and can't wait to hear more of your recommendations!" I call out, waving my hand at him in a sing-song voice Conner has probably never heard. My voice breaks the spell of the tension and Samson, who had been staring intently at Erik, swivels his head towards me. He has a slightly wild look in his eyes, but it shifts quickly to a warm smile.

"Carrie! So good to see you again. I'm so pleased you came back and brought your handsome coach with you this time? Does that mean you both liked the book?" He winks at me and then at Conner, and I hide my grin at his cheekiness.

Conner, my unflappable stud, doesn't miss a beat, walking over to Samson, shaking his hand firmly. "Samson, we devoured it." And winks before saying, "It is so nice to meet you." He turns his head slightly towards where Erik is edging his way towards the literary classic bookshelf which leads to the door.

Erik stops when Conner catches his eye, and Conner nods at him. "Erik, good to see you, man. I know you love to read. This maybe Carrie's favorite place in town, even above my house." He chuckles and pulls me in close to his side. He appears relaxed, but I can feel the tension vibrating through him like a tuning fork.

They stare at each other while Samson and I make small talk. It feels like Erik is trying to decide what to do. In the end, he opts for a quick goodbye.

He meets my eyes and in his delightful accent says, "Good to see you again, Mrs. Vok....I mean, Carrie. I hope y'all are having an enjoyable time together. Right, so I've got some meals to prep for the week, so I'm going to head out." He addresses Samson, and the heat goes up a few degrees in the room when their eyes meet.

Erik gives him the barest of nods and says, "Mate, thanks again."

Conner is trying not to let his gaze bounce back and forth like a ping-pong ball. I can hear the gears in his mind spinning. It's obvious to me what we walked in on, but I'm not about to say anything out of respect for Erik and Samson.

If Erik hasn't come out to Conner, it is not my place to discuss it. I just hope Conner will share what he is thinking and feeling with me later.

I wave at Erik and then step away from Conner's side, to go peruse the fantasy romance table as a distraction even though I've read most everything on it.

With my back turned, I only hear Conner say to Erik, "I'll see you on the pitch Monday morning."

I don't hear Erik respond, and then I hear the front door chime ring as he goes out.

Samson announces, "Well, I need to eat my lunch. I'm starving. Can I trust you two to monitor the place while I go take care of myself in the back?"

His choice of words makes me grin as I raise my eyes to his and say, "Of course you can. I promise I won't take advantage of anything or anyone while you are gone. Scout's honor!" I hold up three fingers and Samson gives a slow chuckle as he walks into the back of the store.

In an instant, Conner wraps his arms around me from behind. His breathing is rapid, just like his heartbeat. I press my head back into his shoulder. He holds me so tight until he finally turns me around and I look up into his face. We don't speak for a few minutes.

He didn't know and is shell-shocked and I know it isn't because he has any issues with homosexuality. He passes absolutely no judgement whatsoever. What I'm reading from him is the shock of finding out this way. I'm sure he would have preferred Erik to come out to him directly. I know his coaching staff tries to keep their personal lives separate, even as he says he knows way too much about Inanna's love life.

I've witnessed the bond the two men formed, and I wonder how this will affect it. So, I say the only thing that comes to mind as I stare into his depthless brown orbs, "Whatever you need, Sweetness, I'm here for you."

I reach up to put my arms around his neck and kiss his lips softly. After a few seconds, he smiles into my lips softly and says, "Not that we needed anything else to talk about, but I guess now have our first 'how do we handle this as a couple,' situation to discuss over dinner."

Chapter 34

Conner

My head is a fucking mess.

I know exactly how Erik feels because that's the way I felt after the photo of Carrie and me kissing after the exhibition match was posted online.

We caught him and Samson in the act. Of what exactly, I don't know, but I know that look.

Samson's face only read desire and Erik's was the same until he saw me. Then it was straight panic.

I don't know how long they've been seeing each other because Erik hasn't ever let on anything about his personal life. He is as private as Inanna is loud. I absolutely detest that it happened this way and there is a worm of distress eating its way through my gut. I can't even wish he had told me. This is his *life,* and he doesn't live it for my comfort.

He has become a good friend, not yet getting into the deep stuff because, well, we are guys.

This changes nothing for me. I've been friends with gay guys my whole life. I have great respect for closeted professional soccer players who not only excel in their sport but also face the challenges of working in a system that nearly forces them to reject who they are.

The stereotypical professional sports player is all about fucking as many women in as short amount of time as possible. I tried to live up to that stereotype until I realized I was the shell of a man. It left me with no joy to rack up conquests. Before the fiasco at Michigan State State, I had one longer-term girlfriend, but after Miranda; I shut it all down because in my mind, no woman, no cry.

Until Carrie, when my universe splintered open and put itself back together around her. Now, with her hand in mine, I can feel the warmth and love flow into me. She keeps glancing at me, no doubt checking on me. She is trying to be sneaky about it, but it's obvious.

It is cute and I tell her so. "Sunshine, I see you looking at me. I'm ok, though."

She snuffles a laugh. "What? I can't admire my amazingly hot *younger* boyfriend while we drive? You are my favorite scenery."

I bring her knuckles up to my mouth as I turn into my neighborhood. "So, you think I'm hot, huh?"

This time, she laughs out loud, a sound I could hear all day long. "Conner Doreland, you know you are hotter than sin. And maybe I am checking to make sure you are ok but really, I'm trying not to be obvious and stare at how gorgeous you are."

I pull into my driveway and park. I turn to face her and say, seriously, and I mean it, "Carrie Volker, I may be hot, but I've never met anyone who radiates love, light and goodness in such a tangible way. If there is ever any doubt who the lucky one is in our pairing, it is me, my only Sunshine."

I can see her melt at my words, leaning close, tilting her head and kissing me. It's a chaste kiss, but behind it is a force of emotion that takes my breath away. The delight in the kiss lingers, and I can't help it. I smile into her lips.

She pulls back, curious, and asks, "What are you smiling about?"

I sigh as I reach up to take her face in my hands and lean forward to give her a peck on both cheeks, then finally again on her lips. Then I look into her eyes and say, "Because you make me feel like no matter what, everything is going to be ok."

She holds my gaze and says, without a shred of hesitation, "That's because it is. How else would we have found each other if it would not be the best possible outcome?'

I smile again into her depthless eyes, and she reaches across to cup the back of my head, lightly using her nails to scratch my scalp.

I groan and say, "God, woman, you are a witch! I'm all yours."

She keeps smiling at me and scratching my head in slow, soft circles before she palms the back of my head and pulls me forward.

Softly kissing me, she leans over to whisper in my ear, "Let's go get ready for our dinner date. We are partners. We will figure out the best way to approach this with Erik." Then she kisses my nose, and we exit the car to get ready.

***

Carrie

We arrive at the same restaurant as the team dinner, but this time, we are seated in a quiet corner on the opposite side of the space, amidst candlelight flickering everywhere. There is a small bouquet of hydrangeas on the table, three to be exact. One white, one blue and one pink.

It is so romantic, and Conner gives me a huge grin as we are seated, with the maître D pulling out my chair and pushing it in for me.

As he leaves, I lean forward to whisper to Conner, "Very well done, sir. You know how to set the mood."

He winks at me, and then our server appears to take our drink order. I order my usual sparkling lemonade, and Conner orders Perrier for the table. The server returns with both sparkling and still water and hands us our menus.

At this moment, I realize I'm starving. We didn't eat lunch, only our early afternoon snack at the coffee shop. I'm grateful

Conner values me healthy and isn't a guy who expects a woman to eat like a bird.

Because I'm going to eat the hell out of dinner. And I know if I am hungry, Conner has to be ravenous.

I rarely order appetizers, since suspect he is going to follow my lead, I ask him, "Sweetness, is it ok if we order an appetizer? I'm famished."

He smiles again, winks at me, already knowing what I was going to say. My laugh is full of delight as I suggest, "Small Charcuterie board, then?" He nods approvingly and tells the server what we want.

I know what I want for the main meal, so I hand him my menu after he takes Conner's.

"You getting your usual steak, soccer god?"

He shakes his head and says, "No, ma'am. I already told them I'll have what she's having."

I chuckle a little about that movie line and wonder if he knows the reference, so I test him.

"You going to give me an orgasm during dinner to make sure I haven't been faking it like Sally?"

Conner grins and then the grin turns into a boisterous laugh, confirming he knew the context of what he was saying. Then he crooks a finger in a "come closer" motion. I lean across the table as he reaches around to grab my chair and yank it next to his.

He leans over to whisper into my ear, "I would be more than happy to make you come again while we wait for our food."

I giggle and shake my head, whispering back, "Definitely another time, my love. Give my pussy a rest. She's gotta have some time to recover."

His smile never changes. "I'll accept that challenge with the time is right."

He leans ever closer and says, "The way your pussy swallows my cock whole, I know it's always been real."

The tone in his voice is so dark and lustful. I shiver.

Just then, our starter arrives. Conner lets me serve myself and take as much as I want. Then he consumes the rest. I enjoy several slices of house made bread fresh out of the oven with my cheese and olives and watch him tuck in. I can tell it takes the edge off, so I ask what's on my mind.

"Conner, how are you about what happened with Erik? We don't have to talk about it if you aren't ready. We have plenty to discuss when it comes to our future."

I give him a big smile, but the one he returns is a little weaker. "No, Sunshine, I need to talk it out. My head is a fucking mess about it."

I take his hand over the table, and he visibly relaxes. I rub my thumb across his knuckles like he usually does to me, and he lets out a long sigh. He begins verbally processing what we saw, what he thinks, and his experience. There were a couple of teammates over the years who felt he was safe enough to come out to and he treated every situation with respect and dignity, lending them his full support.

I say little, only affirm him when there is a break in his stream of consciousness and prompt him with any clarifying questions. As he winds down, our main meal arrives with my second lemonade. We both dig into the house special, a chicken and shrimp dish that is both unusual and delightful. We switch to light conversation about the food, enjoying each other's company and the meal.

It isn't till we are waiting on dessert–house made mint chocolate chip gelato for me and chocolate souffle for Conner, who chose it because he "wanted to see how his stacked up to a pastry chef,"–when Conner says to me, "I really don't know what to do. Should I say something to Erik or just let him come to me?"

I pause and again take his hand. I can tell how much this is bothering him. Erik has become a friend, and I know Conner doesn't want to lose that connection. He doesn't want an employer-employee relationship with Erik. He and Inanna have each other's backs, and he wants that with Erik, too. It is hard for him to trust people after his experience as a pariah at Michigan State.

For anyone, the possibility of losing a friend is scary. As someone with more than enough experience with relationship loss, I tell him what I believe from my heart.

"Conner, you value Erik. Not just as a coach, but as a person. That comes through in who you are, not just in your words. You are a man of integrity and have such a huge heart. I think you will know exactly what to say and do when the time comes.

Give him some time to come to you and I know he will. It's not a one-sided friendship at all, I can tell. Trust yourself and it might just surprise you how easy it will be to reconnect after the troubled waters calm."

He is staring deeply into my eyes, and I see so much emotion swirling in him. The low light makes them almost merge with his black pupils and his expression is so open, accepting and flat-out trusting. It makes my heart clench. I do the only thing I can think of, which is lean over to kiss him.

The warmth of his lips slows my heart that had started to race and stabilizes my breathing. He is quickly becoming my personal source of strength. I know too many of my friends with men in their lives who don't, won't or can't receive advice from women. I feel the emotion crawl up my throat at the reality of being with a man who truly wants to know what I'm thinking and be connected through our shared understanding.

We don't deepen the kiss, but it's extended. So long, in fact, the server awkwardly clears his throat when he arrives at the table to deliver our dessert. We were lost in each other and had no clue. He smiles at me, embarrassed but happy for us. He nods at Conner and then takes his leave.

We share our desserts with each other, both making borderline erotic sounds at how good it is. It is truly divine, and I think I'm going to have to loosen my belt a notch. I'm so full. I don't know what we are going to do next. Conner said we would go out after dinner before heading home.

As we leave the restaurant and get in the car, we are both quietly holding hands. I watch his long fingers maneuver the steering wheel. We don't drive long but go uphill. He puts the car in park and gets out. He comes around to open my door as I unbuckle myself. He offers his hand after he opens my door for me. When I take it and look beyond his handsome face, I gasp.

We are at a park on a cliff side overlooking the ocean. The moon is full, and the light is shimmery and bright. He tucks my hand into the crook of his arm, and we take a long walk, enjoying the view. Our conversation returns to our future together, and he notices when I shiver. He gives me his coat, warm and smelling of his spicy sandalwood scent.

I want to bathe in that scent, here in the moonlight. I mentally add that to my dream wish list of things to do with Conner–take a bath with him in the moonlight. I know he will make it come true.

He stops walking and pulls me to his chest. My head fits neatly into his neck, right at his throat.

We hold each other in the embrace, and Conner hums. He sways as he hums several tunes. He moves us slowly, bringing my hand out in his and using his other arm to hold me securely in a graceful hold.

He starts a small one-two shuffle step, and we slow dance together around the park.

If other people are in the park, I wouldn't know. My mind is quiet, fully present with Conner. This is the most romantic experience I've ever had, and nothing can break the spell. We sway for a long time, even after he stops humming, reveling in the moment. It is like we are on the moon, far away from everything and everyone else.

As the air cools and I shiver again under his blazer, Conner kisses me softly, then leads me back to his car. We continue to hold hands on the drive back to the house, where I go through my nighttime routine. I was wearing my hair up to show off my necklace, and I can practically hear my scalp sigh in relief.

I leave my necklace and ring on and wrap myself up in my robe. Conner is in a pair of sleep pants and is shirtless, man meat all on display. He chooses our movie, this time one of his favorites, which surprises me.

"Sunshine, you haven't lived till you've seen Casablanca. I took a film course in college and the professor blew our minds."

I think about warning him I may not last very long, curled up safe and warm in his arms, so it really doesn't matter what movie he picks. He settles himself on the couch and I curl up between his legs, my head on his chest, the reverse of our position this morning when he found me out here after meditating.

It is the perfect place to fall asleep and maybe ten minutes into the movie; I do.

Chapter 35

Conner

Carrie's ability to fall asleep during a movie is truly majestic. Sleeping so soundly, I don't think she remembers me getting her up at the end and moving her to the bed. I left her in her robe as I didn't want to wake her, taking it off and get into the cold sheets. She lays down in the bed and lets out a long, sleepy, happy sigh when I snuggle up to put my arms around her from behind.

The peace I feel about sleeping with her is going to be sorely missed when she leaves tomorrow. I don't let my mind wander too far down that path as I lie there in the dark listening to her mumble. I bring myself back in a meditative style to this moment with her and drift away to dream.

In the early morning, I wake up to an empty bed. I panic as the bed next to me is cold and my conscious mind immediately thinks something is wrong. It races that maybe I've been dreaming the whole last month and now I'm finally awake. I take a second to gain my bearings. Looking around the room, I notice the bathroom light is on and that's when I hear it.

A small, pitiful sound. It's muffled but clearly, Carrie is in the bathroom crying.

Immediately, I leap up and go to the bathroom door. I knock softly and ask, "Sunshine, are you ok? Can I come in?"

She hesitates to answer me and I'm about to ask again when I finally hear a little, "Ok, come in."

I open the door and walk in, see that Carrie is naked, on the toilet and her robe is on the floor. It has blood on it, which alarms me until I realize she started her cycle. That doesn't explain why she is crying, so I pad over, kneel in front of her and put my hands on her thighs.

"What is it? Why are you crying?"

She sniffles, wiping the tears and her runny nose with some toilet paper. She takes a deep, shaky breath and says, "I started my cycle nearly a full week early. I'm cramping a lot, and I feel so bad for ruining our last night and morning together."

My heart breaks a little if she thinks I'm going to be bothered by something as natural as her period.

I smile gently, kiss her knees, and ask, "Why does this ruin it? It doesn't for me at all."

She sniffles again and leans forward to put her forehead on mine. "It's just messy and unexpected. I saw in my mind about how I was going to wake you up with this amazing blow job and this was definitely not part of the plan."

I chuckle at that, even as my dick, God bless him, gets incredibly hard at the thought of a morning blow job. I take a deep breath to channel the flood of desire coursing through me and she notices.

She lets out a melancholy sigh. "See what I mean? Ruined."

I sit back on my heels enough to take her face in my hands. She looks up at me and I catch the tears as they fall. I lean forward to kiss her lips and softly whisper, "Waking up with you is more than enough. It's perfect, no matter what."

She slow blinks and sighs again. "But I have nothing with me. It is so early; I don't know what to do. It explains my emotional outburst in the car on Friday night. I'm usually sensitive when I'm in my luteal phase. Unfortunately, I didn't know I was in that phase!"

She sounds frustrated and I think fast to walk her back from the edge of being super pissed off at herself. That will not help her body feel better.

"My love, tell me what you need. I'll go get it and while I'm gone, you can take a shower. Let me get you some pain relief. Then I'll run out and when I get back, I'll give you a pelvic massage."

I wink at her, and she laughs.

She takes a deep breath and lets it out, her warm breath coasting over my face and neck. "Some pain relief will help. And for now, I would love a back and leg massage. The pain is intense, radiating down my legs."

With directions to move in, I stand. I turn on the shower for her, the temperature near scalding like she likes. I hand her the pain reliever from my bathroom cabinet and grab the robe from the floor.

At that, she stops me with a word. "Conner, if you have hydrogen peroxide, use that to remove the blood before you wash it. It works the best. You might have to use it on your sheets, too."

She looks embarrassed at that, but I reassure her it's fine as I assimilate this new information into my grocery list.

I pull on a hoodie, socks and my trainers before I realize I do not know what products she uses. Carrie is in the shower now, so I pop my head in, getting an eyeful of the most delicious set of tits as she washes them.

I can't help my grin. She notices me and puts her arms up under her breasts, plumping them together and making them bounce.

I growl, "Sunshine, unless you want me to get in there with you and suck those beautiful tits dry, don't distract me. If you didn't need taking care of in another way, I would do just that." She blows me a kiss and I'm relieved to see the shower is relaxing.

I continue, "Tell me what you need me to get."

She describes a product I've never heard of before, a menstrual disc. She assures me they will be at any drugstore, and she is right. I make quick work of my errand, the brand she usually uses right on the shelf and grab some hydrogen peroxide and a bag of dark chocolate peanut butter cups for good measure. They are her favorite and I figure at a time like this, it could only help to bring her a treat.

I get back as she is getting out of the shower, and I hand her the package. She smiles, leans up and kisses me, face still damp. I pull her into me, and she lets out one of those breathy sighs that I know means she is happy.

I lean down and whisper in her ear, "Get yourself settled and I'll meet you in the kitchen. Wear anything of mine you want."

She emerges from the bathroom looking much better than when I found her, cramps subsiding with the medicine, hot water and the promise of caffeine. I've already mixed in the protein powder into blistering hot coffee.

She comes over to me, takes the coffee from my hand, sets the cup down before she wraps her arms around me.

I return the hug as she buries her face in my neck. We don't move for a little while, content to hold each other barefoot in the kitchen. It feels ordinary but, at the same time, extraordinary.

I want to hold her like this for the rest of my life.

I tell her so and she whispers, "Let's do it, Sweetness." We pull apart and she sighs again as she drinks her coffee. She compliments my preparation and sits across the counter, waiting patiently as I measure out all the ingredients for our breakfast.

After we eat, we move to the couch, and I rub her back, hips, quads, and hamstrings. Years of attention from team trainers means I know what to do. "Still hurting, Sunshine?" I ask as I tenderly knead out the tight right hip flexor.

She shakes her head, relaxing into my touch. Then she asks, "What are we going to do until it's time for me to leave?"

Mentioning going home today breaks a little of the spell we are under, but she's right. We need to talk about our plans, so I suggest, "How about we just spend the morning cuddling and talking through what the next few months will look like? Does that sound good?"

She smiles her big, bright smile at me and my heart catches. I can't believe that smile is all mine. Planning the next few months of back and forth–and meeting for weekend games - is easy and I know that whatever comes, we will work it out together.

**

Carrie

Leaving Conner is bittersweet. Long distance was never something I wanted, but I know it is only temporary. Knowing the game schedule helps because I can plan my travel to see him and Elise. I'd already planned to be away most weekends with Sabrina taking over Schroeder care and house-sitting.

She is there when I get home, and I realize she's been sleeping in my bed. It makes me laugh on the inside because when she was a teenager; she spent more time in the master bed than she did her own some days. It's dark, quiet but still on the ground floor where she can keep her finger on the pulse of the house activities. My middle daughter loves to know what's going on with everyone else, with the option to engage, or not, when she feels like it.

When I get home from the airport around 11 pm, she is sound asleep. I decide not to wake her, just sending a text, letting her know I'm home and upstairs in Maley's room. Maley has the second most comfortable bed in the house, which is another reason Sabrina spends so much time in mine. Her bed is ok, but it isn't as big or as soft as the master bed.

I leave her the rest of my dark chocolate peanut butter cups on the kitchen counter. I head to upstairs to get ready for bed, which doesn't take long. Conner took the edge off my cramps with his care and a long love-making session with several orgasms just before I had to pack up and leave.

It was a little messy, but it didn't faze him in the least. I couldn't imagine a more perfect man who doesn't bat an eye at bodily functions. I tell him at the airport as he was dropping me off, I was good for the blow job the next time I saw him and he pulled me in for a scorching kiss before biting my neck and whispering, "I will hold you to that, my only Sunshine."

After dreaming all night of being in a movie, the scenes changing so rapidly I couldn't keep up. I wake up rested when my alarm goes off. I'm headed into the office and at the end of the week, Gena and I plan to announce the transition of the company into her hands. Sabrina is already gone to work when I come downstairs.

When we make the announcement about Gena buying the company, the feedback is varied but unsurprising.

"I think this is a brilliant move, Carrie." My best client services rep, a woman named Nadia, declares several times. She never fails to see the potential of change.

"I have some reservations. Could we meet to discuss this?" asks an email from our legal counsel, Jerrod, who always has a reservation for anything new.

With Gena taking over, nothing truly changes. She is already–de facto–running the company. We've built a culture on an open feedback loop, accountability and opportunity for all. That will not be any different and most know that.

In our regular lunch meeting, I look at Gena and tell her, "This is an opportunity to clear out those folks who are struggling with the vision and performance. You know who they are."

She nods.

She knows exactly who is of the most value to her vision for this company in the future, and who isn't. She is the COO and the last stop before anything hits my desk. If it doesn't go through her first, I never see it. It is the way we worked best, even when Scott was alive.

We ordered in because we both forgot our lunches and have been taking respite in my office for longer than our usual lunch.

After thoughtfully chewing her turkey burger, she says seriously, "I will take care of this company and see it through to the next level. Your minority stake in it will be lucrative, you know that. Nothing you and Scott have done will be wasted. It will just get even better." She smiles a Cheshire cat grin as she holds up her bottle of sparkling water in salute, to which I respond in kind with my lemonade.

I know this company, that has almost been like another child to me, is in the best hands. It is time for me to think about my next steps. My business plan for my Coaching Practice is in place. I am tracking my goals with the close out of my role in this company and the launch of the new.

It's all up against the backdrop of UCC moving into their NCAA season and I want to be there for it all. Gena switches gears to ask me what I've sketched out for the new enterprise, and she nods in approval.

"Email it to me and I'll give you my feedback."

"Done." I tell her as I press send on the note on my phone. We catch up on each other's personal lives, and I'm grateful to take a mental break from thinking and talking about the company sale, which has been all I've been focused on all week. It's what women do best–fly through a hundred different topics in less than fifteen minutes.

I share my travel schedule, and she laughs. "How are you going to have all the sex you want with all those kids, including Elise, running around?" I shrug and grin. She snorts and once again raises her glass bottle, "Here's to trying, anyway."

She cackles and then looks at her watch. It's time to get back to work. A low-grade stress headache has been hovering around my eyes and temples for the last two days. As I rub some of the tension out of my forehead, I sigh and say, "I'm ready for the weekend. My flight leaves at 7:30 pm."

She snorts and says, "You and me both. Get ready. This is just the beginning." I know what she means. People will take the weekend to process and there will be more questions to answer, especially from a few folks well-known as stirrers of the pot.

As if her comment conjured him, as I'm on my way out to catch my plane, I ride down in the elevator with one gentleman who has been at the company far too long, thanks to being fraternity brothers with Scott. He leveraged that fact nearly every time we saw each other, and his parting shot gives me the opening I need.

"You know Carrie, I always liked you. Well, I liked you because I knew I could trust Scott would be firm with you if you got too far out of hand. He had balls, you know. All the way back in our college years together. Honestly, my pause with Gena is without a male in her life, she will run this company I've seen thrive into the ground."

I look him dead in the eye as the heat of my anger at his words cascades from my scalp to the bottom of my feet. I am coated with righteous feminine rage.

I smile before I say, "John, thank you. You've given me just what I need to set this company up for success." He returns my smile before his face turns into stark confusion at my next words.

"You're fired. I've been looking for a reason to get rid of you for years because of your mediocrity. But the connection to Scott, you never let me forget, kept you employed. However, your words violate our company ethics. As I am still CEO, I can confidently say you have no place here—now or in the future."

We reach the lobby, and I stop him from getting out with an arm across the open elevator bay as I press the button to return to my company's floor with my other hand. "I'll escort you upstairs, where you can pack your shit. You'll get your last check in the mail." Then, I press the number for security in my phone, telling them to meet me at the door to the office.

His shock is palpable, as if I slapped him across the face. It leaves him mute as the beefy security guard watches him pack his desk and escorts him out of the office.

As he walks out, I hold up a hand to stop him. My rage peaks and I reach over to snatch the badge off his belt loop, whispering, "Who has the balls now, John?"

Chapter 36

Conner

Traveling south to play UCLA is an ordeal I am happy to not oversee. I have a passion for coaching women, and while these women are highly skilled, it can still be difficult to get them all on board and organized. They all arrive on time, but the noise level is deafening.

At one point, I hear Inanna mutter, "Freaking cats. It's like herding freaking cats."

Erik and I sit together in the bus's front per usual. Even though we've worked out a few times, we are still recovering from the fallout at the Book Nook. It hasn't hindered his work, or mine, but there is a slight strain on our friendship. He glimpses my audiobook app on my phone, as I put on my noise-canceling headphones, a gift Carrie sent this week. She's traveled with Elise's club teams enough to know earbuds don't always do the trick to drown out the noise.

Erik raises an eyebrow at me when he sees my screen. I shrug because I will not deny my Sunshine her request to listen to the very spicy fantasy book, the first in a series.

Erik chuckles and responds, "I know that book. Samson suggested it. Don't be getting hard next to me on this trip, especially when the pirate finally catches his princess. She stabs him with a pocketknife and then he 'stabs' her with something else." He waggles his eyebrows at me and then cracks up at his own joke.

Thanks to his lewd joke, the tension between us eases a bit.

As an olive branch, Erik tells me how he met Samson - the same day Carrie did. They started texting and finally got serious about ten days later when Samson handed him a copy of Leaves of Grass by Walt Whitman. Bastard is damn good at keeping a secret, I'll give him that.

Carrie is flying in tonight. It won't give us a lot of time together, but I'll take thirty-six hours over nothing. We had an intense discussion about whether she should get her own room. Elise will stay with her suite mates, and everyone knows about us. So, I was in favor of her staying with me. She was uncomfortable about it and kept talking about 'keeping up appearances.'

In the end, it was Elise who broke the stalemate.

On their regular weekly FaceTime call, Carrie mentioned having her own room. She hadn't said a word to Elise about being upset, but Elise has that sixth sense for her mom and put her finger right on the spot.

Apparently, she rolled her eyes and says, "Mama, if you still care what people think about you and Coach, you are wrong. You are together so BE TOGETHER." Then she hung up the phone, and that was that.

In recounting it to me later, Carrie says, "She's going to be a nightmare for her opposing council–and the judge–in chambers."

After we arrive at the hotel near the UCLA campus, I unpack my bag in our room as the team gets settled. We always have dinner brought into the hotel the night before a game. After a game, the ladies go out, unless it's a terrible loss. If that happens, we bring pizza and have a game night. I've learned that after a big loss, that's when the team needs each other the most.

However, that will not happen this season.

Carrie texts me she's arrived right in the middle of dinner. I take my leave to meet her at the check-in desk. When she meets my eyes, my chest constricts. I know it's been a long week and dealing with the news of the company sale with several employees was taxing. Her flight was also delayed because of the weather, but she used the time to fill out paperwork after firing some douchebag in the elevator. It's nearly eleven p.m. to her body clock, even though my watch reads nine.

She hugs me tight around the neck and I feel her relax against me. I whisper in her ear, "I'm here, Sunshine. Don't worry, I've got you."

I know she is still getting used to the idea of someone taking care of her. She doesn't cry, but when she pulls back to look into my eyes; I see the tears swimming in her bottomless blue eyes. I cup her face and we look at each other for a long moment before we hear a familiar voice say, "Mama!" from down the hall.

Carrie's face immediately lights up, the effect of seeing any of her daughters.

Elise and Carrie reunite, and I take Carrie's bag as Elise walks her down the hall to the conference room for some dinner. I saved her a plate, which she takes up to our room but not before commenting on how well the team has made the room look like a sleepover in progress.

The ladies brought down their comfy items after dinner and got settled. Tonight was Inanna's movie pick–so we are watching "Moana." Erik gets the next one, which he has already announced is "Australia," which made everyone roll their eyes. I round out the rotation, and this will be the fifth year in a row I lead off with "Braveheart."

I've been called a cliché neanderthal and I'm ok with it.

Carrie retires to eat and shower while I finish the movie with the team. When I join her upstairs, I find her asleep.

I strip off my clothes and climb in next to her. She gives a warm purr of happiness and opens her eyes as I tell her, "I'm sorry to wake you." She puts my hand on her back and says, "Just touch my skin."

I know exactly what that means, and our connection happens at lightning speed. She might have been dozing, but my Sunshine is ready for me. Gently, dragging my fingertips across her back and hip ignites us both, and we come together quickly. I kiss her senselessly in our favorite position–missionary. I hold myself back as long as I can, but given we've been a part for the week, it's not long.

She cries out with several orgasms, and I join her in the gush. After letting our breath settle together, I push off of her to grab a washcloth and we clean up before I tuck her into my side, and we are both asleep before eleven.

Carrie sleeps through my alarm, which is just as well. This is her chance to rest after such a long week. I quietly leave to meet with my coaching staff for breakfast and pre-game strategy.

Knowing Carrie in my bed is better than six shots of espresso.

The game itself is tough. UCLA is rebuilding their team and recruited a very good striker. They are crisp with their passes and have an eye on our plays. The first half was scoreless, even as my offense took some excellent shots. Both teams have energy to spare, but Erik made sure their legs will never run out.

Going into the locker room at half-time, I say very little. Inanna breaks it down, then turns it over for a team discussion. They all agree to make some adjustments in placement.

I finally speak just before we head back to the field. "Great job defense and offense, you are in the right places. Their defense is softer on the right side. Watch out for that left side fullback. She is a beast. The keeper is getting tired. Keep hammering her and play the game you know how to play. You got this, it's all there. Now it's time to execute."

We break on three and we are off to the races. Being so coachable and game smart, the team immediately adjusts, and we score in the first six minutes of the second half. They continue to follow the plan and stay in majority possession the entire half. The opposing offense gets no real shots as our defense easily handles their attempts. UCLA panics when we go up by two with ten minutes left to go.

At one point, I look at Carrie, and she is looking at me. She places her hand over her heart, and I smile because she told me that when she gives me that signal, it means she loves me. It makes my adrenaline surge.

I make some substitutions, including bringing Elise out, and she gives me a tight smile. She hates to come out when there is still time on the clock, but I need some fresh legs for the remaining minutes. The subs do their job perfectly and we beat UCLA for our first win in division play.

I can feel our momentum picking up speed and I love it.

Now, it's time for the team to celebrate on their own. I have my lady to wine, dine and then make her beg for mercy till its time to sleep.

***

Carrie

I slept till after eight and it was glorious. When I hugged Conner at the check-in desk, it was like all the tension from the week–having to hold it all together–drained right out of me.

I get my workout in and get to the stadium to sit with the other parents who made the trip and witness the first division win for my daughter and her team. We are an obnoxiously loud cheering section, and it bonds us for what should be an epic season.

After the team all depart to find dinner and hang out on the town, Conner takes me to a cute little bistro down the street. It's a nice dinner alone which surprises me. I was kind of hoping Inanna and Erik would join us, so I can get to know them, but both had plans to meet up with someone special. Inanna has an old friend with benefits here in town, and Erik with Samson over Facetime.

I hope UCC benefits from all their coaches channeling their explosive sexual energy. As Conner pays the check, I comment his coaching staff must be the most relaxed in the country.

As the waiter walks away, he laughs and says, "Why is that my only Sunshine?"

He offers his hand for me to stand and leads me out of the restaurant with our fingers interlaced. As we emerge from inside the restaurant to a rapidly cooling night, I tell him, "Because everyone is getting their brains fucked out."

Conner roars and pulls me in for a kiss. He pulls back and looks at me, those golden-brown eyes shining, "To be fair, it was never Inanna and Erik who weren't getting some. It was just me. But that's never going to be a problem again, now is it, my little vixen?"

My core tightens and swirls as he leans down for a searing kiss. Then he whispers, "Are you ready for me to show you what I've learned?"

Conner, as a side quest, has been researching Shabari rope play. I nod as my mouth goes dry. I've never been tied up. I randomly selected 'Oklahoma' as my safe word. This will be a first for us both. As we walk back to the hotel, Conner holds me tight against him.

I am so keyed up with the thought of what he will do to me, my legs are a little wobbly.

He stripes us both bare when we get back to the room. As always, he is tender and sweet before he lays me back on the bed, kissing me softly around my face, ears, until he finally bites my neck on my favorite spot, and I moan.

He pulls the ropes from where he secured them under the bed, and I watch him move. His body is mouthwatering. But I'm nervous and my nerves make me self-conscious. He notices and distracts me.

"Sunshine, you are beautiful. Holy, even. I can't believe I have earned your trust so thoroughly." He keeps talking as he drags the ropes he will use to secure my hands and ankles across my breasts, then down my middle and over both legs.

He ties up my ankles first with a single column tie, then pulls my other leg out wide. Then he pulls my arms out at a similar angle, so I am spread eagle before him. He sits back on his heels to admire his handiwork for a moment, then comes over to kiss me again, this time plundering my mouth with his tongue. The kiss tells me just how much he is enjoying this, and it only heightens my desire. My head swims as he pulls back, and I feel like I have a fever. He touches my skin like he did last night, applying only slightly more pressure, so he doesn't tickle me too much.

I am shivering; he is teasing so much. His fingertips dance and when he adds his mouth, first kissing down my sides, then blowing warm breath over my nipples, I nearly come. Even making love to me, he has never taken this long. I whisper, "Conner, I'm going to go insane if you don't touch me."

He smiles devilishly and says, "I am touching you, Sunshine," as his fingers and lips continue their maddeningly slow onslaught.

I wriggle in my bindings, not uncomfortable but alive like never before. The buildup of pleasure is almost painful, as he finally comes face to face with my pussy. He blows, this time across my clit and I lose my breath. He then softly bites his way down the inside of one thigh to the back of my knee before coming up to the other side.

He leans over and kisses my clit, making me moan low.

I hear him whisper, "So pretty. So wet."

Then he is gone.

My shock knocks the wind out of me, and I call out for him. He doesn't immediately answer, and a sliver of worry crosses my mind. I pick my head up to look around the room, but quickly the angle makes my neck cramp. Turning my head to the left, I finally catch sight of him. He is standing in all his naked glory, just watching me, a self-satisfied smile on his face and his cock hard and pointing directly at me. He doesn't immediately move to me, but with the heat of electricity between us, I relax, knowing it won't be long.

It isn't more than another few beats before I feel his weight come beside me on the bed and suddenly, his hands are everywhere as his mouth crashes down on mine. His fingers find my soaking core and it takes only a second of his stroking to bring me to my first climax, which makes my head feel like it is going to pop off.

Breaking the kiss only to allow me to cry out and breathe, before bringing his fingers up to his mouth and licking all of me off. Bending his head to take my left nipple in his mouth, I cry out from the sensation so soon after such a powerful release. He sucks and then uses his hands to cup both my breasts, taking turns on my nipples till I'm close to coming again.

I want to touch and hold him so badly, but his knots are secure. He flips around, so that his face comes down to my pussy and his thick cock land just above my mouth. Spread as wide as I am, he has easy access, and he goes to work, which feels incredible. I can sense the build deep inside my abdomen and I lick his tip before sucking his length down. He moans into me as I taste his salty pre-cum in the back of my throat.

The image I have of us nearly makes me come again and I'm shaking after he fingers me, while he licks my clit and labia, rubbing just inside the right spot. When he adds his pinky finger into my asshole, I buck off the bed, which makes me take him so deep I gag.

He pulls back to look at me, asking in a low voice, "Did you like that or do you want me to stop?" I pull off his cock and whimper in an urgent, pleading voice, "Don't stop!"

He growls in pleasure and says, "My good girl gets whatever she wants," and comes up to flip around. With one tug, he pulls the ties loose on my ankles. He grabs my legs, placing one knee over each shoulder. He doesn't waste a moment once he is in position, sliding his cock straight into my waiting core.

Conner pumps in and out firmly and reverently as he kisses me. My arms are still splayed out, and he takes one last look at them before I feel him tighten up. He calls my name out in my ear as my pussy closes around him. This time, it is his orgasm that pulls me into mine. We stay wrapped up in each other until he reaches out with both hands to release the ropes securing my arms.

He pushes up and off me and gathers me into his arms. He rubs where the ropes left indentions and then settles me onto the bed. He goes into the bathroom and returns with a washcloth to clean both of us up.

As we get settled into bed, I feel a little lightheaded from the intensity of the experience. I tell him that, so he makes sure I'm comfortable as he spoons me from behind. I sink into the mattress, his warmth comforting me from behind. I turn my face back to his and tell him, "I love our adventures together."

I can feel his smile as he kisses my shoulder. "Here is to a lifetime of more adventures with you, my only Sunshine."

Chapter 37

Conner

The next three weeks of division play are a wash, rinse, repeat cycle of Carrie flying out to our games, dragging in on Friday, then sleeping in on Saturday. After the game, we continue to build our relationship through adventures and the growth that comes from keeping ourselves open.

I've closed myself off because of fear and ego nearly my whole life. I don't want to miss anything with her. That want requires me to do my work, especially put aside my ego. We both are.

When she met us for our game up against Washington State in early November, I took a different flight back from the team and stayed with Carrie an extra day. We did a short hike to Hell's Gate Canyon, on the border with Idaho. It was incredible to see the depth of the canyon. Looking across it, I felt like my life had been an exercise in crossing a space this wide to find Carrie. I told her so.

As the late Fall mid-afternoon sun showered us with light and warmth, she turned to me and said, "Now that you've made it across, never let me go."

I've never wanted to get down on one knee so badly in my life. That's coming, and it's coming soon.

My dreams get closer with every win UCC has. With three quarters of the season gone, we are still undefeated, and that means we are going to have a big target on our backs during the NCAA tournament. It's just over three weeks away, on the other side of Thanksgiving break.

As we have one of our nightly chats, Carrie tells me. "Conner, I think you should definitely see your family. We can work things out for you to come here over Christmas."

"Sunshine, I want to experience this holiday with you."

"Yes, but your nieces and nephews are asking for you! How can you deny them their Funcle?"

I chuckle at that. "Yes, I am definitely the Fun-Uncle. Perk of having lots of disposable income that can be spent on their every whim when I'm in town."

She keeps pressing, "All the more reason for you to go. They need all those candy and toys, pre-Christmas presents."

My chuckle is weaker this time when I say, "I know. Tournament season usually leaves me wiped, so Christmas is hard. I always have more energy on Thanksgiving. And Misti is a fantastic cook."

"Then it's decided, go to see Joel and his family. I'll see you not too long after that in North Caroline for the tournament."

My mild frustration peaks as I growl, "I'm not getting what I want here, Sunshine."

Carrie bursts into song with, "You can't always get what you wantttttt." Her efforts to distract me don't quite hit the mark, but I laugh, regardless. I love she can be as silly and goofy as she wants with me.

She can tell I am still holding on to a shred of hope of coming to see her, so she tries another. "Sweetness, I know you will miss my pussy most of all."

That gets a true chortle out of me, and I tell her, "You know I love being buried inside you any chance I can get. Truthfully, I had a different image in my mind of how this Thanksgiving would go. It completely focused on experiencing your family traditions. I know mine. I only want to be with you, Carrie."

She sighs in that romantic way only women can but holds her ground. "We will figure out how to make both happen next year. I promise."

I sniff, "And I know you always keep your promises, even if you take a little while."

She snickers at that, "Still holding onto a resentment about taking so long to send you that first sexy pic, are we?"

I confirm our inside joke again. "Yep, you are going to get another bite on your ass for it too when I see you."

She purrs, "Oh, yes, Coach. Mark me up."

At that point, our call derails into a phone sex session. I can't refuse my insatiable Sunshine. After we finish and she drifts off into sleep, my mind is crystal clear. I don't know why I didn't think of it before, but it makes perfect sense.

I'll spend the first few days of the break with Joel and his family, then I'll fly down to surprise Carrie on Thanksgiving Day. Here's hoping a local florist will open for me to get her some flowers because what kind of romantic figure would I be if I didn't appear on her doorstep without flowers in hand.

I text Joel my plans and make the arrangements while the love of my life mumbles in her sleep over the phone with me. I can't wait to see the look on her face.

***

Carrie

Thanksgiving, as always, is my favorite holiday. Sure, it's a ton of work but without the added pressure of presents and making sure everything is perfect. The week leading up to Thursday means our house is a revolving door for the girls coming in and out with friends. I make four extra trips to the store just to keep up with the demand for snacks, especially for Elise and her high school teammates, back visiting their families.

Maley and Sabrina join the troupe with their retinue of friends on Tuesday, both having taken most of the week off. Thanksgiving is one of the few times of the year I can count on all of them being in the house for an extended period. I'm grateful for it. It's focused and concentrated time together we all need.

The only piece of the puzzle missing for me is Conner. He debated on coming here for Thanksgiving, but I knew he wanted–and needed- to see his family. I told him to go see his brothers and we would figure out having them down–out of the frigid Upper Midwest winter.

Long distance love is not for the faint of heart. I only saw him ten days ago, but every cell in my body aches for him. I am in the luteal phase of my cycle, which only makes my emotions more intense. This month, it is like I'm enveloped in a cloud of blue. My body feels heavy, lacking my normal energy even as I'm overjoyed to be with my girls, but the sunshine of my personality is tempered with rain. Conner spends each night patiently listening and comforting me as I work through it all. It's so stabilizing to be heard. Conner doesn't treat me like a project to be fixed.

I'll see him next weekend, in our first regional game for the NCAA tournament. Elise is nervous but trying not to let it show. The sisters talk a lot, late into the night, the first night everyone is in the house. They soothe her soul like nothing else, having built a bond stronger than blood after their father's death.

The night before Thanksgiving, just before ten p.m., during my nightly chat with Conner, she comes to my door.

"Hey Conner, Elise wants to talk. I'll call you in the morning."

He calls out his nickname for her in greeting, "Hey El! Ok, Sunshine, sleep well and y'all have fun tomorrow. I wish I was there to see the circus!"

I laugh and tell him, "Soon your circus and your monkeys!"

He chuckles his response, "Indeed. See you tomorrow."

I'm so focused on Elise as I hang up, I miss the comment, "What's up, Buttercup?"

"Mama, I can't stop thinking about the tournament. It's such a big deal. Can I sleep with you tonight?"

I smile, so pleased. Elise more than anyone loves to sleep in my bed, even if it is likely she will return to her own in the middle of the night. Even when she was sick as a child, she would tell me to go back to my bed. "Mama, you make the bed hot!"

I open up the covers and she crawls in, laying her head on my shoulder. I fall asleep first, rolling onto my right side, and when I wake up around seven the next morning, the other side of the bed is mussed but empty. I have my coffee and meditate in the quiet, knowing the work the girls and I did the last two days in food prep gives me plenty of time to relax and take it easy. I also know they will sleep in, so our Thanksgiving Dinner will indeed be at dinner time.

I hear the girls stir in the late morning. After I've worked out and read for a long time, I start our traditional holiday brunch of fruit, egg casserole and pinwheels–our version of cinnamon rolls.

To my surprise, the doorbell rings. Wondering if Sabrina's new guy or one of Elise's friends, I go to answer it with my apron and glasses on, my hair in a messy bun. I am completely floored when I see Conner standing on my doormat, flowers in hand, a huge grin on his face. I practically jump into his arms and choke out through tears, "What are you doing here?"

He laughs and catches my earlobe between his teeth before whispering, "I couldn't hear my only Sunshine be sad anymore, so I told Joel I enjoyed my dinner with them last night, but I had to come be with my girl."

I sag in relief as my body softens against him. I pull back to look at the bouquet in his hands. "Where in the world did you find a gorgeous bouquet on a holiday?" He smirks and says, "I have my ways." Then he kisses me within an inch of my life before I pull him inside to introduce him to the rest of my girls.

Chapter 38

Conner

Thanksgiving with Carrie and her girls is a complete production that borders on chaos. I love every second. They are like a well-oiled synchronized swim team. They each have their parts and move somewhat seamlessly. There are a few sister squabbles, as to be expected, and don't phase me at all. I've coached women my entire career. It's quite amusing to watch them snap and snarl, then go back to giggling with each other in two minutes. The fluidity of them cooking together leaves me breathless in wonder.

I'm also nervous as fuck.

Elise is a known entity. We have a great coach-player relationship, but that allows for a certain distance for both of us. However, being here, in Houston, in her house, is a completely original experience. Also, knowing I'll be sleeping in the same bed with her mom, under the same roof, is enough to have me break out in a bit of a nervous sweat. I can never keep my hands off Carrie in a bed, and she is not quiet when we are together.

We might have to talk about that for the duration of my stay. I hate to muzzle my Sunshine but to lessen the abject awkwardness, being quiet is a must.

Between Carrie's oldest girls, Maley makes me slightly uncomfortable, but it's her middle daughter, the cancer nurse, who scares the shit out of me. I've had to interact with lots of people and no one has ever made me feel the way Sabrina does.

When Carrie introduced me, despite being fresh out of bed, Maley was polite, welcoming and warm. Sabrina, though, looked at me like she had judged my soul and found it wanting. This woman is fierce in a way I couldn't imagine, even being Carrie's daughter. It is like her spine is made of iron and she would rip apart the world to help you if she loved you.

But she doesn't love me yet. Hopefully, we will get there, but she could freeze ice with her stare.

Maley seems to know the effect her sister can have on people, so once we get settled, she shifts into friendly interview mode. She must be a great physical therapist because her bedside manner is attuned to not getting answers. She asks a lot about my family, which I'm happy to discuss.

"My nieces and nephews were sad to see me go. Uncle Conner always has fun tricks and games to play. Misty, Joel's wife, has a lot on her plate and when I'm there, it helps her out because I can keep her kids–and her husband–occupied. I was there for two days and had only planned to be there for one more before I went back to California, but Texas is kind of on the way."

Carrie catches my eye with a beaming smile, and I wink at her.

Sabrina is standing behind her and all she does is raise an eyebrow at me. I feel my balls shrivel a little. Sabrina's whole countenance radiates, "Fuck with her and I will kill you. And get away with it."

I know I must appeal to Sabrina's heart and with a bit of time over this weekend, I'll find the key to it. I already suspect it's showing her I'm taking good care of her mom and sister, as a partner and coach. As if she knows what I'm thinking at that very moment, Sabrina meets my eye and shakes her head.

This may be harder than I thought.

Maley continues asking me about the program, working to diffuse the tension between Sabrina and me. She is very astute and since she is a former top tier high school athlete herself, checks in on how we handle player mental health issues as well.

I brave a comment. "Sunshine, I gotta hand it to you. You've raised some bad bitches." My attempt at deflection works. After a moment of stunned silence at my choice of words, they all break into peals of laughter.

After they each settle down, Carrie tells me proudly, "Well done, Coach. Now, let's bless the food and eat before we must make more food and eat again." She says a quick blessing and we dive into the delicious brunch before the girls go upstairs to shower and I clean up the kitchen.

Carrie comes up behind me and hugs me hard. She stays like that as I resume my soapy washing of the dish; she used to cook the casserole. After a long moment, I ask, "You ok, Sunshine?"

I feel her turn her head to put her nose into my upper back and she takes a long inhale. I hear her mumble, "Never better, Sweetness."

She pours some water from the counter filter jar. Taking a long drink, she meets my eyes. "Let's snuggle on the couch until it's time to cook again." Once all the dishes are clean and I wipe down the counters, that's exactly what we do.

We spend several hours talking and laughing, being joined in intervals by her girls. Sabrina is slightly warmer now that she is caffeinated and put together for the day. She watches a Premier League game with us, while Carrie naps, then showers. Finally, the moment arrives, and she orchestrates the chaos of Thanksgiving dinner. I sit here, longing to help, but since they won't let me, I drift off into thinking about how I want to propose to Carrie.

It's only been four months since we've been together, but it feels four years. I want to spend the rest of the academic year building the stability of our foundation as a couple. I plan to ask her what she wants the rest of our first year together to look like.

Soon, the doorbell rings again, and it's Sabrina's new guy. Maley is recently single, so not expecting anyone. Elise's two best friends, including another collegiate soccer player named Summer, are coming to join us for dinner. Summer plays for Coach G at Texas A&M. I would love to look up Summer's scouting report to see what her skills are, but if she is full-ride for the Aggies, as an attacking mid-fielder, I know she is an excellent player.

We talk through dinner about the highs and lows of sports, and I share with her what it is like to play in the Premier League. I suddenly realize all eyes are on me as I tell Summer yet another story and then the whole table bursts into questions about my time in England.

Carrie doesn't say a word. As the matriarch, she doesn't have to. She lets her kids and their friends grill me. She smiles into my eyes the whole time and I can feel her love and admiration for me like I feel the sunshine soak into my skin, which is why it's her nickname. She beams out her admiration, her pride in me, and I can't look away for a long time.

I realize I've never really talked about this portion of my life with her. She is as enraptured as everyone else. I reach the point of discomfort that I'm talking so much about myself until I catch Sabrina's eye as I relate a story about one of my teammates.

His daughter got child got very sick and needed an emergency operation that could only be done in the States. We did a massive fundraiser because this guy was a first-year player and at the very beginning of his contract; he needed financial help.

I relate how my buddy and I set up the fundraiser and did all the promotion for it, even getting on one of the UK's biggest talk shows. We ended up raising five hundred thousand pounds, which the owner of our team matched dollar for dollar. One million pounds more than covered the medical care for the rest of her life, as well as their travel, and also extended stay for his wife so his daughter could recover for a few weeks before flying back to England.

In listening to this story, Sabrina's face completely softens and by the end, she is smiling at me. It takes my breath away. She looks so much like her mother; I felt like I've been taken back in time to see Carrie in her twenties. It stuns me as the table grows silent. I stared dumbfounded at Sabrina. Her smile fades and she breaks the quiet with, "Conner, ummm, why are you being creepy all of a sudden?"

There is a pregnant pause, and then the whole table erupts in laughter. They can't stop for a while, and Carrie wipes her eyes multiple times. Sabrina just scowls as she looks between me and her family.

Once they stopped cackling, I tell the truth, "Sabrina, I'm sorry. I didn't mean to stare or be creepy. It just struck me how much you probably look like your mom at that age. I felt like I'd been transported back through time."

I heard an audible sigh come from Carrie's end of the table, as well as to my left, where Elise and her friend sit. Sabrina's boyfriend just looks. Sabrina responds in a slightly frosty tone, as Maley chirps at the same time, "I don't look like Mama. Maley does."

"She doesn't look like Mama at that age. I do."

This must be a well-debated topic because Maley rises from the table in one swift motion. She walks around the table to the bookshelf in the corner of the dining room and pulls a scrapbook off a middle shelf. She flips through it, walking back to the table, to stand next to me.

In this moment, it dawns on me I'm seated at the head of the table across from Carrie.

Maley holds the scrapbook out for me to look at. As I look at the picture, I am struck dumb. Indeed, Maley could have been Carrie's twin, but Sabrina and Elise are very close. All three girls strongly resemble their mother in the full blush of youth.

I clear my throat of the building emotion and meet Carrie's eyes. I raise my glass to toast, with everyone joining me. With glasses raised, I say, "To the woman who has held this family together, safer and tighter through unimaginable heartbreak. She has not only passed down the beauty of her physical form but even greater than that, the beauty of her heart and soul. I am desperately humbled to be with you, Carrie, and with your family today. Thank you for welcoming me and I will do my best to honor every gift you've given and still pour into the world."

When I finished speaking, there wasn't a dry eye in the house, and they were by far the most meaningful words I'd ever said.

***

Carrie

If I wasn't already in love with Conner, his toast secures my heart. How in the hell did this man find me? Or I find him?

All I know is - it is a miracle, and I continue to be in awe. Hearing him recount his experiences playing in the Premier League is one thing, but then watching Sabrina's resolve to not like him crumble is magical.

"Conner! You are a guest! You should relax." I tell him this as he is, once again, elbows deep in warm, soapy water.

He only shrugs. "You ladies cooked. I'll clean." He also commandeers Sabrina's new guy's help. He is a doctor, and he doesn't seem happy about doing dishes. That attitude won't win him any points with us at all. I realize there are few men like Conner, and I will thank the Universe for the rest of my life for guiding us to each other.

After dishes, we have dessert, which we eat on paper plates with disposable forks. All our favorites are there: key lime pie for me, pumpkin for Maley and Sabrina, and blond brownies for Elise. Scott's mother, as she always does, sent buckeyes and Conner sighs in contentment.

Peanut butter and chocolate are his favorite.

Once we are stuffed to the max, we all put on comfy clothes or pajamas and it's time to watch our traditional Thanksgiving movie - "Elf." It signals the transition for us into the Christmas Season, and we've been watching it every year since the girls were old enough to sit through it.

It's been a while since all four of us make it all the way through. Even I stayed awake until we start another movie, my personal holiday favorite, "The Family Stone." This time, I did what I usually do. It couldn't be helped with Conner rubbing my legs while I scratched Elise's back. I wake slightly to Elise is covering me with a blanket and Conner coming to spoon me on the couch.

They know me too well, I guess.

The girls all go off to do their own thing: Maley to visit her childhood friend Rianne; Sabrina with her new beaux to his apartment; and with Elise and Summer to hang out at another friend's house.

"I'm in college now, Mama. No curfew for me!" She declares this while she walks out the door, pumping her fists in the air.

It's after nine but my movie nap gave me energy. As I rise from the couch and stretch, most of my joints popping audibly, Conner gets up and sits at the kitchen table. He crooks a finger, beckoning me to him. I am like a moth to a flame and go straight over.

Intrigued, I ask him, "Sweetness, we are alone in my house and you want to sit at the kitchen table?"

He smiles at me, then pulls on the front of my soft pajama top. "These PJs are cute."

I thank him, not exactly sure if I'm supposed to sit or what. He is dressed in a UCC t-shirt and equally soft lounge pants. He smiles at me again, wider this time, and asks, "Got any playing cards?"

I furrow my brows and nod. I walk around the table to our game cupboard and pull out a deck. Still smiling up at me, he nods me into the chair directly across from him and takes the cards. He shuffles and deals us each five cards.

"Conner Doreland, do you want to play poker with me?"

He raises his right eyebrow, "No my Sunshine. Not just regular poker. Let's raise the stakes and play strip poker."

I toss my head back to laugh loudly. "Oh, Sweetness, I could never deny you anything. I'm an awful poker player, so I guess I'm going to be sitting here naked long before you will."

With a devilish gleam in his eye, he responds with, "You might, and that's just fine by me. Let me know if you get cold. Oh, wait, I'm pretty sure I'll be able to tell." He looks pointedly at my breasts because he knows full well what happens to them when I am even the slightest bit chilled.

"That's not really fair, Sweetness. You know all my tells."

With a smoldering glint in his eye, he says, "Don't worry, we will both win tonight."

I shiver, and then we begin. Conner wins one hand, but then I get on a hot streak, winning enough times to leave him shirtless and pant-less, in only his boxer briefs. I gloat as I lick my lips with all that man flesh on display. I'm still in my PJ top and underwear.

I gloat over my good fortune and ogle him.

He is the picture of composure and gives me a sly grin. When he says nothing, I get very curious and ask, "What's that look about, Sweetness?"

His grin turns into a smile and finally responds with, "It doesn't matter who wins, you know."

I am taken aback. "Conner! Of course it matters who wins! It is a *game*," putting all my emphasis on the word. I mean it too. I am a horrible loser and an even more horrible winner. I either pout or rub my victory in the other person's face for hours.

He continues to smile at me, but it turns a little feral. The look in his brown eyes gets darker and he whispers, "Is my only Sunshine going to be a good girl when she wins? Or am I going to punish her till she screams my name?"

My insides melt and I feel the wetness seep through my panties. Thankfully, my cycle hasn't started. Not that Conner would care.

I stand abruptly and throw my cards over my shoulder, stunning Conner until he hears me say, "Last one to the bedroom is a rotten egg."

I take off running and make it to my bedroom first. I make it to the far side of the bed, breathing hard from my quick sprint and laughter. Conner barrels through the door, ever the predator. There is also an amused glint in his eye. I don't get one over on him very often.

I might be safe on the other side of the bed, but I'm also trapped. I realize this at the same time as Conner, who, fast as lightning, leaps over the bed. He pins me against the far wall of my bedroom. He is gentle, but his hands are firm on my wrists. He drags them both slowly upwards in an arc and leans his face just above mine, our gazes colliding in a rush of heat and joy.

While I expect some sort of quip about being a rotten egg, he surprises me by saying, "I've missed you so much Carrie," just before he crashes our lips together. I tangle one of my legs around his hip, pulling him into my center where I can feel his hardness. It makes me whimper against his mouth.

He threads one of his hands into my hair, gripping firmly and tilting my head for deeper access. His hard, warm chest crushes into me and his other hand still holds both of my wrists above my head. He kisses me so hard and for so long, I almost feel like I'm going to suffocate.

It would be an excellent way to go.

He finally makes his move. He spins me around, pins my front to the top of the bed. He has maneuvered me to where he still holds my hands, but now behind my back. He yanks down my undies before kneeling to lick my pussy and bite my backside until I am begging.

He stops and stands up behind me. "Are your arms ok, Sunshine?" My desire for him is so high, I can only whimper. It barely registers when he says, "Tell me if that changes, but until then, I'm going to fuck that sore loser out of you. Ready, my love?"

I don't immediately answer, so he slaps my ass, just enough to sting.

"Yes, oh god, Conner, yes, fuck me, please, please, please!"

"I can never say no when you beg me, Sunshine," he says this as he steps out of his briefs.

We both groan as he pushes into me in one thrust and then, being a man of his word, fucks any kind of resistance or attitude out of me. I come twice, once before and once right after he does, and it is so good; so rough but still sweet. I am completely spent.

Conner must be too, because he collapses on top of me. This is a whole different luxury as we recover our senses, letting our bodies come down from our ecstatic lovemaking on their own.

When the girls come home later, they find us tucked up in my bed. I am already asleep, so I don't hear them come in. He tells me the next morning about how they all responded to finding us there together.

Maley gives him a big smile and a wave.

Elise gives him a thumbs up.

Only Sabrina stands at the door for a long moment, staring. She finally says, "You hurt her - I will kill you and get away with it." She turns to walk away before turning back. "I am happy she is happy again. It's been a long time since I've seen her this way, if ever. Thank you, Conner."

He tells me it is right then I say in my sleep, "Night, Sweetheart, I love you and see you in the morning."

Sabrina, her gaze now falling on me, responds, "Go tell your stories, Mama. I love you too."

Chapter 39

Conner

This season is turning out to be epic.

We are headed into the NCAA regional qualifying rounds following the Thanksgiving break and I couldn't be more ready. I've had to work through some anxiety, especially after leaving Carrie. The weight of it all settled back on my shoulders, whereas when I'm with her, everything is lighter.

The way she expresses her love for me—and for her family—is effortless and it makes everything else feel that way, too. Now that I'm away from her, preparing for the culmination of our season. Without Carrie's soothing presence next to mine, my anxiety is a scratchy wool blanket. I'm uncomfortable in my skin and even exercise isn't taking the edge off.

I knew the heat would be on after Thanksgiving. Carrie is focused on the sale of her company, regardless of the fact she is selling it to one of her closest friends. I'll see her tonight when she flies in for our games. Before I left Houston Thanksgiving weekend, I gave her a key to my house.

She was floored I would make such a grand gesture, but I've given her my heart, so a little key is nothing. She can be impressed with a key for a while because a ring is coming.

I can't wait to see her face when I propose after we win the whole fucking enchilada.

As I sit in the strategy meeting with my coaches on Friday afternoon, a message comes through my watch. It's from Carrie but I shouldn't be getting it now, it's too early for her plane to have landed.

Confused, I make a mental note to text her back when we have a break, which doesn't come for another twenty minutes as we working through several factors, including the return of Maciee Griggs. She bought her way into their program, even into a starting position.

We decide to leave it to the ladies to handle, which I'm relatively sure they will do with poise and grace. Everyone is well aware of who we are playing this weekend, and Arizona State is known for their rough play. We will be ready.

Tournament play is intense, and this one stretches out for a few weeks, so the final four teams can emerge for the last two games in North Carolina. Since college games on a Sunday are rare, if ever, we have the doubleheader Saturday. We are playing teams we beat earlier in the season in both games.

Our game times are ten am and four pm. Between games, we will have a two-hour study hall and then a full stretch session before we go out to warm up again for the later game. As a team, we are all aware of having to be in the right headspace to come out of this weekend victorious.

And we will.

As we finally wrap up our strategy session and get ready to head out for training. I check my message from Carrie and my fucking jaw hits the floor at the same time as my eyebrows hit my hairline. My cock also has a very distinct response anytime she is involved.

She has sent me a collage and the pictures reveal a very naked, very sexy woman sprawled across my bed in a variety of poses. They are all tasteful and clearly; she put in some research on how to do an at home boudoir selfie shoot. The text of the message is,

> I'll be right here waiting for you.

"Hey, Coach, everything ok?" Inanna asks, a few feet ahead of me, as I stopped dead in my tracks.

When I don't respond, she asks again, "Conner, everything alright with the family?"

My mouth is bone dry as I stare at my future wife spread out like a buffet waiting for me to feast upon. I didn't think she could surprise me anymore, but here we are. She must have taken an earlier flight to get here this soon and used her new key to get into my house.

The hand holding my phone flies up to my chest to hide the screen from prying eyes as I feel Inanna touch my arm. I feel little beads of sweat prick my hairline and my cock throbs. I take a deep, ground breath and finally look at Inanna, who is growing more and more serious by the minute.

I clear my throat before replying, "Yes, Coach, all is well. Sorry, didn't mean to concern you. Just a little surprise waiting at home."

Inanna's expression turns from concern to confusion before she shrugs and says, "Ok, well get it together. You aren't getting sick, are you?"

I shake my head as I brush past her. Thankfully, she is looking at my face. She didn't notice my massive erection, thank God.

I channel my lust into a challenging tone and say, "Come on, Coach. I'm fine. Let's take that silly mother-goose worry for me and use it to pound our enemies into dust, shall we?"

Inanna makes a sour face, which was the exact response I was looking for. Even though her legs are half as long as mine, fast as lightning, she is walking beside me. We peel off toward our respective dressing rooms and I hear her mumble, "We are going to rip their hearts from their chests and feast on their entrails."

I chuckle and text Carrie back.

> *Sunshine, you better be a good girl and keep that pretty pussy wet for me. When I get to you, I'm going to make you come so hard you will see the face of God.*

***

Carrie

After a Friday night full of orgasms and snuggles, Conner prepares me to see Maciee Griggs and her slimy Dad. It won't be until the second game. I don't feel nervous because I'll be surrounded by the parent community. They all know what happened and are all in favor of this relationship. Alyssa's Mom has become like a second Mom to Elise and a good friend to me.

It happens like this for sports parents. We may be thrown together because of our kids, but we end up a family, even if it is only for a season.

Conner kisses me and leaves me in bed, as he heads out to meet the team at seven a.m. I packed him a lunch. I wanted him to feel cared for on a big day. I make sure to be up by eight to have time to move my body, which is now sore from riding Conner in reverse, cowgirl–our new favorite position. I put in my earbuds, move to the music, and it sets me up to be ready to watch our team take their next steps towards the championship.

Since UCLA, the games have been fairly easy wins, and we aren't expecting today to be any different.

The first game against Oregon is dull. The Ducks are bland players and while they defend well, there is nothing exciting about their gameplay. UCC is so well-orchestrated in their movements it's like watching a ballet.

UCC wins the game easily, continuing their streak and now off to study hall, rest and refocusing. I give Elise a quick hug and kiss on the cheek before the game and then a high-five after. She didn't play much because the coaching staff wanted to save her legs for the second game against Arizona State.

I grab two prepared lunch boxes from the bakery down the street from the Book Nook and then visit Samson. We talk for a long while as we eat and, as usual, I buy the book he recommends. I am now getting the friends and family discount and tell him if this new business doesn't work out, he can hire me as a cashier so I can get the employee discount.

Samson, in his deep baritone, confirms, "Well, if it comes to that, you and your girls have a home with me!" It made me tear up. I hold him in a hug before I head out to make some phone calls about the business sale. Through the lump in my throat, I tell him I appreciate his loving care as a friend and fellow traveler on this road to a happy destiny, together.

Before I head into the stadium for the second game, I sit in my car and respond to a few emails. I look up to see Nelson Griggs entering the stadium. Yuck.

He is with a younger woman and as I take my seat next to Alyssa's Mom, Marta; I notice the woman he is with could be his daughter's age.

Double yuck.

Marta leans over to me. "He looks almost pickled. He and I are roughly the same age, but his lifestyle is not doing him any favors. I highly doubt his arm candy is doing much to extend his lifespan, either. Hopefully, she gets out of him what she can and finds someone healthier and worthwhile."

I chuckle. "Tell me how you really feel. And of course, I feel the same way."

Conner gives me a little wave from the sidelines as he comes out and I blow him a kiss. I hear a few wolf-whistles from the other parents. Good-natured teasing happens anytime we show our affection in public.

Just then, I hear someone booing. I look up and lock eyes with Nelson Griggs. Marta hisses next to me. Nelson has an ugly look on his face, his eyes are pinched. He is sticking his tongue out. The little tart beside him gives me a frown with two thumbs down.

Just to spite them both, I wave and smile brightly, projecting my voice as I say, "Nelson, I see you are keeping it classy!"

Then I lock eyes with the young woman, whose eyes widen in shock, almost as if she hears me think, *Watch and learn, little girl. You might be his princess for the moment, but I'm a queen for a lifetime.*

Marta, who has my back, whisper shouts, "Oh, Nelson's here? Good, we wanted to see the winner of the smallest dick on the planet contest!"

I adore her.

Everyone laughs and a few people point at Griggs, who turns away in a huff. His girl-toy gives me the finger, which only makes the rest of the parents laugh harder. They both keep their eyes on the field for the rest of the game.

The game itself isn't exciting until the final six minutes. UCC is up one-nil with Arizona State desperately trying to make something happen.

So, they put Maciee Griggs in to cover Elise.

Elise is facing me and I see the look on her face when Maciee walks onto the field. Elise is smiling a great white sized grin, but Maciee looks like she swallowed something sour, just like her father's face earlier.

Huh, that apple didn't fall far, I think.

I've seen Elise take out or outrun a hundred girls like Maciee Griggs. Maciee may think she is the shit when it comes to this game, but my daughter actually is. I take the moment to flick my gaze to my man. He is calm and cool. He signs something to Alyssa, who responds with a swipe across her chest. I don't know their team code well enough to understand exactly what transpired, but I know enough to know that look on Conner's face.

He just gave her permission to do whatever is necessary to handle Maciee Griggs

As the whistle blows, Elise moves with precision and speed Maciee can't match. She and the team have the ball in the open space in no time flat. Maciee isn't struggling, she just isn't as fast as Elise. Her only advantage is she just came off the bench.

It's a testament to Erik's conditioning because even as Elise has played the entire game, her strides are long and full of power. Maciee should remember Elise has plenty of gas in the tank, plus a whole other gear she shifts into when she sees her opportunity to score.

Which she does right this second.

Elise comes into position right across the middle and receives the ball. She flips the switch and is charging towards the goal so fast; her signature upper left-corner goal will blast right past the keeper.

I rocket to my feet as she goes down and restrain myself. I saw Maciee slide tackle right into her left leg–her shooting leg - cleats up. I want to vault the railing to get to her as much as I want to punch Nelson for raising a daughter who is so awful. Marta puts a hand on my arm and drags me back down to my bleacher seat to watch what happens.

The ref blows the whistle, and it's going to be a penalty kick for Elise. I see Elise holding her ankle, and I know Maciee got her good. That'll need ice and some anti-inflammatories tonight for sure.

Marta leans over to tell me, "That little bitch cleated Elise right in front of the ref. That should be a yellow card!" She is right and I wait for the ref to bring out the card.

He doesn't.

"Fucking motherfucker! Is he blind?" I say this low enough that only Marta hears. She reaches over and pats my arm. "Carrie don't worry. I'm sure the ladies will take care of it. In fact, I've heard a rumor they made a deal with Coach Conner when it comes to playing Maciee. Apparently, the play is called 'Ford's Theater.'"

I laugh and ask, "Are we to expect a shot to the back of the head? Marta, where do you hear these rumors, I wonder?"

She smiles at me and says, "Well, when you're the mother of the team captain, you'll know all the juicy details!"

All I do is grin as we watch Elise sink her PK in the top right corner of the net, exactly where she would have put it before Maciee pulled her stunt. The teams then line up at mid-field. UCC is up two-nil. With only three minutes left in the game, it will be impossible for Arizona State to come back. They will just have to play out the clock.

What happens next happens so fast, I almost miss it.

As Maciee Griggs passes the ball back to her mid-fielder, Alyssa comes up across the midline and slides in, unprovoked, straight for Maciee's kicking leg. It is a flagrant, beautiful foul. And one that will probably get her red carded.

It does, in fact, because this time the ref is paying attention. Alyssa stands up, thanks him for finally making a good call, flips off Maciee Griggs, who is watching with murder in her eyes from the ground. Alyssa leans in to say something to Elise on her way off the field.

Elise tells me later what she says. "No one treats my little sister that way. The pleasure was all mine."

After that excitement, the two teams settle in to play out the clock when suddenly, Arizona State ends up on a breakaway. They can't win, but they can ruin the shut-out if they score. Maciee barrels down the field with Elise on her heels, stiff-arming my daughter the whole way. She gets far enough past the defenders that the keeper comes out to take the ball off her feet.

The Keeper does just what she intends and does it legally. But Maciee is so hell-bent on scoring the goal on the school that kicked her to the curb, she tries to follow through. Unfortunately, though, she had planted her back foot so hard it gets stuck.

The Keeper's momentum carries her straight into Maciee, and I watch in horror as Maciee's right leg bends backward the wrong way. She goes down in a heartbeat, screaming. Nelson is on his feet shouting for a foul, but it was all fair play and the ref knows it. He calls nothing as the trainers come out with a board and Maciee is carried off. She is screaming and I look around to see Elise and her team have taken a knee.

My girl is classy till the end. Nelson elbows his way through the stadium to get to the lower deck, trying to get on the field to go to his daughter. I watch as they take her into the visitor locker room, and I know that will be the last time Maciee Griggs leaves the pitch as a player.

I've seen players tear an ACL with less force than that and it is most assuredly a career-ending injury. I heave a sigh of relief that Elise wasn't involved, and I meet my daughter's eyes across the expanse. Her mouth isn't smiling, but her eyes are.

Then I hear Marta whisper, "I wonder who she gets her viciousness from, hmmm?"

I chuckle low, "Marta, my dear, that was all karma."

Chapter 40

Conner

Beating the hell out of Arizona State was a big, fat, fucking middle finger to the entire conference, who had the nerve to let Maciee Griggs continue to play because Nelson Griggs threw his money around. They got what they deserved, and we got the win that puts us on top, heading into the conference championship. Doing it in style by sweeping a double-header weekend is even sweeter.

We have two weeks to prepare to play Stanford for the Conference Title. When - not if- we win the conference title and go into the tournament undefeated, we will have a huge target on our back. Stanford is a national soccer elite. They have money rolling into them like no other school and all the players have proved themselves repeatedly.

Their team is all starting seniors, experienced veterans who know how to deliver. We will have our work cut out for us and I'm going to need Inanna to come up with some of her Futbol magic to keep us in the hunt for our undefeated season. Everyone will want to break our winning streak. This will be our biggest test yet.

"Thinking about Stanford already? Want to talk about it?"

My beautiful goddess rolls over in the early morning light. She adjusts the sheets and blankets of my bed to scoot closer to me. I never knew life could be so full. I am winning in all areas of my life and while I know that's temporary; with Carrie by my side, I don't see how anything could go wrong again.

Unfortunately, she flies out first thing, and when I remind her, she sighs.

"I know, babe. I know. I wish I didn't have to leave you when you are all stressed out. I know so many delicious ways now of lowering your blood pressure." She smiles wickedly at me and then moves so that she is half on top of me.

Her perfect tits on my chest and it's all I can do to not bite her; she looks so delicious. My cock has been awake upon hearing her voice. I palm one breast in each hand, and she shudders. Her nipples perk up hard and straight as my thumbs rub them round.

"Conner, we can talk about what's coming, you know." Her voice is quite breathless, her desire ramping as I continue to play with the breasts that spill over my palms.

"Yes, Sunshine, I know we can. I will do nothing but think about Stanford and what comes after for the next month. Right now, all I want to think about is your body on mine. I won't see you for two weeks. I need to get my fix now."

She must oversee the final transition of her company into Gena's hands. That will take a lot of focus. The documents are ready; she has been working on those with her lawyer for weeks now, often when she is here with me or in the airport. There are still one or two employees who are giving her hell, and part of her work this week is to prepare the paperwork with human resources to let them go.

She will give them a final choice–get on board and support Gena or they've reached the end of their road with her company. She expects those will be tough conversations because the assholes giving her fits are old golfing buddies with her deceased husband.

I've never wanted to punch a dead guy in the face so much.

As I continue to knead Carrie's fantastic tits, she moans and becomes complete putty in my hands. I have to be quick; she is going to need time to get ready before we leave in an hour. I hope I've built in enough wiggle room on our travel schedule for a goodbye fuck.

We let our hands roam and I roll her onto her back. She threads her hands in my hair and then pulls my head down so her lips are next to my ear. Her tongue traces the inside and I can't help but moan. She nibbles down my neck, making my cock swell painfully. I slide a hand off her breast and down between her thighs. I trace lightly, knowing this is going to make her brain short-circuit.

It does. For a minute, Carrie is completely immobile. When I touch her like this, she can't think straight, like I've wiped her memory. I love having that power over her because she does the same for me when she laughs, when she smiles, when I'm inside her and when she shares her heart with me.

With her, my thoughts settle like leaves arcing slowly to the ground, caressed by a gentle breeze at the start of Fall. I never knew being with someone could be this supportive and reassuring, but Carrie gives me all I need and more. I know in my bones if I ever needed it, she would pour out the last drop of her blood to give it to me.

I would do the same for her. I would die to be with Carrie. Or burn the world to the ground to find her, in this life or the next.

As my fingers finally find her sweet heat, she whispers my name. It is eternal music to my ears to hear it. In the next second, she attaches her mouth to my shoulder and sinks her teeth in.

"OH FUCK, Carrie!" I yell loudly, out of a little of pain but mostly pleasure.

She giggles, "I'm sorry, I just love you so much I want to take a bite out of you!" She is completely unrepentant, and I love it.

"Keep biting, Sunshine. Add a little suction to it. Leave your mark on me." As I say all of this, I've grabbed my pillow and am lifting her hips to slide it underneath. She dislodges as I jostle her, but as I position myself between her legs, at an angle where I know I will slide right in, she works on the other shoulder.

"Fuck woman, take everything you want."

She pauses making her mark to moan with me as I slide into her. There is a slight resistance I push past that happens every time and we both love it, possibly Carrie more than me. As I move my hips in a rhythmic motion, taking a few minutes to wind her up, she pulls my chest down to hers.

Morning breath or not, she is going to kiss my lips off and I'm here for it.

Her hips are at just the right angle and as I thrust, it begins to hit her in a new place. The slide of my cock along her front pelvic wall and G-spot is something I knew she would like, and she does. Her noises amp me up and I love looking down into her lovely face, open to me in a way no one else gets to see.

Her open heart is reflected in the pleasure I see across her face, and it brings me to new heights to know I'm the one giving it to her.

"Play with that perfect pussy, my good girl. Make yourself come while I'm inside you."

She reaches between us to run circles over her clit while I thrust into her. Her breasts bounce in front of me as I thrust, and I take her left nipple into my mouth and suck hard while her fingers press into her clit.

We continue to make love for a few more minutes until I feel Carrie's pussy contract and I'm lost. I can feel the waves of her orgasm take her as she yells my name, which then melts into wordless groans I can't decipher.

I feel the pressure in my balls that comes exploding out of my cock straight up into her and I yell, "FUCK, Carrie!"

I collapse on top of her as we pant out our releases. I can feel myself slipping out with our combined fluids and I wish I could stay like this inside her. It will always and forever feel like home, no matter where in the world we are.

I take another few minutes to stroke her back and shoulders, using my other hand to brush the hair out of her face as I gaze down.

"Why are you always smiling when you look at me?" she asks playfully, already knowing the answer.

"Because, my only Sunshine, you are my everything."

We both know our love bubble must burst, and we both have to return to the world of work and planning, so we savor every second.

With no traffic on a Sunday morning to interfere, she gets to the airport in time to check her bag before boarding. Once at the gate, she sends me a blowing kiss emoji and I send her a text back:

> *Good luck this week, my love. It will all be well and then we can begin our new lives together. Just two more weeks and we can secure all those plans while the team achieves everything we set out to. Only twelve days till I can hold your sweet face between my hands and know you are all mine for the rest of our lives.*

***

Carrie

This meeting is the worst.

I am so glad Conner, and I did a Peloton workout early this morning and then I have a stretching Pilates class later because I need to take care of myself. Otherwise, I will go ballistic on these two dudes who think they know how to run the business better than a woman; whether it is Gena or I, it doesn't seem to matter to them.

This makes the third guy full of toxic masculinity, and I'm wondering how they kept it under wraps for so long.

We scheduled several days during this transition period to allow for different people within the company - regardless of rank–to present their ideas for improvement. Even as a boutique firm, we still have nearly seventy-five employees. Today is the last day of it and I'm grateful. Most have stuck to their areas of expertise, and they are aware the board is attending via Zoom from wherever they are this week.

However, the team presenting now is not adding any value. Gena nicknamed them the "Trouble Twins," and that's all they've been up to since the sale was announced. They are buddies with the guy I fired in the elevator and, on their best days, mediocre at their jobs in middle management.

Scott hired them as a favor, and it was one of the few times Scott went against his better judgement–and mine. They want nothing to change because it will require them to step up past their regular minimal effort. The prospect of being uncomfortable makes them loud and impassioned for change. Instead of just finding somewhere else to work, they want to make things difficult.

Hell, hath no fury like a middle-aged white man who's uncomfortable.

I take a moment to gather my sanity and check a text from Conner as Pam, my faithful administrative assistant, gathers a couple of questions from the online Q&A software we are using.

Conner is checking in, and I smile to see it.

> *Good Morning Sunshine, are you kicking ass and taking names already?*

Even though I should give the appearance of listening to these two bozos drone on and one about the glories of keeping things "just the way they are," I have heard it already. I've had two one-on-one meetings with them both to allow them plenty of time to air their grievances.

With a growing smile on my face, which I should keep in check, I send back a quick note,

> *The ass kicking will come swiftly enough. This presentation is the nail in the coffin of the Trouble Twins. To distract myself, I'm thinking of what you will look like under me as I ride you into bliss the next time I see you.*

This is not the first time I've sent Conner a dirty text or two to get through these meetings.

True to form, my sweet lover sends me back exactly what my heart needs to hear. It also wets my panties thoroughly.

> *I can't wait to feel your warm, soaking pussy vibrate around my cock while I look into your beautiful eyes, Sunshine.*

Holding in a long sigh that would undoubtedly make me sounds like I'm a lovesick teenager, I send him back several emojis that describe what's happening in my body - raindrops, panting face and the devil and then say, *I can't wait to talk to you later, Soccer God. I want to hear all about all the training and preparation for the tournament matches coming up.*

He sends me back a winking emoji and then a picture. I know he is at work, so there is no way it's a sexy pic. I keep my phone under the table as I open the picture just in case and have to stop myself from laughing out loud.

He sent me a picture of the planning session he is in, which has Erik and Inanna on the strategy board. They look like they are arguing and as I click on the live photo, I can see they are moving the magnetic pieces around. Erik has a slightly annoyed-yet-bored cast to his face, while Inanna looks like, even though she is nearly a foot shorter than Erik, like she is going to pick him up and throw him out the window.

I tap the "ha ha" on the picture and then comment, *I would love to see Inanna eviscerate the Trouble Twins!*

Conner quickly responds with, *They wouldn't know they lost their balls until she told them.*

I have to look up and check the clock, holding back a huge laugh and I catch Gena's eye. She knows exactly what I'm doing. She nods, then flicks her eyes at the clock as well. Roland has five more slides to cover, but he is out of time. I get to be the CEO for another day before we sign the paperwork first thing in the morning. The Board approved the sale last week, so this week was a formality.

We will have one last celebration tomorrow afternoon and my work here is done.

I take a deep breath and exhale before announcing, "Roland and Geoffrey, thank you so much for sharing your thoughts. Unfortunately, your time is up. Pam, are there questions?'

Roland looks like a gaping fish as I cut him off mid-sentence, and Geoffrey just stares at me with nothing but loathing. I make a mental note to ensure Human Resources finishes their termination paperwork and to remind Pam to confirm my meeting with them both tomorrow morning in order to have security ready to escort them out.

Pam tilts her head, the light catching her eyes. She can't stand these guys any more than I can, and I can see the amusement in them as she announces, "No, ma'am. No one has questions at all."

Gena looks at the Trouble Twins and says graciously, "I appreciate your hard work and passion for the way Carrie has run this company. I will take the spirit of your feedback into this new phase in the future." A clear dismissal. Both Roland and Geoffrey have enough sense to pack up their shit and shuffle out the door to their cubicles.

Pam gives me a nod, confirming everything is prepared for their dismissal meetings tomorrow and we are ready for the rest of today's itinerary. All I have to do is close out the business meeting today and we can head to lunch.

A voice suddenly comes over the speakerphone. It is our most senior board member, Constance Fielding. She built a multi-billion-dollar medical payments practice, first in Britain and then in the U.S. and we've used her model to offer a sliding scale to those patients who need our services the most but have the least resources to pay for it.

Her elegant accent captures the attention of the entire room. "Carrie, dear, a quick question."

"Yes, please go-ahead Constance, your feedback is always appreciated."

"My apologies if this question seems abrupt, but I have to ask. I know big changes are ahead for you following the sale of this company. Are you indeed prepared to leave it all behind?"

For a second, I'm stunned into silence. When anyone has asked about my plans, I've always been clear I was focusing on the sale and transition with Gena and my next professional steps will flesh themselves out soon enough.

Conner, my girls, Gena and I all know what my next step is creating my women's entrepreneur empowerment coaching network, but I've not told anyone else.

I take a beat to recover from such a direct question, especially from someone who usually would take a longer lead up or reach out to me in private. Yet, feeling on the spot is something I've grown used to since I took over after Scott's death. I draw my wits to me and my power up from my center, placing my heated palms on the cool surface of the black lacquer of the modern conference room table.

I don't rush my answer and take an extra beat to look around the room, meeting everyone's eyes, finally landing on the camera so Constance can hopefully see I'm looking at her.

My response is short and sweet, "Well, Constance, I'm going to coach women to become just like me–or even better yet–just like you." I smile and nod and she returns it.

"Excellent. Darling, we all wish you the best and have absolute confidence in Gena. I personally can't wait to see what the future holds for you both, in the great things you will do."

Tears shine in my eyes as I meet Gena's and see silver there, too. It is the biggest confidence boost either of us could have asked for–to get Constance's blessing.

I nod for her to take the reins, and she does, thanking Constance, the rest of the Board.

Come Monday morning, the new sheriff will be large and in charge.

As we walk out together and the doors to the conference room close behind me one last time, Pam pulls me in for a quick hug. She whispers in my ear, "You've been the best boss. Thank you for finding someone equally outstanding." I pull back to smile down at her, as she barely breaks five feet and I lean back into a whisper, "Keep her in line as you've always done for me, ok?"

Tearily, she says, "You've taught me everything I know, Carrie. About being a woman in business, a mother, and how to be the best version of myself. I can't wait to find a love like you've found in Conner. I know I will love working for Gena. And if you need a "New Pam" for your new business, you will let me find her for you, right?"

"Abso-fucking-lutely, Pammy." I hug her close again and try not to blubber into the crown of her head.

Chapter 41

Conner

"Hey Coach–can I talk with you for a minute in private?"

The sound of Elise's voice is so similar to her mother's, and she approached me from behind, so for a split second, I thought Carrie was here.

Elise may be my star freshman, but she is also the child of my love. I can't help but feel my heart swell as I turn to her and say,

"Yes Ma'am, what's up?"

I walk away from the coaching staff with Elise. Erik doesn't look up and Inanna only quirks a brow. She has a right to be curious, player consultations are very much her territory. It's not unheard of for me to speak to one of my players alone. Usually, Inanna is the first stop.

My chest tightens a bit to think this is a family-related issue and I can feel myself shift into gear in my head to solve problems. I remember Carrie telling me it's not that they need us men to solve their problems. They need a willing ear and heart to listen, validate and then, if requested, provide feedback.

When I mentioned this to Joel, he laughs in my face and says, "Of course, Dickhead. Women are smarter than us. Ninety percent of the time, all they need is our support, not advice."

Naturally, I told him to fuck off and took his comment to heart.

Elise and I have had more time together, but our interactions are still very much limited to coach and player. Carrie said Elise wants to be more friendly, but her focus is on her studies and playing well. I hope to grow closer after the seasons. As we walk a little farther away, towards the tunnel that leads out the training pitch to the locker room, I give Elise the space she needs to speak when she is ready.

When she finally does, we are almost to the pitch. "Coach, I am a little concerned about the team's health."

I turn my head so sharply towards her my neck cracks. I was not expecting her to say anything like this, so I don't even have time to think before I say, "What? What do you mean?"

She pauses. My abrupt response is probably a little off-putting, so I try to soften it with, "Sorry, I just wasn't expecting you to say that. Do you mean mental, emotional, or physical health?"

Looking through me, I can tell she is weighing her words. She finally continues after a few agonizing beats, "Well, this is probably something the captain should tell you and you might already be aware, but it's been bugging me, so I thought I would bring it up."

"Go on, Elise. I trust you. You may not be captain–*yet*–"I say that word with emphasis, "But you certainly have the makings of it. Anything you need to tell me is held in the strictest confidence. Of course, I may need to share it with my assistant coaches if it is something we need to address team wise–but anything else stays between us."

She nods and takes a deep breath. She explains, "Well, it's just there are quite a few other teams who are getting hit hard by this latest viral outbreak, the hybrid superbug of COVID and the Flu."

She pauses and mumbles, "Like after the Pandemic, we need that."

Then she comes back to address me. "It's spreading through the dorms like wildfire. A lot of us are wearing masks around campus, but not all of us are. With the games coming up, I feel like you needed to know in case you wanted to mandate for everyone to mask up. It's not a sure thing we won't get infected, especially as some of the girls' room with other sports athletes, but it sure would help."

I continue nodding to encourage her and show I've heard her. I've known about this virus since it started spreading, coming back to campus from the outside after the Thanksgiving. There is usually an outbreak of something, with college students being in such close quarters, so we have protocols in place. It is inevitable, there is always something that hits campus following the start of the semester or the holiday break.

Every university in the country, thanks to the COVID Pandemic, has some level of response protocol to address health emergencies.

This one is a doozy. It spreads quickly and makes you feel run over by a truck, which is the flu component. It is then followed by respiratory congestion and restriction that can lead to bronchitis or pneumonia. Those hit hardest are, as typical, those with issues or are in poor health, but I've heard reports that even the fittest of people can struggle to recover.

It's bad timing to be facing this with the most important games of our season and perhaps career staring us in the face, but we prepared for it two days ago in all athletic town hall, called by my boss, Arlo. She encouraged everyone to take strong precautions and apparently Elise was listening. My team attended via Zoom.

Elise continues, "I just would hate to see anyone get sick, regardless of the time in our season, but this is an especially bad time to get sick, you know, Coach?"

I smile at her and say, "Yes, Elise, I know exactly what you mean. Do you know of anyone on the team who has symptoms?"

Elise shakes her head, her green eyes downcast. "So far, it's just the men's soccer team that's gotten it, but it's pretty bad.

Only the volleyball and field hockey teams on the women's side have gotten hit."

So, I turn it back to her, "Elise, if you were me, what necessary precautions would you take?"

She draws in a deep breath and says, "Well, I've thought about it and talked with a few of the other ladies." I smile because a smart leader always seeks an informal commitment from others before coming to the decision makers.

She sees my smile and takes it for the encouragement to continue. "I think we should all be wearing masks to class–anywhere outside our dorm rooms. We should be fine when we are together as a team and out in the open during training. But we can always give everyone the option to mask up. And it might be a good idea, starting after the weekend, for everyone to more or less quarantine after the game this weekend. We will need the rest anyway before next week, after we win."

She gives me her conspiratorial smile and my smile gets bigger. The entire team is praying, manifesting, affirming, and just living into our mantra of win-it-all. No negative talk is allowed, and the ladies have really gotten into it.

I nod again and she continues, "So, we just go on lock down as much as we can and believe for the best. That's what I would do if I were you–and the rest of the coaches, of course."

I nod and tell her, "It sounds good to me, kiddo. Let me go pow-wow with the other coaches and you do what you can to prep the team. We have a team dinner tomorrow night and will make the announcements then."

She smiles brightly; her face lights up at my encouragement. "I will tell my mom and sisters to do as much quarantining as they can. I know my mom won't have a problem with it after this week. Houston is seeing a lot of the virus spread, so I'll tell her to mask up for her last couple days in the office. I'm sure she will."

***

Carrie

I can't believe those motherfuckers came to the office sick as dogs.

Not only did I have to fire the Trouble Twins right before the company sale celebration party, I had to endure them hacking up a lung while I did it. They both came down with symptoms of this Superbug overnight, yet still showed up to their final meeting. I had to meet with each man one at a time. That means I got double exposure. I immediately put on a mask when Roland started coughing, but he'd offered me his hand and I'd shaken it.

I texted Gena after it happened. They were immediately shown the door, being told we would ship their belongings to them. Everyone at the party was masked, and the mood was now somber. The girls and I had already talked about masking up and quarantining before the Regional Championships. It slipped my mind because I'd seen these two looking just fine yesterday.

I am so pissed.

I would have missed the Conference Championship anyway because of lingering loose ends concerning the business, including cleaning out my office over the weekend. But in the end, I'm glad I didn't have to cancel going because of my exposure to whatever those two Typhoid-fucking-Marys brought into their last meeting as employees, no doubt just to get me sick.

When I wake up on Sunday morning, I know something isn't right. I was unusually tired the night before when I was talking with Conner and told him, "Sweetness, I think it's just all the craziness from this week. I'm just worn out. I might start my cycle early too. Apparently, this luteal phase has been sponsored by stress!"

He was completely understanding, but I felt bad because they played so well and are now Conference Champs. He was on a high and I was so proud of them. I watched the webcast of the match while I was cleaning my office. It was a spectacular three-nil win which cemented their bid for the NCAA tournament.

Sabrina warned me about this superbug that had her on lockdown since she was on two long-shifts this weekend. She said it is patients like hers, the immunosuppressed or compromised that are, as usual, hit the worst. "It's not another pandemic, Mama, but it's nasty. It makes you feel like death warmed up."

Then she told me about talking to Conner about her boyfriend. My heart was practically glowing when she told me about the call, and then Conner told me how she interrogated him. Even with the growing headache, I was just a puddle of love on the floor.

Maley said Dallas hadn't been hit too hard by the virus, yet. She is wearing a mask with all her patients and keeping a low profile, as Elise requested. She and Sabrina are coming up after the first game. It's a risk because anything can happen in a tournament, but I know UCC won't lose in the quarterfinals.

They just won't.

Saturday night, I hung up early with Conner and went to bed. I slept nearly twelve hours and didn't feel any better when I woke up. My head was killing me, and I was nauseous as all get out. On Sunday, I only get worse. Dulce dropped off some soup, but I tell her to leave it by the door because I know I've got the Superbug. From everything Sabrina has told me, I'm down for the count. After a two-hour nap, I text Conner and tell him I am going to the doctor first thing Monday morning to get antivirals.

If I had the energy, I'd be raging at those guys for giving this to me—on purpose, no doubt - but I have no energy. I try to hydrate as much as I can, but with this level of nausea, it's nearly impossible. I only throw up twice and thankfully, the diarrhea doesn't kick in till after that's over, sometime around one am on Monday morning.

Sabrina calls to check on me and says, "I think I should send some goons after them. I'm sure I can find one of my patient's families who'd be willing to take care of them for me."

I don't even have the energy to laugh. She makes me an appointment to see a doctor she trusts for Monday at eleven am.

> I just have to have enough energy to drive myself to the appointment. God, I HAVE to be better by the time I fly out on Friday for the tournament!

I text all this to Dulce, at six thirty on Sunday night.

By seven, she is at my door again with more soup, Liquid IV and fully masked. She even has gloves on.

After medicating me and forcing me to eat her magic soup, I crawl back into bed. She tells me and then confirms with a text she will be there ready to drive me to my appointment at ten am on Monday, after getting the appointment time and location from Sabrina.

I'd like to be irritated by her mothering, but I can't be. I need help. I hate asking for it, but I need it and she is there to do it. What are best friends for if they don't tell AND show you the truth, even if it pisses you off a little first?

After a grueling few hours on Monday at the doctor, with Conner checking in almost every ten minutes, I get home and collapse. Dulce clucks her tongue at me more than once from behind her N-95 hospital grade mask she got from Sabrina before going to the pharmacy, getting my meds and forcing me to take more pain relief, soup and fluids.

She doesn't make me talk, just gets me what I need and comfortable so I can sleep. This pattern of her morning through afternoon visits continues till Wednesday when she shows up and declares, since I'm sitting up watching TV in bed, I'm on the mend.

"You know, it's probably not a great idea to get on an airplane and go to a soccer match. I mean, I get it, but still. You are still a *gato bebe*." She gives me a very serious look and I know just enough Spanish to understand she is telling me I'm as weak as a kitten.

I roll my eyes, which is not as impossible as it has been for the last two days and even feel like arguing with her, a clear sign I'm better. "Dulce, I know that. But I'll be fine. Don't fucking mother me."

She smiles. Bitching at her is a grand sign.

"Ok, well, stay in bed until you absolutely *have* to leave. Conner won't care what shape you are in. He is probably going nuts. He can't be here to take care of you himself."

I huff out a laugh–another step in the right direction - even as it brings on a little coughing fit. "He has been quite overbearing, but very sweet. Remind me to call the doctor in the morning about a Z-pack for this cough. I can feel it may be settling in my lungs."

Dulce is quiet for a second before she says, "I texted Sabrina to get her boyfriend to prescribe it. She said, 'Okie Dokie. Anything to get Mama better.'"

Dulce smiles and my heart flutters. "That daughter of yours might have been *infierno sobre ruedas* – 'hell on wheels' - to you as a teenager, but she sure turned out ok."

I laugh again, this time with a little more gusto. "Sabrina has always been your '*carino*.'"

Dulce smiles warmly, "Indeed, a *miha* after my own heart!"

Just then, I feel my energy drop and Dulce tells me she is going to call her son to check on him and her infant grandbabies and will see them next week to make sure she is in the clear. She has been masked the whole time and her hands are probably chapped from the constant handwashing, but she is nothing but fiercely protective of the people she loves.

She would walk through fire for her husband, Brian, their family, and mine. We are family, after all.

When Sabrina comes to take me to the airport for my flight on Friday, I'm about sixty percent of the way there. If she and Maley could have changed their work schedules to accompany me, I know they would. I also know this trip will tax me, and I let Conner know I will sleep in my own hotel room tonight. He protests until I tell him,

Absolutely not, Sweetness. I will not risk your health with my selfish desire to be with you. I'll be at the game for sure, but we need to keep our contact to a minimum, my love. Your wellbeing is too important to me.

My resolve crumbled. Seeing him in the hallway of the hotel in North Carolina, once I got into his arms, I knew I couldn't leave. It had been over two weeks since we'd seen each other. I didn't realize how much I'd longed for him to hold me while I'd been feeling so crappy until I felt him envelop me in his warm embrace. I moved into his hotel room, and we spent the whole night wrapped up in each other.

It was heaven.

Chapter 42

Conner

I've never been so tired in my life. It's got to be because of all the planning for the NCAA tournament games. The last few weeks of preparations must have left me torched. That's the only reason I am so damn tired.

Well, maybe also because I barely slept when Carrie was sick. I hated, absolutely HATED, being so far from her. I was feeling fine before we won the last game, but ever since then, I've been dragging ass.

Erik even commented. "Dude, man, why aren't you pulling your weight?"

He smirks at me because he is being cheeky, the rat bastard. We are currently at the hotel gym, and although he is implying I am not fulfilling my responsibilities as a coach, what he truly means is that I'm weak. I'm not lifting half of what I normally do, and all he can do is make a joke.

I don't even look at him as I say, "Fuck you man, I'm just tired. You try being a head coach sometime."

He shakes his head and says, "No thanks, that is definitely not a career goal. Inanna can have it all. I'm completely fine with being in her shadow, living my little life. No big visions of grandeur like you two have."

"That's exactly your problem, Erik. You might be the biggest motherfucker on campus, but you think so damn small." Inanna throws this barb his way as she comes into the gym to do her typical six-mile run on the treadmill. She always staggers her travel workouts to start thirty minutes after we start, to avoid us on the cardio machines.

While I was running, I felt like I was going to die. This is not normal.

Inanna turns her attention to me and, with a sneer plastered across her striking Persian features, says, "Conner, you look like shit."

I grunt in response. I'm dead and haven't finished even half the workout. I am seriously considering bailing to go take a quick shower and curl up next to Carrie. She is still recovering from being sick, but the antivirals and the z-pack are taking care of it.

She didn't move when I kissed her as I left this morning. Fortunately, we got to sleep in till seven, which is what I needed. I slept for almost ten hours straight after Carrie and I made very slow, very sweet love, and we were both asleep by nine. Normally that would be too early for me, especially with the two-hour window time difference being on the East Coast versus West, but I guess the week really did me in.

We said we would stay apart last night, but it was impossible. I couldn't and neither could she. The first thing she said when we hugged was, "I know I said I would only hug you, but I really will die if I don't sleep in your arms tonight."

I had to match her energy.

I whispered to her, "Carrie, my soul is lost without yours. Get in this fucking hotel room right now."

Typically, our coaching early morning workouts are sacrosanct. It is a chance to get centered before we take the team for training. We've been here for two days, and these next three games will be the biggest of all. We are in the tournament of the top four teams in the country and it's single elimination. We are still the only undefeated team in the country.

All eyes are on us, and we have to make it.

I just hope I make it through this workout. I need coffee and breakfast with my Sunshine so I can mentally gear up for the game at two pm.

"Hey man, you are not just looking like dog shit but like run over dog shit." Inanna comes over to investigate my face, and I can barely drag my eyes up to meet her. She puts my hands between hers, which feel nice.

"Oh shit! Erik, he is burning up with fever!"

Then the world tilts and goes dark. The next thing I know, I see Inanna bending over me, tapping my face and saying, "Shit Conner, WAKE UP!'" She has a look of alarm I've don't think I've even seen. It's only eclipsed by the frantic look in her eyes I've definitely NEVER seen. This woman is tough as nails, so for her to be acting like this, something must be really wrong.

This is the moment I realize I'm lying on the floor.

"Ugh, how the fuck did I get on the floor?" I grab at my head, which is pounding, and try to sit up thinking that will clear my hazy visions.

Erik, in a hushed tone, on one knee beside me, more gently than I could imagine a man his size could be, pushes me back down. "Don't sit up, Conner. We are going to put a towel under your head and legs. We might have you sit up to drink some water in a second, but you passed out, just tipped off the bench, no warning. And damn, you are burning up!"

Inanna returns with towels, and my eyes close on their own. As she tucks the rolled up, scratchy hotel hand towel underneath my cervical spine, I mumble, "Inanna, what the fuck is happening?"

She doesn't address me, and I wonder if I really spoke out loud or just in my head. I don't open my eyes, but I hear her say to Erik, "I think he caught it."

It takes all my energy to push my eyelids open to look at her and ask in a wavering voice, "Caught what?"

I notice her face flashes annoyance that I'm talking, which is standard. I try to smile and make a joke, "You hate it when I question you–any man but especially me," but the words don't make it from my brain to my tongue.

She continues talking to Erik. She is shaking her head, but I can't watch because it makes me dizzy. I let my eyes close again and fall into a haze. I hear them, but it is in a distant, misty kind of way, like I'm underneath the surface of the pool. It's far away, but I hear Erik tell her, "No, it doesn't work that fast. There's no way he would have caught it from Carrie. It was rampant on campus, so there is no telling who exposed him."

After a pause, another first happens. Inanna sound afraid. "Erik, we have to get him to a doctor. He is not good at all."

Erik must have agreed. I float in and out of unconsciousness for an undeterminable period before I smell Carrie's familiar, soothing scent. Like sweet ocean rain, she is there, kissing my forehead and then hissing, which must mean I am still burning up.

She whispers to me, "Hi, Sweetness, can you open your eyes for me?"

I obey, even when it's hard. I think I say, "Hi Sunshine," but it sounds garbled, like my tongue is too thick in my mouth. Trying a little harder, I eke out, "My chest hurst and I feel bad."

I see her nod a little, her blue eyes calm and comforting, even as her forehead is wrinkled in concentration. She speaks in a soft tone, which is the same I'm sure she has used a thousand times with her girls when they were sick. I must be sick, then. Maybe very sick.

"Conner, my love, we are going to take you to the ER. You fell and are burning up. I have a jacket Erik will help you put on and then we are going to get you to the car. Just let me take care of you now, ok?"

"Ok, Sunshine." I speak more clearly this time, and it makes her smile. Confused for a second, I say, "Who's car are we riding in?"

She leans down to kiss my sweaty forehead and says, "We called an ambulance. It will be here in three minutes. We need to get you in and get seen. Now, let's get you up."

Erik hauls me up and then Inanna ducks behind me to help me shrug on what ends up being my coaching parka. "We brought those because it's going to get cold, right?"

Carrie keeps her eyes locked with me and says, "Yes, my love. You are always prepared. Let's see you take a sip of water, and we will walk out to meet the paramedics, ok?"

I nod and try to take a sip, but my throat locks up. It's like my body is rejecting any kind of nourishment and, truly, all I want to do is lie down and sleep forever.

That's exactly what I tell her as she and Erik get under my arms. We walk like a weird six-legged crab to the hotel entrance, which thankfully is not too far away. "I want to sleep forever with you. I'm so tired."

Carrie takes a deep breath. Even with Erik supporting most of my weight, I know I'm still heavy for her. She wraps her arm around me tighter and shakily says, "We can sleep together, my love. Just not forever yet, ok?"

I babble only, "Ok."

The frigid December air hits my face and makes my head spin. The paramedics take over. They begin their barrage of questions, which Carrie and Inanna alternate fielding. They help me onto the gurney, and I groan as I lay down, barely having the energy to be worried about how shitty I feel. I feel the pinch of an IV needle being inserted and the paramedic, a beefy guy shorter and wider than me, tells me they are getting me started on fluids for the twenty-minute ride to the hospital. Erik stands watching as an icy wind kicks up and bites my legs as. I raise my head and ask him, "Girls, have their cold weather gear?"

Erik huffs a laugh and says, "Yes Coach. We will take care of it. You just get better." The other paramedic is in a discussion with Carrie.

Before I close my eyes, I see her gesturing a lot. Suddenly, I hear my brother Joel's voice on the line before they close the doors, and we are off. Carrie climbs in and I hear the paramedic in the back with me, say something about it being "protocol to confirm everything with the emergency contact."

Carrie reaches for my hand and squeezes it hard. It is cold and I feel her stroking my hair back from my face. She speaks in a tone I've never heard. It's hard and forceful. "I understand, but you will not keep me out. His brother will be here by tonight, but until then, they are going to HAVE to deal with me."

I do not know how long we take to make it to the hospital and once we are there; I am triaged. They take some blood for tests. With fluids, I feel a little better and Carrie is right there the whole time, taking care of everything. When it is just me and her, she makes a soft "shhh" sound that makes me smile. Or try to smile.

She fields calls and texts from the other coaches, Arlo, and tells Elise what is going on. Inanna will keep them informed and focused on the game.

The next thing I know, I'm in a private hospital room and Carrie is there with a mask on. I open my eyes to see her looking tired as she puts down a cup of coffee. She comes over and pops the mask up to give me a kiss on the forehead before she squeezes my bicep.

"Hi Sweetness, you've been out for a while. How are you feeling?"

I try to respond, but a coughing fit overtakes me, and I curl up. Carrie is there, perched on the bed and trying to support me as I fall back onto the pillow. I ask the only question I want the answer to before I know I'll fall back into unconsciousness. "Did we win, or are we out?"

Carrie smiles tightly but still smiles. "They are still playing, Sweetness."

I reply, "Ok, that's good. I'll check in later."

I close my eyes and drift off quickly before I hear her whisper, "Don't leave me, Sweetness."

***

Carrie

Sitting here watching Conner sleep, after he woke up briefly to ask how the game went, my mind keeps running through what I should have done differently.

Thankfully, I can stay here, this isn't Pandemic level protocols. I've been tested and cleared, so I don't have to wear a mask, but this is the slowest kind of torture. I can't imagine Hell, but if it does, it would be exactly like this. Sitting here watching someone you love, someone usually so full of life, lying motionless in a hospital bed with tubes and wires stuck in him. Except for the rise and fall of his chest, Conner could be more than unconscious. He could be dead.

You can't think that way, Carrie. That is a bad, bad, terrible drain to circle.

Suddenly, my dream from my first weekend at Conner's house comes rushing back to me. It wasn't Scott in the hospital, like I thought, but Conner. I had a premonition, and that thought nearly breaks me. It's all so triggering. I thought I'd worked through the medical trauma from everything they had to do to declare Scott dead, even though he was gone before they even loaded him in the ambulance.

Now that I'm dealing with Conner being ill, I'm a few seconds away from going nuts. It will be so much easier when Joel is here. Without Conner and me being married or engaged, the medical staff is only giving me the barest shred of information. What I've gotten is the worst-case scenario until his test results come back.

We will not think about the past repeating itself. Think about how you and Conner are going to live happily ever after.

Try as I might, those cheerful daydreams I've spent hours thinking about won't come to the forefront of my mind. The image seared into my brain is the one before me–Conner is practically dead. I move back and forth in the small private room. Some would call it pacing, but I consider it movement to make sure I don't go crazy, which is a distinct possibility given the amount of coffee I've had and how long I've been sitting here – since before eight am this morning.

He's been out for nearly ten hours.

On yet another trip back across the room, my phone buzzes. Two messages, one from Joel and one from Maley.

Joel says,

I look forward to meeting you in about an hour. My plane landed ahead of this storm that's coming in and I'm in an Uber on my way. It's on Conner's app. {winking emoji}

I chuckle and sigh out a huge breath of relief. He is an incredible guy, like Conner, but in a more "Dad" kind of way. His wife Misty got him on the first flight here, which still took two connections. I take a second and say a prayer of gratitude. I'm a little calmer after I do that and then check Maley's message. She is finishing up work for the day and tells me she will call me when she gets home in an hour.

They've each grown close to Conner since Thanksgiving. They missed a stable male presence in their lives and while Sabrina gives him a lot of grief, Maley calls either him, me, or one of her sisters every day on the way home from work. Elise is playing in the game I could watch out in the lobby, but I won't leave Conner.

I take out my last vegan protein bar from my purse and the last few swigs from my water bottle I've refilled twice now.

I go over to kiss Conner's forehead, which is still alarmingly warm, and he mumbles in his sleep before shifting. He barely fits and I try to smooth out the sheet and blanket he is tangled in. I run my fingers through the longer hair on the top of his head and then down the shaved sides.

I lean down to whisper in his ear, "I love you, Sweetness. Don't leave me. I'm right here."

CHAPTER 43

Maley

"I can't believe Mama is going through this again!"

"I know, right? This shit is intense." Sabrina replies in her usual salty manner.

She started cussing when she was in fourth grade, and she's never stopped. She reins it in around Mama, but she cusses more than most people I've ever met. I take a deep breath.

I know everyone needs me to be strong, but Sabrina knows the real me. She knows how broken up I was after we lost Dad, being away at PT school. Mama nearly went crazy with Elise acting out. Sabrina had just graduated from nursing school and was about to start her specialty training in Houston. She lived at home for a while before she had to get her own place so she could focus.

She joins me on this trip down memory lane with her next comment. "I hope Elise doesn't start drinking again over this. Remember how she was after Dad died?"

I take another deep breath in and blow it out. "Yes, but she's had a lot of help. And she is a lot older. She has a strong group of friends. I think she will be ok. Plus, Conner isn't Dad. He is a great guy and great for Mama, but he isn't Dad."

"Yeah." That's the only reply I get from Sabrina, who can sometimes get so caught up in her thoughts that she says the bare minimum.

So, I fill in the space. "I think he will be ok, though. They already started him on the antivirals and Mama says he is sleeping thanks to the pain meds and fluids. What is your professional opinion, Sab?"

She sighs in a slightly bored tone. "I work on kids, you know. But yes, I think he will be ok. I am more worried about that storm coming in. Have you heard about that? What if Mama gets stuck at the hospital with him?"

I haven't been able to check my phone all day because my patient appointment schedule was full, as usual, since I'm the only PT who works on Saturdays. Sabrina fills me in, and it sounds like a bad winter blast is hitting the East Coast this week. We are planning to fly up there with Mama, but our work schedules wouldn't allow it. We had to risk them losing their first game, which they are playing now. It's a tight one too.

With the weather, though, the tournament may get delayed entirely.

"You know, this storm could end up being a good thing. It will give time for Conner to recover and come back. Have you heard how today's game is going?"

Sabrina snorts, "Of course, Elise has me recording it. It's a great game. They are tied in overage."

None of us knew anything about soccer when Elise started playing, but we are now all in.

"Ok, I am pulling up to my place and I'll turn it on when I get inside. I told Mama I'd call her when I got home, so I'll let you know if I hear and you do the same."

"Right, ok, byeeeeee." Sabrina says our traditional closing and hangs up.

I get inside my condo, thankful to be alone. I flop down on the couch and scowl at the pile of my ex-boyfriend's shit in the corner. He has two more days to get it before I throw it in the trash. Or burn it, whatever I feel like in the moment. He is such an immature asshole, good at masquerading as a grown man.

I need to find a grown-up. I think as I kick off my shoes and press my mother's contact number.

As it rings, my thoughts transition and I send up a small prayer for Conner and my mom, as I know she has to be in hell right now. She picks up and I say, "Hi Mama, tell me what's going on."

***

Sabrina

This game is fucking bananas.

I've watched my sister play a lot of soccer. Well, not a lot because I was off living my own best life. I didn't appear at home for a while; it was too painful to walk into that house without my dad there. Then I moved in during the worst of my sister's behavior. I had to move back out six months later because it was too hard to focus. I felt bad, but I had to make it through nursing school.

I helped Mama get Elise into a therapist and we all stopped drinking. Maley and I will still have the occasional glass of wine, but never to excess and never with Mama and Elise.

Now, watching my sister's team battle it out for their place in the semi-final of the NCAA tournament, I realize soccer saved our family. Without the routine of practice and the rigor of club life, things could have gotten a lot worse. Now, life is so much better–for all of us.

Well, except for Conner. I know he will get better. He is so fit and while this is scary; I have more than enough experience with people who have life-threatening diseases to know that he will be fine. The biggest concern for someone like Conner is that it would anchor in a major organ, like his heart or liver, and wreak havoc.

He will be back to normal in a week, but it's going to be rough till then–especially on my mom. She has worked hard to get over what happened with my dad, but trauma likes to stick. I just hope she doesn't go off the deep end and shut down. Or worse.

As I told my sister, this early winter storm is a blessing in disguise. If they have to delay the games, he should be able to at least make the final.

They need three extra days. Just three extra days, Lord.

I'm not sure who I am talking to, but I spent enough time in a high school youth group to pray.

Most of my prayers are that quick because I'm always on the go and my mind is so busy. I don't think Whoever God is, He or She minds too much. They wouldn't be a very good all-knowing, all-loving being if They were mad at me all the time. As I ponder this for a second before turning my attention back to the game and packing to leave, I hear a brief whisper.

I don't know if it is me or God, in my heart or my ear, but it is there and says,

You've got four days. It's all going to be ok.

I close my eyes and bow my head in acknowledgment of that still, small voice, and I choose to believe what it says.

It's all going to be ok, and I feel an urgent need to let my mother and sisters know that. I send out a text on our family group chat.

Guys, it's all going to be ok. I know things are scary right now, but it is all going to work out.

At this moment, I realize my sister is on the screen. The game progressed to a shoot-out and Elise is lining up to take her shot. It's just her and the goalie, with her team like statues behind her. It's a situation she's been in a million times before, but I can see from her posture she is nervous. The close-up shows her jaw set in a hard line and her green eyes as hard as emeralds.

I put my hand on my heart, like Mama always does and whisper, "Play from your heart, E."

As I watch, her face relaxes. She blows out a breath and does her little pre-kick routine, dragging her cleats through the grass. She dances a little on her toes before she runs up to connect the ball with her left foot.

It soars towards the goal, and I close my eyes to wait for the sound of the ball hitting the back of the net.

***

Elise

The second the inside of my left foot contacts the ball, I know it is going in. My signature upper ninety kick is unstoppable. The keeper goes in the opposite direction, and it sails straight into the net with a whooshing sound.

I hear the keeper hit the ground a split second later.

Then I hear my team erupt behind me. I'm standing there with my eyes closed, listening before Alyssa grabs me by the shoulders, swings me around and pulls me into her. She beats me on my back a little too aggressively and then the swell of the moment carries me away and the team is cheering, jumping and celebrating our win.

We are going to the semi-finals. And I did my job.

I did it for my team.

I did it for myself.

I did it for Conner.

I did it for my mama.

I break from the cluster of my teammates, who are now all on the field. I look around and lock eyes with my favorite coach I've ever played for. She is the only one on the team who knows my full story - the why I stay in on Saturday nights and don't party like some other girls.

Why I don't go chasing after guys or why I only post on social media to promote the team.

She knows my ugly history and accepts me. She expects excellence, and I will not let her down.

I partied hard during my sophomore and junior years of high school. I had lots of bad sex with high school boys. There are enough pictures on the internet of me from those years, I never want to post another personal one ever.

I was so scared it would all come out when Maciee Griggs started digging around. I knew that girl was a bitch the very second; I met her. We'd wiped out most of my socials at the end of my junior year after I made amends to my mom and sisters. But you never know if we got it all.

She knows why I am the job. She knows why excelling in soccer is so important to me. She helps me navigate the toxic perfectionism and shame when I don't live up to my own unreasonable expectations.

She is the only one who knows I go to A.A. meetings every Wednesday night and lets me leave training five minutes early to make it on time. I don't think even Conner knows. Mama said that is my story to tell him.

Why does Coach Inanna do all this for me?

Because soccer saved her too. So, we will give it everything we have until we can't anymore.

It's why I want to be a lawyer–to ensure every girl has a safe environment to learn and grow in this sport. While not everyone experiences what the U.S. Women's gymnastics team went through, it happens in every sport, plus there is still an enormous pay gap. I want to fight for those who can't fight for themselves. I want to leave a mark on this world.

Making that kick was another step towards doing that.

I push my way through my teammates to the sidelines, hustling to stand in front of Coach Inanna. She doesn't have tears in her eyes. That would be too soft for her. What shines in her face, though, is just the same–pride.

She reaches up to hug me. A gesture in and of itself is momentous. "I tried to do you proud, Coach."

She pulls back, no expression on her face but that pride shining through her dark eyes. She says at a volume slightly louder than a whisper, "You did, kid."

"Any updates about Coach Conner, or have you heard from my mom?"

She shakes her head and says, "Let's get to the locker room and we will call her."

Just then, the rest of the team surges around us, carrying us into the locker room on a tidal wave of voices full of victory.

Chapter 44

Carrie

I just bawled snot all over Conner's brother. And he is huge!

I don't think I've ever met a man this big, and that's saying something because Conner makes me feel small. Joel might even be larger than Erik. With Joel hugging me, I feel tiny. It has a very immediate and awe-inspiring effect, as I release all my pent-up emotions and go a little boneless.

Shaking his hand was an effort of will I don't want to repeat. I want to lie down and sleep for a week.

Joel lets go of my hand and smiles. Despite his size–which I'm sure can come with a propensity to do violence- he is very gentle with me. His energy feels like when Conner shifts into

"Coach" mode before a game. With a presence this massive, it feels like Joel is suited up to go to war.

As a nurse walks in the door, it feels like Joel is just about to do that. The medical staff has told me almost nothing, completely standoffish, and from our texts, Joel is pissed. I only want to know what is happening with Conner and how they are going to help him. Making some headway with answers on Conner's treatment plan is a tremendous relief.

The nurse catches sight of Joel and instantly pauses. She gets this deer in headlights look and stammers, "W-W-who are you, sir?" She adds the 'sir' on like she was afraid if she didn't, he was going to pillage the whole hospital.

I step in between them and meet the nurse's eyes. She's been in here a few times and is one of the staff making a point to be short with me. I nod my head and say, "This is Conner's medical contact. Now that he is here, it's about time you give us some fucking answers."

Yah, I might be wound up.

Joel steps up to my side. We both make a wall in front of Conner that the nurse will not penetrate. She narrows her eyes at me, especially given my rude language. I don't feel sorry at all. She starts to clap back, and Joel holds up a massive hand, stopping her mid-breath.

He begins slowly, with a sardonic smirk, effectively knowing that I'm about to blow this whole fucking hospital up if I don't get some answers right this minute. He looks at the nurse directly, which makes her eyes go round as the full moon and she swallows audibly.

"I think what my brother's partner here is saying is that I'm here now and we need to know what's happening with him. I'm also going to need whatever forms to sign to ensure whether it's me or Carrie. One or both of us can get the information we need to decide until Conner can make them for himself. I know it's been stressful, and you've just been doing your job, following protocols. But as Carrie has been sitting vigil all day–almost as long as you've been on shift. I'm sure - you can understand a little transparency will go a long way. So, what can you tell us?"

I'm impressed with the way Joel is handling this woman. Gently, with authority and without expecting me to make any apologies for my words or actions. He is not shaming me for being upset or angry. He is validating that I've been here and making sure I'll be the one who is Conner's contact from now on.

I've never been more grateful for a man's help. I drop my shoulders, unclench my jaw and take a deep breath. Wound up isn't even the right phrase to describe how I've been feeling. I've been ready to fight or run since Inanna woke me up yesterday–or the day before–I can't remember now after seeing Conner passed out on the floor.

Now that I am slightly less tense, I prepare myself to hear what the nurse has to say. She is the charge nurse, which explains a lot. Sabrina has told me enough about her work environment that I should have gone the 'catch more flies with honey than vinegar' route rather than becoming the bitchy mess I have been.

I probably should apologize.

The nurse tells us about Conner's medical state and how serious it is. His white blood cell counts were incredibly low. Joel confirms Conner hasn't been sick in years, not even during the pandemic, so this is the first challenge his immune system has seen for a long time.

They started him on a course of intravenous antivirals and antibiotics because Conner is developing pneumonia, even after only twelve hours. He has been sleeping so much because of how sick he is. Moving around will help him, but they've been giving him anti-nausea medication, which can also make him drowsy.

The nurse tells us, "The intake doctor said it was better that way because this superbug hits not only the respiratory system, but can also affect heart tissue, leading to permanent damage. The doctor thought if we could keep him calm and at rest, he would recover quicker, and it would also keep the virus away from his heart."

All the blood whooshes out of my brain at that statement. *Conner's heart could be damaged?*

I feel like I'm on the verge of panic. A heart attack killed Scott. I don't know if I can handle that possibility happening again with another man, even if he is my soul mate.

The shock of this potential side effect has me almost missing what the nurse says next, a response to this revelation I must have said out loud. "We don't think it is a small possibility, though, that Mr. Doreland has already had major heart damage. We are going to run some tests when he wakes up, but the doctor is almost positive given how low his pulse ox was when he came in, the heart tissue has already been injured."

I see stars forming at the edge of my vision and the room spins. I walk backwards to the chair beside Conner's bed I've been sitting in when I'm not directly in the bed with him. I can't hear what they are saying, as Joel and the nurse continue to talk. All I can focus on is the reality that I'm going to lose another man. I'm going to watch my gorgeous, strong, soccer god deteriorate; his heart muscle already atrophying in his chest, never to regain full health.

Conner is going to lose his health, and it will mean he loses everything he has worked his whole life for.

You can't handle this. This is even worse than death. Get out. Get out now.

The sinister voice yells in my brain. If I wasn't sitting down already, I would collapse. My chest tightens painfully, and my lungs seize. A small part of my brain knows this is an overreaction, and it's probably not as bad as I'm taking it. But I can't take the chance to hear any horrible news again.

Conner may not die today, but his life is over. You can't go through that again. Get out. Get out now.

Before I realize it, Joel is kneeling in front of me, offering me a glass of water. He is waving his hand the size of a bear's paw in front of my face, trying to pull my attention back from the darkness I've sunk into, saying, "Carrie, are you there? Did you hear what our next steps are?"

I mutely shake my head to clear the panic attack and communicate I don't know what's going on.

Joel continues, "Ok, Carrie, that's it. Take a breath and drink some water."

Taking a sip of the water, my hands are shaking, and I almost spill it. Joel takes it from my hand, and I slump back in the chair. My breathing labors as Joel stands up to sit on the side of the bed, next to a sleeping Conner, who is rolled on his left side, towards me.

He looks at his brother for a long time before he says, "Carrie, I know you only heard about the potential heart damage. You didn't hear the nurse say they've all been told to offer only the worst-case scenario for this virus. She said Conner is so fit. She is confident he will be much improved in a day or so."

Joel pauses to see if I'm taking any of this new information in. It is registering, but barely.

After a minute, he continues, "I gave them Conner's full medical history. He is in near-perfect form. His last physical was the best since his professional years. I know we have nothing to worry about. They will be back in a few minutes to get some blood and do another round of tests, which I know will show his immune system is bouncing back, just as it is supposed to."

He is looking at Conner, whose chest is rising and falling rhythmically, peacefully. I close my eyes and try to will into being what Joel is saying. When I open my eyes again, Joel is looking at me with a very soft but critical eye.

"Carrie, you need to go get some food and get some rest. They are going to ween off the medication, making him sleep so he will wake up soon, for a full assessment. You will want to see him open his eyes and talk. You will be the first person he asks for."

He puts his massive hand on my shoulder. "There is more than enough hope. He is strong and his heart is going to be fine. Carrie, are you listening?"

I am looking at Joel but through him. My brain feels like it is underwater. I look down at Conner and I say weakly from somewhere outside of myself, "I know he will be ok."

That's all I can muster as Joel opens his phone to call me an Uber. While I collect my purse and jacket, Joel gives me a list of things to do before I come back to Conner. I appreciate it, but the after effect of my panic has me in a vice grip.

I can't do this. I have to get out of this before I get hurt again. I keep my mouth shut and nearly cry again, as Joel gives me a parting bear hug, which to me feels like a goodbye. My fear is all-consuming,

So, I do the best thing I can think of, I run.

Even as my logical mind knows what I'm doing is the wrong choice, I completely bypass the Uber and get into a Yellow Cab Taxi. I tell the driver to take me straight to the airport. I am going to get on an airplane before this massive storm hits. I don't care where I'm going or that I have nothing with me.

I just know I can't come back to Conner, shriveled like a raisin, that visual haunting my mind. I will figure out what to do when I get home, but I know I am not strong enough to watch them try to revive him. I can't watch the sheet go over his face when they give up. I can't watch history repeat itself. I will not watch the man that I love die.

Again.

Chapter 45

I nanna

After riding the bus back to the hotel, I showered and changed. I took a long look at my bed, longing for a nap. Instead, I got dressed, braided my still damp hair and wrapped it up on top of my head. Carrie needs someone to relieve her at the hospital. Joel's there now so he can catch me up.

I send him a quick text to say I am on my way and all I get back from him is, "I sent Carrie back to the hotel two hours ago. You haven't seen her?"

Huh, that's weird. Neither she nor Elise told me she was coming back. I send him a "thumbs up" emoji and immediately after, "I'll find her." Lacing up my Jordans that match my thickest fleece track suit, I also grab my parka, slinging it over one shoulder as I head to Carrie's room.

When I get there, the cleaning crew is working on getting Carrie's room ready for the next guest. Standing dumbfounded in the doorway, I see her suitcase. Getting the attention of the lady working and after a few fits and determines the best language, we can both communicate in, which turns out to be Spanish. I ask her when the guest who was staying here checked out.

At her response, I feel sick. *The guest called to check out more than an hour ago. She said to leave her suitcase in the office, someone would collect it. She had an emergency out of town and had to catch a flight immediately.*

I thank the woman and tip her with a ten-dollar bill, which she gladly accepts and smiles. I thank her again and as I'm walking away to the elevator; I send Erik an SOS text.

> *Bro, Carrie is gone. She left Conner. What the fuck is going on?*

He immediately responds, telling me to meet in the lobby to plan what the fuck we are going to do if Carrie has in fact left our boss and our friend in the hour of his most dire need.

I already know what I'm going to do. I'm going to find her and carve her fucking heart out.

***

Maley

"Mama, go back to the hospital. You just can't leave him." I'm trying to talk sense into my mother over Facetime. She is vacillating between being paralyzed with panic and the most massive freakout I've ever seen—even worse than over Elise and miles past how calm and collected she was after my dad died.

She is facing all the check-in counters and has her earbuds in, so she can talk to me and search for flights at the same time. After a moment's pause, I know, deep in my soul, she's found a flight home.

She confirms it a second later. "Maley, I can't stay and do this. I can't watch Conner fade. These have been the most wonderful months of my life, but he is going to wake up from this and be a different person. I can't support him; I can barely support myself right now. I have to come home and regroup."

Desperate for her to listen to me, I speak sternly, "Mother! You CAN NOT leave him. We will know nothing until he wakes up and you want to be there for that, don't you? The doctors are going to revise his prognosis once he is conscious and when the blood tests come back."

Saying more than I need to and suspicious she isn't listening to me, anyway; I make myself stop speaking.

She's made up her terror-addled mind and tells me, "Maley, I need you to make sure your sister can pick me up from the airport tonight when I get home."

She means Sabrina and I know she has lost it if she goes back to our childhood pattern of her telling me how to manage my younger sisters.

I try one more time to get her to listen. "Mama, PLEASE stay. It doesn't matter what condition he is in. You love Conner. He is your soulmate. You must go back to him. Think about how he will feel when he wakes up, and no one knows where you are."

She sighs and in a trembling voice says, "Maley, I know it will be awful for him. I'm not stupid. I know it will break his heart. What I'm doing is coming home to regroup. Then maybe he will understand why I can't be with him anymore." Her voice breaks on the last word, and she wails.

I know this is tearing her up, and it's just so unnecessary.

"Mama, you don't have to do this!" One more shot and as I say the words, I pray God takes them straight to her heart.

She clears her throat and sniffles loudly. "It's done, Sweetheart. I paid for the ticket and now I'm going to check in. I need to get on the plane before this storm closes everything down. I love you and I'll see you this weekend."

She says this like she knows I'm going to come home to be with her. I am mad as hell, but I will be there. This is too major a development for me to be four hours away from my family.

As soon as she hangs up, I dial the one person I know who will help me figure out what to do. It goes straight to voicemail.

I dial the second person who can help me—Sabrina. When she answers, the words come pouring out like spilled milk. "Mama has left Conner at the hospital. She is having a breakdown, and I can't get hold of Dulce. Sab, what the fuck are we going to do??"

***

Sabrina

I don't always like being the calm one. I wasn't as a child or teenager, but in nursing school; I learned to become scary quiet. It works well with doctors—especially residents. My charge nurses love me for it because when I finally hit that peak and go low instead of high, then people realize who the boss in the room is.

It's me. I'm the boss.

Right now, I need to channel this energy for my mom and sisters. I get why my mama is freaking out. I also understand why Maley is having such a hard time. She was the one who kept me in line in high school and after Dad died. She stepped in to make sure I didn't go off the rails. It was easy since we were at the same undergraduate university before she went into Physical Therapy school, and I went to nursing school two years later.

But now, she's done enough and needs me to be the big, bad, boss bitch I am and take control.

"Where is she now, Males?"

Maley is breathing heavily, fast. "Males, I need you to calm down and talk to me."

With a voice barely above a whisper, she has to really listen. Everyone does when I speak like this. My older sister finally takes a deep breath in, holds it for five seconds and lets that breath out in a long way that almost sounds like a balloon releasing air. It's one of her favorite calming practices and what she teaches her clients when they get overstimulated during a session. I've incorporated it when accessing a patient's port or changing an IV. I do it with them and it always makes them smile.

Synchronizing my breathing with hers, I ask, "Ok, Sister, are you feeling better?"

"Yep. Yes. Ok. What are we going to do about Mama? She just can't leave Conner."

I have to break it to her as gently as I can when I say, "Males, it's already done. She is already on the plane, and she hasn't taken off yet, but she is about to."

Maley switches gears like she always done when I've used the truth, and she knows I'm right.

"Well, then we at least need to get hold of Dulce. She is the only one who can talk sense into Mama."

"Males, I don't disagree, but as far as what it means for us, we are going to be the ones who deal with this fallout—as she falls apart right in front of us. I will track her flight and get her to the airport. You keep trying to reach Dulce."

"Should we let Elise know what's going on?" She sounds unsure about this. Our desire to soften the blow for our youngest sister may never go away. Neither of us wants to be the bearer of news that could pitch Elise over the edge into a terrible place. She's been doing so well, and I know we must trust she's done her work.

It is very hard to fight the instinct to protect her when going over the cliff edge is an actual possibility.

I mean, my mother already has.

I sigh and think before the best option occurs to me. "Do you have Coach Inanna's number? Maybe she can get on the phone with us, and we can update her and Elise at the same time."

In the end, after a quick call to Elise, who finds Inanna and Coach Erik in the lobby, already deep in heated discussion, that's what we do. It's like a freaking war strategy meeting, not to save a country but to save two people's hearts.

***

Elise

My mother has lost her ever-loving mind.

That's one of my grandma's favorite phrases and it fits here.

"So, you are telling me she just left? Like got on a plane and left? My strong, beautiful mother would never do something so stupid, like leave the man of her dreams on his deathbed."

Inanna coughs loudly and corrects, "He isn't dying. In fact, he should wake up any minute now. They took him off the sleepy time meds and now are just waiting for her to wake up. Joel is watching him like a hawk.

My sisters are quiet on the phone until Erik asks for an update on my mom's flight status.

Sabrina, apparently playing Mama's travel agent, pipes up with, "All I can see is that she is still on the ground. Her flight isn't in the air. It's been over two hours now, so I'm guessing they will take them back to the terminal soon. It doesn't look like the weather is going to get any better and the

Raleigh-Durham Airport is right in the middle of the storm's path."

Maley adds at the last second, "They are only landing flights too close to redirect, is what the news is saying."

I put my chin in my palms. I then move my index and middle fingers to my temples and rub. I've showered, hydrated and eaten after the game, but it's been a long day. This crisis only increases my building headache. I need to go paint or draw, something to still my mind meditatively. I've tried doing meditation with Mama, but I almost always have to have something to occupy my hands.

Mama said I was born naturally caffeinated. Remembering that sweet comment only adds to my confusion. Even in the worst of my acting out, she never got so far over the edge that she, too, acted out. She was always the calm one. Well, her and Sabrina. Maley is steady too but between my mother and next oldest sister, I have known I can always count on them for anything.

Now, it seems Mama flipped out. It's so unlike her–or what I'm used to. It unsettles something deep within me. It feels like a rock has been dislodged and if it slips, the whole slide of the cliff will come crashing down. Soon I'm going to need to talk through this feeling with my sponsor and maybe even my therapist.

But I will make those calls after the most critical one.

I need to know how Conner is doing and without Mama there; I feel like my lifeline is flapping in the wind. After Joel answers the phone and I introduce myself, the warmth in his voice makes that loose rock release and the barrier between me and my emotions comes crashing down. I get up from the table where I was sitting in the lobby with Inanna and Erik, my sisters still talking with both coaches.

I barely squeeze out, "How is Conner?" around the boulder in my throat. Joel makes a soothing noise in the back of his before he tells me in a voice and as soothing as the ocean,

"Well, Kiddo, he just woke up. He immediately asked for your Mama but since we can't seem to get a hold of her, do you want to talk to him?"

Chapter 46

Carrie

I absolutely deserve this.

It's all I can think of on the tarmac, in my small airplane seat right by the bathroom. It was the last one available on the plane and I paid an exorbitant fee for it. Paying through the nose for a plane ticket I should never have bought is another well-deserved punishment.

I let my terror take over. I let the story in my head about how Conner could end up coming out of this take me to the darkest of places. It's not even reality because he is so healthy. Part of me knows everything I heard was just the worst-case scenario the medical staff must give you to cover their asses.

In the tiny, smell seat, I move from the terror-driven flight or fight response to the depressed, shame-filled spiral. I've healed so much, grown so much since those dark days after Scott passed and Elise's partying years. I didn't think I could react so poorly, letting my fear hijack my nervous system and decision-making abilities.

Yet, smelling the scent of the last passenger's potty break and that only confirms one thing: *I absolutely deserve this.*

Several of my fellow passengers are getting fidgety and complaining. The flight deck has been waiting for clearance from the tower, but it doesn't look like it is going to happen. The storm is just too bad.

We are all tired, hungry after two hours on the tarmac and I'm so racked with guilt, I'm not sure I'll be able to stand up when they tell us we are going back to the terminal. They most assuredly will. There is only so long they can legally keep us here, but it is still a long enough period. Everyone will be good and miserable when it happens. They haven't even offered us water or snacks.

I absolutely deserve to go hungry and thirsty. I deserve all of this for what I've done to Conner.

I am bereft because I know he will wake up soon. As I click the button on my phone to check the time, nothing happens. I realize my phone has run out of battery. Now, I'm not only away from him, but with absolutely no way to contact him–or anyone else.

Maley and Sabrina know I'm on a flight home, so I'm sure at least one of them is tracking the status. Someone will be there to pick me up, but if they decide to leave me stranded, I wouldn't blame them.

I absolutely deserve to be left at the airport.

Spinning over all of this in my mind, the desperation to tell Conner - to tell everyone - how sorry I am for making such a rash, emotional, over-the-top decision climbs up my throat and just sits there, like there is a boulder of emotion clogging my esophagus. My vocal cords are so tight, my throat physically aches.

My stomach is completely empty, which is just as well as I might not get anything down–or keep it down. My bones feel so lead and even as I try to put the tray table down and rest my aching head on my arms.

I'm just a little too tall. I don't fit in any way that could make it comfortable.

I absolutely deserve this. All of this. Conner is going to hate me. He would divorce me if we were married, but luckily for him, we didn't get that far.

I contort my upper body sufficiently to rest my head finally on my forearms, and I remain in that position, with my head down and my eyes closed, for a very long time. I'm sure this is what Purgatory feels like.

Or maybe this is just the waiting room for Hell, because it would make sense. I would end up there.

Woman who leaves the love of her life, gravely ill in a hospital bed, to save her own emotional skin. Yep, definitely a one-way ticket to the Eternal Burning Man.

I deserve it. All of it. From here to eternity.

I must doze a little, overcome by sheer exhaustion, because I suddenly feel a pinching sensation in both my arms and hands. I realize my arms have lost blood flow. It causes me no amount of discomfort at rubbing life back into them. The plane itself is quiet. In fact, there is brief sound at all, inside or outside the plane.

It is eerily silent as the blood flows back into my limbs at a glacial pace.

When the full use of my arms comes back, the flight attendant startles everyone with an update. "Attention Passengers! We thank you for your patience and this long wait on the tarmac. We will finally get moving. So, we are heading back to the Terminal to deplane. I hope we get out of the airport before the city itself shuts down. Because this is urgent for all of us, we ask for your complete and total cooperation as we get everyone off in a calm, orderly fashion. Thank you for your willing assistance!"

I have enough energy to snort. We have no choice, which means we can go quietly or go quietly.

The only thing we will be up against is people's impatience to get off the plane and try to make it somewhere else than the airport. At this thought, and since I have nothing but my purse, I stand up in the aisle. I hear a few grumbles while people collect their belongings from the overhead bins, but nothing surprising.

We have been on this plane long enough that the feeling of being prisoners has set in. We all move as one as we embark not to our destination but to where we started.

It takes less than ten minutes for me to get off the airplane. As soon as I step into the Terminal and look through the window at the world beyond, my heart sinks to my shoes. I had geared myself up to rush to the ride-share exit past baggage claim to flag down a taxi. But outside, the world is white. The airport is covered by a layer of snow, with more coming down, like someone is shaking out a feather pillow. The sky is empty of planes, and I know I'm in for a long night.

I see a sole plane taxi and land at another terminal and the loneliness of being without Conner, without my girls, hits me square between the eyes.

I absolutely deserve this; I think once again, for the thousandth time.

There are others who try to get out, but only a few taxis, ride-shares and shuttles to various garages are left. I know, deep in my bones and from the same place I first realized Conner was the one for me, that I'm stuck.

And I have no way of checking in. I realize I need to find somewhere to charge my phone and get in contact with my daughters. Hopefully, the storm hasn't taken out cell service so I can let them know I'm ok.

Right then, my stomach grumbles. It is triggered by the smell of hot pizza and reminds me I haven't eaten since I ate my last protein bar nearly six hours ago. I follow my nose to a long line in front of an airport restaurant–a Sbarro Pizza chain.

The line is so long, there is no way I will get to purchase a whole pizza, which is the only thing they are selling. I walk towards other airport-based food places, but every one of them is full or selling out and there are lots of people getting wasted at the bars.

I guess if humans are going to get stuck, the best thing to do is to eat, drink and be merry. Kind of like what we do for hurricanes in the gulf. This is going to be an airport-wide Hurricane Party.

I think all of this as I trudge along on my quest. With my body moving, my head clears a bit and the tightness in my chest eases. I walk towards the other terminal and everywhere people are camping out, setting up and preparing to hunker down till the storm passes and the roads are drivable.

It has a very end-of-the-world kind of vibe as even the airport staff, including TSA, are standing around, milling about. Every TV in the place has the local news pulled up. We will at least have updates on what's happening on the outside of our temporary shelter, or prison, however you want to look at it, unless the power goes out.

I lift a silent prayer for Conner to forgive me, as I take one slow step at a time. I wonder as I wander. I think about what it would be like if I were here with the girls. That, of course, makes me think about what they are all doing right now. Of course, my thoughts go to Conner and imagine what jokes he would make before he took charge, got us food and got me settled for the long haul, however long that would be.

I picture in my mind's eye that he finds us a cozy, out of the way corner where we can curl up together. My head would be on his shoulder as he cradled me to him, using our jackets as blankets and pillows. In my fantasy, the concrete floor wouldn't be nearly as hard as it is in reality, and there is no issue with us being hungry or miserable.

We would be together and that's all that matters.

At this train of thought, I start to tear up and do my best to hold back the tears threatening to rush out. The more I walk, though, the more the emotions rush to the surface, almost like the feeling of standing up too quickly. I've made it to the other terminal now and before I have a nervous breakdown and collapse in the middle of the walking space, I head to the nearest set of seats by a gate with a smaller group of people.

Miraculously, the seat faces the window, so I don't have to bawl my eyes out where everyone can see. Once my butt hits the beige pleather material of terminal seating, I cover my face and let it all go. My shoulders are heaving with sobs, and I feel like I'm going to throw up, scream or both.

I am in the depths of hell, letting loose the buildup of guilt, shame and self-loathing that has been eating me up from the inside for hours since I got on the plane.

I don't know how long I sit there crying, but I'm startled to feel a hand on my shoulder, and I jerk my head up. I can barely see through my swollen eyes, but I hear the unmistakable voice of my best friend whisper as she comes to sit in the seat next to me. For a long moment, I couldn't process why she was here or what she was saying. Her long fingers wrap around my shoulder and give me a little shake, and then I finally grasp what she is saying.

"Carrie, It's me Dulce. My plane landed and then they shut the city down. It's a fucking mess! But what are you doing here? I thought you were with Conner at the hospital. That's the last I heard from Maley before my plane left Houston."

I don't have the brain capacity to form words for a bit, so she just sits with me. I stare into her soft, cocoa eyes and not quite believing the one person who could understand what I did and call me on my bullshit, then help me figure a way out, is sitting right in front of me.

My face contorts as I feel the torrent of grief overwhelm me. I tell her, "I couldn't watch him get worse. I had to leave. I thought I was going home. But Conner is my home now. I messed up so bad, D-say."

She smiles at the nickname the girls gave her many years ago when we met, both of at church until our spiritual paths deepened and took us along other paths. She nods. Her smile remains, even as it grows a little smaller. She takes my hands away from my face and holds them in hers.

"Oye Tonto, we've been through worse. Yes, you were panicking and yes, it was stupid to leave. It's even stupider to get stuck at the airport with no way for people to reach you. But I understand. More than anyone, I understand. So, let's find something to eat and then we will figure out how to get out of this fucking Walking Dead screen test and back to your man."

I nod profusely as I wipe my nose and eyes on my sleeve. My eyes feel gritty, and my throat is raw and dry. I choke out, "You aren't going to lecture me on how I acted?"

This time, her smile is megawatt. "Oh, don't worry. I'll ream your ass out later, after you've had some food, some sleep, and properly apologized to your man. And I'll take all the time I want to yell at you for being so reckless and idiotic. But now is not the time. You panicked, you left and now we need to get you–back to your home. And of course, by home, I mean Conner. You are his home, too, dummy."

CHAPTER 47

Conner

"How long have I been out and where is Carrie?"

I feel like dog shit.

No, I feel lower than dog shit.

I feel like dog shit that's been run over by a hundred semi-trucks, stuck to both the tires and the road.

I have never felt this bad in my life. My whole-body aches and my throat is killing me. I know I've been asleep and now that I'm not, I must be on the path to healing, but it doesn't feel like it. This superbug I caught, probably from someone on campus before we left for the tournament, is no joke. Carrie had it just last week, and now I know she was in agony. I would have saved her from this. I felt even worse when I couldn't be there to take care of her.

Well, maybe. It could be a draw between how badly I definitely felt not being able to be there to care for her and how I feel now. Yes, definitely a draw and I'm coming up nil-nil.

Fucking viruses. I mean, hasn't the world dealt with enough?

My voice sounds like Hades himself–straight from the underworld. It was a deep rasp I don't recognize, and it gives Joel the shivers.

He puts on a happy, affected tone I see right through. "Hey man! You are awake! Oh, damn Conner, we've been so worried, but this is a great sign. They've kept you out to make sure the meds fully saturate your system seems to have worked. You look good, or at least better than you have been looking, and from what Carrie said, definitely better than when you came in here. It's been all hands-on deck trying to get you well. The girls won their game, you know. Inanna did a great job filling in and even as it went into PKs in overage, they pulled it out. You are going to be so proud of them, playing in the freezing rain like they were. They are just beasts on the field. No one wore out, no one quit. And of course, your star freshman nailed the winning shot. She is already a freaking legend."

His word vomit is grandly suspicious. I know him better than anyone, well besides Misti. He only rambles when he is nervous and wants to avoid answering a direct question that will no doubt mean pissing someone off.

In that still raspy, lifetime smoker sounding, king of the underworld voice, I look him dead in the eye and say, "Joel, cut the bullshit. How long have I been out and where *the fuck* is Carrie?"

His phone vibrates in his pocket, and he has the nerve to look relieved. He takes it out to see who it is. He holds up a finger, like this is the one call he was waiting on. I keep my eyes pinned on him. My gaze is burning a hole in his forehead as he answers, "Hey, this is Joel."

I hear Elise introduce herself from across the room. Joel visibly relaxes as she finishes her introduction and then tells her, "Well, Kiddo, he just woke up. He immediately asked for your Mama but since we can't seem to get a hold of her, do you want to talk to him?"

I can't hear her exact words, and her voice gets very quiet. We've only just forged a bond and go beyond the player-coach dynamic.

Apparently, she assents and Joel extends his arm, shuffles a few feet across the room and holds the phone for me to take. Despite the steel rod in my soul, my hand shakes a little as I grab it. I hold it up to my ear and with a voice I soften from the lord of death vibe to a slightly more cuddly version of his coach tone, say, "Hey Superstar, I heard you won the game for us. I knew you could and would."

To make her comfortable, I quiz her on the status of the rest of the team. It also loosens me up. There is something about small talk, even if you know you are rushing headlong towards a cliff, that can either be an irritant or a comfort.

In this case, when it's about my team and their epic win, it is an enormous comfort.

While she talks, I take more sips of water. My throat is on fire, and I make a note to ask the doctor about that. I hear the pause before she drops the bomb. When she tells me Carrie left, I draw in a ragged, painful breath, but I'm not surprised. When I heard Joel say we couldn't get a hold of Carrie, I braced myself for confirmation of what I already knew.

Carrie didn't choose to fight or freeze when her medical PTSD kicked in. She flew, literally.

I see the look of shock on his face. I hold up my middle finger, which he returns. It's our brotherly version of a "fuck-you-but-thumbs-up."

To Elise, I say, "No, Elise, I'm not surprised. Your Mom has been through a lot, and this probably triggered her in a way she never expected. Don't get me wrong, I'm pissed as hell for pulling this stunt. But I also know her well enough to know she will come to her senses and come back when she can."

As I force down more water, which tastes like it has been sitting in the cup beside my bed for a long while, I can't help but make a face. Everything hurts, even my brain, as I try to focus on comforting Elise.

Even though my heart is a wreck that Carrie left, I am strangely at peace. I know, deep in my bones, she will come back. What I said to Elise is exactly what I know. Carrie watched her husband die, then the medical team crank on him, to no avail.

I'm sure seeing me in this bed was her worst nightmare, besides it being one of her girls.

I have a choice to make. I can either let this kill what is the best relationship I've ever had.

Or I can view this as I feel it - a minor setback. Carrie will have to do some work on this—we both will. It isn't a bad idea for us to get into therapy. Everyone at our age has baggage.

Yet, it was her love for me that called me back from the dark, liminal space I was in. It was her heart that called to me. Even now, I can somehow feel her. I know she is miserable, desperate to get back to me.

My love for her will be the light that leads her out of her own darkness.

I never want to wake up again to find she left me because she thought she couldn't handle what was happening.

I let Elise cry for a little while before bringing her back. She's held it all together for everyone else, just like I know Carrie did before it all came out sideways. Elise has been strong for the team, for her sisters and even for her mom. She's been trying to puzzle out what's happening to explain it to me when I woke up.

When I sense the storm of emotion winding down, I ask her, "Elise, what's happening with the weather?" She tells me about this massive snowstorm that barreled into Raleigh like hell on wheels, shutting the city down overnight. It's been a long time since a blizzard of this magnitude hit this part of the state and at this time of year. Everyone was caught off guard.

I'm quiet for a minute as I process what she is saying, as she closes with, "Conner, even all the flights were canceled. Mama's flight still says it's at the gate."

Despite my low brain power, a small, dim lightbulb goes off and I say to anyone listening, "What if her flight never took off for Houston? What if she is stuck at the airport?"

Elise draws in a breath at the same time I hear my brother, the chicken shit in a grizzly bear's body, who let the little girl tell me the bad news, grunts in surprise.

Joel responds first with, "That's entirely possible. The entire city is down." I can practically hear the wheels turning in Elise's head on how to get her mother from the airport to me. Even though she can't see me, I hold my hand to physically slow her down and let out a hiss as that motion puts pressure on the IV in my hand.

The alarm in her voice is palpable. "Conner, what, are you ok?"

"Yes, yes, I'm ok, just moved my IV hand weird, and it reminded me I'm still an invalid." I make a sour face at Joel as he puts his hand up to his mouth to smother a small laugh. Now that I'm awake, he is not worried at all about my health and despite the sibling's delight at my pain, I am encouraged by his confidence. I know how I feel, how sick I have been, but I also know I'll make a full recovery.

And when I do, I might tie Carrie to my bed and never let her go.

Turning my attention back to the conversation with Elise, I feel buoyed by the thought that Carrie is stuck at the airport. It will only be a matter of time before she can come back because the ground isn't cold enough for the snow to stick around for long. It was seventy degrees in Raleigh last week, as it can be in the South during the early winter months before Christmas.

I know she will come back.

"I seriously don't know if she will come back." I hear Inanna say this and the silence that follows, which means Erik agrees and Elise doesn't want to argue with her. I look at Joel, who can now hear everything because I put the call on speaker.

I let the silence go on; the tension creeping up into my very sore shoulders. Inanna is always the point-counterpoint in every discussion, weighing the sides I don't see. It's why I hired her. She may be a pain in the ass, but her vision for strategy is unparalleled, and she has been nothing but an asset. She just proved to every major program in the country she is head coach material, and I tuck that thought in the back of my mind to deal with how long I have her as my second for later.

After Carrie comes back and after we set out to do exactly what we planned at the start of the season—win the whole fucking thing.

I take one more sip of stale hospital water before I speak through the fire in my vocal cords.

"Let me tell you what I know. Maybe I dreamed this while I was unconscious or maybe only a fool believes in magic, but Carrie and I have something they write legends about.

She may be scared, but she is coming back. The second she can get here, she will. This is a love story for the ages, and we will all welcome her back with open arms. Feel your feelings, but there is only a joyful reunion in the future. And keep in mind, right after she gets back, they will reschedule this fucking tournament. I will be ready, so ask yourself, will you?"

Without hesitation, everyone around the table at the hotel, which I realize is maybe more than just a few players, responds with "Yes, Coach!" Word must have gone out I was awake. I look at my brother, who says the same in his deep, melodious timbre.

Then we hear a strange voice at the door to my room. I swing my gaze over to the door to see a tall man in a white coat, who meets my eyes with mirth in his, and says, "Welcome back, Lazarus. Let's check your heart and get you reunited with your one true love, shall we?"

Chapter 48

Carrie

God, my neck hurts.

My first thought rushes to me as I sit up from spending the night on the airport floor. Groaning softly and trying to stretch gently so my body doesn't seize up, taking care to move my stiff sides and hips slowly.

Dulce, eyes closed and sitting with her back propped against the wall, is only a few feet from where she found me at a random gate. Her eyes pop open as I move and she says, "I wasn't asleep," which is a sure sign that she was. That and she looks pissed off. Not unusual for her first thing. As long as I've known her, she has loved to sleep even when it alludes to her. On days like that, everyone around her would feel her attitude.

That is until she found her man and he would promptly fuck the attitude out of her. She's been in a much better mood these last few years since she met Bryan.

"My shoulder is on fire, and I think my left foot is randomly asleep." Dulce grunts at my complaints. Nothing new for the two of us. We crashed out after talking for several hours about my freak out. It took the mass of travelers stuck in the Raleigh airport as many hours as us to settle and accept our current reality.

The news media is calling it "The Great Whiteout." Southerners are so dramatic.

To unravel my tight muscles, I ease my neck from side to side and roll my shoulders. Thankfully, they turned up the heat and there are so many people around; it is probably close to 80 degrees in our portion of the airport. Despite the temperature outside, this could be a tropical paradise.

Well, could be if we were all delusional.

After I do some very light stretching, I scoot over to stand up and then walk to the window, dodging the bodies around the gate. I step carefully, not wanting to be the asshole who wakes anyone up and. A small girl cradled in her mother's arms opens sleepy blue eyes to meet mine and I smile at her for a second. My heart pangs as it reminds me of my girls when they were that age.

The sun is barely up as I peer out the window and the world, at least in the surrounding Raleigh-Durham area, is covered like a blanket. I sigh, knowing we will probably be here most of the day, if not another night. The ground isn't cold enough for the snow to stick, which when the sun comes out, the city will thaw rapidly.

Knowing I've sealed my fate, I now have to make the best of an unpleasant situation. I resolve to because that's what women do, after all. We make the best of any situation. It's exhausting, but if we didn't do it, no one would. The world itself would cease to function if there wasn't a woman behind every situation working to make everyone comfortable.

My thoughts turn morose as my body wakes up. *That's probably why most of society is repelled by an outspoken woman, in complete control of herself. We no longer work to make everyone feel ok about everything but tell the truth.*

Naturally, this leads me to think of Conner, and one reason it was such a relief to be with him. He never played the wounded little boy or controlling man. Then he gave me a soft place to rest, had his vision of success, and never invalidated me when my emotions made me unpredictable.

I put my hand on my heart and plead silently for him to understand my outrageous reaction. *Conner, please forgive me.*

Everything I promised to do and be for him went out the window when I was triggered and tested. I fell into a pit of despair and didn't bother to look for the ladder on the side wall to climb out. I didn't ask for help, and I wasn't honest with anyone. Not until Dulce found me, and I had no choice but to admit to what drove me to run away from the healthiest relationship I've ever had.

"Hey Dummy–stop your melancholy Sylvia Plath level brooding. Drink this."

Dulce, who knows me better than anyone on the planet, including how I take my coffee–hands me a coffee cup with a hefty dose of creamer, which contrasts to her favorite, completely black. I take a sip and sigh, but then make a face. I look up and meet her eyes.

She shrugs and says, "It's airport coffee the morning after an apocalyptic snowstorm. We are going to take what we can get and be grateful."

She's not wrong. This day would end up much, much worse if there was no coffee. When an ice storm shut the city of Houston down a few years back, knocking out electricity for the entire region, I drove miles to find a coffee shop that was open. By then, it was in the afternoon and my headache was so bad, I could barely see.

I look at her sideways and say, "I know. Remember what I told you when you woke up with the worst hangover of your life the day after that ice storm hit Houston? It was six months to the day after Scott died. It was when the sun was out, and the ice was melting."

She nods and responds, "Stop trying to find the answer. The answer will find you. And it did, didn't it?"

I chuckle because it was a rare moment of divine insight in those dark days. After that, Dulce experienced a massive transformation. She'd realized how big her problem with alcohol had become and got sober. She left teaching, got a new career and met the love of her life. It had all happened so fast; it made our heads spin. By the anniversary of that storm, she had worked her steps and was nearly a completely different person.

By the second anniversary of that storm, she was married, running her own successful educational consultancy company. She had a fuller life than either she or I could have ever dreamed possible during that seeming never-ending darkness.

When Elise's addictive behavior came out, she was the one who took her to her first week of A.A. meetings and got me involved in Al-Anon.

I didn't know I grew up with an alcoholic father or married someone who was well on his way to becoming a part of the program until Dulce told me later. The reason Scott had a heart attack was because of the years of alcohol consumption. It put so much stress on his body, his heart just gave out.

Dulce, still staring out the huge airport window to the snow beyond, says quietly, "The answer has already found you. You know that, right?"

Tears form in my eyes and the lump in my throat returns full force. I can barely speak for a few moments and take a large swallow of coffee, which burns all the way down, leaving me panting for air. Eventually, I nod slowly, not looking at her. I can't look at her because if I do, I'll start crying again.

She calls my bluff, "Carrie, look at me." I turn my still stiff neck slowly, but I don't meet her eyes. She doesn't push me to look at her, just gently asks, "So, we know why you left.

You were scared and couldn't deal. Do you think Conner will understand?"

I shake my head no, then yes. She lets out a little nose breath, a small laugh. "Which one is it, yes or no?"

Her tone, so much the teacher she was for two decades, grates on my frazzled nerves, "Don't treat me like a child."

She turns to face me fully, framed in the vast whiteness of the world beyond. Her face is darkened by the brightness behind her. While I can't see it, I know she is smiling. There is enough mirth in her posture that she will not kill me for my insolence...yet.

She responds, "Well, maybe stop acting like teenage Sabrina when she is in a mood and start acting like the grown-ass woman you are."

I fold my arms in front of my breasts, partly to ward off the cold seeping in from the window and partly to defend myself. "Well, Sabrina got those moods from somewhere."

At that, she shifts, and I can see her face. She is smiling broadly, her tired eyes sparkling. "Oh, I know exactly where she got her attitude from. The source is standing in front of me." I roll my eyes and open my mouth to say something tact turn, my overworked nervous system still holding me over the edge at gunpoint.

She beats me to the punch, though and continues, "Except that I'm not dealing with teenage Sabrina. I'm talking to a healthy, emotionally stable grown ass woman. Notice I did not say perfect. You are human. Freak outs are allowed, but next time, let's take it down a notch."

With a pregnant pause before she continues, "So, what is the answer that found you?"

I sigh and the fight drains off my back like rainwater. She's right. I am not how I've been acting for the last twenty-four hours or more. I am healthy. This has been a blip on the radar in the grand scheme of things. I take another sip of coffee and attempt to form the words.

"Go back and grovel, crawling on my knees so he takes me back?"

She laughs, loud and clear, and several heads turn towards us. "Oh, Conner is going to make you get on your knees alright. But there isn't a question of him taking you back. It's not Conner that is the problem. It's your own fear getting in your way. You are getting in your own way, Carrie. Now, the Divine has given you the opportunity to deal with it."

I scoff, even as I know the truth of her words, but say, "Oh, that's what we are calling this weather hangover, stuck in the airport, 'Divine intervention'?"

She snickers, "Weather hangover, good one. Yes, this time is a gift to get yourself together. When we get out of here, hopefully later today, you are going to take your smelly ass straight to the hospital and make up with your man. Then you can nurse him back to health in a hotel room until they get all the games rescheduled. You will both be fit as fiddles by the time he has to coach again."

Chapter 49

Conner

By the time I finish all the testing—including an MRI of my heart—I am beyond exhausted. Being in the hospital is the least helpful place to recover. As they pushed me—in a fucking wheelchair—between floors, all I wanted and wished for was my bed back in California and Carrie snuggled up close.

That would be the recovery plan I need.

My emotions finally caught up with me, and my anger sparked at the thought of her running. I have been understanding, partly because I didn't have any energy for anything other than her coming back to me. But once the reality of it hit, and I felt slightly better—and her silence went on—my fear reared up. For me, fear turns into anger.

A weak heart, turns out, was what made her a widow. The threat of it again sent her over the age. It's strange to hold understanding and anger together.

Being cooped up like this does not help. I need to get out of the little white box. I am a man who is constantly in motion and whether I have the physical strength to do anything, my body is telling me to *MOVE*.

As I settle back into my room, we've been not affectionately calling 'The Box,' Joel gives me a wry look. He knows exactly what I'm feeling, but he is a man who acts when necessary. He is measured and shakes his head to tell me not to push myself. Here much longer than he expected. I know he is ready to see his family. I finally get the longing he has for Misti.

I let out a long-suffering sigh, which makes him grin bigger. I don't feel terrible anymore and my job is to let the IV bag of fluids and life-restoring meds flow in unhindered.

My brother's grins even wider and reaches into his pocket. He pulls out, shockingly, a tennis ball. I break out the silence with, "Where the fuck did you get a tennis ball in a hospital?"

He doesn't immediately answer, just tosses it to me. I catch it in my IV free hand, a lifetime of sports having developed my hand-eye coordination to a near superhuman level. I turn it over in my hand and notice it has a wide gap in the middle. It's almost as if it was cut open.

"You didn't?" I narrow my eyes and keep my voice just above a whisper. The last thing I want to do is to alert the medical staff, especially Nurse Rachet, as I've dubbed the Charge Nurse on this floor. She has already given Joel and me one lecture about being too loud. This is contraband, but like to any prisoner, it is life-giving. It is a connection to the outside world. I don't want to lose this.

He throws it back and we begin a game as old as time: how many times can we throw the ball back and forth before someone drops it? It is just something automatic guys shift into when there is a ball around. We will even get Misti in on it, when she doesn't have a kid hanging off of her. Or even when she does.

Once we get to a hundred, I add a level of difficulty. I talk again. I ask, "Ok, where did the tennis ball really come from?"

Still concentrating like this game is for the NFL Championship, he grunts, "Stole it off a walker."

That confession makes me almost drop my next catch. I don't, because I'm a professional and there is no way I'm going to cause defeat. But I do pause before throwing it back to him. "You what? Why? Where? Who?"

He smiles and motions for me to throw the ball back. I do and then he says, "Relax, it was off the back leg that already had a rubber stopper. It'll be fine." The game continues as we fall back into amused silence. Our focus is on the ball and how high the count has gone. The game only stops if someone drops it, so when my night nurse comes in, we take a pause as I tuck it under my leg.

We both stare at the door she walked out of for a few seconds before we turn to look at each other. We nod and shrug and begin our game again.

After an unknown amount of time, and after successfully catching the ball over five thousand times in a row, my phone buzzes and I lose my grip on the ball.

"Fucking hell!" I yell, annoyed at the interruption. It felt so good to be focused on something physical. I probably could have played that game for days straight.

Joel laughs and says, "It's because you are better with your feet, little brother. Good time to stop, though. I'm starving and you are, too. I'll get something to eat and find out where your dinner meal is. I need to call Misti and the kids, anyway."

"Get me extra pudding!" I yell to him as I watch his massive back exit through the door. He lifts a hand in confirmation as the door closes. We'd kept the room fairly dim, so my eyes have to adjust once the door blocks the hallway light again. I put the treasured tennis ball down by my left side and pick up my phone that had been silent up till now.

Innana told me everyone was letting me recover. What she really meant was, she had told everyone to leave me alone, especially until they figured out what happened to Carrie. And everyone had. It had been both good and bad. I'm a dude, so I don't want to talk to everyone all the time. The game with Joel had lifted my soul from the pit of despair. But now, only seeing one message made my heart sink.

That was until I realized who it was from—the only person to risk Innana's wrath and break her no-contact order to let me know what was going on outside this cell block.

Elise.

Her message was simple and short, but I heave a tremendous sigh of relief, not realizing how tense I was in waiting for news about Carrie. She said it all in less than twenty words.

Mama never made it out. She is stuck at the airport. She's coming to you when she can.

I lift my IV arm to cover my eyes with my hand, but the bend is painful, so I shift. All I feel is relief that she is safe. I rub my eyes, suddenly tight with tears. She didn't get out and thoughts flood my brain. The one I settle on makes the least and the most sense. It's like the Universe kept her in Raleigh-Durham, kept her in the snow-bound airport, to have the chance to face her demons before she comes back to me.

She hasn't texted me yet and I debate on texting her first. I recognize I don't want to because I'm angry at her and don't feel like she deserves the comfort of me contacting her. I sit with that emotion for a long time, grappling with my own demons of feeling abandoned in my greatest hour of need.

Then one thought bubbles up to the top of my brain space, through the muck of my anger and mire of my fear.

Do you want to be right, or do you want to be happy?

The answer is obvious then. I want to be happy. I am happy with Carrie. If it takes leaving me in a hospital bed and getting stranded in an airport for her to work through her fear, that's what it takes. She is coming back. She wants to be with me. She was overwhelmed and wants to make it right.

She is a warrior–a warrior for love. Warriors aren't perfect. She is not perfect. But she is perfect for me. She has fought through so much pain and not let it make her shrink. If this had to happen so she would rise to become all she was created to be, then I need to support her.

I need to forgive her and tell her to come back to me.

I send the text just before Joel walks in the door with my dinner. It smells surprisingly good for the hospital: a plate of roast beef, mashed potatoes and cooked carrots. I could kiss him for the twelve chocolate pudding cups he stacked in a pyramid and balanced on the tray. I hit send as he slides the tray over my bed and devour the food like it's my last meal on earth.

After my sixth pudding cup, I finally breathe and Joel asks, "So, what did you tell Carrie?"

I hesitate to share. I don't want him to think I'm weak. There was never anyone before Carrie and there will never be after. He nods, knowing my thoughts, and I realize he feels the same way about his wife.

I pick up my phone to act like I need to read this message that burned its way out of me from the depths of my soul.

> *I forgive you. I'm your home. Come find me.*

Chapter 50

Carrie

I can't stop crying as I read Conner's message again and again, even though I can't see it through the waterfall of my tears.

> *I forgive you. I'm your home. Come find me.*

I hadn't asked for forgiveness, yet he freely gave it.

He is right. He is my home.

I don't deserve him.

I feel a hand on my shoulder and a warm squeeze. "Yes, you do, dummy. You are both imperfect people wanting to grow and build a life together. Stop questioning. You fucked up. He forgave you. Now, get out of your mental darkness and live in the light."

My best friend, who I hadn't shown the message to yet, read it over my shoulder as I cradled the phone in shaky hands. Dulce takes the phone from me now and replies with two words.

I will.

"Hey! That's not what I would say!" I protest loud enough heads should turn our way, but everyone stuck in this airport is used to emotional outbursts by now. There is one about every five minutes as people grapple with being stuck and trying to figure out how to get back to their lives.

Dulce gives me yet another side-eye and, in a voice as dry as toast, says, "Like I'd let you send him a novel. Keep it simple. You can confess your sins when you see him, and he is ready for it. He is still in the hospital, recovering from a very scary scenario. What he needs to know is that you are ok and will come to him when you can. That will probably be tomorrow, and you can let him know that when you know for sure. Plus, you need to shower. You stink. Now, let's see if we can find some food."

"You keep complaining I stink." I mumble as I stand up to follow her. As we stand in line at the airport branch of the local coffee shop, I meditate on the real question as my gut twists.

Conner forgave me, but can I forgive myself?

We wait fifteen minutes because food is scarce, over twenty-four hours into our lockdown. People eat partly from fear and boredom. The authorities reported over the loudspeaker that we only have a maximum of one more night here; the roads are already salted and thawing. What Dulce said is true. I'll see Conner tomorrow at some point.

Catastrophe opens the doors for price gouging, but I pay twenty dollars for coffee and a measly breakfast sandwich. At least there is still some powder creamer available. If I had to drink my coffee black, it would be salt in my self-created wound.

Black coffee is a true misery.

I spend an additional seven dollars on a twelve-ounce water bottle and sigh. I am fortunate to have the funds to pay the borderline extortionary prices the vendors are charging. I look at Dulce and she nods, already knowing what our task will be today–which will get out of my head.

Find some people to help.

It feels good to stretch my legs. Yesterday I was solely focused on the deep hole I'd assigned myself and then trying to get even remotely comfortable to get any sleep possible. Today, with the help of lukewarm coffee and feeling the love from Conner, I am clearer headed.

It is always the ability to help someone else that gets me out of the funk. In the darkest moments after Scott's death and Elise's addiction, I kept steady through a regular rotation of volunteering at different women's shelters around Houston. There were days when it was all I could do to bring diapers to young mothers, but I did it. If that was the only good thing in my day, it was still something to be grateful for.

Service is a tradition we maintain. Every holiday season we serve. Last year, we cooked a whole Thanksgiving feast for the fire station down the street. I might have majorly fucked up, but it's not the end of my story. The end of my story is with Conner, and I will accept nothing less than to close out my days on this earth in his arms.

Empowered by our restored focus on finding a mission to make our time here worthwhile, Dulce and I make small talk. There have been various camps set up and everyone seems to work together, watching each other's stuff - until we are set free. There are only friends in crisis, and everyone seems to be on their best behavior.

Dulce comments, "This makes me feel warm inside. Humans can be so, well, human, warts and all. This could have been so ugly. Maybe it's ok because everyone knows the end is near. But honestly, living in Houston has shown me repeatedly, when bad things happen, humanity rises to meet the challenge and help each other."

I nod and respond in full agreement, "We've done our fair share of serving during those times. Think we can find so folks to help here in North Carolina?"

Dulce nods, "Heck yes. I see someone just up your alley right now."

I follow her line of sight and instantly know exactly who she is talking about. A young woman, who looks like she hasn't slept in days, is cradling a baby with a toddler in her lap on an iPad. She looks as if she might pretend to sleep, but I see the tears rolling down her cheeks.

My heart constricts in my chest, and I look at Dulce. "Oh, my god. How many times was I like that with the girls?"

Dulce looks at me and says, "Too many times. Let's see what we can do."

We slowly make our way to the woman and her precious children. The toddler is a boy with a full head of tight black curls. The baby is in yellow, so could be a boy or a girl, until I catch sight of the pink pacifier she is gently sucking in her sleep. We approach slowly, not wanting to startle any of them. The tiny boy doesn't raise his head, but I can see from the light of the screen, he has shadows under his eyes.

With an encouraging nod from Dulce, I quietly clear my throat and say, "Excuse me." The woman's eyes fly open as she sits upright, coming up off the wall she was leaning against. She jostles the baby, who lets out a small but sharp cry. Thankfully, she doesn't open her eyes. Her mother quickly puts the pacifier back in place. The little boy looks up from his screen listlessly, and I know Dulce wants to feed him, wrap him up and sing him a song until he can settle down to sleep.

We have to convince his mother to let us help her first. She quickly reaches up to shove the tears off her cheeks and quakes, "C-c-can I help you?"

I smile warmly and start with the truth. "Well, we are stuck here just like you. I have three daughters myself, albeit they are older. I remember this age well. We only came to help." I quickly add, "If you need or want it."

The woman's brown eyes dart between Dulce and me, disbelief and incomprehension marking her pretty brows as she tries to process what I've said. I give her a second rather than jumping into over-explain myself. I learned a long time ago; people will catch up faster the less you talk.

She finally finds her voice, her eyes round. "Do you want something from me?" I look at Dulce, whose long years in education have honed the skills to deal with confused parents. She steps in with ease. "We were taking a walk to stretch our legs and noticed you and your beautiful children. I have a son myself! We were wondering if y'all needed anything to eat or drink."

Her brain fog of sleep deprivation and exhaustion clears, and she says exactly what I expect her first response to be, "No, no. We are fine. Thank you, though."

I offer her my unopened water bottle and say, "Here then, take this. Like I said, I remember the days when I could barely catch my breath when my girls were this age. And I was never stranded at an airport for two days. We will be just over there, whatever you need." I point to two empty seats about twenty feet away. Certainly not our makeshift site, but I don't expect it will take her long to acquiesce.

Dulce and I both give her warm smiles and go sit down to eat our meager rations and drink our coffee in the woman's line of sight. With my mom-sense hearing, I hear the little boy whine about being hungry and the mother trying to comfort him.

Less than five minutes later, she and her precious children are standing in front of us, telling us how they ended up here.

Her name is Jayden. Her son is Carter, the baby named Calia. She was flying home to Boston to visit her parents while her husband is on active duty with the Coast Guard.

The poor thing can't help herself as we share our stories and our food with her and Carter. She cries again, and that kicks us both into action. Dulce stays with her and the kids while I go to find them food. She is not only out of money but out of formula for the baby. I end up finding everything they need and more, haggling my way to a much better price for lots of fun snacks plus lip balm for Jayden.

When I arrive back to the spot I left them, Dulce is not only holding the baby, but she is also playing thumb war with Carter. Carter is winning, and he is beaming. Jayden is watching with a smile and when she sees me, she bursts into tears again.

"I have had nothing to eat in two days. This is a miracle!" She reports.

As she cries, we give her the space, just sitting with her. Carter hugs his mom and says in that very loud child-like whisper, "It's ok Mama. These ladies are the angels we prayed for!" That makes her cry a little harder. Dulce puts her arm around her.

Once we all settle down, and Carter is sleepy in Dulce's lap. I pose a simple question. "Jayden, do you work beyond being a wonderful wife and mother?"

She nods solemnly, and her answer comes out in a whispered rush. "I've always wanted to start my own business. I'm a talented artist–I won awards in high school. I had a scholarship to an art school in Boston, but James and I got married and I got pregnant. I don't know how to find the time or what exactly I should do." She sighs mournfully and continues, "I adore my family, but I want something of my own, like I dreamed."

Dulce and I meet each other's eyes, and everything clicks into place. I look back at Jayden, touch her shoulder and tell her, "Well, it seems we meant to meet. I'm a women's business coach. I've had my success and now I want to help other women like you find their purpose and make an impact."

And just like women do, we take care of the children while we plan to help Jayden change the world one project at a time.

Chapter 51

Conner

"Bro, I have got to get the fuck out of here."

I inform my brother of this, and he nods, like I'm speaking a truth he knows in his soul. He needs to get out of here, too. We've both been cooped up too long.

The window shows the sun is setting on a world that is still white, but less so than when we woke up. We've played as much ball toss as we both can stand. I've eaten, I've walked around, and I even tried to do some pushups. I got to twenty before I had to stop. I'm rapidly healing, but I'm not resurrected.

Misti and the kids should be able to fly in by tomorrow. The city is rapidly thawing, and I know Carrie will be on her way to me soon. We've been texting, and she told me she is in a better place, mentally and emotionally. She even met someone she can help as she launches her new business.

God works in mysterious ways.

Now, I need Him to get to get a move on for my discharge papers. Sixty hours in the hospital is far too long. I flat out told the charge nurse I would check myself out as soon as the road between the hospital and the hotel was clear.

She smirked at me, threw a hand on her hip and says in a flirty voice, "Try me, Big Boys and see what happens." It's a good thing she is old enough to be my mother, if not my grandmother. I'm certain she would do everything in her power to make sure I only left when I was certified well enough to go.

I let out a sigh of frustration and decide one more loop around the floor I'm on will do me good.

I tell this to Joel, who informs me, "Conner, I'm dizzy from watching you walk around. Sit your ass down. Evening shift change is happening right now, and we will have news on when you will be let out not long after. Nurse Rachet promised."

Our nickname for the head nurse amuses her. She isn't mean, only bossy. She's also been stuck here with us, as have all the medical staff. They are getting overtime but want to leave as much as we do. Still, her professional code won't allow her to promise anything until it's a real deal.

We get the news of release just after eight-thirty. It took over two hours for staff to come off their in-hospital downtime to get their shit together, review my chart and consent to me leaving to recuperate somewhere other than here. No time is wasted in packing up our meager belongings. I catch a whiff of both of us as we move and groan.

"Dude, we both need showers, pronto."

Joel smiles and says, "I got dibs." I groan again, forgetting the number one rule of brotherhood–make sure you stake your claim early and often. "Fine, but you better make it quick. I'm going to see Carrie as soon as she walks in the door. I don't care how gross she is. She won't smell nearly as bad as I do."

Joel nods and says, "Yah, I don't know how they do it, but even when they are gross, they still smell good."

Nurse Rachet enters the room and announces I need to stay away from everyone for another twelve hours.

"It is protocol because this virus is so dangerous. I wouldn't see anyone other than Joel to keep them from being exposed. Once you've been on the anti-virals for forty-eight hours, you are no longer a risk. It's as much for their safety as it is for yours, especially going back to your team."

I grunt in acknowledgment of what she has said, with my mind whirling through possibilities. I land on one and lob it to her. "But what if someone has already had the virus? That won't be an issue, right?"

Carrie was sick last week–which feels like a hundred years ago. That should exempt her, or at least get her to quarantine with me rather than my stinky oaf of a brother. I love him and all, but I want my girl.

Nurse Rachet gives me a ray of hope. "The best option, if you don't want to make anyone else sick, is to keep your distance. If they've had it recently, their immunity should suffice. It will be another few days–at least till the weekend- for them to reschedule the tournament games. You'll be clear for that."

Turns out Nurse Rachet is also a rabid soccer fan. She's been keeping us up to date not only on the city but also on the university's plans to reschedule the NCAA final two games we still have yet to play.

I agree to follow her directions, that are also reiterated by the doctors. I text Inanna to tell her the plan. Last, I text Carrie I'm headed to the hotel, and that's where she can find me when the road out of the airport is clear and she can get a car.

Apparently, Dulce had a reservation when she landed and has already confirmed it with the rental car company for the moment they are released to drive.

Which should be any minute now.

The message to Carrie keeps saying "not sent," until we arrive at the hotel, even though I click it a hundred times. Joel and I walk in the room I was sharing with Carrie, and he shoots me a grin. "Just for funsies, want to share the bed?"

I flick him off. "We haven't shared a bed since you grew past six feet a million years ago, moron."

Still grinning, he flips me the bird as he walks into the bathroom. I hear the shower turn on and I feel my skin itch. I walk to the door and pound on it. "You better be fast, dickhead! I'm the one who has been in a bed for nearly the last three days!"

I walk back over to the bed and realize just how tired I am. I need some food and order a pizza.

Two, to be exact, one for each of us. This is not the time to watch my carb intake. I can feel that I've lost strength and muscle mass. I'm not dehydrated thanks to all the fluids, but I am ravenous.

All I want is to be clean, full and hold my love till we both fall asleep. Well, maybe after a gentle but fast fuck to make sure she never wants to leave me again.

I try one more time to text Carrie and the message finally sends. I don't immediately get a response, and I assume the cell relay systems, like me and the entire city of Raleigh, are recovering to full power.

Lying on the bed, I must doze off because I'm startled awake by my phone buzzing. I immediately check it, hoping it's Carrie. It is and fuck. We have another problem.

She never got my text about being out of the hospital and back at the hotel. Her message is only four words: "Conner, where are you?"

My stomach drops a bit, and I hit the call button. She picks up and while I can tell she is in a bit of a panic; her overall energy is light years better than the last few days.

When she answers, I tell her, "Sunshine, God, it's good to hear your voice. Where are *you*?"

She laughs in a tight, small way and says, "Well, I came to the hospital to rescue you from your confinement, only to discover you checked out over an hour ago. Why didn't you tell me?"

I sigh, slightly frustrated, "I did, but I don't think all the texts are going through. I didn't want you to have to run around the city after being cooped up in an airport for three days."

She says the part I left off, "Even if that was my fault. Look, Conner. Dulce is driving and I'm going to have to tell her everything anyway, so I'll just say this in front of her, even though I've said it many, many times over text. I'm sorry. I'm so so so sorry. I left you out of fear of history repeating itself when I know, deep in my heart, that the past does not determine the present or the future."

She takes a deep breath before continuing, "I know you are going to be fine, and I truly hope you will accept my whole bonehead, running scared, idiotic outburst. I know if I would have made it to Houston, I would have just come straight back because you are right. You are my home. I love you more than I can truly comprehend, in ways and on levels I don't even realize. I love you with my entire being and from now and until the end of time, I will always be right by your side."

She chokes up, making her pause. She is right; she has said all of this before but if my Sunshine needs one thing to move forward; it is that I've heard her and that I see her–all of her. So, I tell her just that.

"Carrie, I see you. I don't judge you. You were scared. You made a choice to preserve yourself and I don't fault you for that. Do I wish this had been different? Yes, but all we have is now. We have each other. I am fine, the doctors declared it. And while I need to stay away from everyone else, you are ok to be holed up for another twenty-four hours because you've already had this. Seems you getting sick first was divine intervention."

I hear her mumble, "There's that phrase again."

I chuckle and say, "Indeed. Sounds like you've got a tale to tell me about your time away."

Joel comes out of the bathroom with a toothbrush in his mouth. This guy is a psychopath. He brushes his teeth in the shower. He has a towel barely hanging on above his hips. He has just the slightest hint of a round belly, but it's more like a turtle shell than a gut. He is solid muscle and I doubt he will ever lose it.

I turn my attention back to my partner, who is making plans to get a hotel room for Joel and Dulce. I say a silent prayer of thanks for Carrie's best friend finding her, because without her, Carrie would lose her mind. She tells her Joel can take care of himself, to stop trying to manage everything for everyone and calm the fuck down because, "We will be there in less than an hour."

My gut tightens in anticipation, and I tell Dulce, "You can order all the Door Dash you want on my tab as a thank you for rescuing my Sunshine from herself."

Dulce hears me loud and clear now that Carrie put me on speaker phone.

Her retort is priceless. "Well, Coach, I'll tell you this. If you ever almost die again and make me have to deal with her ass like this, I'll make sure you are dead."

I take my time in the shower, getting ready for my girl. I'm still worn out and will probably sleep like the dead with her in my arms. The pizza arrives. Joel takes his and goes down to get himself another room.

As I try not to devour the whole thing and leave a couple of slices for Carrie, I do a mental check in. My need to see her overwhelms my need to talk through a plan of how best to communicate in the future. That discussion can happen after we win. Right now, all I need to focus on is her.

Right then, comes a knock on the door.

***

Carrie

When the door opens, I fall and Conner catches me.

As relieved tears flow, I blurt out, "I'm home."

As he pulls me inside and tight to his chest, he strokes my hair. I loop my arms around him and we hold each other for a long time, not saying anything. Once the swell of emotion subsides, while wiping the tears off my face and my hair out of my eyes, he says, "I know."

Then he kisses me. It is nothing like our first kiss, full of passion and raging want. This kiss is tender and full of forgiveness. Even as our lips part and our tongues meet, there is not any push. This kiss isn't a windup for sex.

This kiss is an amends–a reconciliation. I know I need to return to therapy to deal with my fear and I pour my promise to do into the kiss.

Conner is the first to break contact, but only to take me by the hand and lead me to the bed. I perch on the edge, unsure exactly of what he intends, but trusting him absolutely. Staying silent, he kneels down and unlaces my sneakers. He takes them off, then my socks, and then takes my left foot into his hands. He massages it out, careful not to tickle my sensitive arches, and after a bit, switches to the other foot.

I look at him while he focuses his attention on my feet and let the rest of my awareness fall away.

He is still the same Conner. Broad shouldered, the muscles under his t-shirt moving and flexing. My gaze drifts down to his arms, watching as his sexy forearms work in all their strength. Then I watch the hands that give me so much pleasure and make me feel so safe as they hold me close, graciously tend to the feet that took love away, only to be drawn back like a magnet.

Finally, I can't help myself, as I reach up and run my fingers through his hair. Conner finally meets my eyes. There is so much to say, so much that could–and should–be said, but in this moment, we are beyond words.

Our hearts communicate through our eyes and when he finally stops, I pull him between my legs, on his knees. We wrap arms around each other as I stroke his hair, his shoulders and back. His arms come around my waist and lower back. I feel surrounded and whole. It feels so good, so right to hold him.

The words come out of their own volition, in a whisper, "I don't know why I thought I would ever be home anywhere else but with you."

Conner tilts his head up, then straightens to press a soft kiss to my lips. He smiles at me, eyes glinting, "Me either, Sunshine. Wanna shower?"

After I take a long, hot shower, then put on one of Conner's t-shirts, I eat the two slices of pizza he saved for me. I know I could probably eat more, but my body is telling me it is time to rest. We say little, just touch each other. Whether it is hand in hand or leg to leg, as we sit on the bed, we surrender to the tangibility of our love.

Coming back from putting the pizza box outside the room, I look at Conner to see his eyes drooping a bit. Just then he yawns, so I ask, "Ready for bed, Sweetness?"

He yawns again in answer, so I pull back one side of the covers and crawl in. It's late, after eleven p.m. and the chaos of the last few days is catching up. Plus, Conner is still recovering. As we tangle ourselves up together under the blanket, neither of us makes a move towards sex.

Tonight isn't about sex. It's about coming back together, heart to heart. There is something so vulnerable about sleeping with someone, and it's exactly what we both need. We both fall asleep in record time and don't move all night long.

***

We both sleep late until after ten am. We order room service, which ends up being lunch. Conner orders a grilled chicken wrap with fries and ranch for us both.

We snuggle after we eat, watching a movie before my body tells me I need to get up and move. Doing some light stretching, making space where we can, Conner joins me after taking his oral meds. I watch him move and I'm pleased to see he is rapidly gaining his strength back.

Not stopping his flow, he asks, "Ok, Sunshine, tell me about Jayden and how you are going to help her."

"Well, she is my first client, so it will definitely be a challenge. She is going to be my guinea pig as I develop my coaching system and skills. I'm going to charge her fifty percent less than I plan to going forward. Her parents gave her the money to start her business, but she is doing as much for me as I am for her, so we will really be partners in it all. I truly hope I can help her be successful."

"Oh, I have no doubt you already have. You believe in her–her business. Just by being you, you show her she can live her dreams. You've never settled for what society tells you to be happy with and you know life is meant to be lived to the fullest. You are the system, Carrie. Don't stress too much on the methods. You know what you've been through, what it takes to have a work-life balance."

I chuff out a laugh, "Only because I didn't for so long."

"Yes, but that's exactly how we learn. We must experience pain in order to course correct. You already have 'the why' and 'the what.' Trust me, 'the how' is the easiest part."

Delighted to have his support, I ask a question that's been in the back of my mind, "Sweetness, how is the team doing? Elise has told me spirits are up, but they are getting eager for you to return. She says they are so ready to play, it's like they are jonesing!"

He sniffs and tells me the truth. "They are. Soccer women dislike to be cooped up. They need the heightened experience of a game. I'm sure other athletes are similar, but soccer chicks? They are a breed all unto themselves. Alyssa is about to drive everyone bonkers."

Just then, Conner's phone vibrates. It's Inanna, and he holds it up apologetically. I smile and nod at him. It's as if the team knew we were talking about them. They need their head coach, so I wave him off. He sits at the desk, engrossed in the conversation about how rescheduling the games is going.

Feeling suddenly overwhelmed with gratitude; I get on my knees on the side of my bed. I offer a simple prayer to the Spirit of the Universe.

I am grateful for Your love, Your care, Your provision and Your guidance.

Guide all those I love in everything they do.

Keep my heart open and soft to all that is to come.

I dedicate my life again to doing the best with what you have given me.

A few tears trickle down my cheeks—happy ones. It feels good to be me again, having made it out of such a dark place back into the light of this incredible life I get to live, with people I cherish and witnessing them living their best lives too.

Coming back to sit on the bed, I pick up my phone and see I've missed messages from the girls, Dulce, and the parent group chat.

Next game is scheduled for 7 pm against UNC. It's go time!

I breathe a sigh of relief and meet Conner's eyes. He looks like he is alive again, eyes aflame with purpose.

I respond to the group chat with three words.

Let's fucking go!

Chapter 52

Conner

"We have our game time."

I say it out loud as I hang up the phone and turn to see Carrie staring at me. Her smile is blinding, and she is nodding. "The parent group chat already knows."

I laugh because, of course, they do. The word spread like wildfire while I was on the phone with Inanna and Erik making plans. The team is antsy, so my assistant coaches braved the remaining chill from the storm and mostly empty roads to take them to the UNC workout facilities.

I made plans to meet with the team in three hours at the stadium, two hours before we are supposed to be on the pitch. I respect what the doctors said, but I've been on the anti-viral long enough. No one else has come down with symptoms since we've been in North Carolina, so wearing a mask would be out of an abundance of caution. Plus, they've all been cooped up together.

If anyone else was going to get sick, they would have by now. My team is in the clear.

We are playing UNC. We've never faced them. Both Inanna and Erik have been reviewing game tapes with the team because we've had plenty of time to prepare. In their down time, each of our players was given their counterpart on the other team to research and that's revealed some important game intelligence.

Quickly, we discussed what they've discovered, and it confirmed the truth: UNC is going to be really fucking hard to beat.

They run a clean program and at a level very close to ours. They are ranked number three in the nation, just behind us and Florida State. Florida State had their one and only loss to UNC earlier in the season and the Rams have been decimating their opponents every step of the way to this NCAA tournament semi-final game.

Other than Stanford, who got knocked out of the tournament early in a surprise upset, UNC looks to be our toughest opponent. Florida State has struggled with injuries to their All-American goalkeeper and striker, so they've been limping their way to their own semi-final game against UCLA. The top four teams are battling it out and it is up to myself, my coaches and my team to persevere all the way to the top.

And we get to play the hometown favorite, on their home turf, after a natural disaster that has had everyone–including me–stuck in a box for a week.

UNC players and the fans will be rabid for victory.

Knowing my team as well as I do, they will be in their heads. I need to be ready to help them get loose and ready to play our game.

We are not going there to play the Rams; we are going there to win. We've been working for this all season–really for the last five years.

My plan takes shape as I do my own homework. If the players have to research their counterparts, then I'll do the same.

I kiss Carrie quickly, who kisses me back hard. My cock stirs to life, reminding me we haven't completed our reunion yet.

She takes my face between her hands and looks me in the eye as she says, "I want you so bad, but you've got a job to do. You get one hour, then I get the rest of the time before you have to leave to meet the team."

I kiss her to seal the deal and sit back down at the desk to research the UNC head coach.

Anson Dorrance has had the career I want. Before coming to UNC, he was a U.S. Women's National Team head coach. I spend most of my time on his wins instead of losses. I want to know how he won, how he leads, how he inspires. The dude is fucking brilliant and if I'm going to live my own dreams of coaching the USWNT to a World Cup Victory–the holy grail of soccer–I need to know how he did it.

He has one of the most successful coaching records in the history of athletics. When I say this out loud, Carrie tells me, "Elise was recruited by UNC before signing with UCC. I've met him. He is a class act. And he has been married to his wife for over fifty years."

I cluck my tongue as I process this. Maybe I want to BE Anson Dorrance - to have a career and personal life that successful. I not only need to beat this guy, I need to get him to show me how he did it.

Carrie, as if reading my mind, walks up behind me, puts her hands on my shoulders and kisses the back of my neck before she says, "You be you, Conner Doreland. Dorrance is someone to admire and learn from, but you have your own brilliance. You have vigor and connection to this new generation, more so than he does. You bring things to the table in this current climate of soccer he doesn't. I bet he'd be open to a conversation with you, and wouldn't that be incredible?"

Inspired by her words, I grunt and literally bang on my chest. I have been hyping myself up since Day One. Now, I get the added boost of the most amazing woman in the world, who pumps even more wind into my sails.

I realize I missed a piece of what she says, "Whaddya mean, my Only Sunshine? What would be incredible?"

Now standing behind me, rubbing my shoulders, she laughs softly. "It would be incredible if the winning-est coach in the history of U.S. Women's soccer passed the mantle on to you."

The air rushes out of my chest and my ribcage constricts at the thought of becoming the Anson Dorrance for the next generation, in the age of Women's soccer. I close my eyes, leaning back into the chair and her body behind me, feeling secure.

My parents taught me and my brothers to always go after what we wanted, and that has served us well. They wanted us to be happy and encouraged that, while letting us discover what that meant for each of us.

It took me a while to figure out—as it did Joel. Our older brothers settled for the safer, more run-of-the-mill lifestyle. Yet, it's not enough for me. I want to take the risk. I want to chase my dreams. I want to live this short time on planet Earth to the max. Carrie wants the same thing. I am aligned with a partner who helps me grow, cheers me on and will be at my side till the end.

Who am I to stand in the way of all the goodness the Universe wants to bring into my life?

As I take a moment to contemplate the possibilities, dreaming of a win against UNC and Anson Dorrance becoming my mentor, Carrie stands vigil behind me, continuing her lovely ministrations to my hospital-stiff upper back.

It settles me and I feel my energy shift beyond the restless. I feel it shift into the highest gear: *hope*.

After a few moments, Carrie leans down and whispers into my ear, "Wherever you go, I am with you."

Still leaning over, she nips at my earlobe and then licks the shell of my ear, immediately making my cock surge. Then she whispers, "You have ten minutes."

I turn my head back to meet hers and say, "I don't need it. Back up, Sunshine."

She does, and I push back and up from the chair. I turn around to a beaming smile. It's like seeing coming out into the sun after being a dark room for ages. I squint and before I can stop myself; I wrap her up in my arms and smile down into her gorgeous face.

Her breath is minty clean, having just brushed her teeth, and all she says, "My, my, Mr. Wolf, what big teeth you have."

My response comes out just as quick, "The better to eat you with, my Sunshine."

I scoop her up in my arms, bridal style like the first time we were together, and take her to bed.

It's time for the Big Bad Wolf to feast on my favorite meal.

***

Carrie

Conner, as always, is worth the wait.

In what feels like forever, he teases me, first with his tongue and then rubs his cock all over my pussy. He delivers me to the first of many highs.

He narrates the whole encounter, saying things like, "Fuck, I have missed every sound you make." And "Hearing you moan for me over and over again has me so hard, Carrie."

Finally, when I can't take anymore, I beg him. "Conner, please, please please, please."

He smiles, but looks like a madman takes over. He leans forward, above me and says, "Does my good girl want me to slam my cock home in her soaking wet pussy?"

All I can do is whimper.

He laughs, a little maniacally and says, "As you wish, my love," and thrusts himself in all the way, easily because I am so wet. The sheets are soaked and as he enters, I come again.

The orgasms flow from one into the other. I am not sure where one stops, and another begins. I was hard up for him as always, but given what we had been through, it is the connection between us that sends me into orbit.

It was like we were outside of time, in an eternal realm, just the two of us, forever.

It doesn't take Conner long to join me and he yells my name till he is hoarse.

We both shake from our release and Conner pants into my hair. I breathe hard into his shoulder with red teeth marks from where I had bitten him in my ecstasy. I tighten my legs around his middle and squeeze. He grunts with the pressure. I laugh and do it again, this time a little harder. I feel our combined release slip out a little and as he kisses my ear and whispers, "I want to stay inside you forever."

I sigh out of happiness and desperation, wanting that more than anything, too. After another few minutes of holding each other, feeling his weight I missed, but feeling a leg cramp coming on, I wiggle, and Conner gets the hint.

Rolling onto his side and taking me with him, we relax into each other, milking the moment together. Thankfully, he is still inside me, and I can relish in the feeling of fullness–no, completeness–a little longer.

Just then, I glimpse the clock and laugh out loud.

Conner picks his head up and looked at my face before he says, "I know it's been a while, Sunshine, but I did not expect you to laugh or use your abs after all those orgasms."

Reaching up and putting my thumb and middle finger on either side of his chin, I gently turn his head to look. "Sweetness, look at the clock."

"Holy Shit. That's not possible."

I giggle loudly and tell him, "Well, it has been two weeks since we've been together. But I swear to God in heaven we were in it for longer than twenty minutes."

He holds my gaze, then tilts his head to lean down to kiss me softly. "Carrie, if I only ever get twenty minutes to make love to you every day for the rest of my life, I will make sure it is like that–or better."

I believe him and telling him so. I say, "You're the only man who can make me come that many times in such a short period."

He puts his forehead against mine and says in a low, serious voice, "There will never be another who gets a chance."

I tilt my head back to kiss him and say, "I'm yours. Forever and always."

With his forehead still pressing into mine, he responds with, "You better be."

We lie together for a few minutes longer before I realize my arm is asleep. Fidgeting, I tell him, "Sweetness, as much as I hate what I'm about to say, I think it's necessary. I need to move."

He chuckles, "Not willing to lose a limb on my account?" Then he rolls to give me more space, and that dreaded sadness invades the moment as he pulls out. He props himself up on his arm, staring into my face.

I look at him and, in a voice as serious as a heart attack, I tell him, "I'll lose a limb if it means being with you for the rest of my life."

He laughs, leans over and says against my lips, "That's the spirit. Good girl."

I'm ready for him all over again with that praise, but unfortunately, we don't have time. Cuddling instead, Conner says he wants to save himself for later after the game, but I can tell our whirlwind fuck-fest took a little too much out of him. He was pounding me into the bed, so I'm not surprised. He needs his strength for the game.

It feels idiotic now, given what we experienced, that I could have thought I would lose him before it was time, but I try to have grace for myself.

I reacted out of fear, and I wasn't myself. But I am home now and will never leave again.

I've grown used to the moment I feel his energy shift as he turns to what's ahead. In my mind's eye, I can see him strapping on his coaching armor. Then he moves, just as I knew he would.

In the barest breath, he announces, "I've got to go, Sunshine."

I nod, even as tears form in my eyes. One slips out, and he catches it on his finger, puts it to his lips and states, "But I will be returning here as soon as possible." He gives me his megawatt, soccer god smile, and I can't help but return it.

I choke out, around the knot of emotion in my throat, "I know. Besides, you aren't meeting me here after the game, anyway."

In the whirlwind of the last two days, I forgot to tell him I booked an Airbnb for myself and the girls. Elise will stay here with her team, obviously, but the older girls can finally fly in and we will stay right near the stadium.

I smile at my man and say, "I made other arrangements for us tonight," as I wink at him. He cocks an eyebrow at me but only replies, "You lead, I'll follow, my only Sunshine."

"God, only a special man can say that. And I'm glad you are mine. I'll text you the address and I'll meet you there after the win and the post-game wrap-up with the team."

He nods but is already up and moving, his energy alchemized into intention. He is back in the proverbial coaching saddle, due for his return to his team. I stand up to shower and start packing, but first give him a blessing.

I stop his movements and take his head between my palms. I kiss his forehead, both his eyes, his cheeks, and finally his lips. "Via Con Dios, my Sweetness. Beat the hell outta UNC."

He smiles and says, "I'll take your Texas blessing and make it so."

He heads out to make our dreams a reality.

I meditate, visualizing any lingering fear, doubt, or worry about anything in my life go down the drain.

As I prepare to leave the hotel room that sheltered me and reunited me with my love, I say "Thank You" over and over again. Whoever is up there must be listening, because a deep sense of peace and serenity envelopes me.

It's time to enter my new life. It is a whole new season to come. It is about to start with a win against UNC. The best is yet to come, and I am ready to receive it.

Chapter 53

Conner

Leaving Carrie after just getting her back is the most exquisite torture.

My shoulders are tense as I arrive in the stadium to meet the team in the locker room. This is the first time I've seen my players in almost a week, so when I walk through the door, the noise of their welcome is deafening. There is so much screaming, yelling, and "Hell, yeah Coach is back!" it nearly knocks me off my feet. Then the wave of bodies hits me, and I'm carried off my feet into the middle of the room. I find myself lifted on Erik's shoulders while the team swirls around me, chanting, "Coach is back! Coach is back!"

From my vantage point, looking down, it's like a tornado of burgundy as the players meld into one through the tears in my eyes.

I know how much these ladies and their efforts mean to me. It's humbling to know they feel the same way.

Finally, they put me down and the sea of color parts to reveal Inanna standing about five feet away. She takes a few steps forward; the players giving her room to move towards me. She doesn't say a word. Coming to stand two feet away, she raises one hand, and the room falls silent.

She brings it down as she raises her other hand.

In it is my playbook I'd made sure she'd gotten from my hotel room when I got to the hospital. It was the one coherent thing besides Carrie's comforting presence I remember from that day.

She thrusts it up to me and only then breaks her silence, intoning in an uncharacteristically somber voice, "By the old gods of the pitch, this instrument of power is by right and rule yours, Coach Conner Doreland."

The hush that falls on the room turns into a swishing sound as each player takes a knee and bows their head. I want to laugh and nearly have to cover my mouth to keep it in, but this is something they'd choreographed for my return.

I meet Inanna's eyes and there is an unusual sparkle in them. I know she did an incredible job winning the quarterfinal game. I tell her, "There wasn't a better coach for the last game, Inanna. Are you sure you don't want to take the reins?"

The humor comes through in my voice and her mouth turns up at the ends as the players raise their heads to look and listen to our exchange.

Still serious but knowing the bubble will burst if one of us laughs, Inanna replies, "Only if we win it all."

On that note, the instant my hand touches the playbook, the whole room breaks into a cacophony again as the ladies explode to their feet. It's a melee of dancing and cheering with Inanna and I in the middle, laughing our asses off. Erik is doubled over, having contained his amusement as long as he could. We let the celebration continue for another minute and then I speak for the first time to the complete team.

"Ok! Ok! Let's talk, team."

The room quiets with only a few "shh's" and then I've got all eyes on me. It's time for my pre-game Braveheart speech and while I'm no orator, I try to make it as meaningful as possible.

"I know you've been in expert hands. Whatever Coach Inanna has prepared for this game, I know it's going to take every ounce you've got. UNC is not only the home team, but they are also the favorite. We've prepared all season for this."

I pause to breathe in before continuing. "What t I know is this–I have never coached a more capable, more successful, more willing team than you. You play together like a symphony, and you play from the heart. It's going to be our greatest challenge, but we are up for it. You each must be ready to play the best you ever have. This is your next level and your only chance.

We, as your coaches, have taken you as far as we can. It's up to you now. Are you ready?"

There is a contemplative silence before our team captain puts her hand into the middle and says, "Ready on three!"

The sound of the word "Ready" reaches the heavens, and we all run out the door to the pitch. It's time to win.

As we emerge onto the field for warmups, tensions are high, and the energy is palpable. You can see it on the players of both teams as they bounce from foot to foot. I shake hands with Coach Dorrance and to my surprise, he says to me, "Glad to hear you are back on your feet, Coach. It's been a history-making week in a lot of ways here in Raleigh. I'm excited to play your team. Let's have a great game."

Feeling like a tween meeting her favorite popstar, undoubtedly with hearts in my eyes, I can only respond with, "Thanks so much, Coach. Have a great game."

I walk back to Inanna and Erik and can think of nothing but *God, I'm an idiot.*

Erik catches the look on my face and grins. Inanna, fangirling herself, asks, "What's he like?"

I shake my head and tell her, "The nicest person you've ever met."

She snorts and says, "I'm sure we will see his dark side in nine minutes." She is no doubt correct as our players finish their warmup drills and take their positions on the sideline for the coin toss. We win the toss, and we decide to deal with the rowdy UNC student section for this first half. The two teams take their positions on the pitch and the whistle blows. We immediately press the ball and take position.

My team looks stiff and hesitant as they string the passes together. UNC looks loose and ready until their Senior All-American collides with one of our defenders thirty yards out and has to be taken off the pitch. Inanna whistles low. We will know this player. She is top tier, having played at the youth national level and just earned her spot on the senior team. It's called a foul on UNC, which the captain, encouraged by Dorrance, argues vehemently.

Things are getting heated. There is so much on the line for both teams. This will put one of us in the national championship game. This is the key to the next level for many players – and coaches. I look at Inanna and she nods, reading my mind.

In a surprising move, I signal to let Elise take the free kick. She nods, places the ball in the no-man's-land between the six and the eighteen. The UNC keeper, who also plays for the U.S. Women's National Team, makes a brilliant save of the torpedo Elise launched with her left foot.

She is probably the only one in the country who could make that save.

One shot missed. We can't afford to miss any others. The game continues, the clock ticking upwards. It gets more physical, but the players keep it clean. There is some frustration, but that is typical of women's soccer.

Each team gets a couple of shots, but the defenders and keepers are doing their jobs well.

There has never been so much on the line. I want to chew my fingernails off, but it's still too cold so I keep them stuffed in my pockets as I wear a small patch of grass out. Inanna bounces on her toes and Erik stands as still as a statue.

With two minutes left in the first half, the ball ricochets off the foot of our midfielder, who was out of position, trying to assist in blocking an offensive kick. The ball goes out, giving UNC a corner kick. Everyone quickly gets into their space, as our keeper directs.

I find the bottom of my parka pockets and feel like trying to rip through the seams, nervous as fuck. These shots are a UNC specialty, with the most goals scored off corners this season. The cold has been creeping in again with another front coming through and just as the kick comes in, a chill runs down my spine.

My players clear it but not well. It falls to an Uber talented UNC freshman defender who hits it on a onetime volley into the lower left corner from twenty yards out. Immediately, my captain loudly and angrily appeals for offsides, but the referee denies it.

The goal stands at one-nil with less than a minute left to the half. We hold the ball so we can get into the locker room and regroup. As we gather in the locker room, everyone's faces varying shades of pink or red. My team is all sitting, looking down at their cleats. It feels as if our collective pet dog has passed over the rainbow bridge and we are mourning.

Even Inanna is sitting, with Erik standing behind her, one foot braced on the wall and his eyes locked heavenwards as if pleading for help. We stay like that for most of the break.

Everyone swimming in the waters of letdown and potential loss.

Finally, I can't take it anymore and walk to the center of the room, searching the depths of my soul for something inspiring to say. I can feel my team hurting and suddenly an emotion I don't expect rises within me. The force of it catches me off guard, threatening to explode, as if I'm a soldier in the heat of combat, on the verge of dying more than I ever was in the hospital.

I'm furious. We are not going out this way.

But instead of yelling, I feel it quietly. We didn't make it here to just lay down and lose. I didn't make it through a health scare in record time just for my team to give up. So, I speak from my heart and a stunned wave of a different silence makes its way across the locker room. Even Inanna stands up when she hears what I have to say.

My voice is barely above a whisper. "I'm here. I'm breathing. I'm coaching. It wasn't only because of my will to live, but you added yours. You believed I would make it back, and I did. It's time to believe that now. We are going to make it back and we are going to win. Do you believe it?"

No one responds for a long moment.

So, I repeat my question, meeting every pair of eyes and pausing between words for emphasis. "Do. You. Believe. It?"

Then finally, from her seat at the end of the bench in front of the lockers, Elise Vokler, who has no business saying anything as a freshman, says exactly what I need to hear.

"Yes, Coach."

I walk over to her, standing in front of her and with the voice of a drill sergeant say, "What did you say, Freshman?" She looks shocked for a second before her mind clicks.

Then, standing, she says even louder, "Yes, Coach!"

"Yes, what?"

"Yes, Coach! I believe!"

"You believe what, Vokler?"

"I believe we will win! I believe we will win! I believe we will win!"

She starts the chant, and it takes only a split second before the whole team joins in. The energy from before the game, during the reunion, takes hold and everyone is yelling "I believe!" as we move into the center to break, but the chanting doesn't stop.

The team, with the coaches trailing, doesn't do our usual huddle, they just rush the field, now only saying one thing, "Believe!"

Our visitor crowd picks it up and as I come onto the field, even amid the huge stadium, I catch Carrie's eyes and see her mouth moving. She is chanting right along with everyone and that is the moment everything changes.

We are five minutes early on the pitch, ready for kick-off. Everyone can feel the intensity. As UNC walks out onto the pitch, the team's bearing changes. I see Elise look into the stands and watch as she responds to her mother's prompting, their routine. She taps her hand over her chest, then all of UCC follows suit. As the UNC players take their positions, my team is communicating to each other without words the message that tapping gesture means.

Play from the heart.

And we do.

The first fifteen minutes are about position and rhythm, which we find easily. On a pass that wasn't hard enough, UNC makes a break and ends up in a three versus two breakout. In a brilliant move that redeems the first-half corner kick debacle, our midfielder, Paisley, takes the ball off the feet of the attacker. She moves it out to our captain, who switches feet and hits Elise mid-stride, coming down the left flank.

Elise sees her opening and hits a perfect cross kick to Paisley, who makes her own signature upper nineties kick to tie the game with twenty-five minutes left.

There are several well-executed plays on both sides, with shots taken, but the keepers are again on point. No more goals are scored until the last two minutes of play. Things have gotten rougher and more aggressive as the countdown marches on. Both teams know this is the last gasp and I signal for a trick play we haven't done all season.

Inanna asks me out of the corner of my mouth, "You sure?" I nod and Erik pats me on the back.

Time to be bold. Time to be brave.

They execute it perfectly and the defender kicks it out exactly where we need her to, for a shot at a corner kick. Elise nails the ball out to our left midfielder near the center of the pitch, nutmegging the other teammates. It confuses the UNC players and with them off guard, our striker shoots at the goal. The keeper, as good as she is, doesn't know where to look and the ball sails past her into the net.

UCC players, coaches and fans alike erupt in celebration and the referee moves the ball down the field. All we have to do is keep the ball away from UNC for the next sixty seconds. It all comes down to what these ladies learned in their first game as four-year-olds.

Control the ball and we win.

Their long years don't fail them. With expert precision, my team controls the ball till time runs out.

It's an upset that will send shockwaves throughout U.S. soccer and put my program on the map.

We are playing in the final.

Chapter 54

Maley

Packing for the flight to Raleigh, after the emotional roller coaster of this week and watching the semi-final, while at work, is enough to make me want to go to bed at eight pm. I have to get up at four am to get to the airport.

I *want* to be in bed early, but I'm so keyed up. Watching Elise and her team outrun and outplay their biggest rivals–and arguably the best team in the nation–and knowing there are scouts in the stands reminds me of when I played in the college softball world series.

After I get my carryon packed for the long weekend in Raleigh, which is still colder than usual, I spend some time flipping through my high school and college yearbooks. It was such a great time, even if it was stressful trying to keep my grades up to get into PT school. I think about all my family has been through since that time and even when she was at her lowest, my mom still showed up for me.

She's had it rough–more difficult than she has had in a long time. I was mad at her for running away from Conner until Sabrina reminded me she is human. I don't have to hold her to a higher standard than I should. It's still so new for all of us, even as it is the best it has been since my dad died.

I sharply inhale as a picture from that senior year game catches me off guard. It's Mama, in the stands with the other parents, yelling her face off. Her yelling always got on my last nerve, especially when she mouthed off to the umpire. More than once, I had to put her in her place after the game about that.

Still, looking at that picture, I realize she showed up the best way she could for me and my sisters, and she deserves more than forgiveness. She has earned my understanding, especially now that I'm an adult. She isn't perfect, but she is the best. Finally, my body settles down about eleven p.m. I drift off to sleep, saying a prayer of gratitude and a petition for strength for our family as we walk into this new future together.

I know whoever is up there is listening.

***

Sabrina

I send my boyfriend home at nine pm because I'll be up super early for my connecting flight from Houston into Dallas to fly up to Raleigh with Males. He wanted to stay over and drive me to the airport, but I'm not ready for that kind of closeness yet. He is a good boyfriend, a truly nice guy and despite some awkwardness at Thanksgiving, has turned out to be pretty healthy.

I've rushed into so many relationships, though, that I want to take this slowly. If it's meant to be–and it's a love like I see in Mama and Conner–it will happen. No need to force it or trade attachment for actual connection.

Huh, I'm really growing up if I have those kinds of thoughts.

I haven't told my mom and sisters that I'm back in therapy yet. They would only ask me a million questions about it. What triggered it? Are you ok? Is there anything we should know?

That's the problem with being close to people who love you so much–they always want to know what's going on with you. I did a pretty good job keeping my therapy sessions in college secret until Mama asked me why I was so much happier.

She says, "I don't think this is because of a guy. You are different, more peaceful, and settled. Serene even. So, what's up and what are you doing differently?"

With that, I had to fess up. She cried in happiness, which was so weird, but it was when Elise was in the thick of her acting out phase. Males was also struggling, holding in her stress and anxiety like she always does till she explodes. I guess Mama was just happy one of her daughters was getting healthy. She told me I was the beacon for the other two and, as usual, she was right.

Mama has always helped me see my way to happiness, peace, and joy. I know we are going up there to see Elise play and her team win the championship after that grueling semifinal.

But I have a secret. I'm going to make sure Mama gets her happy ending.

Conner is going to propose, whether they win or lose the final.

And I'm carrying the ring.

***

Conner

The game itself was so intense. I know I'm not back to full strength. Then the emotional roller coaster of the win had me completely drained. We celebrated with the team at dinner. I made another, very short, speech about how proud I was of all we'd accomplished, then gave the girls the curfew they knew was coming because, well, we have a game today.

Back-to-back game days are not unusual for any elite athletes. It is part of the gig. You might be the one at the top of the heap, one game and at the bottom of the pile the next.

We celebrate, but also move forward. It is the blessing and the curse of playing sports.

You always have to keep one eye on tomorrow's game plan. Inanna, Erik and I meet briefly after dinner to confirm the meeting to discuss strategy before they head back to the hotel, and I meet Carrie at our Airbnb. Maley and Sabrina arrive around noon, so we have the place to ourselves.

As much as I would have loved to have all my strength and vigor back, to fuck Carrie into oblivion, we have other business to attend to. I still plan on pleasing her, and myself, but she takes that pressure off.

As soon as I walk in the door, she pulls me into a tight hug and then whispers, "Tonight is about restoring us to being us. I am guessing you are probably worn out, too. I could feel you drooping at dinner. Let's get comfortable. No pressure to do anything else, ok?"

I pull back to smile into her face and say, "I love you are back on my wavelength, Sunshine."

She stands up a little on her toes to kiss my nose and says, "It helps I'm back in my right mind, Sweetness."

I take a shower, a long one, while Carrie putters around, arranging her clothes and essentials the way she likes. She had groceries delivered for the next couple of days and cements our cooking menu. I plan to go back on Sunday, leaving Carrie to have some time with her older girls. They are going to do some sightseeing and shopping and fly back to Houston and Dallas, respectively, on Tuesday.

After I get out of the shower and ready for bed, I prop up the pillows and motion for Carrie. I could feel her relax as her body comes in contact with mine. I give her a minute to settle and our breathing to sync before I say, "Tell me why you were so afraid you had to leave?" I am careful with my words because I trust her with hers.

She sighs and snuggles a little closer. After a heartbeat, she tells me about how overwhelmed she was at the idea I would have heart damage as the result of the virus. She details how it brought up all her fears from the experience of her husband dying. She had that dream memory months ago and that seed of fear was planted that the same thing would happen to me.

"It felt like confirmation I was doomed to lose the love I just found. I wanted to spare myself the pain, so I ran. It was so wrong of me. I knew I should have waited, trusted in our love, to overcome anything. At that moment, I just couldn't do it. I couldn't handle it, and my instinct was to flee. I know I need to work on that. I'm so sorry, Conner. You didn't deserve that, and I don't know how I'll make it up to you. I don't deserve you."

I feel a tear or two slip from her eyes onto my chest. I give her a minute to feel her emotions. She doesn't need me to rescue her, just hold her steady. So, that's what I do. A few minutes pass and as I feel her body and breathing settle again, I use my forefinger to tilt her face to mine. I kiss her softly and tell her what I've been feeling for days.

"Carrie, you absolutely deserve me, as I deserve you. I only want you to do the work to grow to feel worthy of all the good things in and coming into your life."

Her beautiful ocean eyes stream and she swallows as she looks up at me. She stretches her neck up to kiss me but before her lips touch mine, I whisper, "But I'm not fucking around, Sunshine.

I need complete honesty from here on out. No more 'gotchas,' okay?"

She sucks in a breath as she pulls back to look up into my face. She stares deep into my eyes, her own darting back and forth to read my look. I smile at her, still with a serious look, and she nods. I pull her in close and whisper into the top of her head, "We are just getting started, my love. Let's keep growing together."

She wraps her hands in my hair and suddenly, I'm overwhelmed with a desire for her. She opens to me in every way, impossibly more open than ever before. Both of us are. We both pull off our pants, with her PJ top still on, and she straddles me. I watch as she pleasures herself with her fingers as she rides me and again, in no time flat, we are both carried over on the wings of climax. As she falls over me, her hair fawning over my face and neck, we both breathe into each other.

The next thing I know, Carrie is crawling back into bed with me. She makes small, quiet noises as she tucks herself into my side, covering us both with the blanket. All I know is the comforting presence of her beside me as we peacefully sleep together until the morning light peeks through our room's curtains.

Carrie and I both depart the house near Chapel Hill at the same time. Erik and Inanna pick me up for breakfast planning and Carrie is off to get her older daughters from the airport before the game later.

My coaches and I spend the next ninety minutes mapping out our strategy against Florida State and then we head to the stadium to meet the team. As we arrive at the stadium to play the current National Champions, the energy of the team is tangible. As we get ready to warm up, everyone is locked in and doesn't even notice FSU on the other side of the pitch.

After warmups, my senior captain asks if she could have a minute with the team without the coaches. I nod and the girls walk in the locker room. Erik, Inanna and I expect to hear cheering, but it is quiet with only a brief rumble.

After ten minutes of cooling our heels, we walk into the locker room. The team is ready to go. Each coach takes a minute to tell them how honored and proud we are. We gather for our huddle, and they chant "UCC" as they line up to take the field.

As we exit the tunnel, the stadium erupts with cheers. I notice more than a few UNC players in the stands cheering for us. This is the best of the sport. I see Elise and Carrie do their exchange, each tapping their hearts. I catch Carrie's eye and repeat the gesture back to her.

She blows me a kiss, which I catch, only to hear Inanna groan next to me. "Stop being a simp."

I chuckle and pat her on the back. "Get ready to have all your dreams come true, Coach."

As the whistle blows, our senior right back makes an overlapping run and revives the ball, laying it off to Elise, who is matching her stride for stride and hits one time to score the fastest goal in NCAA men's or women's soccer. The UCC fans erupt while the FSU side goes silent. The FSU keeper is yelling at her defense and their coaching staff looks stunned.

The ensuing kickoff by FSU in the first ninety seconds has them attempting to string passes together. They take five minutes, but they finally move the ball into our half. They take a hail Mary shot to catch our keeper off our line, but our goalie expertly plucks the ball out of the air and rolls it out.

We effortlessly move the ball down the pitch and take a shot. Their keeper saves it and at the twenty-five-minute mark, FSU has had one shot to our five.

I tell my team to settle with a few shorthand motions. We play aggressively and FSU fouls in response. The refs are getting frustrated with their tactics.

Just before the half, they take out our standout sophomore, who comes off injured. The FSU player gets a yellow card, which may not be their last the way her team is playing. With a free kick from thirty-five yards out, Elise easily sends it into no-man's-land between the penalty spot and eighteen yard line, where her big sister volleys it home with a swish in the back of the net.

Our fans are going ballistic.

With one minute left before the half, we are up two-nil. FSU scores on a breakaway but it is called back for offsides. Our keeper distributes it and sends our captain on a breakaway. With ten seconds left, she scores and the halftime whistle blows.

We are up three-nil to defending champs. The crowd on our side continues to be off the chain while the FSU side sits in frustrated silence.

As we enter the locker room, the girls are ecstatic. The seniors are telling them it's not over and we still have forty-five minutes to play. I say little, this is the senior's game. Our strategy is in line with theirs, so I let the leaders do their thing. I turn it over to my captain and she takes it from there. She asked each player what they want out of the second half.

They give it to her in one word: VICTORY.

As the second-half whistle blows, FSU comes out ready to play. Their coach inspired them, and we end up pinned in our own half, defending but defending well. They make three shots on goal before the twenty-minute mark, but our keeper handles each with expertise.

I hear Elise tell them all, "Get out of your head and play with your heart!"

That was the message they needed because it's like a switch is flipped. Two minutes later we score again and now FSU is frantic, going after each other. The clock winds down and I can feel another goal coming.

In true UCC fashion, my captain and her little sister, my freshman stand out and one day stepdaughter, puts the final nail in the coffin with ten minutes left to play. Elise makes an incredible cross-kick assist and her big sister scores with a power drive to the left upper ninety.

We are now up five-nil, and I look at my coaches in utter disbelief. We know we didn't coach this. The ladies did this all on their own.

The final whistle blows and the University of Coastal Cove–my team- are the new national champions.

Epilogue

Conner

My plan was to propose on Christmas Eve.

But since we are only a few weeks away, and on the high of winning the National Championship; Carrie getting her first business coaching client and all that has happened in the last week...it only feels right to do it now. It feels like we've shifted into a different timeline, where things we've worked for that seem to be years away, are now happening at lightning speed.

I still can't believe it. All our dreams are coming true.

Even one I never knew I had: someone to walk through this life with, hand-in-hand, to build and grow more than we ever thought possible.

So, I decide to propose tonight. The night I got out of the hospital, I texted Sabrina to bring the ring I'd bought with her over Thanksgiving. We told everyone we were going for ice cream to discuss her boy situation. That was partly true, but really, she went with me to a vintage jewelry shop where I found the perfect ring.

The owner of the shop met us there and told us the story of the two carat, emerald cut sapphire.

It was previously owned by a woman who had been happily married for over fifty years, who passed away three months after her husband died. She was a friend of the owner and was in good health, but knew her time was short.

She told the owner she was taking care of her estate and specifically wanted him to sell her ring only to someone who had the chance to experience true love like she had.

He had it in his shop for three years and Sabrina asked him when he got it. I hear her sharp intake of breath and see the tears come before I hear her whisper, "That's the day my dad died."

The owner winked at her and then looked at me before he says, "I guess you are the ones I've been waiting for." I smile at him and love the romantic back story, but there was only one reason I bought this ring.

It matches Carrie's eyes.

After we come back to the house following the game win and celebration, Sabrina made Maley put her shoes back on, just moments after she'd kicked off by the front door. She said in an airy tone, "We are going to some club my nurse friend told me about."

Giving me a knowing nod, she makes sure her mom doesn't see; they rush out the door, giving us the Airbnb all to ourselves.

Carrie and I are both still aglow from the win and our faces are a little chapped from the cold. She is in her wool socks and jeans from the game, lounging on the couch with a huge smile on her face.

Pulling my phone out of my pocket, I sync it with the house speaker and put on the song, "One and Only" by Teitur. Sabrina chose it for this moment, the love song from her favorite movie, *Aquamarine*. She said her mom would know it because she'd watched it with her hundreds of times, often with her when she was low.

The ring is in my back pocket as I reach for her hand.

"Sunshine, will you dance with me?"

Carrie giggle-groans and only drags her feet a little, fitting into my embrace effortlessly. We are made to fit, and dancing is a natural extension of that.

I press my face into her hair and whisper, "I want to dance with you through the rest of my life."

She hums the song and slides her hand up the back of my neck to rest her hand in my hair. We sway to the music till the song ends and when she pulls back to smile up into my face; I know this is my moment.

***

Carrie

The second the song, which Sabrina must have picked out, stops, I pull back because I want to ask Conner to move to Houston with me. I don't know why I would ask him now when he is the winningest coach in UCC history, but it feels right. As I smile up at him and the words form on my lips, he pulls back and drops to one knee. He brings a square velvet box out of his back pocket and offers it to me before he speaks.

My mouth goes dry.

When Scott proposed, I knew it. We'd talked about it endlessly and he seemed to drag his feet until he finally popped the question. I had to wait through his long heart-felt speech when I just wanted him to ask me already.

But this proposal, with Conner, is totally different.

It can't be anything else, and I am completely surprised. Of course, I'm going to say yes.

Of course, I'm going to spend the rest of my life with him. I've known that from nearly the start.

I just expected to celebrate the win for a little longer. And after the week we've had, with my actions at the top of mind, the tears spill down my face.

In true Conner form, he doesn't give me a long speech. All he says is, "Carrie, will you be my one and only Sunshine for the rest of our lives?"

I sink down to my knees, which couldn't hold me up any longer, anyway. He removes the ring from the box, a stunning sapphire that matches my taste, and places it on my left ring finger. It slides on easily and rests perfectly on my left hand. It feels like it was made for me. I look up into his face and cup it in my hands. I'm utterly speechless, so all I do is nod.

He smiles and says, "So, that's a 'yes'?"

I nod again franticly, as he pulls me into him.

Everything in me settles and I know we've both gotten the happily ever after we never expected.

Acknowledgements

I write my stories to give women hope and a vision for a better future. Every single one of my books starts with a question and through the process of writing, the answer finds me. It's always one word: **vision**.

The Assist gave me a vision of the love I wanted for my life. I was married at the time I started writing it, just for fun as a Kindle Vella story (a good portion of the original is still out there!). I thought this vision was going to come true with my then-husband. Less than two months into the creation of this story, my marriage crumbled so it could not be rebuilt. No, I am not a widow like Carrie, but that relationship died in an instant.

Yet, I kept writing. I kept writing for the love I knew was out there and waiting. I kept writing, praying, manifesting and healing for this outrageous love. It was so painful, and entirely liberating. Seven months after I started writing, I was officially divorced, as a woman in my late 40s. I was not even a year into building a new career and business. The outlook on the many fronts, including the relationship one, was bleak. But something in me said my own Conner–my epic Conner-Carrie love story was out there.

And he was. I met him just as suddenly as Carrie meets Conner, but in a totally different and unrelated way.

The first person I have to thank for being with me in this book writing process is myself. You see, my Mom had only two choices in mind for names when I was born: Amy and Carrie. So, Carrie is me. I wrote this Vella-turned-book as a love letter to myself. There are so many easter eggs in this book about my real life.

But in the end, Carrie stands on her own. She will always be the character I wrote myself into, but became her own person. This little birdie is living a life all her own. As am I, my girls and everyone else who will see themselves in this book. Because there are many people who filled in the lines of the characters for me.

Except for Inanna. I've met no one like her. I *think* I would like to and maybe my youngest will have a coach like her someday. She could use a Mama Bear amid all these raging bulls.

Speaking of people, there is no such thing as a book written in isolation.

Ok, maybe there is. But not for me. I cannot write without my people.

First and foremost – Blair, this is as much your book as mine. May all your love and support for my books (and what's in them) come back to you tenfold, Sister-Friend.

To my soccer ladies–Dana and Brittany, thanks for being patient with me. I finally came around and love soccer. God definitely has a sense of humor since I'm now a keeper's mom.

THE ASSIST

To my daughters and my Mom–don't read this. You are in it, of course. But don't read it. It will scar you for life. But that doesn't change how much I love and admire the women you are. Thank you for just being you.

To Ellie/Jen: you've read this from the beginning and guided it through the ugly edit. I hope I did you proud.

To my family at Next Page Publishing, led by Larissa- becoming the coach I am today would have never happened without you, however we met. I could envision Carrie's business because of what we do and who we help write books. And to those clients who might read this–y'all have changed my life. Thank you and I'm ALWAYS grateful and humbled to work with you. You put your trust in me to help you write your story and midwife it into the world.

To my Conner, who goes by another name–whether you manifested me or I manifested you, doesn't really matter in the end. What matters is that you give me a chance to experience healthy love and say with confidence, men like the one I wrote in this book exist in the real world. The dedication is true because of you.

Finally, to the readers. You are all good girls and you all deserve a love like this. I pray you it finds you.

About the Author

Amy W. Vogel's passion is to help other women achieve their dreams, whether that is through the realities she creates or publishing yours. At her core, She is a spiritual storyteller who empowers readers and authors to heal and find their voice.

She is an accomplished author, speaker, and coach who has been immersed in the world of stories for as long as she can remember. And helping women is her passion and purpose. She began writing on a whim at 35 after she recognized the transformative power of storytelling. With six published books, both fiction and nonfiction, through a variety of channels, she aims to inspire and empower others, for maximum impact on the world.

With three daughters and a tiny dog, she also aims to make sure there is plenty of nonsense to go around. Just look at her Instagram stories for proof.

At the time of printing – Amy has written 5 books and featured in an anthology. Her next book, **Bejeweled**, a historical romance that retells Queen Jezebel's story. In Amy's version, Queen Jezebel will be the archetype feminine queen who must

THE ASSIST

battle, in her own unique way, against insidious religious patriarchal forces to help her people not only survive, but thrive.

Look for **Bejeweled** in 2026.

To learn more about Amy, her other books, coaching practice and to follow her on social media, visit her website: www.amywvogel.com

Surprise Bonus Section

Receive **TWO exclusive Assist bonus chapters**, along with excerpts from Amy's other books, sign up for her newsletter here: https://books.bookfunnel.com/readerschoicebundl

Did you know??

There is an **Assist Playlist** on Spotify! It is the music to fit the mood and more than enough songs to get you in the reading mood! Find it here: https://open.spotify.com/playlist/35c9v754mTwvl14D0QwoFB?si=IZCWUv0uTeeiyfdW5wWyFw

AND.......last but not least.

It helps authors–especially self-published authors (like Amy)–**to get reviews** on Amazon, Goodreads and for an extra special show of support, on social media!

If you loved this book:

    1. Review it,

    2. Promote it on social media and

    3. Tell your friends!

THE ASSIST

If you'd like to get in touch with Amy about this book (or anything else), find her on social media or email her at info@amywvogel.com.

THANK YOU!

Made in the USA
Monee, IL
06 March 2025